Superman pulled up to the decrepit rowhouse in a black '78 Econoline van. The needles crunched on the sidewalk along Avenue C when he got out. It was a piss-numbing, subzero night down in Alphabet City, and at half past two in the morning, the streets were dead. Superman looked around before he slid the van door open. There was enough gasoline inside to take down a city block.

The two red cans looked black in the night scope as Eddie Burke watched him from the roof across the street. He had been tracking the psychopath for months now as he wreaked havoc across the Lower East Side, lighting fires, smashing boilers, and breaking water mains. Landlords would hire the fearsome Dominican to clean out their rent-controlled buildings and Superman (born Dagoberto Rojas) did it with the efficiency of a surgeon cauterizing a wound. Still, half a dozen people got burned in his fires; among them an elderly woman and three-year-old twins. When told of the death toll, Superman would just cackle through yellow teeth and say *"Muerte a los bomberos . . ."* Death to the firefighters who think they can stop me . . .

FIRST DEGREE BURN

Peter Lance

BERKLEY PRIME CRIME, NEW YORK

"It had to be you" by Gus Kahn and Isham Jones, Gilbert Keyes music (ASCAP), Bantam Music (ASCAP) both administered by The Songwriters Guild of America. Used with permission.

FIRST DEGREE BURN

A Berkley Prime Crime Book / published by arrangement with the author

PRINTING HISTORY
Berkley Prime Crime mass-market edition / July 1997

The Putnam Berkley World Wide Web site address is http://www.berkley.com

ISBN: 0-425-15698-2

Berkley Prime Crime Books are published by The Berkley Publishing Group, 200 Madison Avenue, New York, NY 10016.
The name BERKLEY PRIME CRIME and the BERKLEY PRIME CRIME design are trademarks belonging to Berkley Publishing Corporation.

PRINTED IN THE UNITED STATES OF AMERICA

10 9 8 7 6 5 4 3 2 1

For Bina and Joe
who taught me how to start fires that
always burn hot and bright.

And for Christopher, Mallory, and Alison
who help me keep them under control.

ACKNOWLEDGMENTS

THE GENESIS FOR *FIRST DEGREE BURN* CAME FROM A remarkable documentary produced more than a decade ago by my sister, Mary Lance. In researching *Artists at Work*, a film history of the WPA art projects, we came across a little-known incident in which thousands of canvases by American artists from the 1930s were later destroyed or sold as scrap. Plumbers bought them and used some of the great paintings to wrap pipes with. There were secrets buried in these works that lesser men in later years decided shouldn't come out.

I'd like to thank Mitch Douglas at ICM for believing that an ex-reporter from *ABC News* had the chops to write fiction and Denise Silvestro, my dedicated editor at Berkley, who first discovered the manuscript.

The research that went into the novel was extensive. Eddie Burke is an arson investigator, and the fire marshals of the FDNY live heroic but dangerous lives. In order to enter their world, I was aided by Dick Berry, an ex-fire-fighter who is now an insurance investigator. He gave me access to the Bureau of Fire Investigation where I had the benefit of meeting with fire marshals Bill Manahan, John Knox, Fred Taylor, Tom Morano, and Gerard Trimboli of

Brooklyn Base. Chief Fire Marshal Michael Vecchi sat with me at headquarters and was immensely helpful in giving me an overview of the BFI.

The man who walked me through the arson scenes and helped make sure that the manuscript was bulletproof was Louis F. Garcia, now assistant chief fire marshal, who was the former executive officer of Manhattan Base.

Louie is an extraordinary man. The exact antithesis of Mike Kivlihan, the ferretlike executive officer of Manhattan Base who torments Eddie Burke in the book. The time I spent with Louie convinced me that the fire marshals of the FDNY are a unique breed of investigators. Like their precinct detective brothers in the NYPD, they dress in plain clothes, carry Smith & Wesson nines, drive unmarked Chevy Caprices, and arrest felons for violent crime.

But every marshal is an ex-firefighter with years in a ladder or truck company. They've ridden the trucks through subzero, ice-covered streets. They crawled on their bellies through smoke-filled tenements. And every one has lost a buddy or carried out a half-dead child from an arson blaze. Of the 30,000 structural fires that break out each year in the city of New York, more than 4,000 are intentionally set.

Somebody has to track down the demented torches who start them. So the fire marshals of the FDNY come to the job of arson investigation with an emotional commitment that's unlike anything else in law enforcement. Men and women who walk through the char of an arson scene with experience, dedication, and real heart.

Beyond all others, this book belongs to them.

Bel Air, California
March 1997

ARSON IN THE FIRST DEGREE 1. A person is guilty of arson in the first degree when he intentionally damages a building...causing an explosion or a fire and when (a) such explosion or fire is caused by an incendiary device (or liquid) propelled, thrown or placed inside such building and when such explosion or fire either (i) causes death or (ii) serious physical injury to another person.

–SECTION 150.20
NEW YORK PENAL LAW

PILOT   NURSE   STEVEDORE

WORKERS OF THE WORLD UNITE, SKETCH FOR

FARMER   TEACHER   MINER

TWO-PANEL MURAL, 1938. A. GROVESNOR

Everybody has something to hide....

–DASHIELL HAMMETT

FIRST
DEGREE
BURN

1

SUPERMAN PULLED UP TO THE DECREPIT ROWHOUSE IN A black '78 Econoline van. The needles crunched on the sidewalk along Avenue C when he got out. It was a piss-numbing, subzero night down in Alphabet City, and at half past two in the morning, the streets were dead. Superman looked around before he slid the van door open. There was enough gasoline inside to take down a city block.

The two red cans looked black in the night scope as Eddie Burke watched him from the roof across the street. He had been tracking the psychopath for months now as he wreaked havoc across the Lower East Side, lighting fires, smashing boilers, and breaking water mains. Landlords would hire the fearsome Dominican to clean out their rent-controlled buildings, and Superman (born Dagoberto Rojas) did it with the efficiency of a surgeon cauterizing a wound. Still, half a dozen people got burned in his fires; among them an elderly woman and three-year-old twins. When told of the death toll, Superman would just cackle through yellow teeth and say *"Muerte a los bomberos . . ."* Death to the firefighters who think they can stop me.

This bothered Eddie Burke, who had a particular problem with arrogance. And when he transferred from Brooklyn

Base to Manhattan, where he worked as a catching fire marshal, he pushed Superman up to the top of his chart.

So now, on this frigid night in December, he lay on his belly as the arsonist hauled the gasoline cans into the vacant tenement.

"Squad four-eight to four-one," Eddie whispered over the three-inch Motorola Handie Talkie clipped to his turn-out coat.

"Four-one. You got him Burke?" Supervising Fire Marshal Mike Kivlihan was on Avenue A and Houston Street, standing in front of Sixteen Engine and Five Truck. There were thirteen firefighters behind him, waiting for the word.

"Yeah," said Eddie. "And it's gasoline again, which means a fast in and out."

"So? What about it?"

"I asked for two *blocks*. You're five minutes away."

"Who gives a shit? The place is unoccupied." Kivlihan was a nasty little bantam rooster. A short man in a big man's job.

But Eddie kept pressing. "A lot of crack heads use the buildings down here."

"I thought you said the windows were covered with tin."

"They are."

"Then it's empty." Kivlihan turned and played to the men behind him. "Look, this is *your* party, asshole. I got two pieces of apparatus, and we're on the clock. Now, you gonna do this or not?"

Eddie shook his head. Among the marshals, Kivlihan was known as an empty suit, a house marshal who'd gone on light duty after a minor injury his third year in an engine company. He'd ass-kissed his way through the ranks ever since.

"Just *be* there." Eddie punched out.

He grabbed a Haligan tool and a nylon lifeline and

pushed down off the roof, while below in the shadows Superman used an eight-inch crowbar to pop open a basement window. The building had been boarded up for months now. It was the end town house in a block of brownstones designed at the turn of the century by McKim, Meade & White, a row of six-story Belle Epoque buildings that had been granted landmark status in 1995. And that was their death sentence.

You see, the law was designed for preservation, but arson investigators like Eddie Burke knew that it was an open invitation to burn. Landmark buildings could only be renovated along precise lines approved by the HPD, the city's Department of Housing, Preservation and Development. You couldn't just do a spray job or slap Sheetrock over these babies. They cost ten times as much to bring back to life as a conventional structure, and many landlords, finding themselves with an expensive "old lady" to take care of, simply put out the word for a torch.

In this case, no one knew that the landlord had already drawn up the plans for a twenty-story tan brick high-rise of Section Eight housing. He'd get an insurance payout for the burn and federal matching funds to replace the glorious old brownstone that was too expensive to renovate.

Once again, a little piece of the city would die. That's how things ran in New York, and after twelve years in a truck company watching Manhattan burn away, Eddie Burke was disgusted. He could get his revenge with a gun or a bottle, but for now it would happen when he finally put the bracelets on this piece of shit from Santo Domingo.

They called him Superman, in part because no one could touch him and in part because he'd survived a six-story jump into an alley when Eddie had cornered him on the top floor of a tenement. The man just refused to get hurt or get collared, and he was always four steps ahead. But tonight, Eddie would grab him, arrest him downstairs in the boiler room as he set up the incendiary device. That way the charge would be Arson One.

The first-alarm response was on standby with Kivlihan just in case Eddie was late or the fire-starter beat him to the match. But Eddie Burke wouldn't let that happen. And he had the Dominican fuck in the Trigicon sights of his Smith when Rojas disappeared in the basement doorway.

Inside, the arsonist worked quickly. He went straight to the boiler room and switched on an overhead bulb dangling from a cord. There was still power in the building so the landlord could keep the boiler on low and prevent the pipes from freezing. In the fire investigation that would follow, he would have to prove that he fully intended to renovate the landmark but that fate or some faulty wiring had intervened.

Superman switched on a hand spotlight and unscrewed the bulb. He screwed a Y extension into the socket and replaced the bulb. Then he found an old plastic garbage can and moved it next to the oil storage tank. He hit the side of the tank and smiled. It was three-quarters full of number-four heating fuel, enough of an accelerant to break windows three blocks away when it blew.

Eddie was moving through the alley at the side of the building now. There was a vacant lot next door from an earlier three-alarm blaze, and he saw a half-dozen rotted out mattresses where the crack addicts would lie on a summer night and blow rock. But not tonight. The temperature was fifteen below.

At the back of the building, there was a fire escape with a pull-down ladder. Eddie reached up with the Haligan tool and yanked it down. Then he climbed up and began making his away along the old, rusted fire escape.

At one point it shook, and one of the second-floor bolts sheared. The thing rocked.

"Jesus Christ . . ."

Eddie said it under his breath as he grabbed the rail. Fire escapes were an afterthought on a building like this, and they were the last part of the infrastructure that ever got serviced. This one had rusted out years ago, and Eddie wasn't sure if it would take his full weight, so he moved up cautiously to the third-floor landing and headed for the roof.

Down in the boiler room now, Superman opened a Glad drawstring trash bag and pushed it into the garbage can, taping the mouth of the open bag around the rim with duct tape. Then he pulled out two white extension cords. He plugged one into the socket and took out a small house timer, the kind people use to try and fool the home invaders when they take a trip. Superman plugged the timer into the first extension cord and then the second cord into the timer. He stripped the ends off, exposing the wires, then twisted them into a pig's tail and taped it so that the exposed end was directly over the open garbage bag in the can.

Eddie was two steps from the top landing of the fire escape when it buckled again. Christ. The thing shook. Eddie fell back a few rungs and hung on. The old wrought-iron stairwell made a creaking sound, and down in the base-ment, Superman stopped cold. He looked upstairs, cocking his head like a predatory beast, and listened again. He moved out of the boiler room and panned the spotlight. A rat darted across the floor, and he smiled.

"El ratón . . ."

Outside now, Eddie held his breath and moved up the stairs, touching them like eggshells. The fire escape creaked one more time, but he lunged up, grabbed onto the edge of the roof coping, and pulled himself over. He hyperven-tialted, staring up at the World Trade Center to his right. Then he got up and moved to the bulkhead that led to the top-floor brownstone landing. He inserted the Haligan tool in the door and was about to pop it when he saw smoke.

"Mother of Christ."

Eddie jumped on the two-way.

"Four-eight to four-one. There's somebody in the building."

Kivlihan clicked back. "No shit. The fuckin' torch."

"No. I mean somebody's on one of the *floors*. A civilian."

"That's bullshit."

"Hey. I'm on the roof and there's smoke from a cooking fire coming out of one of the chimneys."

"Maybe the maggot decided to have a fuckin' burrito before he blew it."

"No. I'm goin' down to see."

"That's a *negative*," Kivlihan hissed at him, so Eddie hit the transmit button.

"Sorry. You're breakin' up . . ." He punched out and popped the door.

Now, down below, the arsonist was certain he heard a noise. He rushed back into the boiler room to finish the job as Eddie made his way down, two steps at a time, through the darkened building. Because Rojas was downstairs, it was too risky to use a Maglite. But seven years with a forcible entry rescue crew had given Eddie an instinct for moving in the dark. Coming in with the first response on Four Truck when the smoke was so thick you had to crawl across the floor on your hands, sucking compressed air through a Scott's bottle with temperatures hitting eight hundred degrees, you felt your way through as you searched for bodies. The smoke was so dense that you had to tie a lifeline on the first piece of iron inside the door just to pull yourself out.

Now, by instinct, Eddie moved down along the cast-iron stairwell, checking each door along the way for a line of light. Then he smelled it—the smoke he'd seen on the roof. He saw the flicker of light beneath the transom. Eddie felt the door. He turned the knob and inched it open.

Inside, there was a fire smoldering in a rusted fifty-five gallon drum. Someone had started it with the wood from a shipping pallet. Across the mouth of the barrel there was a piece of chicken on a crude spit that was burned to a crisp. The smoke was traveling up through the ducts of the old forced-air heating system. Eddie flicked on a penlight flash and shined it across the room.

"Oh Jesus . . ."

In the opposite corner he saw a woman in her early twenties, Black, lying on her side, her eyes wide, tongue out . . . the crack pipe was on the floor beside her. An overdose. Eddie pushed in and rushed over to her. He felt for a pulse.

"Fuck." He pulled his hands away. The body was stone cold and stiff as a board. He was about to take off for the basement when he saw something move under a ratty old blanket. He grabbed the butt-end of the Haligan tool, figuring it for a rat. Then he pulled the blanket away to smash it and . . .

"Holy Christ!"

It was an infant, lying in urine soaked "feety" pajamas and turning blue from the cold.

He pushed the two-way and whispered.

"Burke to four-one. There's one DOA and one living . . . a baby. Can't be more than three months."

"Leave it and get down to the basement. I'll have Rescue there in five minutes."

"Christ, Kivie, no. If it blows—"

"He won't risk it. He's got to get out first."

"But this kid's gonna freeze to dea—"

Kivie stopped him.

"That is a fucking *order,* mister. Now get down there."

Eddie hesitated. The tiny baby was trembling now. He felt like it could die any second in his arms. He looked down below where the target was and . . .

"Fuck it."

He ripped open his Nomex turnout coat and shoved the baby inside. Then he pushed out, down toward the first-floor landing.

Now in the basement, Superman moved toward the boiler. He knelt down and looked inside at the blue flame from the pilot light. He took a hammer and came down on the thermostat housing. *Bang.* The light went out. He didn't want any fucking fire burning when the gasoline vapors started to rise. Next, he opened the first can of gas and poured it into the bag.

When the garbage can was half full, he poured in the second twenty-five gallon can. Then he plugged in the timer and checked his watch. It was 2:32 A.M. He set the timer for 2:40. Eight minutes. Plenty of time to get out. Finally, he plugged in the second extension cord. Now, as the gasoline fumes began to fill the room, he'd created a circuit.

The highly flammable vapors would rise from the can. When the timer hit 2:40 A.M., it would trip and complete the circuit, causing a short. A spark would flash along the twisted wire pig's-tail above the can. This would blow the gasoline and set off the storage tank full of heating fuel. Superman would be having a Bustello at a social club full of witnesses six blocks away, and he'd laugh through his yellow teeth when the dominoes fell on the table nearby from the shock of the blast.

He poured a few extra ounces of gasoline in a line from the can to the tank as a trailer and then grabbed his light. He started to exit the basement when he heard the sound of a nine millimeter round going into the pipe of a Smith & Wesson on the floor above him.

Superman stopped in his tracks. He ran his odds and thought fast. If the *bomberos* were on him, he'd give them a little *regalo* when they walked in. Take the fucking skin off their faces. So he ran back into the boiler room, shined the light on the timer, and shortened the blast time to 2:36.

Less than four minutes away and just enough time for him to climb out through the basement window.

Now, up above, Eddie was moving down the pitch-black stairwell. He was on the second floor landing, about to step down, when he stopped. Instinct held him back. Instinct and the draft he felt at the landing's edge. He reached out for the railing and there was nothing. The baby inside his jacket was beginning to cry now. It was just warm enough to feel pain. And as Eddie switched on the penlight flash, he rocked back.

"Fuck me . . ."

He holstered the gun and looked down. Scavengers had been in the building. They'd taken out the first-floor wrought-iron stairwell for scrap. Now there was a fifteen-foot drop to the first floor, and Eddie had an infant in his coat.

He hit the two-way.

"Move in."

Kivlihan jumped on the radio. "You got him?"

"Not exactly. But this kid here's about to die. Send EMS. Thermal blanket. The full loadout."

Kivlihan almost exploded. "Where the fuck's Rojas?"

"I don't know, but the fire escape's gone, and I'm a little short of a first-floor landing here." He looked down at the open drop to the basement when just then, through a hole in the floor where the scavengers had hacked away at the stairwell, he saw a light flash.

Superman.

Eddie dropped the lifeline from over his shoulder and snapped it onto the second-floor railing with a carabiner. He held his right arm around the baby and slid down the line with his left. . . . boom . . . to the first floor.

Superman was just at the basement window when he heard the noise. He ducked back into the shadows as Eddie drew the Smith and moved down the stairs to the basement. He stopped when he smelled the gasoline.

Ten feet away in the boiler room, he could hear the timer. *Click, click, click.* He looked around left, then right, searching through the dark with eyes that few other men had. That's when he saw it. The flash of silver as Rojas pulled out a narrow blade.

Eddie pointed the Smith at the shadow just below the window and cocked it.

"That's it, Rojas. Come out where I can fuckin' see you."

From the dark he heard. "Fuck you man, and fuck your mother."

Eddie turned toward the timer, which was just clicking past 2:34 with less than two minutes to go.

"You shoot me, this whole fuckin' place's gonna blow," said the arsonist.

"That's *one* way to end your career," said Eddie. "Now get the fuck out here."

Click, click, click.

"Two-thirty-four, man. It's set to blow in two minutes."

Just then, from outside, they heard the sirens. Now Superman had to make a decision. He could take his chances up the back stairs with a piece-of-cake jump from the first-floor landing or run into half a dozen six-foot Irishmen with turnout gear and fire axes coming in the front door. It wasn't even a choice.

"Fuck you, man."

And with that, he darted out through the dark toward the back of the basement.

In a second, Eddie was after him, drawing the baby to his chest as he chased the Dominican psychopath down along the basement hallway toward the back. Superman was almost at the foot of the stairwell when, suddenly, Eddie lunged forward and threw out the Haligan tool. The axlike blade spun end over end and knocked the arsonist down. Eddie ran up to him, about to pull out the cuffs, when the baby cried. Rojas smiled like a pit viper. He knew that Eddie was vulnerable, so he slashed out with the knife.

"Christ," Eddie went down in agony.

Rojas had cut a six-inch slice across his thigh.

"Fuck you *maricón*," said Superman. "You coulda had me, but you stopped for some fuckin' kid that was dead before it was fuckin' born. You deserve to blow."

And with that, he jammed the knife into Eddie's thigh, kicking past him and taking off up the stairs.

Eddie was almost in shock now from the pain. The narrow-bladed stiletto was buried up to the hilt. But the baby was crying, and the fire marshal knew that there wasn't much time.

He looked at the luminous dial on his black plastic Casio. 2:35 A.M. Less than a minute to go. With all the strength that he had, Eddie pulled himself up by the stairwell railing. The little baby was bawling now as Eddie backed up the stairs, one at a time. Blood was pouring from the knife wound, and across the basement, the timer ticked away.

Finally, Eddie got to the first-floor landing. He pushed to a hallway window and, with his good leg, kicked away at the tin. A flap opened in the corner of the window, and he looked down. It was twenty feet to the pile of rubble in the lot next door where he'd come in.

The baby was starting to convulse now, and Eddie wasn't sure it could survive the fall. He couldn't even feel his leg. The blade of the stiletto was buried down to the bone. He checked his watch—thirty seconds—and kicked out at the rest of the tin.

A unit from Rescue One screeched into the lot next door, and a four-man team jumped off. They shined their lights up at the building as Eddie climbed onto the window ledge.

He looked down at the mattresses in the lot below and yelled, "Get back. Its about to bl—"

And with that, the timer clicked. The circuit was made. The line shorted out. The sparks flashed, and the gas fumes ignited, blowing Eddie Burke, arms across his chest to protect the baby, out the window and down twenty feet to the mattresses as the Rescue One team rocked back from the blast and the landmark brownstone erupted in flames.

That was all Eddie remembered. The sight of the rescue truck and their lights and then blackness . . . until he woke up ten minutes later on a gurney. An EMS paramedic leaned in over him and flicked on a flashlight to check his vitals.

Eddie coughed up some blood and wheezed out, "The kid?"

The paramedic shook his head.

"It was gone before the thing ever lit."

"What was it?" said Eddie. "A boy or a girl?"

"Little girl. Sorry, Eddie. . . ."

Eddie started to get up, but then felt the shooting pain in his thigh. Just then, Bobby Vasquez pushed in, smiling. Vasquez had worked with Eddie back in Four Truck. He'd broken his back in a three-alarm and was now on light duty, the house watch who manned the board at Manhattan Base.

Bobby held up an evidence bag with Superman's pearl-handled stiletto. "Right down to the fuckin' femur, Burke. This is definitely gonna affect your golf game."

"I don't play golf."

"That's good,'cause you sure as shit can't start now."

A half dozen firefighters nearby laughed. Vasquez moved over and patted Eddie on the back.

"The old man'd be proud."

For some reason Eddie nodded bitterly, when just then, Kivlihan, the rat-faced executive officer, rushed up to him.

"Goddamn you, Burke. There's a chain of command here."

Eddie pushed himself up on the gurney as Vasquez turned to Kivlihan. "Hey Kivie. Lighten up, for crissakes. He oughta get the Bennett Medal for this."

"What he's gonna *get* is a goddamn write-up with IAB." Kivlihan looked across at the burned-out hulk. "Landmark building. Six alarms. Half the fuckin' block almost blew."

"So, what was he gonna do? There was a kid in there."

"Yeah, a dead kid."

Eddie managed to brace himself on his good leg. He gritted his teeth from the pain. The morphine was just kicking in.

"You know somethin', Kivie?"

"What's that?"

"I don't *like* you."

And with that, Eddie hauled back with his left and broke Kivie's jaw. The supervisor went down like a sack of shit as Eddie staggered and dropped back on the gurney.

"Jesus Christ," said one of the probationary firefighters, just pushing in to see. "What the hell was that?"

Vasquez looked down at Eddie and shook his head, smiling.

"That, my friend, was a goddamn left cross."

The probie smiled.

The EMS guy strapped Eddie onto the gurney and nodded to his partner to wheel him off. As they moved past Kivlihan, the partner looked down.

"What about *him?*"

Kivlihan was on the ground now in agony. He was holding his jaw shut with his hands.

The paramedic smiled. "This fuck can wait."

2

THREE DAYS AFTER EDDIE BURKE WENT ON SUSPENSION,
Alex Sloane lay on her bed in the loft on Prince Street. It
was late. The bedroom was lit by the dull blue light of a
lava lamp. Alex's hands were tied behind her back with
leather thongs. She was dressed in a black leather bustier.
Her legs were covered by the sheerest of stockings, and she
was jammed into open-toed platform spikes. Carlos was in
the next room doing coke. By now he'd graduated from
powder to rock.

It was hard enough for Alex to squeeze into the bustier,
but the four-inch heels were murder. He had been buying
her leather and silk outfits for weeks now; form-fitting,
cinched at the waist, with ties up the back. Whore clothes.
Mostly black, with garters, tiny satin G-strings, and platform spikes. Clothes that pushed her breasts out and her
ass up and made her walk in tiny baby steps to the bed.

She felt like a hooker from Avenue A. But Carlos liked
it. He wanted her trussed up in satin and spandex. Submis-
sive. Ready to come when he called. His *puta*. His whore.

And that wasn't the worst part, because this was a crime
of consent. He would pick the clothes, dress her up, and
force her to do things that made her retch. But Alex would

never fight back. That's what hurt her the most. That *she*
was the co-conspirator. Still, Alex Sloane had no choice.
The man owned her. From the moment he pushed up
against her at Odeon.

She was in black that night; heels and a short leather skirt.
She could feel his breath on her neck as he leaned in and
whispered.

"It's a sin."

"What is?" said Alex, without turning.

"That someone like you should be here alone."

Oh God, she thought. Not another one. And she pulled
away. But he grabbed her arm and turned her around. Then,
when she saw his face, her heart jumped.

He was a young Tyrone Power. Right off the screen from
that movie she'd seen at The Thalia. *Blood and Sand.* Tall,
with dark eyes, and there was some kind of accent. Maybe
Latin or French? He touched her arm and she hesitated, but
then he smiled—white teeth—and he had her.

He threw a hundred down on the bar to cover her tab,
then cocked his head toward the door.

For all his strength, Carlos was gentle with her that first
night. He picked her up at the door and carried her into his
bed. He lit candles. He put on a little Keith Jarrett and he
took his time with her, moving his thumb and forefinger
up and down on either side of her backbone, finding each
crevice, until she was so relaxed that she almost came. He
was a painter, he said. Superrealism. An airbrush artist. And
in between kisses, he asked if she'd let him paint her. Alex
just wiped the cum off her belly and laughed that he already
had.

But all the danger signs were flashing that night. The
way that he ripped her silk blouse open. The animal sound
that he made as he went inside her, and the tiny vial of
white powder that he reached for after he came. She re-

membered, when he found that the vial was empty, he cursed in Spanish and flicked it onto the floor like a cigarette butt. But still, Carlos took her again and again that night. For a man in his thirties, he had incredible staying power. Alex was sore for three days, and when the phone didn't ring on the fourth, she went to him.

He was distant at first and then at dinner he started to laugh, and when they went back to her loft he made a ritual out of opening the wine. He took half an hour to light every candle in her place before pulling her into the bedroom.

He kissed her softly at the edge of the bed and then, just when she thought that she'd opened his gentle side, he thrust her down by the shoulders and told her to take him into her mouth.

On their third date he made her wear a Chinese silk dress slit up the side to her thigh. He had seen it in a shop on Mott Street that morning and bought it for her along with the first pair of shoes: red stiletto heels; fuck-me shoes with tiny satin straps that Carlos took pains to buckle.

That was the first night that she knew for sure he was a sadist. The first night that he'd pounded her so hard that she almost cracked her skull on the headboard. And the first night that he'd come in her long red hair.

She jumped up and rushed from her bedroom that night and he ran after her screaming as she shot to the elevator, stabbing at the button. She had to get out. To leave her own place. Anywhere. Just to get away from him.

When the lift didn't come, she pushed into the stairwell and started running; racing down the twelve flights of stairs. And he went after her, screaming for her to stop. But she didn't until the door opened on eight and Raphael came out in his pajama bottoms, demanding to know what was wrong. Raphael, the tall Black painter who managed the loft co-op, hugging her as Carlos raced down to kill her, taking the stairs two at a time. Finally, at the sight of the

Black man, Carlos stopped, demanding to know who he was.

Alex said he was a friend and Carlos rubbed some coke across his teeth as he buckled his pants and pushed past them down the stairs.

"This guy's bad blood for you Alex," said Raphael holding her in his arms. And she started to weep.

It was another week before she saw him again. She'd come up to the twelfth-floor loft where she worked as an art restorer and found a big pink box tied with a black satin bow. There was a tiny card attached that said Alex Sloane.

Inside the box was an airbrushed drawing of her in platform heels and spandex slacks with a bustier. He had signed the picture himself and he'd made her look like Annie Lennox. Drop-dead gorgeous—though she'd always been the type who had to push for good looks. Beneath the picture, under some tissue, there was a black silk teddy. The note said simply: "I'm sorry . . . Carlos." And it was as much her own sickness and need to be coveted that caused her to pick up the phone.

After that, he virtually moved into her loft on Prince Street. And every night there was another present, another piece of rubber or silk for her bondage and discipline. She kept promising herself that she'd end it and change the locks, but after years of repression, he'd opened her up and she'd found herself getting wet in the middle of the day just thinking of how he was going to take her that night.

This had been going on for weeks now, but tonight he'd gone way too far. As Alex lay tied on the bed, she looked out through a crack in the door. Carlos jammed a crystal into a crack pipe and set it on fire. His head fell back as he toked. It was weapons grade.

"Baby, it's getting late," she said. "Why don't you come in here and untie me?" Then, in a flash, he was in the room behind her. Quiet. Watching her. She heard a switch and off went the lava lamp.

"I don't like the dark, Carlos," she said. But there was no answer. "Untie me now. . . . Really . . . I mean it, baby." But there was nothing. It seemed like a minute went by and her pulse began to race.

"Goddamn it, Carlos, don't leave me tied up in here." And then in the dark, she heard his footsteps as he moved toward her face. She heard the sound of his belt opening. Then the fly coming down as he reached in and pulled it out. He called her *puta* and grabbed her by the hair, pulling her toward him. He told her to eat it and she opened her mouth. But he was pushing too hard and she choked. So he came up behind her and told her to lift up her ass. She did as he said, but it wasn't high enough, so Carlos pulled off his black leather belt and he slapped her.

Alex heard him pop a cap off a jar and she smelled something sweet. "What are you doing Carlos? I'm serious. If you don't turn that light on right now, I'll scream."

He slapped her across the calves with the belt and then lunged for the switch on the lava lamp. Suddenly, the bedroom was blue again. But there, on a table beside the bed, she saw it: the jar of K-Y jelly.

"Oh God." A shock cut through her heart. She had never used rubbers with Carlos before because he'd been to the clinic and tested HIV free. But now this. This was different.

She struggled to pull away, but he held her down and mounted her from behind, pumping, pumping until her head was off the bed and she started to scream. "Carlos . . ." He cracked the belt and told her to shut up, but she screamed even louder, and finally, she heard Raphael pounding hard at the door.

And then it was over.

Alex was bawling, barely able to get out a whimper as

Raphael used his passkey and rushed into the loft to find her. Alone on the satin sheets, trussed up from behind, as the window onto the loft roof lay open. The escape route of Carlos Guzman: Bolivian airbrush painter and black leather sadist.

3

ON THE SAME NIGHT THAT CARLOS TERRORIZED ALEX SLO-
ane, Dr. Caroline Drexel had the dream—in her bed up on
Sutton Place in teal silk pajamas, her blonde hair spilling
over the pillows as she lay half asleep. She had seen pieces
of it now for almost twenty years. The dream had begun
when she met Dr. Helen Liebman.

Caroline was ten. Her mother had been dead just a year,
and she could still remember the sound that the coffin made
when they slid her body into the mausoleum on Ocean
Drive up in Newport. The little granite sepulcher with the
name Drexel in five-inch letters, modeled after the big granite "cottage" they lived in.

For months after her mother was gone, she'd been unable
to sleep, tormented by demons that came to her in the dark.
Her grades had begun to slip and she'd lost almost fifteen
pounds, so the headmistress had contacted her father and
recommended Dr. Liebman, a Jungian Therapist on the staff
at Mt. Sinai, who was just beginning her seminal research
into regression therapy.

The doctor was a heavyset woman with a shock of white
hair and piercing blue eyes. Her accent was Austrian and
her voice was gravelly from too many packs of Gitanes.

She had an intimidating presence, but the little blue numbers from Auschwitz were still on her wrist, and she knew what it meant to suffer. Also, though the doctor's practice was exclusively adult, she was barren from her years in the camps, so she welcomed the chance to help this beautiful little child.

The sessions began quietly at the doctor's apartment on Central Park West. Caroline remembered that the place smelled musty at first, as though no one had lived there. And when she first met the big woman, she pulled away. But Dr. Liebman just smiled. She told Caroline to call her Helen and took her into a small room with a collection of porcelain dolls. Each one had white skin with pink lips, just like Caroline's, and the doctor let her hold one.

Helen made her hot chocolate and told her to caress the doll as she laid down on a soft brocade couch. It was so soft that the little girl almost sank down inside it.

This was a Saturday morning, and most children her age were at play. But Caroline was ever so tired. The nights were a frightening time for her, and nobody seemed to understand how exhausted she was, but the doctor just smiled and pushed the blonde hair away from her eyes. She put on an old recording of Chopin and told Caroline that it was perfectly fine for her to just sleep.

That's how the sessions would start: with hot chocolate, Chopin, and sleep. For weeks it seemed. Every Saturday morning. And Caroline could never remember the doctor talking to her or asking her any questions. She'd just go there and get comfortable and start to rest. Later, Dr. Liebman would read to her. And in the months that followed, as her grades improved and she put on a little weight, Caroline began to sleep through the night.

That's when the dream started.

The first night she saw it in fragments; a face here, a brush stroke there, but never the full picture. She didn't know back then that any of it was connected. But then, over the years, with the doctor's help, the dream fit together.

In the beginning, she saw parts of it in black-and-white, with slow dissolves like a movie. But as time passed, the image focused and it became more precise.

Now, on this night, in December of '97, it was all in color. So vivid, so sharp, that Caroline was there with them, in that studio in the Village, and it was 1938. She knew the approximate year from the style of the mural they painted. The work was enormous, ten feet tall by forty feet wide. A diptych in two panels, mounted on canvas. It must have been commissioned for a special event, because most of the New Deal artists painted frescoes, and this work was meant to be moved.

It was raining in the dream and she could hear it coming down on the frosted-glass skylights of the studio.

The three artists were almost finished now after months of hard work. They were joking and playing around, flicking paint on each other and laughing. But Caroline never heard their voices, only the music coming out of an old Philco upright in the corner.

It had to be you. . . . It had to be you. . . .

From the first night she heard that song in her dream, Caroline began collecting the blues singers. Bessie Smith, Libbie Cotton, Lady Day, trying to identify the singer that was belting it out from that radio. By the time she was twenty, she owned dozens of blues LPs from the thirties. Cuts on Decca, Chess, Bluebird, Aladdin, and Biograph. But she hadn't yet found that recording. It tore at her for years, and the dream stayed in fragments. Then one night in 1988, she did better than locate the record. She found the singer herself.

Caroline was down in New York for a weekend. Down from Providence where she studied painting at the Rhode

Island School of Design. Her boyfriend at the time was a young turk in the bond business and they'd gone to a little place on Eighth Street for dinner. There was an old Black woman at the club who'd come back to singing after years as a nurse. Her name was Alberta Hunter. She was eighty-three then, and Caroline almost died when she started her opening set:

It had to be you. It had to be you. I wandered around and finally found, somebody who . . .

And that night, in her room at the Hotel Carlyle, after the young bond trader had pushed himself into her and left her alone, Caroline slept and went into the dream. And then, for the first time, she could see it in color.

The artist's studio, an old paint-splattered warehouse with huge, frosted-glass skylights facing north. The walls were a dingy off-white with mahogany wainscoting, and in the corner, there was the old Philco upright tuned to WNEW with the young Alberta singing it live:

It had to be you. It had to be you. I wandered around and finally found the somebody who . . .

When Caroline was old enough to know what hypnosis was, Dr. Liebman explained what was happening each time she went to sleep in the office. Helen was taking her back, regressing her into childhood to get to the root of her trouble. Somewhere, buried in her subconscious, was some terrible incident. Something that has caused her great pain. Somehow, this dream with the artists held the key to that trauma, and over the years, she got closer to it.

Caroline tossed and turned now and exhaled hard. She was back in the thirties, in the studio. Along the south wall the painters were putting the finishing touches on the enormous ten-by-forty-foot mural, a huge canvas in two sections, celebrating the dignity of American workers.

The mood was upbeat and randy, almost sexual, as the

three artists moved with the music. The Depression was almost over. Happy days were here again. The Dodgers were winning and these kids were young: full of heart and testosterone.

Could make me be true. Could make me be blue . . .

There were always three painters at work in the dream: two men and a woman. The female had striking blue eyes and black hair. Liz Taylor at twenty. She was finishing a part of the canvas where a crowd of workers were waving red flags.

And even be glad, just to be sad, thinking of you.

The woman looked up and blew a kiss to a rugged young painter on a scaffold above her. Tall and preppie with tortoiseshell horn-rims and Yankee good looks, he was completing a factory building at the top of the canvas.

Some others I've seen, might never be mean . . .

Meanwhile, a short, thin painter with curly brown hair came over and pinched the female artist in the ass. The woman grinned like a cat and rubbed her hand along his thigh. The thin painter shrugged as if to say, "Not with me, babycakes," then turned to finish a section of canvas with a coal miner.

Might never be cross or try to be boss but they wouldn't do . . .

Caroline Drexel could see it all clearly now as she slept in the enormous bed on the second floor of her Sutton Place co-op. She was in the dream, lost in the 1930s, moving with the music along with the artists. At peace for a few seconds, seeing the dream as a whole.

And then, as it always did, a back door to the studio opened and she saw *herself* walking in. Or maybe it wasn't, but the woman looked just like she did at twenty; a tall young blonde with high cheekbones and hazel eyes. She was carrying a bucket of ice and some Veuve Clicquot; dressed in tan jodhpurs and boots under a red riding jacket.

Old money. Newport. Just like Caroline. She seemed out of place in this paint-covered dingy old studio. But then she took off the jacket and picked up a brush, approaching the mural to touch up the face of a pilot.

For nobody else gave me a thrill, with all your faults I love you still, it had to be you, crazy old you, it had to be you. . . .

And then, as they did every time, the artists would finish the mural and the cork would pop on the champagne. Each of them would hold up a coffee cup and the pretty young blonde would pour in the bubbly as they clicked cups and stood back to admire their work, that enormous two-panel diptych.

A New York labor rally with workers full of energy, muscle, and hope. There were six figures across the front, representing American labor:

A pilot, a nurse, a stevedore, a farmer a teacher and a miner. Behind them, the crowd of workers was waving banners and crimson flags and behind them there were farms and factories. Social realism in the classic Thomas Hart Benton style. One of ten thousand murals commissioned under FDR's Works Progress Administration to decorate some public building.

Caroline had written her dissertation on the period and the lead chapter had been excerpted in *Art in America*. A spectacular achievement for an art history scholar her age. She'd taken her doctorate at Columbia to be in New York where most of the work had been done.

Her sessions with Dr. Liebman had continued right up to the early nineties when the doctor had suffered a stroke. Now, every Saturday, Caroline would visit her at the chronic care hospital on upper Fifth Avenue where the old woman lived, bringing her porcelin dolls and sneaking her thermoses of hot chocolate. Helen had been forced to give up her practice and her own doctor from Lenox Hill had sworn her off Gitanes. She spoke with a slur for a time and her left hand was paralyzed, But after months of therapy, she'd almost recovered. Still, she was in her late seventies and needed around-the-clock help. A clinical practice was out of the question. Besides, Helen was tired.

So every Saturday, Caroline would come. Helen would hold her arm and they'd walk to a terrace overlooking Central Park. The young Art Professor would light a Gitane and Helen would push close just to take in the smoke. They would talk. Helen would demand to know why Caroline was still single, and Caroline would say that the men who were rich enough not to care for her money were bankrupt in other ways. Helen would smile and they'd both cry when Caroline had to leave. She was as much a daughter as the Auschwitz survivor had ever known, and for the Sutton Place heiress, Helen was her surrogate mother.

Whatever it was that had sent her to Dr. Liebman had been buried years ago. Caroline functioned well and almost always slept through the night. The little girl with insomnia who'd been terrified of the dark now held a tenured chair in art history at Columbia University. The first woman in her line for six generations with an actual paying job. She was nationally ranked; a consultant to the Museum of Modern Art, a visiting curator at the L.A. County Museum, and few people knew that it had started one night with this dream.

Caroline Drexel, it seemed, had it all: the face of a runway model, a tenured professorship, and a fortune worth thirty million. But there was a problem. Once every month or so, she would wake up wondering. Not so much troubled as unfulfilled.

You see, for all she tried, she could never get to the end of that dream. She'd get as far as the champagne toast and then the door to the studio would fly open. The cold rain would pour in from the street and a young, violent man would storm up to the artists. A young man whose face she couldn't see. He would shout in a loud, muffled voice with words that she never made out and then rush across the studio, slamming down a newspaper in front of them. For years, that front page had seemed like a blur and then once in graduate school she'd seen Marcel Ophuls's film, *The Sorrow and the Pity*, and that very night the front page became clear. The eighty-point banner headline read, "Nazis Invade Austria."

Then the moment was shattered. She'd shoot up in bed and the dream would end the way the dream must have ended for those artists that night in the thirties. Caroline Drexel, beautiful, blonde, and exceedingly rich, would lie back down in bed, shivering and alone.

4

BROADWAY ON THE UPPER WEST SIDE OF NEW YORK WAS
quiet in the first hours of New Year's Day 1998. Bitter cold.
A few drunken revelers roared by in a taxi, blowing big
plastic horns. But it was late, almost three A.M., as two
figures walked south near the corner of Ninety-second
Street.

Hector Cruz was a seventeen-year-old Puerto Rican with
a hard cock and a bad attitude. Sonia Ortiz was fifteen.
They'd just come out of a social club at Ninety-third and
Amsterdam. Sonia had on gold plastic heels and a gold
spandex minidress under a red leather jacket. She'd bought
the dress at Loehmanns with her lunch money from Holy
Rosary. The jacket was really vinyl.

Sonia's Poppi had forbidden her to see Hector, who'd
spent a year in Spofford for grand theft auto. The kid liked
to jack Beemers. That's all. "Was da big fuggin' deal?"
said Hector. "It's not like I'm boostin' Trans Ams." But
Sonia's Poppi said he'd take out his straight razor and cut
him if the little prick ever got near her again.

Hector had to find a place to go with her. His old lady
worked days as an LPN at Morrisania, and Sonia's Poppi

was always home, so he had to find someplace to take her after the clubs. Someplace warm.

"Don't worry, chica," said Hector as he pulled her along toward the subway grate at the corner of Ninety-first. "I got a spot."

One of Sonia's heels got caught for a second in the cross-hatched metal of the grate, but he helped her pull it out and then bent down with the flashlight, searching.

"Shit . . . where the fuck is it?"

And then he found it: the padlock across the hasp at the edge of the grate. He looked around, making sure nobody on Broadway could see them.

But it was late. Three fuckin' thirty and there was nobody out. He shivered as he took out the pick and started working the lock. It was so cold, his fingers stuck to the metal, but he couldn't do it with gloves.

"Come on, baby," said Sonia. "My tits are ice cold. You said this wouldn't take long." Her red-painted lips were starting to turn blue.

Then she heard the noise of the lock as Hector flicked it open and pulled up the grate. He panned the flashlight down, revealing a short set of stairs. The passenger escape exit from an abandoned subway station on the old IRT Broadway line. Down below, they could hear the sound of a train roaring through.

Hector looked around one more time, checking to see if they'd been spotted, and then pulled Sonia down, letting the grate fall slowly over his head as they made their way down the cold metal stairs.

"You jus' wait, chica. Hector make you warm."

They came down onto the platform of what was once the Ninety-first Street station. Arc light flashed from the third electrified rail as a southbound train roared by, and Hector pulled Sonia across the deserted platform, shining the light until he came to a corner near the old token booth.

He stopped and shined the light down to show her: the sleeping bag that he'd laid out that morning. Next to it there was a Coleman lamp filled with kerosene.

"Check it out," said Hector.

He took out a plastic lighter, turned the gas cock on the lamp, and lit it. Right away, he could see the smile on Sonia's face in the hot yellow glow from the light.

"The bag was a bitch to boost. But it's goose down. Hundred percent. Soft, jus' like you."

Sonia smiled as Hector dropped the flashlight and threw his arms around her, easing her down onto the sleeping bag. They started to tongue-kiss when, just then, arc light flashed again across the tracks and a northbound IRT train roared uptown.

Hector pulled down the top of Sonia's spandex dress and moved her right breast out of the little black bra. He licked her nipple. Then he worked his way down and tongued the silk vee of her panties. She let out a little sigh and pushed him back. But Hector wouldn't stop now, and he knew that Sonia didn't want him to. This wasn't date rape or forcible entry. It was pure, postpubescent animal lust.

He pulled down the satin panties and undid his belt. The zipper dropped and then:

"Ahhhhh."

He put it inside her, grabbing her by the waist and nailing her against the platform floor as Sonia let out a gasp.

"Oh baby, oh baby . . ."

The train screeched past them and the old station rattled for the two billionth time.

Suddenly, up above the spot where Hector was taking her, an old pipe wrapped in canvas began to leak.

"Oh baby, oh baby . . ."

She was panting now. Then, "What was that?" She stopped, looking up toward the street.

"What?" asked Hector, also panting.

"I felt a drop on my face."

"Forget it. Jus' tell me it's good. Say it's good . . ." He started pumping her again.

"Hay qué bueno baby. El mejor . . ."

They fucked for another few seconds and then, "Shit." She pulled back as another drop fell on her face. The water was cold. Almost freezing.

"What?" said Hector, stopping.

"Fuckin' water." She looked up. "Shit."

Hector pulled out of her now, grabbing the flashlight. He panned it up toward the pipe.

"It's nothin'. Pipes always leakin' down here."

He switched off the light and moved her down a few feet.

"Here's a spot. Jus' relax."

He buried his tongue in her mouth and in another few seconds he was in her again, only now she was standing up and he was pounding her against the cold tile of the station wall.

"Oh baby, oh baby. . . . Pick me up . . ."

Hector pulled up the gold spandex and reached under her buttocks as she lifted her legs and crossed them around his bare ass.

"Oh baby, oh baby, so big."

"Does it hurt?"

"Yeah, but I love it."

He bent his head down to suck on her tit.

Meanwhile, up above, the drops were getting bigger.

"Oh baby, oh baby, fuck me."

As the water from the pipe began to fall now, their passion started to build.

"Uh, uh, uh, uh . . ."

Pretty soon the drops were getting bigger and the sound of fucking was getting louder and louder until, finally, the tear in the canvas insulation became a rip and . . .

"Oh baby, oh baby . . ."

"Uh, uh, uh, uh . . ."

Hector and Sonia hit climax and the pipe burst, drenching them both in a hundred gallons of ice-cold water.

5

TWO HOURS LATER A ROAD CREW SHOWED UP FROM THE
New York City Transit Authority. They were pissing and
moaning about being dragged from their beds on the coldest
New Year's morning in memory.

The head of the crew was a 300-pound Italian beast from
Kew Gardens named Smaglia. His sidekick was a red-
headed Irish runt from Bensonhurst named Sullivan. The
third man was a skinny Black kid named Leon who was
wearing colors under his TA jumpsuit and a Knicks hat in
gang-style reverse. Leon knew that he'd rather be home
pulling pud, watching those 900 ads on cable than down in
this freezing hole, but he was the junior man on the crew,
so he kept it quiet and worked on the scaffolding while the
other two biscuit heads shot the shit.

"Hey, Smags, how much OT we get for this?"

Sully was nosing up to the big Italian as Leon finished
setting the scaffold.

"Fuck, I don't know. Soon as that phone rang after midnight we were on double golden, plus there's your holiday
differential. I figure, what? Maybe sixteen, seventeen an
hour, plus the short turnaround after that main break at Wall
Street."

"Beautiful."

"What? I could give two fucks for the money tonight. It's New Year's Eve."

"Yeah. You're right," said Sully, suddenly disinterested. "All's I wanna do is get home, play hide the mouse with my Paula."

"Don't forget to smell the cheese first," said Leon.

Sully shot a look to the Black kid.

"What's that s'posed to mean?"

"It means I seen your wife."

"Hey, fuck you, Leon."

"Hey, fuck your sister."

The Irish runt lunged for him, but Leon just pushed him off. Sully turned to make another pass at him when Smaglia jumped in.

"What've I gotta do with you two? I'm freezing my fuckin' stones down here and you're giving me Macho Camacho and Cesar Chavez?"

"Spic boxers? No way," said Leon.

Sully shoved his middle finger into Leon's face, so the young Black gave him the under-the-chin Sicilian gesture for "fuck you."

"You tight with the Eye-tye, maybe you understand this."

"Cut the fuckin' shit, Leon. It's late," said Smaglia. "Now, where's that goddamn scaffold I asked for?"

Leon shrugged and pushed the stainless steel scaffolding up under the break.

Smaglia climbed up on the first stage and panned the light along the pipe. It was frozen now with ten-inch stalactites of ice.

"Christ, it's a fuckin' hemorrhage."

"Good thing it was down below zero," said Sully. "Otherwise we'd be friggin' hip-deep in here."

Smaglia checked a set of dirty blueprints.

"Goddamn ten-inch main," he said. "They haven't used that kinda stock since the fifties."

"Where we gonna find pipe like that? said Leon.

"Gotta get the fuckin' canvas off before we can get to the break."

Smaglia climbed to the second stage. He looked down to Leon.

"Hey, numbnuts. Throw me a box cutter."

Leon bent over a toolbox and whispered "Fuck you, Homes" under his breath.

He took his time searching for the little tool while Smaglia shivered and Sully tried to set fire to a Lucky. Just then, the IRT Local roared by, heading south, and the station lit up. In the momentary glare of its headlamp, Leon located the box cutter and tossed it up to his boss.

Smaglia made a long slit in the canvas insulation near the break. The noise of the train was building, and the light in the station flickered on and off like a strobe. At long last, Smags completed the incision and pulled away at the canvas.

"What the fuck?"

"What is it?"

"I dunno. Gimme some light over here."

Leon shined a second searchlight from below as Smaglia scored around the pipe with the box cutter. He grabbed hold of the second layer of canvas and pulled.

"Holy shit. Look at this."

"What the fuck *is* it?" asked Sully. He was halfway up the scaffold by now.

Smaglia gave one more tug to the old insulation and then, finally, it came out.

"Mother a Christ . . ."

It was some kind of picture. A painting. The thing was covered with plaster, but it looked like some people in front—workers maybe—and factories in the back.

• • •

Later that morning, Caroline Drexel was pouring Vienna Roast from a Braun coffeemaker into a Spode china cup. She was in the white tiled kitchen of her Sutton Place co-op. *Channel 4 News* was on in the background, but the sound on the TV was down, so she didn't hear the report. She was about to leave the kitchen when she took a sip. The coffee tasted bitter, so she turned back for some sugar.

Then, as she crossed the travertine marble floor, she looked up and caught a glimpse of the newscast. On the screen next to the anchorman, there was a graphic. The letters below the graphic said: Mural Found.

Caroline rushed to the TV set as they rolled a taped news report. There was a picture of workmen in a subway station holding up a large canvas. The canvas had pictures of a crowd waving red flags. In the foreground, covered in plaster, she saw what looked like the figures of workers. Caroline grabbed for a remote and frantically tried to turn up the volume. She caught the last words of the reporter:

"... mural was believed to have been painted in the 1930s during the WPA."

Caroline dropped the cup full of coffee.

"Oh my God."

The cup shattered across her floor and she covered her mouth with her hand.

It was the mural from her dream.

6

THIS WAS GOING TO BE THE FIRST NIGHT FOR ALEX, THE night her new life would start: after three weeks of therapy, four stitches to the edge of her lip, a hundred bucks on new dead-bolts, and two separate visits to that awful police precinct.

The way they had questioned her. God. She'd been too embarrassed to tell them he'd gone up her ass. Besides, her blood test was negative. Still, with HIV it would be another six months before she knew for sure.

Alex wondered why they didn't arrest the sick fuck. Lock him up. The doctor at the Bellevue emergency room had said another quarter inch and that gash on her lip would have scarred. But the cops put it down as a domestic disturbance. Shit. The goddamn lawyer had cost her a thousand just to get the protective order—order of protection—whatever the hell it was called.

But all that was behind her now. The stitches had come off yesterday, and with a little Revlon 32 and some blush-on, there was no way to tell. Her old roommate Sasha from Parsons had called and they were going to meet for drinks.

Sasha'd been seeing a young associate from Skaaden Arps and his best friend, David, from Yale, was in town on a case. Sasha had pointed him out to Alex across the bar at Spring Street, and she'd never seen blue eyes like those on a man. She wondered what his cock was like and felt a little twinge down below. She touched herself between her legs and she was wet. God, it had been so long now. Anyway, Sasha was going to try and set up a meeting tonight.

Just a week ago, Alex had checked her monthly reading in *Elle* and the box for Sagittarians had promised a "momentous event" in January. She thought maybe it would come in her personal life and then, three days later, she'd gotten the greatest commission of her life: a referral from Leo Castelli through a professor in the art department at Columbia, Dr. Caroline Drexel. She'd been called in to consult on this mural they'd found.

Alex knew the Castelli connection would pay off when she'd done that John Singer Sargent for him. She'd turned it around in a week. The big gallery owner had wanted it cleaned for a Japanese buyer, a real estate mogul who'd become enamored of American masters. The Sargent was a rather weak oil from his middle years. In fact, it had languished for decades in the basement of the Gardener Museum in Boston, unworthy of exhibition. But then, back in '89, after that big theft had cleaned them out, the Gardener board put the Sargent up on the block.

Leo had seen her book and was best friends with her mentor, Dr. Rothstein, at Parsons. So he'd given Alex a shot, and she'd pleased him beyond his expectations. She'd been working with a new line of solvents that raised the impurities without searing the pigment, and that dingy old Sargent had come back to Leo as if it had been sealed under pressured glass for a century.

When the mural turned up in the subway, the city commissioner of arts & restoration went into apoplexy. The mayor had just been pilloried after four priceless murals were found painted over and covered with bulletin board cork in the Williamsburg Housing Projects. How could the city allow its art treasures to die like that?

So Rudolph Giuliani picked up the phone and called Columbia, where Dr. Drexel was the reigning queen on the New Deal Arts projects. Rudy wanted the subway mural brought back to life in time for a Metropolitan fund-raiser to kick off his reelection campaign. And when Drexel called Castelli, the gray eminence had not forgotten Alex Sloane.

Now there it was, at center stage in Alex's loft, half-caked in plaster but spread wide on stretchers as she dusted it off with a number ten foxtail brush and began the painstaking process of bringing it back to life. It was mildewed, and the canvas was badly deteriorated, but there was no mistaking the outline of the workers in front: A pilot, a nurse, and a stevedore.

She'd been working on it all day and had succeeded in removing just the first layer of plaster from the upper right quadrant when the phone rang. It was Sasha.

"You ready? They're going to meet us at seven-thirty."

"Are you serious? I thought you said nineish."

"Robert's deposition was canceled. Besides, what's wrong with early? This way maybe drinks first, then dinner."

Alex shot a look into a mirror. "God, I'm covered in solvent."

"That's why they invented the shower massage."

"All right." Alex checked her watch. "Six-thirty. I'll be there by seven-forty-five. Just keep his motor running."

"Okay, hon. Odeon."

"Wait a minute. I thought we were meeting uptown."

"Robert likes the gravlax at Odeon. What's the dif?"

"What if Carlos is there?" Alex asked, suddenly worried.

"So what if he is? The sonovabitch doesn't *own* you."

Alex hesitated. "No . . . you're right."

"Good. Quarter to eight, then. Bye."

"Bye." Alex hung up and quickly dropped her brushes into a plastic container of kerosene. She pulled a large section of cheesecloth over the mural and rushed toward the shower.

She set the knob on the shower massage to pulse and stepped into the black marble shower. She'd bought the loft on Prince Street raw when the building had first turned co-op. All there was on the floor back then was a water riser, a 220 electric line, and five thousand square feet of space. She had to bring up the gas line herself. Broke her nails putting down the number-four common oak floor. Her brother, Jason, down from Syracuse, had done most of the work and it had taken every bit of her share of their mother's life insurance to finish, but now it was done: the perfect postmodern space for living and work, and she'd never leave. Never. You couldn't *find* a finished top-floor loft in SoHo with north light and a certificate of occupancy for under a million. Even if this David got down on his knees and *begged* her to marry him, she'd stay put. Oh God, here she was picking out her china pattern and she hadn't even met the guy yet.

The warm water felt good on her face. Alex checked her fingers for any smell of the solvent and poured a small pool of rose oil into her hand. The dull, numbing drone of the shower massage blocked any outside noise, so she didn't hear it when the plastic ruler was inserted into the window lock and the man came in from the fire escape.

Slowly, he made his way toward the bathroom to make sure she was still in the shower. Good. The bitch was still zoning out on the water. He saw her reflection through the steaming glass of the shower door and felt himself getting hard. He wanted to do her right there against the shower tile, but he had business first. The man put the plastic ruler back in his trench coat and walked up to the mural. He lifted the cheesecloth and pulled on a pair of latex surgical gloves. Then he ran his finger along the plaster-covered faces and smiled. He was about to set it on fire when, just then, he heard the shower stop. The man knew she was defenseless now. Soaking wet, groping for a towel. If he wanted to hurt her, this was the perfect time. But destroying the mural would hurt her much more. So he darted his head left, then right, until he found it. A closet off her bedroom. Someplace to hide.

It was seven-thirty by the time Alex Sloane had pulled on the little red Nicole Miller and finished painting her face. When she'd first come out of the shower, she'd made a move toward black leather, but then she thought about Carlos and decided on silk.

The man was across the loft inside the closet, but the door was open a slit and he watched as she pulled on the red stockings and clipped them onto the red satin garter. She tied the tiny red G-string at the side of her leg, and he rubbed a latex-gloved hand along his stiffening penis. The G-string was the kind that could fall away with the tug of the bow.

Shit. With all this red on, she must be making plans for later on. Would *he* love to fuck her right now. Push her down at the sink so her face was pressed against the mirror. Her lipstick would smear on the glass and he'd stick it hard up her chocolate channel. But no, he had work to do.

Alex checked her watch. Seven-thirty-five. It was a three-minute cab ride to Odeon. That's if she could *get* a cab at this time. She had on heels and she didn't look forward to walking it. But God, she felt lucky tonight. There'd be a cab waiting when she came out on West Broadway. She could feel it.

Alex pursed her lips and checked her face in a mirror. She closed the little red Chanel bag and thought for a minute, then opened a drawer and pulled out a package of Trojans. She snapped open the bag again and dropped them in.

The man watched as she hit the lights, moved to the freight elevator, and stabbed at the button.

Suddenly, a bell went off on the elevator down on eight. Shit. Alex checked her watch. Seven-thirty-seven. She pulled open the metal cage door across the front and looked down. Damn it. The elevator was parked four floors below and Raphael was loading canvases on board.

"Raffie. Send it up, will you?"

He dropped one of the canvases and looked up. "Sorry, Babes. Gotta get these out for a show. Figure another ten minutes."

Alex checked her watch again, clearly pissed.

"Come on Raphael, I've got a date."

She stabbed away at the button again and the bell rang.

"What the hell's wrong with the stairs?"

"I'm twelve goddamn floors up. That's what's wrong with the stairs," Alex said as she pushed out her front door and started down the stairwell surrounding the elevator shaft. The heels sounded like machine gun blasts on the cast-iron steps.

Then, as the big fire door slammed shut behind her, the man came out of the shadows and moved toward the mural. Because the canvas was so badly damaged, the faces of the three figures up front were covered in plaster. But behind them in the mural, he could see the crowd of workers. They were marching with clenched fists and waving red flags. He thought about the bitch in high heels on the stairwell and rubbed himself again.

As Alex rounded the eighth-floor landing, Raphael opened the fire door from his loft and smiled.

"All right, take it. Just tell that boyfriend of yours to stop pissing in my hallway."

"Carlos is history. It's over."

"Hey, now you've come to your senses."

"Right."

Alex got into the elevator and stabbed at the down button. The elevator motor roared up above and then the car began to rise.

Alex said, "Shit."

"You pushed the up button, Babes. Gotta go up before you go down. And speaking of going down, who's the new boy-toy?"

Alex smiled like a cat.

"I'll let you know later. Wish me luck."

She waved at him with her painted red nails as she disappeared up toward twelve, and Raphael slammed the cage door on eight.

Meanwhile, up above, the man opened his trench coat and pulled out a can of Ronson's lighter fluid. He popped the red cap and began spraying it over the mural.

As the elevator moved up toward ten, Alex was checking her watch.

The man saturated the old canvas with fluid.

The elevator moved up past eleven.

The man took out a gold Dunhill lighter. He flicked it once, twice, then put the flame to the edge of the canvas.

Just then, the elevator hit twelve and Alex flung open the metal cage door.

"Oh my God!"

The mural was on fire. The three workers were engulfed.

Horrified, Alex rushed from the elevator and saw the man.

"Goddamn you . . . noooooo!"

Down below, Raphael heard the scream.

"Alex? Alex? What's wrong?" He started up the stairs

two at a time while up above, Alex ran to a wall and grabbed a fire extinguisher. But before she could get to the mural, the man pulled her back by the hair and slammed her savagely against the brick wall. She hit her head and went down.

He checked for a pulse, but there was blood coming from the edge of her eye. She was dead.

Raphael called out from the stairwell.

"Alex. What the fuck's wrong? I smell smoke."

The man rushed to the front door and thrust it open. That Black prick was two floors below and closing. So he shot back into the loft and rushed across to the window, making his way out onto the fire escape and up toward the roof of the building, just as Raphael burst into the loft.

The smoke was too thick now to see anything.

He covered his face from the heat as he yelled out her name. "Alex!" There was no response, so he felt his way along the wall until he found the fire alarm. Just then, the sprinklers went on. Raphael smashed the glass and pulled down the alarm trigger. A fire bell sounded.

In seconds, the smoke cleared and Raphael saw her body lying against the brick wall. The sad little art restorer who trusted too much, dressed up in the red silk minidress, with the blood streaming down from her eye. She looked like a limp, broken doll.

Alex Sloane's horoscope had said that a "momentous event" would happen in the month of January, and tonight, for once, the astrological signs had been right.

7

THE RIVALRY BETWEEN THE NYPD AND THE FDNY RAN broad and deep. Historically, both departments were manned from the Irish enclaves, filled with the progeny of immigrants from Kerry, Mayo, and Cork. But, as in all tribes, there was a pecking order, and among New York cops it was commonly held that "the blues got the best and the reds got the rest."

If you were Italian and you came up in the city, you had several options: become a cop, become a priest, or get made. But when it came to public service, there was only one choice for the working-class Mick: you wore a gun and chased predicate felons or you screamed through the streets in an American LaFrance and chased fires.

Somewhere along the line, the fiction developed that cops led a more dangerous life. God knows, enough of them went down in the line. It seemed like every week there was another TV news story of blue men in sad rows at a gravesite.

But the truth was that the life expectancy in a ghetto engine company was far shorter. Inner city firefighters put their stones on the line ten times a day in the hot seasons. They got blown out of windows, suffocated by toxins, crushed to death under floor joists, and drenched in burning inflammables with such regularity that death had become a routine and the funerals almost never drew airtime. They were rewarded for their heroism by having their hoses slashed with machetes or trash cans of burning swill thrown at their trucks, and more than a few men had been shot off their ladders by snipers angry that any representative of the man would venture into the hood.

The myth was that they spent their days shining firepoles and watching *Oprah*. But firefighting was a dangerous life, and emotions ran deep in these men who resented the attention cops got. You see, unlike their uniformed brothers, firefighters had none of the opportunities for "private advancement." Except for a few inspectors, the rank and file in a ladder company had no chance for a bribe. The unmentioned pad didn't exist for these men. So, in their minds, they took all the risks with few of the residual benefits.

Though their base pay, health, and pensions were comparable, the men of the New York Police Department seemed to always come first in the hierarchy. The Police Academy took the first and the strongest sons. The cops always marched first past St. Patrick's on March 17th. And many an Emerald Society communion breakfast ended in fistfights as the men of the FDNY sought to correct this disparity.

There was an incident back in '95 captured with a front-page *Daily News* headline that read: "Battle of the Badges." Rumors had been floating that the NYPD's Emergency Services Unit was about to take over all rescue work, a large part of which was handled by the FDNY's elite rescue companies. On this particular day, there was an entrapment in Brooklyn, meaning a motorist had been pinned in his car after a crash. The FDNY's 105 Truck responded and immediately deployed a Hurst Tool (the jaws of life) to cut out the poor man before he bled to death.

Suddenly an ESU unit pulled up and an argument broke out over who was going to save the guy first. Well, one thing led to another, and one of the firefighters knocked a uniformed cop to the ground. The blues radioed their precinct and were ordered to withdraw. The motorist was freed. Finally, 105 Truck took up, as the reds call it when they leave a scene.

Then, on the way back to the firehouse, a pair of police radio patrol units literally cut the truck off. Two sets of uniforms jumped out and grabbed the firefighter who threw the punch, off the rig. He ended up back-cuffed under his Kahn's helmet with his turnout coat and boots on.

There was simply no love lost between these men.

And so it was that when the unmarked Chevy Caprice pulled up outside the crime scene on Prince Street, the driver was prepared for a fight.

Eddie Burke looked for all the world like a cop. He dressed like a middle-grade detective in the same single-breasted wool worsted, $255 off the rack at Sy Syms. He carried a Smith & Wesson nine in a Pachmyer holster at the small of his back. There was even a shield in his wallet, and clipped to the roof of the Chevy with a magnet was the same blinking red Mars light, known to cops as the Kojak bubble. He had the same face: the ruddy complexion from Bantry Bay; the cobalt-blue eyes, and the same killer smile you see in all early thirties Irish-Americans before the drink kills their will. In fact, the only thing about him that would set him apart from a precinct detective was his shoes. There was a standing joke in the Bureau of Fire Investigation that the one sure way to tell a fire marshal from a cop was by looking down at his feet. The marshal was the one with the dirty shoes.

Eddie Burke was FDNY, and even though he'd come from a family of blues, even though his old man had been a legend in the NYPD, he knew that he was not welcome here.

This was his first night back after the suspension for clocking Kivlihan, and he'd celebrated by having dinner at a gin mill on Columbus.

He looked tired as he ducked under the yellow crime scene tape and moved up toward the cast-iron steps of the old loft building. He had a two-day growth of beard on his face and he'd been nursing a cold.

Eddie stopped at the edge of the steps while the EMS boys rolled out the gurney with the body bag. He flashed his shield. One of the body handlers stopped as Eddie unzipped the top of the bag. Just then, a big bull in uniform named Carney cut in front of the body.

"Sorry, crime scene."

"I'm working," Eddie told him.

"And who the fuck are you?"

"Fire marshal."

"What's your name?"

"Eddie Burke."

The bull laughed. "You wish. There's only one Eddie Burke."

Eddie looked up at the black New York sky. He had the same name as his father, and this kind of thing happened five times a day.

"Look, it's cold, man. I just came off leave." *Suspension* didn't sound right under the circumstances.

"So?"

"So how about giving me a break."

The big bull just grinned.

"Sure. Just wait over there by the curb and when Crime Scene is finished, I'll let you by."

But Eddie had had it. His blue eyes went dead and he pulled out his tin again.

"I told you. I'm working."

He started to push by, but Carney stopped him.

"Fire marshals don't count for *dick* here."

"Is that right?"

"Yeah."

Eddie lunged forward and grabbed the big Harp by the balls. He squeezed and then whispered in Carney's ear, "You know, if you're gonna use the word 'dick,' you'd better have one."

The cop exploded. He swung out with his right, but Eddie ducked and shot a left jab to Carney's abdomen. The big bull went down to his knees.

"Jesus . . ."

Just then, a detective sergeant named Jelke came out of the loft building.

"Aw, Christ . . . break it up."

"But boss, he just—" Carney stood up now.

"What? Threatened your manhood?"

"But Sarge, the fuck—"

"I told you. Forget it."

Jelke pushed Carney back, and Eddie unzipped the body bag. He pulled the penlight flash from his raincoat and looked at the blackened remains of Alex Sloane. He ran his fingers along her cheek and drew off some of the soot, rubbing it between his fingers and smelling it. There was the caustic hint of accelerants. Next, Eddie shined the light in her nostrils. They were clean. She'd died before the smoke got too thick. He looked for petechial hemorrhages in the whites of her eyes—small exploding blood vessels that are always the sign of death by asphyxiation. Not there. But he saw a small clot of blood at the edge of her left pupil. He turned to one of the EMS guys.

"The ME clean her up?"

The paramedic nodded.

"Took a blood sample from under the left eye. He's saying trauma to the posterior lobe."

Eddie pulled the red hair away and saw the contusion at the base of her skull.

"That's where she hit the wall," said the paramedic. "Splatter on the brick upstairs."

Eddie looked at him for a second and said nothing when Carney, the bull, jumped in.

"Come on, Burke. Make a decision. Either close the bag or fuck her right here."

Eddie was about to lunge at him again when suddenly there was a small commotion at the door of the loft building. Two uniforms walked out followed by a stunning blonde in a brown leather trench coat.

As she came face-to-face with Eddie, she stopped for a second. There was a flicker of interest and then she moved toward a blue and white.

"Thanks for your help, Dr. Drexel," said Jelke. "My men will take you uptown."

She nodded without saying a word and got into the car. But Eddie Burke couldn't stop looking at her. He had given up with most women. After Mary Rose had taken off, he'd gone through the requisite period of self-pity and then started to hunt again. But after two years of dating, he'd come up empty. The ones that got him hard never challenged him, and the ones that made him think left him cold.

But this one . . . she had to be some kind of model, and Jelke had called her *doctor.* Christ. Before he could think about it, the woman was inside the unit. She stared back at Eddie. He could swear for a second that she looked at his cock, and then the squad car screeched off.

8

EDDIE BURKE POPPED A VITAMIN C AS HE STABBED AT THE
elevator button in the hallway of the loft building. A pair
of detectives stood by the stairwell smoking, and Eddie
heard one of them whisper, "Big Eddie's kid. Best he could
do was FD."

Eddie shook his head. Christ. When will this ever stop?
He started moving toward them to finish what he'd begun
with Carney, but the freight elevator arrived and the metal
cage door swung open.

As soon as he got off the elevator, Eddie knew that this
had been a flash blaze. It had ignited quickly, burned hot
and yellow, and incinerated the point of origin. But there
was little more than smoke damage everywhere else.

The photographer from the Crime Scene Unit stood on
a ladder to get one last high shot. He bounced the flash off
the smoke-charred ceiling and banged off a picture.

When he finished, Eddie pulled out a battered Polaroid
and popped off his own set. No sense asking NYPD for
copies.

After the wide shots, he approached the metal table next
to the easel where Alex had stored her jars of paint thinners
and solvents. He took a picture showing the table in relation

to the canvas, and then took out a small microcassette recorder.

"Marshal Burke, four January, ninety-eight, at one twenty-five Prince Street Apartment twelve-B. Commencing BFI physical. From the spread of char on the proximate walls and ceiling joists, it appears that the point of origin was an easel located approximately ten meters from the north wall and six meters from the east. Period. The depth of char, blistering, and the absence of alligator burning suggests a white-hot flash fire of between twelve hundred and fourteen hundred degrees Fahrenheit, extinguished within minutes by overhead sprinklers. Paragraph.

"The rate, direction, and extent of the spread, coupled with odors present, indicate the use of accelerants in the burn. Period. There is a metal table located one half meter from PO. Period. It contains a number of solvents and paint thinners, presumably used in the decedent's work as an art restorer. Period. Among those solvents visible, there is kerosene, turpentine, and the degreaser trichloroethylene. One container says AB-Fifty-seven solvent. Period."

Eddie clicked off the recorder and bent down near the mural, now reduced to a pile of black char. He pulled out a pair of hemostat tweezers, gently picked up an inch square section of the blackened canvas, and dropped it into a shiny, one-pint sample can. The orange BFI sticker on the outside said Evidence. Just then, he felt Sergeant. Jelke looming over him.

"You're wasting your time."

Eddie stood up. "Is that right?"

"Yup. It was a homicide. Intent to kill."

"I don't think so."

"What was it, then?"

"Arson with a manslaughter chaser. You can smell the accelerant two blocks away."

He started to exit the loft, but Jelke stopped him.

"Look, Burke, you can pick up all the little pieces of dirt you want, but I'm telling you, this case is down."

"We'll see." Eddie pushed past him.

Jelke waited until he got to the front door.

"You're blowin' the call, kid."

Eddie stopped.

Jelke lit a cigarette. Cocky. Confident.

"Normally, I wouldn't say anything, you being FDNY and all, but—

"What?"

"I knew your father."

Eddie turned to face him now. "You and half of New York."

"Yeah."

"So let me get this straight. You're trying to save me from fucking up because of Big Eddie?"

"Why not? The man broke me in."

"Okay," said Eddie. "Let's hear it. You've got one female DOA, an arson fire, and no prints. What else?"

Jelke strutted up and whispered into his ear, "We know who did it." He cocked his head toward the bedroom.

Inside one of her bureau drawers, under a tangle of silk bustiers and garter belts, Jelke pulled out a framed color snapshot of Alex Sloane. She was hugging a dark Latin male. The picture had been taken with a wide-angle lens as the Latin male held out the camera in front of them and stuck his pointed tongue into Alex's ear. She was wearing a studded dog collar.

"The boyfriend," said Jelke. "One Carlos Guzman. Would-be Bolivian painter and crack head. The neighbors said he'd come up to the girl's loft every other night and knock her shitless. She got an order of protection with the Sixth Precinct, and the last time he beat her, he went out through the window."

Jelke turned to the open loft window where a CSU tech was dusting for prints.

"Yeah?" said Eddie. "So why the fire?"

"You kiddin'? The fuck came here. They fought. He hit her too hard, and she cracked her skull. He set the fire to cover. Case closed."

Eddie just shook his head. He wasn't buying.

Just then, one of the uniforms rushed up to Jelke.

"We got him, boss. Rooftop, two blocks away on Canal."

Jelke smiled. He kissed his middle finger and pointed it toward Eddie. Then he tore out of the loft.

Eddie rushed to Canal Street on foot as Jelke pulled up in a blue and white. Searchlights panned the top of the building.

On the roof, Carlos Guzman shivered as he crouched behind a standpipe. Was this the man who crushed Alex Sloane's skull as he slammed her against the wall? From the manic, half-dazed expression on Carlos's face, it was hard to tell. But one thing was certain; he was terrified. Carlos popped a vial and shoved a crystal of rock into a pipe as the scene played out like something from an old Cagney film.

Down below on Canal Street, Jelke grabbed a bullhorn and hit the switch.

"It's finished kid. Give yourself up."

He nodded to a Puerto Rican uniform for the translation.

"Alto piricuaco! Rendirse, ahora!"

Beggar dog, thought Eddie. Those fucking PRs had such a flair for high drama.

Up on the roof, Carlos Guzman got the message. He lit the pipe, sucking in hard. The hit took him up for a second, but he was starting to shiver again. He thought, fuck, he never should have come to this place. Never should have left La Paz. He took another hit and coughed out the smoke as he heard the scream again from below.

"Rendirse. Rendirse, ahora!"

Suddenly, an exit door flew open across the rooftop and the uniformed bull named Carney rushed out. He was followed by two detectives.

Carlos took off like a shot as the three cops drew their guns and gave chase.

Carlos zigzagged across the asphalt of the roof, moving in and out of the skylights that lit up so many artists' lofts down below. He came to the edge of one roof and dropped down half a story to an adjoining roof where he did a broken field run across the black graveled surface.

The cops were maybe twenty yards behind him now when one of the detectives cried out, "Police, halt."

But Carlos kept moving, so Carney crouched down into a modified Weaver stance and capped off a shot.

It fractured a brick chimney inches from Carlos's head and he stumbled. Then he got up and rushed to the edge of the roof.

Down on Canal Street, the searchlights showed Carlos balanced on the sheet-metal ledge. He was staring at a lower roof ten feet across an alley, thinking about whether he could make it, when Carney fired again. This time the bullet got so close that Carlos could feel it whizz past his ear. So, with the cops gaining on him, Carlos ran back to give himself distance, then jumped off the roof.

Down below, Eddie saw it almost in slow motion as Carlos got halfway across the alley and Carney fired a third time. The .38 slug ripped through the painter's left shoulder and slammed him forward against the ledge of the building across the alley.

Eddie watched as Carlos hung on the ledge for a second. He watched as the three cops stopped on the roof ledge, holstering their guns. And he watched as Carlos weakened.

The blood spurted out of his shoulder wound as he reached for a piece of ornamental coping on the ledge, but the sheet metal gave way, and Carlos, the sadist, dropped ninety feet to his death.

Eddie tore across Canal Street and a westbound car had to swerve to avoid him. He didn't even hear the brakes of the car as it screeched to a stop. He didn't hear Jelke's voice bellowing behind him to get away.

All he heard was the final gurgle and the death rattle as Carlos Guzman spit blood and stared up at him bug-eyed.

Then, as it always does when the heart pumps out through an open wound, the red pool under his shoulder got wider until the dirty cobblestones on Canal were sticky with blood. And Carlos Guzman just died.

Eddie was alone with him for two or three seconds before Jelke came up behind him.

"Just like I told you. Case closed."

Eddie reached into his pocket and ran his thumb across one of the Polaroids.

"Yeah. Right."

He said it. But that's not what he thought.

9

MANHATTAN BASE WAS LOCATED IN AN OLD GARAGE ON West Forty-fifth between Tenth Avenue and the river. Before the fire marshals moved in, the city's Department of General Services had given it over to the Board of Education to store schoolbooks.

The location near Hell's Kitchen and the building itself said a lot about where the FDNY was on the pecking order in New York. Among the uniformed forces, they were number two. All you had to do to see that was contrast Fire headquarters in a seedy office building on Livingston Street in Brooklyn with the gleaming tower that was One Police Plaza.

Brooklyn, the city's second borough, was good enough for the red men, and when the white hats (as the chiefs were called) went searching for a building to house their Manhattan fire marshals, they didn't bother to look past this old garage.

The thirty-three marshals who caught cases there worked in pairs on the chart, meaning they rotated in three-day shifts of nine, ten, and fifteen and a half hours. During that time, whatever team was first up took the call.

But Eddie Burke was different. He worked a single. And

until Kivlihan had replaced his old boss, Supervising Fire Marshal Louis Garcia, Eddie had enjoyed the best clearance rate in the borough. Garcia, a big, gregarious New Yorican who'd put his own son through Harvard, was beloved by the men. He shot straight, and he understood that a force of nature like Eddie Burke could do him a lot of good. But Eddie was short on the social skills, and he always made his own cases. To a bureaucrat like Kivlihan, who hated independent thinkers, that was anathema. So when Louie "got made" and went to Brooklyn as assistant chief fire marshal, Eddie lost his rabbi.

Now, as Burke sat at his desk in the squad room, Kivlihan glowered at him and gritted his teeth through a wired jaw. The little executive officer got up and walked over to Eddie.

"When the hell are you gonna call the scene?"

Eddie looked up. "Soon as I get back from the lab."

By law, fire marshals held all fire scenes (meaning they controlled them) until they determined whether or not the blazes were incendiary (intentionally set).

Until then, the police had to wait, and this often drove the precinct detectives up a wall. You see, whenever a body was found in a fire, the cops hoped that the marshals would declare the origin accidental. That way there wasn't some unsolved homicide that they'd have to clear. Arson murders were a bitch to break because motive was so hard to prove.

Let's say a guy is pissed at his girlfriend for humping the super of her building. The guy pours liquid Sterno outside the super's door on the first floor and tosses a match. The fire starts and within minutes the building is consumed. If some wheelchair-bound grandmother dies on the top floor and the fire marshal calls it arson, then the cops have to track down her killer. Since the little old lady probably never even *met* the torch, the cops have one helluva time showing motive. And motive is the key to breaking 95 percent of all homicides.

In this case, Jelke and the boys from the Sixth Precinct were *convinced* that they had a homicide and that the killer, one Carlos Guzman, was now also dead. But the fire could have started accidentally. The victim, Alex Sloane, could have come in, seen the flames, and hit her head as she tried to escape. So Eddie had to decide.

Still, the cops were getting impatient.

"The PD wants the crime scene released." said Jelke. "They got a lot of people with juice in that building."

Eddie got up with the sample can.

"Fine. Soon as Aggie runs the numbers, we'll know."

He started to take off for the Lab when Kivlihan called after him, "Don't take all night."

Eddie stopped. He turned around and looked at Kivie, who was rubbing his wired jaw. "Let me ask you something."

"What?" snapped the supervisor.

"In the morning, when you're eating breakfast . . ."

"Yeah? What about it?" growled Kivie.

"Do the cornflakes get caught in those wires?"

Eddie shot a look over at Bobby Vasquez, who laughed.

"Get the fuck out of here, Burke."

Eddie grinned and took off.

It was another sign of the pecking order that the FD didn't have its own lab. All volatile evidence seized by the fire marshals was tested by chemists at the police lab located on Twentieth Street between Second and Third in the building that housed the Police Academy. Eddie Burke knew the place well. In fact, he'd first come there as a cadet, bound for a career as a cop, the son of a legend. The first in his class . . . before he washed out and joined a ladder company. The reason for that gnawed at Eddie like the pain in

his thigh from Superman's knife. As he entered the elevator
for the trip to the ninth floor lab, he popped a pink and
gray Percodan capsule into his mouth.

Ten minutes later, he was drumming his fingers on a lab
bench while Aggie Stein, the night duty chemist, performed
what the marshals called a heated head space test.

Aggie inserted a hypodermic syringe into a bladder at
the top of the sample can. She extracted the vapors from a
section of the mural canvas, which she'd heated to 210
degrees. Then she injected the vapors into a Hewlett Pack-
ard 5890 gas chromatograph. The test would determine
whether Eddie's sample contained any LPDs, or light pe-
troleum distillates, often used as accelerants to start fires.

Pushing sixty, with her gray hair tied into a bun that
she'd fashioned with a number two pencil, Aggie was one
of those hardened midlevel bureaucrats unique to New
York. A public servant so battered by paper and policy
changes that comedy was her only response. The kind of
old bird that could cut a desk sergeant in half with a look
or send a rookie out running for barf bags. She was funny,
aggressive, and brilliant, and she took no prisoners when it
came to incompetence. For almost thirty years she'd sat
witness as the city ignited and burned down around her.

Aggie Stein was on duty the night back in '62 when
they'd brought in a body from the crash of TWA Flight
435. It was locked in its chair with the seatbelt melted,
fused to the armrests by the explosion that ripped open the
Lockheed Electra. The body had cooked in the heat, like a
frank on an outdoor grill, expanding to the point where its
skull had burst open. Aggie remembered how the skin on
the face had stretched out so tight that the eyes had swollen
to slits.

She had seen that same face almost thirty years later on
another body, this one retrieved from the Happy Land Social Club fire. It was found standing rigid and upright, lean-

ing against the bar, a cigarette still in its lips as the firestorm roared through the tenement packed with people. Eighty-seven illegal aliens had died that night—most of them from El Salvador. Aggie had to coat her nostrils with Vicks Va-porub to hide the smell of roasted *pollo* and burning flesh.

Aggie was close to retirement now, but she still visited fire scenes, picking through the ash and char in her raincoat and boots. She ran the night tour at the lab like an old bird of prey, and Eddie Burke was the only one to suspect she was soft inside. He was the only one in the bureau who remembered her birthday and the only one who showed up at Temple Emmanuel in Bayside when her husband, Saul, had passed away. Aggie knew the shadow that Eddie lived under because of his father, and though she had the mouth of a stevedore, she did what she could to mother him.

"You look like shit tonight," she said as the printout emerged from the machine.

"Sorry. I haven't been to the health club in weeks."

"Yeah, right. I can just see you at the Holiday Spa. You and Joe Piscopo."

"You trying to say I'm out of shape?"

"Come on, Eddie. You haven't exercised since Frankie Valli was young."

"Don't need to. I've still got a thirty-four waist."

"What? On Miller Lite and meatball subs?"

"God gave me a high metabolism."

"He should have given you a Trac II. When's the last time you shaved?"

"I've been up for two days now."

"Yeah. I heard about the suspension. Somebody said he saw you up at McGlade's toasting your return to duty."

Eddie rubbed his thigh. "The leg's been hurting, okay? I needed a little hair of the dog."

"Go home, Eddie."

"As soon as you read me the printout."

Aggie looked up to heaven. "The man's always pushing me. Pushing . . ."

Eddie smiled as she shuffled over to the chromatograph and pulled out the test results. Aggie put on a pair of blue rimmed glasses that she kept on a string around her neck. She checked the peak spread on the printout against a series of control specs for certain chlorinated hydrocarbons. By comparing Eddie's sample against a control sample, she was able to pinpoint the accelerant.

Aggie moved her lips silently as she ran down the list.

"You were right. It's sixty percent dimethylbromide."

Eddie cracked a smile and jumped up to nuzzle her neck.

"I'm gonna have your children, Aggie."

"You're a little late, hon."

She ripped off a copy of the printout and handed it to him. Eddie kissed her on the cheek and was about to push through the swinging doors when he ran into Kivlihan.

"They said you were down here."

"Where *else* would I be? I'm working the SoHo thing."

The little pit bull moved up to Eddie.

"Uh-uh. It's dead."

Eddie stopped. "We just got six-o worth of DMB on the sample." He started to take off.

"Hold it right there."

Eddie stopped again.

The little shit came up behind him. "Look at me."

Eddie winced and turned to face him. Kivie held up his index finger and flicked it, indicating for Eddie to come closer. Eddie shook his head, then complied. Christ.

"I'll say this just once. NYPD has a suspect with motive who died in flight."

"They're wrong. Listen—"

"No, *you* listen. I got a half dozen burns on my hands right now. Some fuckin' Lebanese pricks are lightin' multiples down in the leather district."

Kivlihan turned to Aggie.

"They do one and collect for water damage on three hundred K worth of pocketbooks. Then they move the damaged goods to another location, set off a hot plate fire and collect again when the sprinklers go off."

"Sounds pretty imaginative," said Aggie. She turned to Eddie and winked.

"Anybody die in those fires?" asked Eddie.

Kivlihan shook his head. "No."

"Then my ten-forty-five down on Prince takes priority."

"Bullshit. You do what I tell you."

"We'll see." Eddie started to leave again, but Kivlihan stepped in front of him. He could barely talk through the wired jaw.

"Look, you fuck. If those shits on 105 Truck hadn't backed you, I'd have your ass up in Rikers right now."

Aggie stepped between them. "Backed him on what, Kivie? Way I heard it, you tripped running into that lot and broke your jaw on some rubble."

Kivlihan spat bile. "Yeah, well, then you tell this hump somethin' for me. He's Eddie Burke, *Junior,* Fire Department. Not a homicide cop. If he's got a problem with that, he can go back to the academy. He can see the department shrink. Maybe challenge the old man to a fight. But while he's workin' for me, he does fires."

He turned to Eddie. "You get that?"

Eddie turned away. "Yeah."

Kivlihan threw the Lebanese file on a lab bench and stormed out.

Aggie came up behind Eddie. "What a dickhead." She barely kept it under her breath.

"I can't believe that fuck," said Eddie, holding up the printout. "What am I supposed to do? Ignore this?"

Aggie sat down in front of him. "Look. There's the battle and then there's the war. This guy wants you out because you're the only one at the base with any balls.''

"So what's the good of staying in the bureau if I can't do my job?''

"Come on. This isn't about the case. It's about control. Kivie has to know that he owns you. You can't deck a guy in front of his men and just walk.''

"Yeah . . . right.'' Eddie shook his head.

"Look. Take the long view,'' said Aggie. "He's ambitious. I mean, the man has his nose so far up the commisioner's ass that if Von Essen stopped short, Kivie'd be on his belt line.''

Eddie pulled away.

"Right. Why don't I just wait till they make him chief?''

Aggie put her hand on his arm.

"Then do this for *me*. You're the only one left in this place I can talk to. You go, and I'm done here.''

"Oh Christ, don't pull that shit on me.''

"Why not?''

Eddie exhaled hard. " 'Cause it works.''

Aggie squeezed his arm. "Come on. Another day, another fire. Right?''

"Yeah.'' He took another look at the volatiles printout, then shoved it into his jacket. Resigned to it now, he walked to the lab bench and picked up the Lebanese file.

"Let me ask you something.''

"What?'' said Aggie.

"We've got major medical, right?''

"Yeah? So?''

"Does it cover curvature of the spine?''

"Go home, Eddie.''

"Right.''

10

EDDIE WAS ON HIS WAY UP BROADWAY IN HIS CHEVY THE next morning. The pile of files from Kivlihan was in the shotgun seat when the two-way crackled.

"Manhattan to Squad four-eight."

Eddie picked up the Motorola and came back to him.

"Four-eight to base"

Bobby Vasquez, the house watch, was on the radio board.

"Supervising Fire Marshal Kivlihan wants your location."

Eddie surveyed the neighborhood. He was just passing Columbia University at 116th Street.

"Broadway and One-one-six. On my way to interview that witness on Lenox."

"Right. He wants you to call in when you get there."

"Why doesn't he just jerk my chain?"

"Didn't copy."

"Forget it, Bobby. Ten-four."

Eddie punched out and switched on the car radio.

"This is WINS, Westinghouse Broadcasting Company, serving New York, New Jersey, and Connecticut with all news all the time. Our top story this morning: Police say the perpetrator of a brutal SoHo arson murder is now dead.

"Meanwhile, a police consultant says the mural burned in the fire appears to be part of an exhibit painted for the 1939 World's Fair."

Eddie heard a woman's voice. "The mural had been missing for years. Its discovery was a major event in the art world. The loss now is beyond calculation."

"That was Professor Caroline Drexel of Columbia University."

"Drexel."

Eddie jammed his foot on the brake and the Chevy skidded to a stop on the corner of 123rd. He switched off the radio.

"Drexel . . ."

He thought about it for a second, knowing that he should take Aggie's advice. Lay off and keep going up to Harlem. Shut up, keep his head down, and do Kivie's work. But he couldn't. It wasn't in him. And besides, he wanted to see her again . . . Dr. Drexel . . . see what she looked like in daylight.

So Eddie Burke slammed the Caprice into a squealing left turn. He almost scraped the side of the elevated track as he spun it around and roared back down Broadway toward Columbia.

The girl in the registrar's office smiled as he showed her his fire shield. She was tall, Puerto Rican, attractive. Seventeen, maybe eighteen, with thick lips and long hair frosted red. The nameplate on her see-through blouse said Alma. She was wearing stone-washed Guess jeans and black heels to match the blouse, and she eyed Eddie up and down as she tapped her inch-long red nails on the counter.

"This professor," said Eddie. "Where do I find her?"

Alma ignored the question. She ran her nails across his badge and looked up.

"If you're a fireman, where's your little ax?"

"I'm not *that* kind of fireman."

He was getting impatient.

"Look, I'd appreciate it if you could tell me what class she's in. I'm working a case, and I need to see her. It's important."

Alma pushed the shield back across the counter and smiled.

"Sorry, officer, but the policy at the university forbids me to give out that kind of information."

Eddie had two choices here.

He'd been dealing with bureaucrats all his life, and it was always one way or the other. You could get tough or use sugar. He hesitated, then looked into Alma's eyes.

"Policy, right?" Eddie flashed the killer smile.

Alma nodded, smiling.

"Uh-huh."

He studied her nameplate.

"Alma Rios. River woman. *Haslo para mi.*"

She looked at him, surprised.

"You speak Spanish?"

"Just enough to keep from getting my face slapped."

Alma smiled. "I'll bet."

Eddie touched her arm. "Come on."

She stuck one of those long red nails in her mouth and twisted it coyly.

"I don't know . . ."

"Please . . ."

Finally, she smiled and ran the back of her nails against his beard.

"All right. How'd you know?"

"What?"

"Men who don't shave . . . they're just . . . sexy, you know?"

"Really?"

"Yeah."

Alma spun on her heels and clicked her way over to the card file. The stone-washed jeans were skintight.

"Christ, where were *you* when I was in high school?" Eddie said it under his breath.

She kept eyeing him as she rifled through the file. Finally, she pulled out an index card and clicked back to the counter.

"Let me ask you something?"

"Anything."

She was holding the card back, taunting him with it.

"If I had a fire at my place, would you come put it out?"

Eddie flashed the smile again. The cobalt-blue eyes were bloodshot now, and he had all he could do to keep from lunging over the counter and grabbing the card with his teeth.

"Absolutely."

She giggled and tapped her nails on the counter.

"So, what do you say?"

Alma thought about it.

He stood on one foot and then the other now, hungry to get the card while this girl tried to hustle him. Finally, he squeezed her arm and said, "Alma, I need this."

That did it. He was a man who *needed* something.

She pushed the card down in front of him.

"All right, hon. This is Tuesday. At ten o'clock she teaches Twentieth Century in Avery Hall. One oh two."

"Twentieth Century?"

"Art."

"Okay. Where's Avery?"

"Building to the left, behind Low Library."

"Thanks," said Eddie. "Gimme a rain check on that fire?"

"Maybe."

She checked out the curve of his ass as he split from the office.

The lecture hall was half dark as Eddie slipped into the last row of seats. He could see cigarette smoke wafting up through the white light of the slide projector below. He knew the smell. In fact, he'd smoked them himself for years, until he quit. Gitanes. Twice the kick of Gaulois with half the bite. He could see the halo of blonde hair as she stood below with the slide remote in her left hand and the cigarette between her two fingers. She was wearing an off-white silk blouse, a sheath skirt, and high heels. There was a double string of pearls around her neck atop the lavaliere mike. Christ, if the teachers had looked like this when he went to City College, he'd have his Ph.D.

The room went to black as the projector engaged, and a black-and-white slide appeared on the front wall behind her. It was a photograph from the 1930s showing hungry men in a soup line. They were unshaven like Eddie, and he wondered if they were as horny as he was right now.

"To understand the full impact of the New Deal art projects, you have to consider America in the 1930s, caught in the grip of Depression."

Her voice was deep and throaty. You get that from smoking Gitanes. Another slide flashed, showing women on street corners selling apples.

"Fully a third of the country was unemployed," she said. "There were breadlines everywhere."

Now she punched through a series of slides showing construction crews building roads and bridges. Eddie saw a shot of what he thought might be Hoover Dam.

"When Roosevelt created the Works Progress Administration, he put millions back to work building highways, bridges, and hydroelectric plants."

Next came a slide showing a half dozen WPA artists painting a mural.

"But he also gave jobs to artists. From 1933 to the middle of World War Two, thousands of murals, paintings, and statues were created for government buildings."

She shook back that head of blonde hair and Eddie bit the edge of his hand.

More slides appeared now, showing murals in post offices, train stations, and schools.

"Artists like Willem de Kooning and Alice Neal were paid twenty-six dollars a week to produce public works of art—art that reflected the hope of the time for recovery."

Eddie couldn't take his eyes off her. She looked like an angel standing there in the smoke. But she was strong, tough, confident in her words. The projector changed again, and now a slide of the subway mural appeared behind her.

"As best we've been able to tell, the mural destroyed last night was commissioned for the Labor Pavilion of the New York World's Fair. It had been missing since 1951."

Just then, she looked up at a wall clock. It said 10:55.

"All right, people. Next time, we cover social realism." There was a scramble among the students now to exit. Even with the microphone, Caroline had to raise her deep voice.

"Remember, the exam's in two weeks."

She walked to a panel by a door and turned on the overhead lights.

Now Eddie could see her clearly. He felt his jaw drop as she bent over to shove some files in a briefcase and her skirt hiked up to her thigh.

A teaching assistant packed up the projector. By the time Eddie was halfway down the lecture hall stairs, Caroline was at the door.

"Dr. Drexel?"

She turned to face him. There was a flicker of recognition. And then, without a word, she took off.

He caught up to her outside in the quadrangle as she moved through the throng of students changing classes. She walked with her shoulders forward and her arms back, taking big strides as she made her way along the brick path toward Amsterdam Avenue. Christ, even in heels, this woman moved like an athlete.

"Dr. Drexel, could you give me a minute?"

She kept walking.

"Sorry. I've already told the police all I know."

But Eddie stopped her, flashing his badge. It was gold with an eagle atop his number (526) and the words "Fire Marshal—Fire Department—New York" in a red circle around the FDNY crest.

"I'm not a cop, I'm a fire marshal, and there's one thing I don't understand."

"Yes, what's that?"

She seemed preoccupied now, impatient.

"If that mural was so valuable, how'd it end up in a subway station?"

She bit down on her lower lip, deciding whether or not to continue. Another small flicker and this time Eddie could tell. She was interested.

Caroline smiled.

"How did it end up in the subway? That *is* a good question. Marshal—"

"Burke. Eddie Burke."

When he pronounced his name, he almost hesitated to see if she recognized it. She didn't. That was good. They moved on.

"What do you know about the 1930s?"

"They came after the 1920s."

Caroline smiled again.

"Back then, many of the New Deal artists were leftists."

"You mean Communists, don't you?"

Caroline looked slightly offended.

"It was the times they lived in. In the thirties, people joined the Communist Party the way students joined SDS in the sixties."

"Yeah? So?"

"When the McCarthy era hit in the fifties, certain politicians began to see things in the murals . . ."

"Like what?"

"Hammers and sickles. Pictures of Lenin and Stalin . . ."

She stopped now.

"Thousands of murals were painted over or destroyed. Sculpture was smashed up and thrown into the Jersey Meadowlands. At one point, they literally sold hundreds of canvases for pennies a pound as scrap. Plumbers bought them for insulation to wrap pipes with."

Now he got it.

"Pipes. That's how the mural got—"

"Yes, Mr. Burke. Some of the greatest art of the twentieth century, wasted because of the Red scare. With communism in pieces now, it would be comical if it wasn't so tragic."

She started to pull away.

"Now, as I said, I'm late for class."

She turned and got maybe twenty feet away. Then Eddie let her have it.

"The McCarthy era ended forty years ago, lady. That girl was murdered last night."

Caroline kept on walking.

"Somebody wanted that mural burned so bad, he was willing to kill for it."

This time, she stopped and turned to face him.

"What are you talking about? The police said there was a lovers' quarrel."

"The police were wrong."

He walked up to her and took out the lab printout.

"Whoever torched the mural came in with his own incendiary liquid. He wanted the *canvas* destroyed. The girl's death was an afterthought.''

She looked confused.

''I don't underst—''

''Look, if the boyfriend had killed her, he could have used any one of a dozen solvents she had hanging around to clean up her brushes. But this guy brought lighter fluid.''

He pointed to the reading on the printout.

''Dimethylbromide. It was arson first, then murder. Not the other way around.''

Caroline looked shocked, trying to let it sink in. She started to go, but Eddie went face to face with her.

''An innocent girl's dead, Doctor, and the killer's still out there. You want to walk away, or you want to skip a few classes and help me find this guy?''

Caroline Drexel hesitated. She moved her hand through that lustrous head of blonde hair, then ran her right index finger under her cherry-red lips. Christ. He wasn't even sure he was right, but he had to see it through, and he wanted to do it with this woman.

Finally, she lifted her perfect white wrist and checked the time on a platinum Patek-Philippe.

''It's too late to change my next class. I have students. But if you'll give me an hour, I'll do what I can.''

Eddie looked up toward heaven. He was sure now that all those years as an altar boy, getting up in the snow to serve seven o'clock mass, had paid off.

11

IT WAS HARD FOR EDDIE TO TAKE HIS EYES OFF HER. SHE was sitting at his desk in the squad room, poring over black-and-white stills of the mural. Pictures taken just after the mural showed up in that subway station. Eddie had wangled the shots from a buddy who worked for the transit cops. It was late now as she sat at his desk, legs crossed, the sheath skirt hiked up to her thighs. Eddie could just see the top of her stocking with the little clip that fastened to a garter. Christ, she didn't wear panty hose. This was a woman who lived for adventure. She tapped her long red nails on the desk as she moved from the pile of stills and searched through an art history book she'd brought along. The book was titled *A New Deal for Artists: Murals of the WPA*, a coffee-table-size collection of color plates from the thirties.

Caroline closed the book and checked her watch. It was after eleven now. They'd been at this for hours. She started looking around Eddie's desk, searching for something. She spotted the Pez dispenser with the head of Goofy wearing a fire helmet; the autographed ball that said Reggie from the day Eddie shagged that foul in the Bronx; the wire baskets full of files he'd forgotten; and the framed picture of Eddie with his mother, Mary DeAngelo Burke. She picked it up.

"This is your mother?"

"Was. Yeah. She died about ten years back. Had a stroke."

"She was very pretty. She looks . . . Italian."

"Sicilian. Her father came from Catania."

Caroline looked at Eddie, who was as Irish as Paddy's pig.

"And your father?"

Eddie turned away from her.

"Third generation. County Cork."

Caroline walked around to face him.

"You don't have his picture?"

"No."

"Is he still alive?"

Eddie rolled his eyes. "Oh yeah. He was with the . . . He was chief of detectives . . ."

"For the police department?"

Eddie was anxious to change the subject.

"Yeah. So listen, did you find anything?"

"Not so far. She sat on the edge of the desk and crossed her legs. "Look, I know this is the Fire Department, but I'm dying for a smoke, do you think I could . . ."

"Sure. But I'd have to cite you."

He pointed to a wall sign with the picture of a cigarette. It said: Don't Even Think about It.

"Terrific."

Caroline turned back to check the stills.

Eddie smiled and grabbed Goofy's head.

"Here. Have a Pez. I kicked Gitanes with these."

Caroline looked up at him.

"*You* smoked Gitanes?"

"Yeah. I dated a stew from Air France for awhile."

"A stew?" She looked back down at the book. "You mean flight attendant, don't you?"

"Yeah. You're right. Christ, I'm always doing that."

"What?"

"Saying things that are politically incorrect. I mean, are they Native Americans or Indians? Is a person disabled or physically challenged? One wants to be *tolerant* but not a slave to some interest group."

Caroline looked up at him now.

"You're rather knowing for a fire—"

"Marshal. Yes, well, I've been known to read the *New Yorker*. I mean, don't get me wrong. I don't *buy* it. But they sell it at the liquor store where I go, and once in a while when I'm standing in line with my bottle of muscatel, I pick it up."

Caroline laughed at the joke. She reached down, flipped back the head on the Pez dispenser, and took a candy from Goofy's mouth. Then she turned back to the book. There was lipstick on Goofy's face now. Christ, Eddie Burke was in love.

Five minutes later, she found it.

"Here it is."

The book said *Art of the 1939 World's Fair*, and Eddie had to lean over her shoulder to see it. He could smell her perfume now. What was it? Something he'd seen in a magazine. Panther maybe. Or was it Obsession? Eddie was good at smells.

"The original title was *Workers of the World Unite*."

Caroline was pointing at a small, three-by-five-inch color plate taken when the mural hung in the Labor Pavilion. The picture was shot wide, from at least twenty yards back. With both panels together, Eddie could see the six figures in the foreground. In the left panel there was a pilot, a nurse, and a stevedore. In the right panel, a farmer, a teacher and a miner. Because the picture was taken from so far back, Eddie couldn't make out their faces.

Caroline picked up one of the stills from the fire and compared a fragment of the stevedore's legs to those in the book.

"Here, you can see . . . in the left panel of the diptych."

"Diptych. You mentioned that earlier. What is it?"

"A mural represented in two sections." She showed him the picture from the book with both halves.

Eddie feigned seriousness and studied it, allowing himself a quick look at Caroline's cheek. Her skin was flawless. He had all he could do to focus, as she continued the lecture.

"It says here that the original was ten feet high by forty feet wide. Most works of that size were painted directly on plaster walls, fresco style. But this was a World's Fair commission, designed to be moved in two sections."

She stopped and turned, catching him watching her.

"Are you listening?"

"Of course."

"What did I say?"

"It wasn't a fresco. They needed to move it." Eddie picked up a notebook, getting down to business. "What about the name of the artist?"

"On projects this big, there were usually teams."

Caroline opened another book entitled *WPA Artists Rolls*. She began flipping through the pages as Eddie mentally traced the outline of the Lancôme gloss around her lips. A few minutes later, she looked up.

"Here it is. The left panel was credited to two artists: Julian Krane and Esther Schi—"

Suddenly, she went pale. The color seemed to drain from her face. "Esther Schine."

Caroline closed the book abruptly and got up.

"What is it? What's wrong?"

"Nothing. It's late. I've got to go."

She shoved the art books into her briefcase.

Eddie didn't understand her quick change in mood.

"Wait a minute. Let me give you a ride."

"That's all right. I'll get a cab." Christ. She couldn't wait to get out of there.

"Then I'll walk you up to tenth. You don't want to be on Forty-fifth Street this time of night.

"I'll be fine." Caroline pushed past Eddie and hurried out of the squad room. She went down the stairs two at a time. He started to go after her when suddenly, Kivlihan stepped in front of him.

"You got to Harlem an hour late today."

"Traffic up Broadway." Eddie tried to go around him, but Kivlihan got in his way.

"Who's the blonde?"

Eddie didn't answer. He craned to see past him as she disappeared down the stairway.

"Hey. I'm talking to you. Who's the blonde?"

Eddie ignored him and pushed into the hallway, but by the time he got out there, Caroline was gone.

Kivlihan walked up behind him.

"What about it?"

"What?"

"That woman."

Eddie had to think fast.

"Hey, look. It's after hours. You want to read my little black book, pay me overtime."

Eddie turned and exited into the stairwell.

Kivlihan, the pit bull, just stood there shaking his head.

"The ice is gettin' thinner, fucker. Keep it up."

12

IT WAS BRUTALLY COLD NOW AND WEST FORTY-FIFTH WAS
deserted when Caroline Drexel headed east toward Tenth
Avenue to hail a cab. She knotted the belt of the brown
leather trench coat and tightened the silk scarf at her neck,
but it wasn't enough. God, it was empty out there. Dead
still, and then came a flash of lightning.

A few seconds later she heard the thunder, and then it
started to rain. Caroline pulled the scarf up over her hair
and rushed up toward Tenth. The art books in the leather
briefcase were heavy and her heels were slipping.

The lights of an oncoming cab hit her face, but it roared
by, full of people, taking the corner on Forty-sixth heading
east.

Julian Krane and Esther Schine. She kept repeating the
names of those artists over and over.

When she'd first seen the report of the subway mural,
Caroline was in shock. Years ago, when the dream began,
she assumed that the painting she saw was imaginary. But
then, when she studied the period, Caroline realized it was
a well-known piece. In 1939 the Labor Pavillion was one
of the showcase venues at The World's Fair. The mural
had disappeared in the '50s during the Red scare, and like

so many other pieces from that time, she assumed it had been destroyed.

When Giuliani's office gave her the go-ahead, she contacted Leo Casteilli. He recommended the Sloane girl, and Caroline had been thrilled at the prospect of seeing the original, damaged or not. She'd visited the loft on Prince Street twice as Alex was removing the plaster. The young woman had just begun to expose the faces of the artists when the tragic fire broke out. Caroline had met Alex for lunch just the day before it happened. The police found Caroline's card from Columbia inside a drawer next to Alex's worktable. She was called to the scene within hours of the blaze.

Now, as the rain poured down, she thought back to the mural and that other rainy night so long ago. There was another flash and another thunderclap and Caroline thought she heard music off in the distance.

It had to be you . . .

She saw the lights of another taxi, but when it got close enough, she realized it was just a passenger car.

Caroline drew the trench coat around her and shivered.

Eddie didn't see her as he rushed out of Manhattan Base, looking up and down Forty-fifth. The old garage at 522 was in the middle of the block, so she could have gone either way: east toward Tenth Avenue or west to the river. He wanted to stop her; to figure out what set her off. But the streets were empty now and it was pouring.

"Shit."

He looked up toward Tenth, but the rain was coming down in sheets, and he was soaked to his Thom McAns. He thought about how many times he'd gotten his feet wet, slogging in and out of fire-charred buildings, trying to keep people from using "the poor man's gun." That's what they called it in the street. Arson. But Eddie knew it would never stop. You might outlaw weapons, but how could you keep people from using gasoline or a match? It was impossible, and even if you stopped the fraud, the arson for profit, there was always some sick fuck who'd get pissed at his mother, douse her with kerosene, and set her on fire. It was tribal, almost barbaric. But revenge fires like that happened five times a day in New York.

Eddie saw the lightning flash and thought, Jesus, she couldn't wait to get out of there. He wondered if he'd ever see Caroline Drexel again.

He was drenched now, so he walked back to 522 and went upstairs.

The rain was blowing cold across Tenth as Caroline raised her hand to an oncoming cab.

"Taxi!"

The light on top was on. Thank God. It was free. But then, just as it passed her, the driver switched on the Off Duty light and roared by.

"Damn it."

The music was getting louder.

I wandered around and finally found, somebody who . . .

She watched, shivering, as the cab disappeared uptown.

Now, soaked to the skin, Caroline started to walk along West Forty-sixth Street. Maybe she could catch something going east or at least find a taxi on Ninth. It was so cold, her teeth were chattering. Behind her, she could just feel the lights of an eastbound taxi. She prayed that the cab would be free.

Make me feel blue, make me feel true . . .

And then, as she turned around to hail it, she noticed a man in the dark back on Tenth. He was walking under a flickering streetlight, alone in the pouring rain.

There was a felt hat pulled down over his face and he was wearing an overcoat. Caroline moved into the street and the man did the same. She could see he was coming toward her.

"Taxi!"

She shouted it out as another cab roared by her full. She picked up the pace, but then, so did the man. She was sure now. He was following her.

That's when the music stopped in her mind and Caroline started to run.

But the man took off after her.

The high heels and the slippery pavement were holding her back, and the man was gaining.

Finally, she stopped to kick off the heels and tore out onto Ninth Avenue as a gypsy cab approached, heading downtown.

The man was only twenty yards back now when she raced headlong in front of the cab. As it screeched to a stop, the cabdriver, a Rasta, stuck his head out to scream at her, but Caroline quickly jumped in the back.

"Please," she said. "I'll give you a hundred dollars to take me to Sutton Place."

The Rasta smiled.

"Sutton Place? Make it two and you got it."

Outside, the man was getting closer.

Caroline couldn't believe how this bastard behind the wheel was holding her up. But she didn't have many options. She checked her purse. She had fifties.

"Sold. Now let's go."

"First let me see the cash."

The man was almost behind the cab now as Caroline shoved the money through the slot in the plastic divider.

"Just get us out of here."

The Rasta smiled.

"Hang onto the strap, miss."

He popped it into first and the cab spun into a screeching left turn.

As it roared off, the man crossed to the curb and leaned into a doorway. He took out a Marlboro, cupped his hands from the rain, and set it on fire. He used a gold Dunhill lighter.

13

EDDIE BURKE FELT TIRED, WET, AND DEFEATED AS HE
pulled up to the bar near the corner of Ninety-seventh and
Third Avenue in Bay Ridge. Tam O' Sh nt r. Two of the
vowels were missing from the flickering blue neon sign
over the place. But Eddie had no trouble finding it. The
Tam was wedged between an OTB betting parlor and
McMurphy's, a store selling religious artifacts. The location
allowed you to lose your paycheck, pick up a statue of St.
Jude, and get shitfaced without having to cross the street.

Eddie smelled it as soon as he pushed through the door.
The strange aroma of vomit and beer that was common to
gin mills like this. The place looked cheesy, with quarter-
inch ply veneer on the walls, a black and white checkered
linoleum floor, and bar stools in forest green Naugahyde.

The Tam was way below his old man, thought Eddie.
Big Eddie Burke was a "cut glass" Irishman and this place
was decidedly "shanty."

When he retired from the NYPD, Eddie's father had
taken a position as vice president of security for Merrill
Lynch. But soon he began to miss it: the action, the edge.
And most of all, he missed "the boys." From the time he
played fullback for St. Brendan's in Red Hook, Big Eddie

Burke was a mixer, a natural leader of men. He lasted exactly two years on Wall Street before cashing out his stock options and buying the bar. He'd had it with board meetings, and offices filled with Japanese art, and polite cocktail parties where no one went past Chardonnay.

Here, there were pickles in wooden bowls on the bar and a dish full of hard-boiled eggs. He'd hung a green Harp flag on one wall, a couple of Aer Lingus posters on the other. There was a steam table at the end of the bar for hot corned beef sandwiches, and four brown Formica tables in back. But except for the TV over the register, that was it. No pool table, no dart board, no video games. This was a place where grown men came to smoke and bet and take alcohol, and there was no sense confusing the process. It was the kind of place where Big Eddie Burke had finished many a night in, too high from the job to come home, too full of the hunt and the homicide scenes. At the height of his career, Edmund Burke, Sr., was a prince of the city, a man who could walk into any borough unarmed and get answers. He cleared hundreds of cases, but he'd never been able to solve the mystery that broke his own heart.

Here was a kid, a chip off the block. Number one in his class at the academy, and he flushed it. Walked away. How come?

The old man never understood it when Eddie dropped out, and he never forgave him for joining the second team. Firefighting was an honorable profession for some men, but not for the son of Big Eddie Burke.

Now, as he entered the bar, the fire marshal noticed that most of the crowd was in uniform. They'd all just knocked off from the four-to-twelve tour and their hats and nightsticks were under the bar. Almost everybody was armed. The TV was tuned to ESPN. The Rangers were at Vancouver. Eddie heard a small whoop go up through the crowd as New York scored and wet money hit the bar.

He settled onto a stool and looked around for the bartender, but there was no one behind the counter, so he got up and reached over for a rock glass and a bottle of Jameson's. He was just about to help himself to a shot when a thick, beefy hand grabbed his wrist. Eddie looked up and shook his head. The man standing over him was big. Six three and maybe three hundred pounds. He was sixty-seven, but he looked fifty-five; tight and ruddy with the same jaw as Eddie, the same cobalt-blue eyes, and the same killer smile. He spoke in a loud voice so everybody could hear him.

"Christ, will you look at this?"

All eyes in the place turned on Eddie now.

"I go out for a pee and come back to find this? Fuçkin' larceny. The kid hasn't paid his tab from the last time he was in."

Eddie just shook his head. "I knew this was a mistake." He threw a twenty onto the bar and started to exit.

"Hey. Where's your sense of humor, kid?"

"I lost it in the third grade at St. Pat's."

The big man waited until Eddie was five feet from the door and then let him have it.

"Little Eddieee!"

The place came to a hush.

Eddie froze. He had heard those words from over his shoulder a thousand times before. He looked up at the ceiling and then turned to face his father, the man who'd broken the Kitty Genovese case and put the bracelets on the Son of Sam. Here now, presiding over this gin mill in Brooklyn as his son stood there seething.

"Six months you don't come to see me and all I get's twenty bucks? That's it? No hello, Pop? Good-bye? Christ, you don't even ask how I've been?"

"I know how you've been," said Eddie. "You're always the same. You're *Eddie Burke.*"

The off-duty cops traded looks. Nobody talked to the chief this way. Not even blood.

"Why'd you come, then? You need money? Mary Rose hit you up for more alimony?"

"No. No it's just that . . . Fuck. What's the use?" Eddie turned and started to go.

"What is it, kid?"

Eddie stopped. "You had to do this . . ."

"What?"

"You had to do this in public, didn't you?" Eddie was grinding his teeth, almost whispering.

A few seconds passed before Big Eddie got it. "Oh shit, kid."

He walked up to Eddie and motioned him into an alcove by the door. He was suddenly tender now.

"What is it son? Why'd you come?"

"You didn't say you were sorry yet."

"Mother a Christ. I'm sorry. Now, what are you doing here?"

Eddie shook his head, not wanting to do this.

"Come on," said his father. "You wouldn't have hauled your ass out to Bay Ridge if it wasn't important. What's wrong?"

"Nothing. It's just . . ."

"What?"

"A case."

Big Eddie brightened. "Christ. Why the hell didn't you say so?"

The fire marshal had just warmed the cockles of his father's heart. The big man put his arms around Eddie and hugged him.

"Come on."

He gestured toward the back, beaming now, pointing at

Eddie and nodding to the blues as they made their way into his office.

"Chip off the fuckin' block."

Twelve miles away in Manhattan, Caroline Drexel was into her dream again. Lying in the big bed on Sutton Place, silk pajamas on linen, as she tossed and turned.

She was in the '30s again and the rain was coming down on the skylights above the loft. Alberta was singing from the Philco upright and the three artists took their turns on the mural. But this time she heard the voices distinctly. This time she heard the thin painter with curly brown hair as he pinched the Liz Taylor look-alike.

For twenty years now, he'd pinched her and just mouthed some words. A name maybe, but Caroline had never been able to make it out. Now, almost as if in slow motion, she watched as he pinched her again, and this time she heard him say "Esther." It was crystal clear.

And she watched as the gorgeous painter with black hair and blue eyes rubbed her hand along his thigh. She, too, uttered a name. It was "Julie." Julian Krane and Esther Schine. Caroline heard the words now, distinctly. The way the music had found its rhythm the night she'd met old Miss Hunter and the way the headline had come into focus after she screened the Holocaust film.

She saw Esther so clearly: her tan rayon blouse and brown slacks, the chocolate-color mules she was wearing, and her tiny pierced earrings, two baby-blue Stars of David that seemed to flash as she smiled and ran her unpainted nails along Julian's thigh. And Caroline heard his voice, too, soft like a woman's, as he turned to finish the section of mural showing a coal miner. He shook his head. "Not with me, babycakes."

And then the dream went on as always: the tall blonde with the bottle of bubbly, the toast, then the violent young

man storming in with the terrible headline. And Caroline
shot up in bed again, her heart pounding, shivering with
the memory of the workers waving red flags, the factories,
the farms, and all those clenched fists. She knew for sure
now that the mural they found in the subway station was
the mural she saw in her dreams.

14

BIG EDDIE BURKE SAT BEHIND HIS OLD DESK IN THE OFFICE
in back of the bar. He dropped a pair of rock glasses in
front of his son and unscrewed the cap on the Jameson's.
Behind him on the wall were the trophies from Big Eddie's
life: his gold detective shield was mounted on black velvet
with the five-inch line of service ribbons below. One of
them was an OIS citation from when he'd been shot in the
line of duty. There was a framed black-and-white crime
scene photo of the townhouse on West Eleventh that members of the Weather Underground had turned into a bomb
factory. There was a shot of Big Eddie standing over Joey
Gallo's body at Umberto's Clam House after they'd made
the hit. There was a charcoal courtroom sketch showing
Big Eddie glaring at Bernhard Goetz and a framed *New
York Post* headline that read: ''Burke Breaks Preppie Murder Case.''

As chief of detectives, Eddie Burke, Sr., had presided
over more than three thousand investigators, the second
biggest detective force outside of the FBI. For seventeen
years he had ruled it with tenacity, wit, and an iron will.
He had held the line for New York against mad bombers,
crack heads, rapists, heroin dealers, and serial killers, but

somewhere along the way, he had lost his own son.

Because for all his mementos, for all his trophies, headlines, and plaques, there was only a single shot of his boy on that wall: a picture of Eddie at eight with his dad in a fishing boat off Sheepshead Bay. Big Eddie had just made lieutenant back then, and it was the last time he'd been able to break away on a Saturday, the last time he could remember that his son held his hand and hugged him, laughing there in his Yankee cap with the bluefish he'd just caught. And Big Eddie kept that shot on the wall because it meant more to him than all of the other honors.

But when Eddie saw it, all he could think of was the Saturdays that they'd lost. The times when his only glimpse of his father was a sound bite on *Eyewitness News.* So he looked away from the wall and tried to stay with the case, filling in every detail until he'd come up to that night.

". . . anyway, when Kivlihan put the brakes on, I wasn't sure what to do," said Eddie. "You know, with the suspension and all, I figured—"

Big Eddie interrupted. "So that's why you came here? You want me to fix it with Kivlihan?"

Eddie looked up at the ceiling and shook his head. "Are you serious?"

"What?"

"You think I'd crawl out here for that?"

"Hey, look, kid, I'm sorry. I was the one that called *you* the last time. Remember?"

"Right. What? Christmas Eve?"

"Doesn't matter. You never got back to me."

"Hey," said Eddie, "I was busy at work."

"Fine." Big Eddie turned away.

Eddie shook his head, deciding whether or not to go on. Christ, this would never end. Then, finally, he got up.

"All right. You want to help me?"

"Sure."

"I need to find out if there's any paper on those artists at NYPD."

"That's it?" his father asked.

Eddie nodded.

"And you want me to pull the files?"

Eddie looked away and nodded again, embarrassed that he even needed to make the request. Then Big Eddie laughed.

"Shit. All right, kid, I'll play."

He filled the two rock glasses with whiskey.

"What'd you say their names were?"

"Esther Schine and Julian Krane."

Big Eddie wrote the names down on a small pad. "Schine . . . that's S-C-H, right?

"Yeah. And Krane with a K."

"I'll see what I can do."

He clicked his glass with Eddie's and took a shot.

"Anything to help you get lucky, right?"

"What do you mean?"

Big Eddie flashed the smile now. The eyes twinkled. The white teeth showed. The jaw jutted out like Jack Kennedy's. He picked up a copy of the *Daily News* from his desk and opened it up to page three. There was a picture of Caroline Drexel next to a story about the burned mural.

"The broad from the paper. Jesus. How come they didn't look like that when I was in heat?"

Suddenly, Eddie jumped up. He leaned over the desk.

"Is that why you think I came *out* here? To ask your help so I could get lucky with some broad?"

"Hey. Time out, kid. I just—"

But Eddie was out of the office now, pushing through the bar, trying to get as far away as he could from his father.

Big Eddie got up from the desk and shot to the door.

"Eddie. I'm sorry . . . Eddie . . . Christ."

He was shouting through the crowd of blues now, shouting over the noise of the hockey game. But his son was already out on Third Avenue, already into his Chevy, and Big Eddie stopped, unwilling to chase him in front of his men. The pride. His position. Even now in retirement, he had a rep to maintain, and if you couldn't control your own kid, you were weak.

So Big Eddie stood his ground as his son gunned the Caprice and screeched off. The other cops in the Tam drank up and pretended they didn't see it.

The master suite in the three-bedroom duplex on Sutton Place was right out of *Architectural Digest* and decorated just like its owner: expensive, with impeccable taste. Caroline was staring at the ceiling now, unable to sleep. She switched on the light above the night table and lit a Gitane. Next to her bed, there was a biography of Frida Kahlo, the dark-eyebrowed wife of Diego Rivera, who'd suddenly become the rage out in Hollywood. Such a brilliant and twisted painter, thought Caroline. Decades before her time.

What a pity she'd married that giant. The Mexican Communist. The muralist who'd painted for all the big capitalists: Rockefeller and Ford. Perhaps if she'd come of age now . . . Outside of Diego's shadow . . . But Caroline didn't have the patience for Frida tonight. Her mind was still racing from the dream. So she stubbed out the cigarette, turned off the light, and dropped back down on the pillows.

She tried her left side and then her right, but she couldn't stop thinking about the two painters, Julian Krane and Esther Schine.

She thought about calling Helen at the chronic care hospital, but it was too late. She'd see her this weekend and ask her about the mural.

Maybe if she opened the window, perhaps the cold air would do some good. Caroline got up and pulled back the drapes and then . . . oh God. There he was. Down below in the shadows across Sutton Place. The same man who'd chased her along Forty-sixth Street. He was staring up at her window now. God . . . She touched her heart. It was pounding. So she ripped at the curtain, pulling it back across the window as she rushed across the room to the phone.

Manhattan Base was almost empty now. Tyrone Diggs, the marshal who worked House Watch on the Night Tour, was in the kitchen. He was reading The *Post* and watching *Letterman* when he heard the phone ring on Eddie's desk. But he let it go. Anything significant would come through the radio board from dispatch. The other marshals were out in the field. Whatever it was could wait till the morning.

The phone rang three times, then stopped. Then it rang again.

Across town on Sutton Place, Caroline Drexel just shivered. She let it ring one more time and hung up. She was worried now. Not just because there was a stranger outside, but because deep down, she knew that Eddie was right.

At first she didn't want to admit it. When the murder happened, she'd let herself believe that it was a crime of passion. But then Eddie had pushed her to check the artists rolls. Julian Krane. Esther Schine. These were names that she somehow remembered.

And then there was the mural itself. A woman had *died* for that painting. And in the pit of her stomach, Caroline knew that others would die as well.

She went to the window again and looked out. The man was still there, in the shadows.

Caroline picked up a phone and called downstairs. She told the doorman she'd seen a prowler outside. He said he'd check. But when he got to the street, the man was gone.

15

THE RENTED TV ON TOP OF THE RENTED CHEST OF DRAWERS was spewing white noise. The studio was located in the front of a brownstone on West Fifty-first in Hell's Kitchen. There was a rented table in the kitchen alcove littered with Chinese food containers, pizza boxes, and beer cans. A half dozen U-Haul file boxes were stacked full of clothes in a corner. There were three or four pieces of charred wood in sample cans on the sink.

The home of Fire Marshal Eddie Burke existed in marked contrast to the triplex on Sutton Place. It was the kind of place usually reserved for recently divorced men or serial killers. The the white noise from the TV gave the place a warm eerie glow as Eddie slept on a pullout couch. The sofa was green, stained, and frayed at the edges—one of the few things in the place that didn't rent by the month.

He had rescued it when he gave up his share in the Borum Hill co-op, after Mary Rose had sent him the papers. Well, "sent him the papers," was a bit of an understatement. The marriage had been shaky for quite awhile, but they'd been to a marriage counselor and Eddie had resolved to make it work. Then he had to go to D.C. for a week. A training seminar in crime scene analysis at the FBI Acad-

emy in Quantico. He'd taken the Delta Shuttle down. Mary
Rose was supposed to pick him up at La Guardia when he
got back, but she'd called that morning to say she was sick.
Since Brooklyn was an expensive cab ride away, she asked
Eddie to take a car service. He agreed, and when he walked
off the plane, he saw the driver, a short Asian man, holding
a sign up that said Burke.

Eddie was tired after the long week and anxious to get
home. He grabbed his bag from the luggage carousel and
rushed over to the guy. Then, something happened that he
would never forget. Something that hurt him as much as
the death of his mother. The ''driver'' looked away from
him and said, ''Hey man, I'm sorry.'' Then he handed
Eddie a summons and complaint. Mary Rose had filed for
divorce. But worse than that, she'd obtained an ex parte
temporary restraining order alleging domestic violence. A
TRO that prevented Eddie from even going home to see
his dog.

It was a nasty little preemptive strike that only hurt more
when Eddie went to a cash machine to get money for a
cab. The little card that came out said ''account closed.''
And when he finally got through to Citibank customer service, Eddie learned that Mary Rose had cleaned out their
savings.

In the space of five minutes, he found himself separated,
broke, and on the street. It took him six months and most
of his pension fund before it was over.

After he finally hired a lawyer, Eddie remembered telling
him what it felt like to get coldcocked.

''It's like two guys walk into a bar. One guy comes up
from behind. He hits the other guy over the head with a
chair, knocks him down, and kicks him in the nuts. Then
he helps him up and says, 'Let's start the fight now.' ''

This divorce without notice was a new tactic used by a
certain breed of domestic attorney. Lawyers who special-

ized in handling women, convincing them early on that their husbands were all to blame for what was wrong in their lives. They used domestic violence to grab the quick high ground in the dispute, and many men were forced to spend all of their energy and all of their savings just to catch up.

These predators fed off the very real headlines of spousal abuse, and though Eddie had never laid a finger on Mary Rose, except maybe to rub her back, he found himself on the defensive from the start.

In the end, he gave her everything. The co-op, his black Lab named Charcoal, even his jazz records, and Eddie would have been on the support hook for years to come if she hadn't met Mr. Right.

He was a dentist in his mid-fifties with a Dodge Viper and a condo in Boca Raton. They'd met at Club Med Martinque, the place Mary Rose went the day after the decree had gone final.

Eddie had gone to a gin mill instead. A failed marriage didn't seem like a cause for celebration to him. But she'd taken off to get a tan and came back engaged. The new guy was Jewish and divorced with no kids. A professional man who kept regular hours. Someone who didn't stop in the middle of a sentence when he heard a siren go by. A mature man who liked Woody Allen films and did the Sunday *Times* crossword in ink. Confidence. That's what the dentist had, and that's what Mary Rose sorely needed in a husband. Someone who could make a decision. Decide in a split second whether to save the incisor or go with a cap.

Eddie had loved Mary Rose at the start. The tall, leggy Italian girl from Font Bonne Academy. They'd run to St. Malachi's the day she got pregnant. But even after the miscarriage, he'd loved her, and it hurt him that he'd been unable to make her happy.

• • •

Now, eight months after the final decree, he'd sworn off women, retreating into this rat hole, making do with a *Penthouse Forum* now and then, ending each night alone with white noise.

But as he slept, he saw Caroline Drexel: the brown leather trench coat, the spike heels, the stockings snapped onto the garter, and the lipstick stain on the Pez dispenser. Christ, she was beautiful. And smart. An angel with a Ph.D., rising out of a cloud of Gitane smoke. She was coming toward him now, and he felt his heart pounding and then Caroline undid the belt on her trench coat. He could smell her perfume. Obsession. Definitely Obsession. She dropped the coat to the floor, and underneath he saw the stockings and the garter and the little satin push-up bra on top.

She extended her finger and flicked it toward him the way Kivlihan had done in the office, and Eddie felt himself moving toward her. Just then, in the smoke, he heard Mary Rose's voice. She was calling to ask if he'd be working late again, but Eddie couldn't hear what he told her because his words were drowned out by the sound of a dentist's drill. Then Caroline touched his stubbled face with her long, red fingernails. She ran her hand down his chest until she got to his belt buckle and his heart kept pounding, pounding until he heard his fly go down, and pretty soon she had her hand on his cock. That perfect hand with the red nails, nestling into his pubic hair. And then she dropped to her knees . . . pounding, pounding . . . as she pulled it out. Now his ex-wife's voice didn't matter. He no longer heard the dentist's drill and Caroline was about to take him when . . . pounding, pounding . . . he suddenly woke up and looked around the apartment. The light from the TV was blinding, and he had to adjust his eyes.

But the pounding was still there. *Boom. Boom.* So he jumped out of bed. Christ. Somebody was out in the hallway. He grabbed his Smith & Wesson from the night table and went to the door in his Speedos.

"Who is it?"

"Monsignor O'Neil . . . I'm here to go over your Latin, kid . . . *Ad Deum qui laetificat juventutem meum.*"

Eddie looked through the peephole and shook his head. It was his father.

"Your first mass is in two weeks. You better be ready."

Eddie pulled the chain off and threw the dead bolt. When he opened the door, Big Eddie was staring at him, half lit, with a folded *Daily News* in one hard and a bottle of Jameson's in the other.

"I brought the wine. Thought maybe we'd practice the Offertory."

"You're drunk, Pop."

But Big Eddie just stood there, bobbing and weaving.

"It hasn't been right since they put it in English. You know that? The Mass? It was meant for a language you couldn't understand. The priest with his back to you. Stained-glass windows. Incense. There was mystery then. There was fear."

He walked in and slammed down the bottle on the kitchen table. Then he looked around.

"What the hell's my son doin' in a shit box like this?"

"It's where I live, Pop. I don't need much anymore."

"Not since the wife ran off with that ortho—what was he?"

"Periodontist."

"Yeah that tooth fairy. Christ, if you hadn't knocked up that little bitch, you'd be a detective by now."

Eddie walked to the TV and shut it off.

"You still blame Mary Rose for the academy, don't you?"

"Why the hell not? Two weeks before graduation you wash out? First in your class?"

"I couldn't take it."

"Bullshit. It's in your blood. You're my son. You could have been commissioner. Fuck. You could have been mayor."

Eddie turned to face him now.

"I don't think so. There's only one Eddie Burke."

Big Eddie ignored that.

"It wouldn't have been so bad, you did something else. Fuckin' longshoreman . . . a mechanic. I'd even take a goddamn insurance salesman. But no. You had to join an engine company."

"We had a kid on the way. I needed work."

"Hey. She lost it. Remember?"

Eddie remembered, all right, but he kept his mouth shut while Big Eddie went on.

"You took a gun and you pointed it right at my heart, kid. A goddamn fireman . . . Shit."

Big Eddie turned to walk out, then he stopped to think. He opened the *Daily News* and pulled out a file folder hidden inside. He staggered to the kitchen table and tossed it down next to the Jameson's. It had the NYPD seal in the upper right corner and it was stamped Closed across the front in inch-high red letters. Eddie picked it up.

"What's this?"

"Missing persons file on that painter."

"Julian Krane?"

"Negative. Couldn't find a thing on that bastard. It's the girl."

"Esther Schine?"

Big Eddie was at the door now.

"Yeah. Too bad, kid. You won't be able to play cop and question her."

He slammed the door and exited into the hallway.

Eddie gnashed his teeth and then shouted from behind the door. "Why the hell not?"

"Cause she's *dead*."

"What?"

Eddie rushed to the door and opened up.

"When?"

"Nineteen hundred and thirty-eight. And guess what?"

"Tell me."

"It was murder."

16

THE OLD JEWISH CEMETERY IN QUEENS SAT ON A RISE NEAR
the LIE. Eddie had come through the Midtown Tunnel and
taken the Maurice Avenue exit to Sixty-first Street. He
didn't have long before Kivlihan yanked him back, so he
drove past the headstones quickly. An old friend of Aggie's
in the ME's office had supplied the plot number. She had
to go into the microfiche from the thirties to get it, and
Aggie had said that Eddie owed them both dinner.

He checked his notebook now against granite and marble
headstones at the corner of each row: 37 AA 3; 37 AA 4.
There it was. The fifth column in the AA row of the thirty-
seventh section. He stopped the Chevy, got out, and walked
up through the city of headstones. And then he found it: a
dark slab of granite with a star of David on top and the
name Schine carved under Hebrew characters.

The stone was blackened from fifty-nine years of pollu-
tion and acid rain. So old that the names were barely visible. But what did it matter? No one had put flowers on the
grass here for decades. Eddie ran down the names of the
Schine family members until he came to the one at the
bottom.

Esther, Beloved Daughter: 1912–1938

She must have been the last of her line. Eddie stared at the name and wondered how it was that a young female painter had ended up dead on West Twenty-eighth Street. That's all the file had said: Deceased. Probable Homicide. She'd been twenty-six, much too young to die.

He'd come out here to see if she might have some relatives living, but Esther Schine was the last name on the stone. Shit. It was a long shot, anyway. Eddie closed his notebook and returned to the car. Then he stopped. In the next row there was a freshly dug grave. The headstone said Saltzman, and it was covered with flowers. Wreathes made of roses, and green plastic vases full of tulips, irises, and mums. There must have been a funeral that morning.

Eddie thought for a second and then smiled. He looked around and picked up a vaseful of mums. In another hour, they'd be frozen anyway. He walked back and put them in front of the headstone below Esther's name. Then he stood and said a short prayer, the one his mother had taught him that he'd said every night as a child:

Angel of God, my guardian dear. To whom God's love commits me here. Ever this day, be at my side. To light and guard. To rule and guide.

Nobody should die at twenty-six. He made the sign of the cross and started walking away, then he looked back and saw it, a name carved into the back of Esther Schine's headstone.

Nathan: Loving Son: 1913–

Nathan Schine. There was another one still alive. Just then, his beeper went off. Eddie ran to his car. He picked up the two-way, and called in. Instead of Vasquez, he got Kivli-han.

"Where the fuck *are* you?" Kivie rubbed his jaw. It was aching again.

"I hit traffic in the Midtown."

"Bullshit. I checked with Bridge and Tunnels, and it's been clear going east since rush hour."

"Look, I'm on my way."

"I've had three guys from SIU at Roosevelt Island for over an hour."

"I'll be there."

"You fuckin' better be."

17

IT WAS AFTER 10:00 P.M. AS EDDIE COMBED THROUGH A half-dozen phone books from the tristate state area. It had been a bitch of a day, and he didn't get a chance to make any calls on the mural case. Kivlihan was off now at some testimonial for Commissioner Von Essen, so it was safe for Eddie to work from his desk.

He circled a name in a Queens directory and picked up the phone. It rang once, twice, three times before somebody answered on the other end. There was a woman's voice and Eddie knew that she'd been asleep.

"Hullo."

"Yes. Nathan Schine, please."

"Who's this?"

"Edmund Burke. New York City Fire Department."

"Oh, my God. Did something happen to my Nate?"

"No, ma'am, I'm just looking—"

"Did he get into trouble up there? I told his father Brandeis was too far to send him."

"Brandeis?"

"I wanted NYU, but his father insisted—"

"Wait a minute. How old is Nathan?"

"How old do you think? He's nineteen."

"And his father?"

"Forty-two, but he doesn't live here anymore."

"I'm sorry, Mrs. Schine. I've got the wrong number."

"You're sorry?"

Eddie hung up sheepishly. Christ.

It went on like this for three hours. Investigative work. It was boring. A crapshoot. People watched TV and the cops always put the case down in an hour. They'd work a few witnesses, roust a few snitches, and get it. But the truth was, this work was a bitch.

It took patience and tremendous tenacity. When you sat there staring at ten inches of phone directories, you had to believe that you'd pull out the name. Otherwise, why would you do it? Why wake all those people up? And nine times out of ten, you were wrong. But you still had to lie to yourself and believe that you'd crack it. Otherwise, you might as well sit in a ladder company and wait for the bell.

But that wasn't enough for Eddie Burke.

He'd done his time as a smoke eater; rode the trucks, pulled the line, strapped on a Scotts bottle, and jumped into fires so hot that his eyebrows got singed. He'd lost the hair on his face twice. Another time the flames were so intense that the rubber in his mask melted. In six years on a forcible entry team he'd pulled out more than a dozen people. And a third of the time, when he split open a door or broke through a window, he smelled accelerants. Volatile liquids. Evidence that the fires had been set with intent.

Eddie was working 102 Truck in Bed Stuy back then, and some twisted fucks had come up with yet another way to rob Uncle. They were using a federal program called the Fair Plan. Set up after the sixties riots when ghettos like Bed Stuy were in flames, the Fair Plan was a government-insured risk pool.

The law said that in order to sell fire insurance in affluent neighborhoods, the big carriers like State Farm, Aetna, and

Firemen's Fund had to offer policies in the ghetto. So the three-hundred-odd insurers in the state of New York pulled together and kicked into a fund. It meant that the little guy in the hood could now get a policy on a brownstone or a barber shop that had once been uninsurable.

But like so many federal programs, the Fair Plan turned into a well-intentioned experiment gone bad. In fact, it was a goddamn gold mine for arsonists.

Since no *one* insurance company bore all the risk, no *one* company would push to investigate if a fire started suspiciously. So little fires started happening all over the city from the South Bronx to Greenpoint.

One night, a torch got caught in a blaze of his own making, and Eddie pulled him out. Eddie knew it was a Fair Plan building, but he didn't understand the scam. So he shook down the torch for it. The bastard could live with the third-degree burns on his arms, but he didn't want to go back to the joint, so he told Eddie how it worked.

"Say State Farm's holding six million bucks worth of paper on an office building. The place goes up, you *know* they're gonna call a PI. He'll go in, take his samples, his pictures. He'll look for accelerants, any evidence of arson, so State Farm doesn't have to pay on the claim."

Eddie nodded. He was listening.

"Now, take a Fair Plan insurer," said the torch. "They got what? One three-hundredth of the risk? Fuck. They could give two shits if a building gets hit for fifty K in a burn. It doesn't pay to contest the award."

Eddie understood now. Keep the payouts small, and nobody asked for the cause. Who cared that a two-year-old Spanish kid got caught in the blaze? Or a pregnant mother from Haiti? Or an old Black granny confined to her bed? Fuck. These people didn't have standing, and fire made money. Case closed.

A small group of urban terrorists had figured this out and

made a fortune through arson. They'd start buying buildings. They'd trade them among themselves, inflating their value on paper. After that, they'd hire bust-out specialists like Superman to clean out the buildings. They'd destroy the boilers in the middle of winter, fracture the water pipes, play ear-shattering music till dawn; anything to get the tenants out. Then, pretty soon, tenants or not, the fires would start. Twenty-two grand worth of scorched joists in the basement; six months later, an electrical fire on the third floor; and ten months after that, a grease fire on five. Each time the Fair Plan would cut the check without an investigation and each time the payout would go to a different landlord because they were swapping these rat shacks like Monopoly deeds. It didn't matter that a pair of young twins got trapped in their cribs or an invalid died in her wheelchair. The Fair Plan would kick out the checks and nobody'd be the wiser.

But Eddie got curious about some of the Bed Stuy fires. Working as the outside vent man on a first-alarm assignment, he'd break the side windows of a tenement. The smoke would come out from the stove fire and he'd smell toluene or he'd pick up the scent of dibenzofurane in the basement. Accidental fire, his ass. Someone was torching these places. He didn't know how or why until he saw the headlines about the Fair Plan scam up in Boston and the one on the Near North Side of Chicago.

So he did his homework, checked the payments, and shook down the torch. He took the package to the Deputy Chief, and the DA got a string of indictments. Eddie had been with the Bureau of Fire Investigation ever since.

Still, there was something he missed about fighting fires. Something clean about roaring up to a working fire in progress. All you had to do was kill it, smother it, take the oxygen away. And though it could burn you and people died, when it was over, you were *done*. It was Miller time until the next one.

But investigative work was different: a tedious, detail-ridden bitch of a job, and on nights like this, as he went blind poring over the names in those phone books, pissing people off, waking them up, and getting phone after phone slammed down on him, Eddie wished he was back in his turnout coat and bunker pants, crawling into some old-law tenement that was on fire.

It was almost one in the morning when he got the hit.

18

HE'D GONE THROUGH AT LEAST THIRTEEN NAMES. WHO would have thought there'd be so many Nathan Schines in New York?

Of course, it could have been worse. He could have been looking for Burkes. Eddie had counted them up one night during one of these sessions and stopped at 116 in the Brooklyn directory alone. With Schine, he had found 14 names, and he was half asleep when he grabbed the phone for one last call.

It rang six times before he heard the pick-up.

"Who the hell's calling this late?"

"Hello. Mr. Schine? Fire Marshal Burke, FDNY."

"FDN what?"

"The fire department, sir."

"I don't smell smoke."

"No, sir. I'm sorry to bother you so late, but I've been trying to locate the brother of an Esther Schine, and I wonder if you could help me?"

There was silence on the end of the line; not a hang-up, just silence. He could hear the old man breathing now. Wheezing almost.

"Mr. Schine, you still there?"

Another interminable pause and then: "My sister . . . She died years ago."

Bang. He got a hit.

"I'm aware of that, sir. Look, I wonder if I couldn't ask you—"

"What the hell are you doing bothering me at this hour? I'm an elderly person. I've been sick."

"I'm really sorry, sir, but I'm working a case—"

"Case? You know what you can do with your case? You can stick it up your ass."

Eddie just sat there for a second, staring at the receiver. Then he said, "I don't think I could do that, sir. We're not allowed to put things into our rectal cavities while on duty."

Click. The old man hung up. But Eddie jumped up and screamed *"Yessss!"* so loud that Tyrone, the house watch, turned around at the radio board and shook his head.

Eddie looked over at him. "Sorry, Ty." Then he smiled and wrote down the old man's address in his notebook: 452 Avenue A. He checked his watch, got up, grabbed his jacket, and tore out of the office. The clock on the squad room wall said 1:03 A.M.

Seven minutes went by and then the phone rang on Eddie's desk. No answer. It rang again. Nothing. Then a third ring.

On the top floor of the triplex on Sutton Place, Caroline Drexel stood by the window in a silk robe. She had a glass of wine in her hand and she was shivering, hidden behind the curtain as she looked down through the blinds and saw him again. The street had been deserted all night. She'd decided to take a peek before going to bed, and there he was, in the shadows, standing below the stairs of a co-op across the street. She'd called the police and they'd sent a squad car, but by then the strange man had disappeared. And now he was back again. If she could only see his face.

The phone rang a fifth time and then a sixth and then, finally, back in the squad room, Kivlihan rushed in and picked it up. He was still in the tux he'd worn to the testimonial dinner, and he was chewing on a Danneman cigar.

"Fire Marshals."

That wasn't Eddie's voice. Caroline was silent.

"Hello? This is Manhattan Base," said Kivlihan. "Who the hell *is* this?"

But Caroline just let the phone fall into its cradle and the line went dead.

Kivlihan slammed it down and then looked at the phone books on Eddie's desk. He walked over and cocked his head to Tyrone on the board.

"Hey Diggs, was Burke in here tonight?"

The Black man shrugged. "Yeah. He just left."

Kivlihan narrowed his eyes and sucked in on the cigar so that the tip glowed red hot. Then he flicked the ashes on Eddie's desk and stormed out.

This fuckin' guy was dead.

It was 1:56 A.M. when Eddie stepped off the elevator on the eighteenth floor of the old Jacob Riis Housing Project on the Lower East Side. An immigrant Dutchman, Riis had been a crusading reporter at the turn of the century who ripped the lid off crime in the teeming Chinese and Jewish ghettos of lower Manhattan. He had thrown open the doors to the sweatshops on Delancy, taken Police Commissioner Teddy Roosevelt on a tour of the opium dens along Pell Street, and exposed America to *How The Other Half Lives*. Along with Upton Sinclair and Ida Tarbell, he represented a new breed of investigative reporter, branded muckrakers by the yellow journalist press of the day. Like his contemporaries, Riis, the crusader, died broke, in obscurity. It wasn't until the 1930s, when FDR's New Deal pumped federal cash into the cities, that the teaming slums Riis wrote about were cleared.

The project that bore his name was a series of twenty-four story towers in tan brick that went up just east of First Avenue between Avenues A and C. Eleanor Roosevelt herself cut the ribbon for the dedication in '36. They were the first high rises in U.S. history to be built with public funds. And for the first time in decades, needy families had housing that was safe, clean, and crime-free.

Now, more than sixty years later, the Jacob Riis Projects had turned into Mogadishu on the Lower East Side. A graffiti-painted, garbage-strewn ghetto ruled by gangs. A kind of urban free-fire zone, loaded with welfare families and terrified senior citizens. If Riis were alive today, there's no doubt this is the place where he'd bring his rake.

Eddie walked down the filthy hallway and noticed that all but one of the overhead lights were out. A single neon tube flickered as he came up to a door with a mezuzah on the jam. The word *joo* had been written in crayon just under it and there was an arrow pointing toward the battered metal front door. It said Schine in a tiny box over the mirrored peephole. Eddie checked himself in the two-inch-square mirror. His hair was combed. Good. His tie was straight. Fine. All he had to do now was wake up an old man and tell him his sister had been murdered half a century ago. He checked his watch. It was 1:57 A.M. Then he knocked at the door.

"Mr. Schine?"

A few seconds passed and Eddie heard something fall to the floor. Eyeglasses maybe or a bottle of pills on a night stand. Then he heard shuffling. A pair of slippers across the cold floor. Then a voice. Old and feeble and full of phlegm.

"Who's out there?" The old man cleared his throat. "Who the hell's knocking on my door at this hour?"

Eddie pictured him inside, peering through the peephole.

"Fire Marshal Burke, Mr. Schine. We just talked. Remember?"

"I got nothing to do with the cops. Not this late."

Eddie held up his shield to the mirror.

"I'm not a cop, sir. I'm a fireman."

Eddie heard the sound of the dead bolts turning. One, two, and then three.

"Fireman schmireman. You work for the city don't you?"

He opened the door, still held in place by two chains.

"Yeah," said Eddie.

"Well, tell Koch to fix my heater."

With that, Nathan Schine slammed the door and Eddie bit down on his lip for patience.

"He's not the mayor anymore, Mr. Schine."

Eddie knocked again. "Mr. Schine . . ."

"Go 'way now. Leave me alone."

Eddie stopped knocking. Christ. What was he doing here in the middle of the night, rousting some scared old man on the thinnest of leads in a case that was closed years ago? What the hell was he trying to prove?

Eddie exhaled hard, then turned and walked back down the hall. He felt broken; just like he did in the Tam O' Shanter. Who was he kidding? That uniformed bull outside the loft building was right. "There's only one Eddie Burke."

Then he flashed on Caroline and he stopped. Caroline Drexel. He wondered if *she'd* ever walked down a swill-covered hallway like this. There were things he was willing to do for her that he might not do for someone else—like stay up late and go blind with the phone calls.

But that wasn't enough. He needed something more to turn him around, and he found it sticking out of his pocket as he stabbed at the elevator button. The file on Esther Schine. That twenty-six-year-old girl they found dead on the street. Somebody had cut her wide open, and Eddie had to know why. He'd come too far on this to stop now. So he straightened up, headed back to the door with the mezuzah, and knocked.

"Hello. Mr. Schine."

There was no answer now. Just the sound of the slippers shuffling across the floor.

"Mr. Schine, I visited your sister's grave today. It looked good. They're keeping the grass cut and there's a beautiful view of Manhattan.

Inside, the shuffling stopped. A moment went by and then Eddie heard the three dead bolts thrown open.

"You saw . . . you went to the grave?"

The old man was holding the door open a crack.

"Yeah. You see, Mr. Schine, one of your sister's old paintings was found and—"

"A painting . . . My Esther?"

There were tears in the old man's eyes now. Eddie could just see his face. It was hollow, the face of a death camp survivor who'd never again learned to eat.

"You think maybe I could come in and talk?"

Another moment and then, slowly, Nathan Schine undid the two chains and swung open the door.

19

FIVE MINUTES LATER, EDDIE WAS NURSING A GLASS OF MO-
gen David as Nathan Schine showed him a picture of his
sister Esther, right out of high school.

He was leaning in over Eddie now, a birdlike man with
mottled brown skin drawn tight over his bones and tufts of
hair in his ears. There was a white stubble on his face and
a wisp of white hair under his blue knitted yarmulke.

"A real beauty she was," said Nathan. "Dean's list at
CCNY. Full scholarship to Yale for the masters. She even
won this award, what d'you call it? The Prix de Rome. . . ."

"Is that right?" said Eddie.

"Absolutely. She was supposed to have a year in Italy
to study. But that was in thirty-eight. . . ."

He wiped his eyes.

"The Panzer Divisions were moving by then. I mean,
what Jewish girl in her right mind's gonna walk into that?"

The old man stopped and touched the picture.

"Still, people said she was destined to be a great
painter." He turned away now and began to weep.

Eddie put his hand on his shoulder.

"What happened, Mr. Schine? How did she die so
young?"

Schine wiped his eyes and picked up the picture.

"No one knows. They found her body on West Twenty-eighth. Everywhere there was blood. Whoever it was used a knife."

"Did they ever find . . . ?"

"What? The animal who did it? Never. Back then, a young Jewish girl was not a priority for you Irish cops."

"I told you. I'm not a cop."

"Yeah, but you're Irish."

Eddie didn't have a rejoinder for that one. He just stared at Schine as the old man put the picture back on the mantel.

"What about the other painter she worked with?"

Eddie checked his notebook.

"Julian Krane. Did you ever know him?"

Suddenly, Nathan Schine stopped. He started itching the back of his hand.

"Krane? Never heard of him."

Eddie could see he was lying, so he pressed him.

"You sure about that, Mr. Schine? He and your sister worked on that mural for months. She must have mentioned—"

"No!"

The old man was breathing heavily now. He shuffled to the door and pulled it open.

"You should leave."

Then, as if realizing he'd overplayed it, he stopped.

"Look, I'm sorry. It's just . . . you bring back too many memories."

"Yeah. Well I'm sorry if I caused you any . . . You know . . ."

"Please . . . just go."

Eddie complied.

"Right. Fine. Thanks for the wine."

The old man nodded. Eddie was sure he was hiding

something, but he smiled as Nathan Schine opened the door.

Eddie heard the chains engage and the three dead bolts turn as he walked down the hall. Then he checked his watch. It was 2:07 now. If he was lucky, Big Eddie would just be closing up.

Eddie stabbed at the elevator button and waited. Ten seconds, twenty. Half a minute. Nothing. No light at the button. No sound of the motor engaging. He leaned his weight on one foot and then the other. He stabbed at the button again. Still nothing. So he pushed through the door marked Exit and ran down the eighteen flights.

The bartender was upending chairs at the Tam, and Big Eddie was at the cash register going through the night's receipts when the Chevy screeched to a stop on Third Avenue. Eddie jumped out and hit the door. The bartender looked up and pointed to the Closed sign. Then he saw that it was Eddie, so he smiled and let him in.

"What do you say, Paulie?"

"Eddie."

"Where is he?"

The bartender nodded toward the bar and Eddie rushed up to his father.

"That file on Esther Schine—"

"Christ, didn't I ever teach you to say hello first?"

"Sorry, Pop. You know that file on the dead girl?"

"Yeah?"

"It just had the date of death."

"So?"

"I need one more favor."

Without skipping a beat, Big Eddie slammed down a pair of rock glasses and smiled.

"The fuckin' prodigal son."

• • •

The wind blew hard off the Brooklyn Bridge as Eddie took the Center Street exit and pulled off past Borough Hall.

"Go 'round to the back and we'll park by the MCC," said Big Eddie. "I don't know who's on tonight."

Eddie pulled the Caprice up to a parking space marked NYPD Police Business. They were outside the Metropolitan Correctional Center, the federal jail in Manhattan. The feds had a good piece of turf here, where downtown Manhattan met the river. There was a triangle of buildings joined by walkways: The MCC, U.S. Federal District Court, and the Office of the U.S. Attorney for the Southern District of New York. They shared a plaza with Manhattan Borough Hall, St. Andrew's, an old Roman Catholic Church, and the police headquarters, known since the eighties as One Police Plaza.

Big Eddie had always thought it was funny. The Vatican still held most of the blues in its grip, and it was the pastor of St. Andrew's who rented the square outside his church to a half-dozen food vendors. The row of tan stalls had little red, white, and green stickers on their sides. Italian flags, meaning the food sellers all came from Little Italy, three blocks away. On any given day, you could grab a sausage and peppers sandwich or a paper dish full of fried scungilli. The cuisine was first rate, but half of those food stalls were controlled by the Mafia and almost all of their customers were cops: customs and treasury agents from the Southern District, FBI guys from across Foley Square, and the hundreds of uniforms based at headquarters.

Big Eddie used to joke that if the "Siggies wanted to wipe out half the cops in New York, all they had to do was lace their ziti with strychnine." It was just another one of those curiosities in a city that thrived on irony.

Anyway, at 3:12 A.M., all the food stands were closed when Eddie and his father made their way across St. Andrew's Square. As they passed the front of the church, both of them bowed their heads out of habit, even though neither man had been anywhere near an altar for years.

Big Eddie didn't have to bother flashing his badge at the entrance to One Police Plaza. A legend was welcomed at any time of the day or night.

He ended up schmoozing with so many cops that it was almost 3:30 by the time they were inside the records room and checking the microfiche as they searched through hundreds of old cases.

A few stalls away, a young African-American policewoman was sitting in front of another machine going through files. She was wearing a silk blouse and a short skirt made of suede. Her detective's shield was folded over a thin leather belt. The woman checked her watch, then stretched back and yawned, revealing a beautiful figure.

Big Eddie wet his lips and nudged his son.

"Affirmative action," he whispered. "You gotta love it."

Eddie winced, then turned back to the machine as the cases rolled by in a black-and-white blur.

Two hours later, they were deep into the final quarter of 1938 when they found it.

"Here it is. Schine, Esther. Eleven November, nineteen thirty-eight."

Big Eddie put on his glasses and checked the screen.

"Yeah. It figures. Assailant unknown. That's why it was in the dead files. Get me a printout will you?"

Eddie found a button that said Print and pushed it.

Seconds later, a laser printer nearby spit out an ME's photo of the once-beautiful girl.

There was a second crime scene photo of Esther lying on West Twenty-eighth Street. A white, bloodstained sheet covered the body. The four-page police report came out next, and Big Eddie grabbed it, checking it with his bifocals.

"Is it me, or did they make the print smaller then?"

"Gotta be the print, Pop," said Eddie. "Let me see it."

He started reading out loud.

"The subject body shows invasive tears of the left and right labia attendant to massive arterial hemorrhaging . . ."

He looked up at his father. "Christ, she was butchered."

"Go on."

"The gravid uterus is buoyant with particles of conception due to an incomplete scrape of the uterine wall."

Suddenly, Big Eddie grabbed his son's arm.

"Wait a minute. Read that back."

"The gravid uter—"

"Christ. That's it."

"What?"

"She was pregnant."

"I don't get it."

Big Eddie got up and started to pace. "Look. A nice girl gets knocked up today, she takes a cab to the clinic."

"Yeah?"

"Back then they used coat hangers."

"A back-alley abortion?"

"You got it. The bastard nicks an artery. She hemorrhages. Goes into shock. He panics. She bleeds to death on the table, and he dumps her on Twenty-eighth. For all the beat cops wanna know, it's a mugging."

"What's it mean?"

"Are you kidding? You just cracked open a murder case sixty years old."

Eddie was quiet.

"First the Sloane girl, now this. How's it tie into that mural?"

Eddie shook his head. "I don't know."

He picked up the picture of Esther Schine lying on the sidewalk and stared at it. There was a small white hand lying under the bloodstained sheet.

Then suddenly, his beeper went off. Eddie reached for a phone and punched in numbers.

Bobby Vasquez was on the board now at Manhattan Base. He picked up after the first ring.

"Fire Marshals. Vasquez."

"What is it, Bobby?"

"I just came in, Eddie. You got a pile of messages."

"Kivlihan?"

"No. Some woman. A Caroline Drexel. Been calling every twenty minutes since three."

Eddie hung up and looked at his father.

"What is it, kid?"

Eddie didn't answer. He just turned and took off like a shot.

20

THE SUN WAS JUST COMING UP OVER THE EAST RIVER AS THE two Burkes entered the marble lobby at 120 Sutton Place. A doorman was sitting in a leather wingback chair smoking a Camel and reading the *Daily News* when Big Eddie flashed his shield.

"Police business."

He started to move toward the elevators when the doorman jumped up.

"Wait a minute. Let me see that."

Big Eddie held it out to him with his thumb covering a word at the bottom of the badge.

"Burke. Chief of Detectives."

"Retired," said the doorman with a sneer as he pushed Big Eddie's thumb away. "The people who live here don't like to be bothered. Get lost."

Just then, Eddie pushed up to him.

"Retired or not, he was a cop once."

The doorman started to turn away. "Fuck off."

Suddenly, Eddie lunged forward and grabbed the man's tie.

"What the fuck?" said the doorman. "Cops aren't supposed to do that."

"He's retired," said Eddie. "And I'm not a cop. So stop pretending you live in this place. You're a working-class stiff just like us."

He let go, and the doorman did his best to recover.

"Sure, sure. What can I do for yis?"

Eddie produced his Fire Marshal's ID.

"Caroline Drexel. Ring her up."

"Anything you want, Chief."

"Marshal," said Eddie, gesturing to his father, "he's the Chief."

Big Eddie beamed at his son. Chip off the fuckin' block.

After a ten-second ride in an elevator framed in gold leaf, Eddie and his father arrived at the third-floor hallway. The foyer alone was gigantic, bigger than Eddie's apartment, with brocade wallpaper, crystal sconces, and tiny framed etchings. Eddie didn't know much about art, but he'd heard the name Degas before.

"Christ. These are real."

Big Eddie rubbed his thumb and forefinger together and rang the bell, instinctively standing to the side of the door, the way all cops do in case the person inside decides to answer with a sawed-off Remington. But not in this place.

Finally, a tiny Asian maid opened the door. Her skin was like porcelain.

"Burke, Fire Department, to see Miss Drexel."

"You wait inside, please." The maid bowed and gestured them into a foyer with an alabaster stairway leading up to the second and third levels. The floor had a black and white checkered pattern like the one in the Tam, only this one was done in marble.

"Christ, I wonder who decorated this place?" said Eddie.

"Same guy who did the Sistine Chapel," said his father. Big Eddie proceeded into the neoclassical living room.

It was just slightly smaller than the old Bonwit Teller's.

"Hey, Pop. She told us to wait out here."

"Don't worry. I'm not gonna steal anything."

Eddie looked around the foyer. The walls were covered with mirrors from floor to ceiling. He smoothed back his hair and tightened his neck muscles. Christ, he hadn't worked out in months. The skin was getting flabby under his chin. He grabbed an inch of it and pulled it tight, imagining what he'd look like if he had a jaw like, say, Alec Baldwin. Then he heard her behind him.

"Thanks for coming."

Eddie spun around as Caroline stood over him at the top of the stairs. She was wearing a silk robe and pajamas. For someone who'd been up all night, she looked like five million bucks, and that's just about how much her apartment was worth.

"They said you'd been calling."

Eddie thrust his hands to his side. He clutched them behind his back as she came down the stairs in heels below satin pajama legs. Christ. Eddie folded his arms. But then, when she stepped into the foyer, he decided to put his hands in his jacket pockets—the way Bobby Kennedy did.

Caroline came up to him.

"I haven't been able to sleep. There's a man. . . . He's been following me."

"What man?"

Eddie pulled out his hands now.

"I don't know. I saw him two nights ago near your office. He chased me and I got away. Then he showed up outside the building here. I tried to call you, but I couldn't get through. Anyway, last night he came back again. He was . . . watching my window."

"A guy chased you two nights ago and this is the first that you *tell* me?"

Caroline lit a cigarette.

"I told you, I couldn't get through. I was at school all day yesterday and didn't get back till very late."

"Why didn't you call the police?"

"I did. When they came, he was gone." She inhaled and put the Gitane in a marble ashtray.

Just then, from the living room, Big Eddie called out.

"Christ, kid. You didn't *tell* me who her father was."

Eddie looked at her. "That's 'cause she didn't tell *me*."

Caroline turned away nervously. Her face flushed like it did that night in the squad room when she found those artists' names. Then she touched her throat, not thinking Eddie would notice. But he did. There wasn't a thing this woman did that he *didn't* notice. Eddie had suspected it that first night when she left so abruptly. Now he was sure. She was hiding something.

She lit another cigarette and Eddie said, "Something wrong?"

"Why no," said Caroline. "Why do you ask?"

Eddie cocked his head toward the ashtray. "You've already got one going."

Caroline stubbed out both of the cigarettes and they moved into the living room. Big Eddie was standing in front of a Steinway grand covered with pictures in silver frames. One of them was a shot of a white-haired Brahmin in his early seventies. He handed it to his son, who shook his head.

"Black Jack Drexel? He's your old man?"

Caroline nodded faintly as Eddie set the picture back down on the piano. She turned to the father.

"And who are you?"

"Edmund Burke, miss." The old cop flashed the Kennedy smile. "NYPD, retired." He took her hand. "You must be Caroline."

Eddie watched as Big Eddie looked her up and down,

the perfect hair, the silk robe, the Lancôme lip gloss and the heels. Christ, the old bastard was undressing her with his eyes.

"Your father . . ." said the ex-cop, "the papers say he's gonna buy the Yankees."

She looked nervous at the mention of the well-known industrialist.

"There's some talk of it. Why?"

Big Eddie responded with acid.

"I just want to know if he does, so I can defect to the Mets."

Caroline touched her throat again.

"I take it you don't like my father."

"What? The arbitrage king? What's not to like? He wrecks a multibillion-dollar company, busts the unions, gets bailed out by Uncle, and now he's looking to sell short to the Japs. The man's a regular patriot."

"Hey, Pop."

"Relax, kid. She can talk for herself. She's got a Ph.D."

Caroline walked to the piano and moved her father's picture half an inch to the left, precisely the place where it had been before Big Eddie touched it.

"Not that it's any of your business, Mr. Burke, but I haven't seen my father in months. We don't speak."

Eddie tried to change the subject. "What's this about you being followed?"

But before she could answer, Big Eddie took over. "First things first, kid. I've got a few questions . . . regarding the mural that burned."

"What about it?"

"You gave my son the names of two artists. Schine and Krane?"

"Yes."

"The report said that the mural was big. What? Ten feet high?"

"That's right."

"Lot of work for two artists. You sure Schine and Krane were the only two that worked on it?"

"Why, no. I . . ." Caroline touched her throat yet again. "It's possible there were others."

"Could you check it for us?"

Big Eddie was inches away from her now, so Eddie stepped between them.

"Look. She said she was being followed. The investigation can wait."

"Yeah?" said Big Eddie. "So what if the guy who's after her had something to do with the SoHo death?"

Caroline put her hand on Eddie's arm.

"No. It's okay. I'll do what I can. But all my research is up at Columbia. I could meet you there later."

"You sure you don't want me to stay with you now?"

It was Big Eddie's turn to step in. "Hey. Last time I checked, you still had a job, kid. You're not in by nine, Kivie'll have your ass."

Eddie turned red now, but Caroline pulled him aside.

"It's okay. I'll take a cab to my office and meet you at, say . . . three o'clock?"

"I'll be there."

As they exited, Big Eddie moved into the foyer, but Caroline called Eddie back.

"Eddie . . ." She was almost whispering.

"Yeah?"

"It was wonderful meeting your father. But later on . . . when you come to see me . . . come alone."

Eddie nodded as his father called out from the foyer. "Come on, kid. This place is too rich for my blood."

In the elevator on the way down, Eddie faced away from his father. He was pissed.

"And *you* wonder why I never lasted with Mary Rose."

"Hey. What'd I say?"

Eddie just shook his head.

The doorman waited until Big Eddie and his son left the building. Then he picked up a phone and started to dial.

The Bell Jet Ranger was just breaking the TRACON air corridor near La Guardia, roaring toward Manhattan from Greenwich, Connecticut. There was a gold logo on its side that read, The Drexel Group.

The cabin phone rang and a man named LeStadt answered. He was tall and expressionless, well-built and dark complected, in a Savile Row pinstriped suit. He wore no jewelry, and the skin on his face bore the scars of a bout with acne in his teens. This was Drexel's secretary.

He listened and then nodded across the cabin to Black Jack, who picked up an extension.

"It's Miss Caroline, sir," said the doorman. "She's had visitors."

There was a long pause as Drexel heard the doorman describe the retired chief of detectives and the young fire cop. He nodded politely and thanked him, then hung up. LeStadt, put the phone back in its cradle. He noticed the almost imperceptible change on the industrialist's face as his jaw muscles tightened.

Here was a man who looked like an Under Secretary of State. A world-class CEO. With silver hair somebody cut for a hundred bucks every week at the Hotel Pierre. He wore Kilgour, French & Stansbury shirts with monogrammed cuffs, two-hundred-dollar silk Sulka ties, and thousand-dollar custom-made shoes. He drank his Chivas in Waterford crystal and once a day he allowed himself a ten-dollar Upmann rolled in Cuba. But for all that, there was something "street" in the way he moved, something larcenous that betrayed his history.

Few people knew it, but Black Jack Drexel was a man who had climbed to the fiftieth floor through the sheer strength of his will. He was made of the same stuff as Carnegie, Mellon, and Vanderbilt: robber barons who had taken the mountain a century ago. He was vain, vindictive, and above all, territorial. He rarely saw his daughter, but that didn't stop him from coveting her, and he didn't like it when strangers came into her life.

As the helicopter crossed the East River, LeStadt watched Drexel's face before he turned away to look down on the FDR Drive. And for just a millisecond he caught it . . . Something behind the eyes. A look on the old lion's face that said, "Don't fuck with me and what's mine."

21

KIVLIHAN SPENT THE WHOLE DAY TAKING HIS REVENGE. Eddie may have gotten a pass for the broken jaw, but Kivlihan was now going to choke him to death with paperwork.

Burke sat chained to his desk, gnashing his teeth as he matched claim reports with estimates from the fire adjusters. There were X number of two-by-eight floor joists burned in this fire; an undetermined footage of 220 conduit destroyed in another. Eddie had to check the crime-scene photos against a printout on building-material costs to see if the property owners were in collusion with their adjusters to pump up the damage. Since most policies paid on replacement cost, the higher the price tag at Home Depot, the bigger the payout. If an adjuster was fudging the numbers on damage, an alert investigator just might find a motive for setting the blaze.

It was mind-numbing detail work, and Eddie was bored shitless, but this was the crap that Kivlihan thrived on. Statistics were a law enforcement bureaucrat's birthright. They sent them to school for this shit. A paper-pushing superviser like Kivie was successful only so far as he knew how to work the spread, and right now the stats on unsolveds for December didn't look good.

But what Kivlihan failed to acknowledge was that arson was a seasonal crime. It was calendar driven, and just like the Fair Plan, its frequency was rooted in statute.

New York State allowed its corporations to set one of two fiscal years: either January to December or July 1 to June 30th. As such, there was always a rash of arson at year's end. Everybody wanted to close their books with a loss when the enterprise was in trouble, and this past December had been one of the worst months in memory. Suspicious-origin blazes were tied to insurance losses in the hundreds of millions. These were big-ticket blazes that burned down entire half blocks, but they were largely confined to industrial areas. They tended to take place at night or on weekends, and there was rarely a loss of life. So Eddie Burke didn't come to them with the same rabid passion he brought to the Fair Plan fires.

He was at his desk, staring at an uneaten meatball sub when Big Eddie walked in.

"Pop, what are you doing here?"

"It's two o'clock, kid. We got an hour to get up to Columbia."

Eddie covered the sub with some papers and stood up.

"Last night you said this was my case."

"Yeah, well, it's a little more complicated now. I thought you could use some help."

"Is that right?"

"Yeah."

"You mean you got a load of Miss Drexel."

Big Eddie feigned innocence. "What's that supposed to mean?"

"Oh, come on. I saw the way that you looked at her."

"Christ. You're still bustin' my hump for that thing—"

"Why not? You never change."

Before Big Eddie could answer, Kivlihan rushed into the

squad room and stormed up to Eddie's desk. His small, feral face was red. He was livid.

"I wanna know what business you got with Jack Drexel!"

Eddie was dumbfounded. "What are you talking about?"

"He claims you're harassing his daughter. The Commissioner just got a call. I can tell you right now, Burke, with the monthly stats what they are, I don't need this."

Before Eddie could answer, his father stepped in.

"Relax, Kivie," the old man said.

"What the hell's *he* doing here?" said Kivlihan.

"Hey," said Big Eddie. "Since when can't a man see his son?"

"All right, fine. Just tell Junior here that he's off the SoHo case as of now."

"What?" said Eddie, jumping up. "That's bullshit."

"Slow down, kid." Big Eddie put his hand on Eddie's shoulder to calm him.

"Fuck you," said Kivlihan. "The goddamn thing was tighter than a nun's ass and you had to go kicking rocks."

"He *made* the thing, Kivi, when NYPD was ready to tag the wrong guy."

"Yeah? Well let's just say the kid lacks a certain . . . discretion. He's off the case. End of story."

Kivlihan shot back to his office and Eddie jumped up.

"That's it. I'm out of here."

He threw his shield down on the desk and started to exit when Big Eddie stopped him.

"Whoa. Hold on. Where you going?"

"To get a life."

Big Eddie smiled. "Hey, kid. I know how you feel right now. But you gotta pick your moments. You throw your tin down every time some asshole breaks your balls, you'll never make it to pension."

Eddie tried to push past him. "I'm not doing this for a pension."

"Wash your mouth out on that one, kid. You work for the city; a pension's your birthright. You go out after twenty, you get half plus your medical. That's the deal. Chipped in stone. You start taking an attitude, pension be damned, and the next thing you know, your palm's out for a bribe. Lot of men got rich as chief of detectives, Eddie. I wasn't one of them."

He handed the shield back to him.

"Okay," said Eddie. "Fine. But I've got a case to work."

"No." said Big Eddie, grinning. "*We've* got a case."

Eddie exhaled hard and then looked at him. "Listen, Pop, I appreciate what you did. I needed some records. You got them, and it helped me. I'm grateful. But I can handle it now."

Big Eddie turned around and pointed at Kivlihan in his office. "You're doin' one helluva job."

Eddie moved away, but Big Eddie came up and put his hand on his shoulder

"Look, kid. Relax, all right? He can jerk your chain, but he can't jerk mine."

"Uh-uh." Eddie was shaking his head.

"Come on. Let me work it awhile. If I get anything, I'll lateral back to you."

"Sorry."

"Hey, thirty seconds ago, you were gonna walk out of here."

"Okay. So I listened to you. Now I'm back."

Big Eddie came face-to-face with him now. He put his hand on Eddie's forearm and squeezed.

"Look. I thought this retirement thing'd be easy. Relax. See the boys. Have some laughs. But I was wrong. I'm going batshit at the bar, kid."

Eddie looked away from him as he thought about it.

"Kid. It's your *old man* asking. I really need this." It was more like he was pleading.

Finally, Eddie nodded. "All right. Go ahead."

"Great."

"But just for this afternoon. When Kivlihan looks the other way, I'll be on it."

"No problem."

Big Eddie's eyes twinkled as he picked up the file from Eddie's desk and took off.

Eddie stood there burning as he sorted it out. Then he looked down at his desk and shoved the uneaten meatball sub into the wastebasket. Shit.

22

IT WAS FIVE TO THREE WHEN CAROLINE DREXEL GOT BACK
to her office from class. She checked the time on the little
Patek-Philippe. God. He was going to be there any second.
She put down her briefcase and opened the top right-hand
drawer of her desk. There was a mirror inside. She took it
out and ran some gloss over her lips. Then she found the
brush and began running it through her hair.

What was she doing? Did she actually *care* what he
thought of her? This fire marshal with the thick Brooklyn
accent? Caroline stopped brushing for a second and thought
about it. Yes. She had to admit it. She did. Other men had
tried to penetrate her defenses, but with Eddie it was simple: she didn't have any. The class division was just too
great. The gap between culture and standing so wide that
there was no reason to expect an attraction. Of course, he
had a good face. But that didn't matter. They all did. The
polo players and investment bankers and Bermuda racers
who had entered her life. Each one had pedigree and good
taste and a killer smile.

They'd been coming at her for years. Even back at St.
George's when she was just in her teens. She'd been tall
and gangly then, a head above most of the boys on the JV

lacrosse team. But they'd come at her anyway. For her money at first, she was sure of it, but then later for the way that she looked.

She was thirteen the first time it happened. The first time that a boy had kissed her without asking her name. She'd just had the braces removed from her teeth and her second or third period had just come. One night in June, just before summer break, there was a clambake near the school at Third Beach. Some boys had come down from Exeter, and they'd all gone for a swim to the raft. She'd lingered there after the others had left, and it was dead still when a boy named Anthony swam up from the back.

It was dark that night, just a half moon in the sky, and she felt the raft move as he climbed up onto it. Caroline didn't say anything as he lay down beside her. Then he rolled onto his back and started naming the constellations: Ursa Major, Ursa Minor. The easy ones at first and then the obscure ones: Scorpio, Boötes, and Casseopeia. He talked about how the white man could only see three stars in the belt of Orion but the American Indian could see six. And she asked where it was and he said that they couldn't see it right then. Orion was visible in the winter sky. And then he touched her hand.

Caroline pulled away at first, but then she turned and looked at him, long and thin and perfect in his little soccer shorts. She let her hand go back and he squeezed it, but this time she didn't resist, and in another second he kissed her.

Up till that night, boys would always approach her after they'd heard her name was Drexel. ''Isn't she the daughter of . . . ?'' God, how many times had she heard them whisper? But this boy was different. Motivated by lust—pure, simple, juvenile lust. And on that half-moonlit night, he taught Caroline what it was like to be kissed the French way.

It was that summer in Newport when Caroline finally turned from a gangly lacrosse player into a tall, leggy debutante. After that, the young men came for her beauty. The trust fund was just a bonus.

But Eddie Burke crept up on her slowly. He seemed vulnerable yet determined, and when she'd met his father, she understood why. God, to come up behind a bulldog like that. Even to *simulate* his line of work took great courage. Deep down, Eddie had to have some kind of strength to pull the sled of his father's legend. It was something that *she'd* learned from Black Jack Drexel.

Still, for Caroline it was easier. For one thing, she was a woman, and for another thing, she'd never tried to go head-to-head with Black Jack at *his* game. But Eddie had done it; he'd taken on his old man. His brass and tenacity excited her. And she found herself looking forward to his visit as she brushed her hair and checked her watch one more time. Three more minutes. Good. She'd have just enough time to redo her eyeliner. But then she heard the knock at her door and looked up.

Eddie's father was there in the doorway. Her heart sank.

"Miss Drexel."

Standing there with the brush in her hand, she felt strangely vulnerable.

"Where . . . where's Eddie?" said Caroline, quickly putting the brush and the mirror away.

Big Eddie didn't say anything. He just sauntered up to her desk. So she tried again.

"I said, where's your son?"

Still nothing from Big Eddie. She was getting annoyed now as he reached into his pocket and dropped a small package onto her desk. It was the size of a cigarette pack, wrapped in brown paper and tied with a string.

"I didn't have time to get it gift-wrapped," he said.

"What is it?"

"Open it."

Caroline burned a look at him and then pulled off the string. She opened the small white box inside and lifted the flat piece of cotton. Underneath was an old police whistle.

"What's this?" She picked it up.

"Next time you're followed, just blow it."

He took it and showed her how.

"See? If the guy doesn't run, he'll figure you're an ex-mental patient and leave you alone."

Big Eddie tossed it to her. She looked surprised. Then, after a moment, she smiled.

The old cop had broken the ice.

"To answer your question, my son couldn't make it. So I'm here." He leaned over her desk and she looked at his arms. The hair was white, but his muscles were taut. For a man in his sixties, Big Eddie still had a presence. She looked up.

"All right. How can I help you?"

"You got the names of those artists?"

"Oh yes." Caroline looked flustered again. She fumbled around on her desk, searching for something. Finally, she opened an art book and pulled out a piece of paper.

"Here. You were right. Two others worked on the mural."

She handed him the paper with two names.

"D. Hampton and A. Grosvenor," said the old cop. "Hmm." He started pacing around her office. It was lined, floor to ceiling, with bookshelves. There was an old KLH turntable in the corner next to a shelf of blues records. On one wall hung a small collection of Art Deco match strikers next to an old Bakelite radio. Most of the art was from the thirties; brooding, dark, industrial studies.

Big Eddie took one of the thick art volumes off a shelf and flipped through it. Then he examined a framed reproduction of a WPA mural on the wall. It was full of factories with smokestacks and workers bending under the weight of their labor. Finally, he shook his head.

"Is there something wrong?"

"Yeah. All of this. Somehow . . . you're not right for it."

Caroline got up from her desk, slightly indignant.

"Oh, really?" She lit a Gitane. "And why not?"

"Because the art from back then was depressing. Everybody was broke. People sold apples to live. It wasn't Newport and it wasn't Palm Beach. It wasn't anything you've ever known."

She inhaled deeply and started to walk toward him now.

"You really think I'm a Sutton Place bitch, don't you?"

He sat on the edge of her desk. She expected an attack, but he surprised her.

"No, it's just that I don't see you with pictures like this. I see you studying something . . . old and Italian. French maybe. Ballet dancers and horses. But not this."

She rubbed her throat nervously.

"It's a vocation I rather inherited. You see, my mother was an artist during the WPA."

"Is that right? Maybe I should talk to her."

Caroline turned her back to him and stubbed out the cigarette. "That's impossible. She . . . she drank herself to death years ago."

Dr. Drexel bit down on her lower lip. But instead of showing sympathy, Big Eddie came up behind her and spun her around.

"Look. Something's wrong. You've been backing away from this case from day one. Eddie had to twist your arm to get the names of those painters. Now, every time somebody mentions them, you shut down."

Caroline kept quiet.

"You *know* something about this, don't you?"

Still nothing from Caroline, so Big Eddie grabbed her by the shoulders.

"You're hiding something."

She looked down at his big hands as they squeezed her. There was something electric about this old man.

"No . . ."

He released his grip and she turned away.

"All right. Have it your way."

He stuck the paper with the two painters' names in his pocket and started to walk out.

She waited until he got to the door, then called out, "Detective Burke . . ."

He turned around to face her. "What?"

"Those two names I gave you . . ."

"Yeah?"

"I know where one of them lives."

23

IT WAS JUST GETTING DARK AS CAROLINE DREXEL'S VINtage Mercedes 180 turned off Route 22 into the village of New Preston. She sat at the wheel of the old forest green roadster and Big Eddie rode shotgun as they moved past the tiny white clapboard buildings along the single main street.

New Preston, Connecticut, was a stone's throw from the spot where Lafayette had once engaged King George's men. It sat on the edge of Lake Waramaug, a wide L-shaped pond up in north Litchfield County. The centerpiece of the village had been an old mill powered by the race from the lake's overflow. Like so many pieces of Connecticut history, it had been abandoned and then later renovated. Half the mill now served as an art gallery. The other half divided into an espresso bar and a real-estate office.

The latter establishment had opened back in the mid-eighties, when arbitragers and junk bond traders with money to burn exploded out of Manhattan each weekend on the hunt for a second-home tax shelter.

With virtually every square foot of Long Island taken and New Jersey just unacceptable, the caravans of Range Rovers would roar up the Henry Hudson Parkway each

Friday, cross I-80 into Connecticut, and tear up old Route 22.

For years, Lake Waramaug had been a sleepy outpost for old Yankee money. A haven for broad, green-lawned estates spilling down to the lake's edge, ten-bedroom summer homes built by textile barons from Watertown and Danbury. Many of them had gone to rack and ruin in the fifties and sixties, but the crush from the city was so great on summer weekends that three of them had been converted to inns. The real change began around '85. That's when *New York* magazine ran a cover story entitled, "The New Hamptons." Word got out that Bill Blass had bought a place here and then the late interior designer Angelo Donghia, and pretty soon the hunt was on. Suddenly, the three inns, The Boulders, The Birches, and Hopkins, all sprang open. Hopkins, the biggest of the inns up on the hill, even opened a vineyard, and by the late eighties, they were offering their own Cabernet. Now the town coffee shop that once catered to farmers was taking reservations for Sunday brunch. Smith Barney was sponsoring an annual 10K race. The local market was selling balsamic vinegar and endive and there was even talk of a Benetton store.

But all this activity was seasonal. It was cold now. And as Caroline rolled through the town up onto the lake perimeter road, most of the weekend places where shuttered for the winter.

Big Eddie shook his head.

"Christ, up here even the air smells like old money."

Caroline smiled. He had kept her enthralled with his exploits for two hours now. How he began in plain clothes, back in '64. He'd just made detective back then, after six years in uniform, and the gold shield still felt hot in his pocket. Nobody called him Big Eddie in those days. It was Eddie or Ed. But he would soon break a case that would make his career: the sad rape and murder of Kitty Genovese.

It was just after four A.M., on the morning of March 13, 1964, when he heard the alarm. There was still dirty snow on the ground and Eddie was the first in plain clothes on the scene. The first to hear how a young woman had been attacked on the street in Kew Gardens. How a tall slender man had stabbed her, once, twice, and how she'd screamed for help. Thirty-eight people had looked down on her from their windows that morning, but nobody would come out. Thirty-eight people heard her call out, "Help . . . Help me . . . Oh God, he's stabbed me." But only one even threw open his window.

"Let that girl alone!" he had shouted, and the assailant in the overcoat and stocking cap disappeared. Then thirty-eight people watched as Kitty got up and walked, "not staggering," one later said, "but walking, almost in a dream . . ." along the row of storefronts on Austin Street and then on into the doorway at 82-62. Not a single person phoned the police. Nobody got up and ran down to see if she was all right.

But every one of them was up ten minutes later when the man returned, this time wearing a strange Tyrolean kind of hat. They watched as he stalked along Austin Street, trying the doors. First at 82-60 and then the door that Kitty had stepped into at 82-62. A few of the thirty-eight heard what sounded like a woman's voice crying out. But it was muffled and low.

It wasn't until 3:55, thirty-five minutes after the first scream, that one of the thirty-eight went to a neighbor's apartment to phone the 104th Precinct.

When Detective Eddie Burke arrived, he ducked under the crime scene tape and went into the hallway at 82-62. The body of Katherine Genovese, a waitress who worked at Eve's Eleventh Hour Bar in Jamaica, was lying on the stairs, legs spread. Her suede jacket and blouse were ripped open along with her black half slip and cotton panties. The ME later found two entry wounds in her back where the killer had come at her first on the street. Wounds determined to be deep but not fatal. Made with some kind of thin metal object. Not an icepick but larger . . . a screwdriver maybe.

It wasn't until the assailant returned, under the watchful eye of those paralyzed thirty-eight, that he had punctured her chest.

She was still alive when Eddie got there. Murmuring low and sucking in, trying to breathe, not knowing that her lungs had collapsed. Eddie bent down and asked her, "Who did this?" But she just shook her head, murmuring.

She was saying something. What was it? And he put his ear next to her mouth. That's when he heard it. The prayer. "O my God, I am heartfully sorry . . ." Then she stopped. She was saying it over and over again, unable to finish. So Eddie knelt in the pool of blood at her side and whispered the words in her ear. The Act of Contrition.

For a Roman Catholic it was the price of admission at death and clearly this woman was in extremis.

> O my God I am heartfully sorry for having offended Thee. And I attest to all my sins because I dread the loss of heaven and the pain of hell. But most of all because they offend *Thee*, my God, who art all good and deserving of all my love. I firmly resolve, with the help of Thy grace, to confess my sins, to do penance, and to amend my life. Amen.

He thought that he caught just the glimpse of a smile on her face and then she closed her eyes. Later, he heard that she'd died on the way to Queens Hospital.

There had been plenty of time to save her that night. If only one of the thirty-eight had run down or called the police. But they just sat there in their little apartments.

Little people. Bugs. They'd reminded him of roaches as he'd canvassed the building to take down their statements. And right then and there, Eddie vowed that he wouldn't go to bed until he put the fucker who'd done this in a cage.

It took him five days to make the collar.

All they had gotten from the thirty-eight watchers was the thinnest of profiles. The assailant was a slender man, somewhere between 120 and 140 pounds. He drove a light gray or maybe a white compact car and he was either white or Negro. People didn't use the word Black back then.

Young Eddie Burke was just a third-grade detective. There were dozens of other senior men assigned to the Genovese Task Force. But he burned that paper-thin profile into his mind, and every waking moment he thought about the man who had stabbed her first on the street and then returned to finish the job.

Five days later, he was working a routine 10-31, a burglary at a furniture store on Queens Boulevard, when he heard the radio call. It was the morning of March 18. A man named Fulton in East Elmhurst had heard noise in the apartment of some friends who were away. He then saw a "Negro" carrying a TV from the apartment. Fulton questioned the man who said that he was giving the friends some help with their move.

The Black man proceeded casually to put the TV into his car parked down below. A white Corvair. A white compact car. Fulton called the police, and Eddie shot across Queens. This wasn't his case, but he had a feeling. By the time he got to the scene, the suspect had fled, but his car was still there, the keys still in the ignition. Detectives from the 104 were handling it, and Eddie heard Fulton describe the man. A Negro. Tall, maybe 130, and thin.

Eddie stared at the white Corvair and jumped back into his unmarked Plymouth Fury.

He was due to go back to the station house for a photo show, but he had a feeling. Eddie called in to say he'd be late. He started driving up and down the blocks of East Elmhurst. The routine would have been to take Fulton with him. Let him ID the perp. But the 104 detectives still had him, and twenty minutes had already gone by.

There was a subway stop near the corner in East Elmhurst where the suspect had disappeared and there was no reason to believe that he'd be on the streets. It was a racially mixed neighborhood and there was no reason to believe that Eddie would know the guy, even if he saw him.

But as he drove up and down the blocks, he kept thinking of Kitty in the hallway; thinking about the blood and her Act of Contrition, and something just drove him forward.

By 11:25 A.M., Detective Eddie Burke had just about given up when he turned the Fury onto Twenty-third Avenue, six blocks away from the crime scene. A tall, slender Negro was casually walking along. Eddie pulled up ahead of him and got out.

When the man was six feet away from him, Eddie showed him his badge and asked if he wouldn't mind stopping. The guy was cool. Chewing gum. He said, "No problem, Officer. What seems to be the problem?"

Eddie had to think fast now. He had no probable cause to stop this guy and therefore no right to search him.

So he turned to his wits. He told the man there'd been a shooting nearby. Somebody had seen a Negro with a Luger.

"You know, one of those German guns?"

The Black man nodded. "Yeah. Like in the war pictures."

"That's it," said Eddie. "You wouldn't be carrying, now would you?" He was smiling at the man.

"No way."

"Good," said Eddie, keeping the grin on. He held his breath now.

"Look, I'm sorry to bother you, but I've got to do my job here. Would you mind emptying your pockets so I can see there's no gun?" This was a big chance to take.

If the man had said yes he would mind, Eddie would have to back off. Otherwise, anything he found on the guy would be tainted and inadmissible. But Eddie was playing a hunch here. The guy was acting so cool.

"Mind? No, I don't mind, Officer."

And with that, the man emptied his pockets. It was now a consensual search. Eddie let the man put the contents of his pockets on the hood of a nearby car. A wallet with an ID in the name of Winston Moseley, a couple of pieces of Double-Bubble gum, and a half-empty package of Camels. But no keys. Eddie asked about that, and the man said he left his keys home. Then Eddie asked the man to open his jacket. It was a short corduroy Mighty Mac with a hood. Winston Moseley complied, and Eddie patted down the outside pockets.

He was about to let the guy go when he felt it. Something long and thin in the inside jacket pocket.

Eddie asked Moseley to take it out, and the man's face froze. But by now he'd consented to the search, so Eddie pulled out his handkerchief and reached in for it: an eight-inch Black & Decker Phillips screwdriver with a yellow plastic handle.

There was blood on the tip, and it came off on Big Eddie's handkerchief. Suddenly, he grabbed for his .38 and cocked it next to Moseley's right ear. He slammed him down over the hood of the car and whipped out the cuffs with his left hand. Big Eddie remembered that his hands were trembling.

Six hours later, in the precinct detective's room at the

104, Eddie Burke stood in a corner, arms folded, as a team of veteran interrogators worked the suspect. Winston Moseley, the accounting machine operator from Yonkers, admitted that he was a rapist and home invader. He confessed to forty burglaries in Queens alone. He confessed to two recent gunpoint assaults on women: one in Jamaica, one in East Elmhurst. Then he admitted to sodomizing a woman on Rockaway Boulevard back in January. Eddie ran out and pulled the case file on that one. At the time the victim reported that the assailant, ''a tall thin Negro,'' had forced her down and told her to ''suck it.'' His weapon had been a screwdriver. Bang.

A few minutes later, the forensics report had come in on the blood sample from the Black & Decker Phillips-head. It was a direct match to the blood that poured out of Kitty Genovese in that cold freezing hallway on Austin Street.

The time was 5:57 P.M., and the squad room was filled with detectives by now. When Mosely bent his head down and finally whispered, ''Okay. I killed her,'' all eyes turned to Eddie Burke. But nobody seemed to notice, as he covered his face, that there were tears coming down his cheek.

Later on, over beers at O'Connell's, the veteran detectives toasted him for ''busting his cherry'' and the legend of Big Eddie Burke had begun.

24

IT WAS ALMOST 4:30 P.M. WHEN CAROLINE PULLED UP OUT-side an extraordinary Georgian manor house at the top of a hill overlooking the lake. The cast-iron gate was open, but she stopped the Mercedes and turned to face Big Eddie.

"He's in there."

The stone pillar at the gate had a brass plaque that said Grosvenor. Big Eddie pulled out the piece of paper and looked at the two names.

"D. Hampton and A. Grosvenor."

He surveyed the estate, then the name Grosvenor, and finally, he looked at Caroline.

"So, who is he?"

Caroline looked away. "One of the last surviving realists from the New Deal."

Big Eddie eyed the estate again.

"I thought they made twenty-six bucks a week."

Caroline managed a tiny smile. "He gets a lot more now."

"Yeah? Like, say, how much for a picture?"

"When he paints . . . Well, his last show was presold. The Germans love him. I think the smallest canvas went for one point two."

"Million?"

Caroline nodded.

"Jesus. So how do you know this guy?"

Caroline looked nervous again. "He was a friend of my
. . . mother's. They met on the mural projects."

"Okay, that's good. He knows you. That'll help with the
questioning. Let's go."

He started to get out of the car, but Caroline shook her
head.

"No."

"What?"

"You go."

Big Eddie stopped. "How come?"

She turned away. "If you want to talk to him, fine. I just
don't feel comfortable—"

"Why the hell not?"

She reached across and opened the passenger door. "Go
ahead. I'll drive up to Hopkins Inn. When you're finished,
just call me."

Big Eddie climbed out and turned to look at the mansion.

"You sure about tha—?"

But before he could turn back to face her, she drove off.

It took him another two minutes to walk up the crushed
gravel driveway. Christ. It look liked one of those places
where heads of state met to negotiate treaties.

There was a huge lawn running down to the lake with a
boathouse the size of his place in Bay Ridge. Big Eddie
cleared his throat and put his shoulders back. Then he rang
the bell. Immediately, as if he'd been waiting behind the
door, a butler answered in full morning coat.

"So, who died?" said Big Eddie.

"I beg your pardon, sir?"

"Forget it. I'm here to see Mr. Grosvenor."

"Who shall I say is—"

"Edmund Burke. Detective. NYPD."

This time he used one of his old business cards. It had the chief of detective's badge raised in gold with three stars under an eagle and oak-leaf cluster.

"One moment, sir."

The butler disappeared into a back room and picked up a phone, leaving Big Eddie to pace across the marble foyer. He had never read much, but he'd been a stickler for self-improvement. Years ago, he'd been glued to that PBS series, *Civilization*. The story of how all those kings in Europe had made it. How they'd raped and pillaged and bought their own titles. And Big Eddie flashed back on something that Englishman, had said. Lord Clark, the host of the show, standing in a huge drawing room at Versailles.

"I wonder," he said. "I wonder if anyone ever had a *great* thought in a *small* room?"

Just then, Big Eddie heard the sound of an inboard engine. He raced to the door, threw it open, and saw a man down on the dock of the boat house by the lake. He was frantically untying lines to a vintage Chris Craft. It looked like he was in a hurry to leave. Suddenly, the butler returned.

"I'm sorry, sir. Mr. Grosvenor is indisposed."

"Yeah," said Big Eddie as he tore out the door. "Thanks for warning him, Jeeves."

He ran down the driveway toward the boathouse, almost slipping on the gravel in his leather-soled shoes, as the man jumped into the old mahogany runabout and cast off. He was forty feet off the dock when Big Eddie got there, huffing and puffing. He hadn't chased a suspect like this in ten years.

The old cop looked around. Nothing on the dock, so he rushed back to the boathouse. Inside, through a window, he saw a ski boat. It was metallic blue with twin four hundred-horse Evenrudes, a pure racing machine. But the boathouse was locked. So Big Eddie wrapped his hand in his handkerchief. He said "Exigent circumstances" under his breath and smashed a pane in the door. It was the second time in his career that he'd seen blood on a handkerchief, but he didn't have time to think about that.

He jumped onto the Ski Nautique now, searching for . . .

"The key. Where the fuck did you put the key?"

The Chris Craft was halfway across the lake when Caroline heard the noise. Up above on the hill, in the lobby at Hopkins Inn, she ran to the window and looked down. Oh God. She'd suspected something might happen when Big Eddie met Grosvenor, but not this.

She rushed out to the Mercedes as the old artist cut across the lake. Grosvenor was in his early seventies, but he was still tall and preppy with tortoiseshell glasses. The young, rugged blond painter from Caroline's dream, screaming toward the opposite shore as he opened it up full.

He looked terrified.

Inside the boathouse, Big Eddie had the Ski Nautique's hood up. He found the two ignition wires, pulled away at the insulation, and touched them together. Suddenly, the engine roared to life.

Caroline spun out of the Hopkins Inn driveway, careening down the hill toward the lake just as a door to the boathouse opened and the Ski Nautique tore out.

Big Eddie Burke, the man who'd caught bluefish in Sheepshead Bay, was a bit out of his depth here, but he was doing his best to hold on as the twin inboard screws erupted underwater.

The Chris Craft was making for a dock at The Boulders, another inn across the lake near the main road, as the Mercedes rounded the turn from the bottom of the hill to the lakefront road.

Out on the lake now, Big Eddie opened it up. The Nau-

tique left a rooster tail as it sliced the small lake in half
and Big Eddie let out a war whoop.

"I'm on you, you fuck."

Big Eddie was back on the chase, and he loved it. The
adrenaline was pumping now, and he was gaining on the
pleasure craft, but the sun was dropping behind the Litchfield hills and the ski boat didn't have any running lights.

Then, suddenly, down on the lakefront road, the Mercedes screeched to a stop in front of Boulders Inn, and
Caroline jumped out just in time to see the Ski Nautique
pull up alongside the Chris Craft.

The two boats were racing dead-on for The Boulders'
dock, neck and neck now, when Big Eddie yelled for Grosvenor to stop.

"Pull over, you sonovabitch."

He held up his shield.

"Police."

But the old painter ignored him.

So Big Eddie throttled down and roared ahead of the
Chris, cutting him off.

"Stop it. *Now!*"

But Grosvenor took out a flare gun and fired.

Big Eddie had to duck as the red tail of the flare missed
his head by just inches. He swerved the Ski Nautique into
a radical arc to avoid it and swamped the boat.

The Chris Craft made it to shore and Grosvenor jumped
off running, leaving the boat to a dock boy.

"Hey mister . . ." said the stunned teenager, but Grosvenor ignored him and disappeared in the night.

Just then, Caroline rushed onto the dock.

It was dark as the dock boy searched the murky waters
with the Chris Craft's headlamp, looking for the man who'd
gone overboard.

Caroline was almost frantic.

"Do you see him?"

"Not yet, ma'am."

"My God, you've got to."

What was she going to tell Eddie?

For a time, it looked like the old cop was finished. He had to be. Nobody could survive for that long in water that cold. But, just then, they saw something at the edge of the light.

"Quick. Over here," said Caroline.

She pulled the dock boy's hand and he panned the light to the left. There was nothing, but then Big Eddie surfaced and came into the light.

The dock boy reached out with a gaff and pulled him onto the dock.

The old man was shivering now, teeth clenched, when Caroline ran to the water's edge and cradled him in her arms.

25

THE BOULDERS WAS APTLY NAMED: A FIFTEEN-ROOM LODGE built from Connecticut fieldstone. It was decorated in Adirondack style, with birch railings on the stairs, hickory wainscoting, and chandeliers made from the antlers of local white bucks. Suite Nine, the old master bedroom, was usually booked in advance. But this was a cold Wednesday night in January, and Caroline had no trouble securing the room.

She sat in a high wingback chair in front of a fire while Big Eddie Burke sat on the floor nearby, leaning against the sofa in a terry cloth robe. The breast pocket of the robe said The Boulders in blue embroidery, and there was a tag attached to the sleeve that said: "This robe is provided for the use of our guests. Should you wish to purchase it, please see the concierge."

He had a Waterford crystal rock glass in his hand, filled with three fingers of bourbon. Caroline was sipping white wine. They hadn't said much since he'd come out of the shower. She'd been waiting downstairs in the lobby and asked him to call her when he was done. The wine and whiskey had just been delivered by room service.

When they'd first brought him in, Big Eddie was soaking

wet and red with embarrassment. All this wasn't necessary. He'd be fine. Just let him dry off and they could shoot back to the city. But Caroline wouldn't hear of it, and she'd rented the suite while the dock boy helped him upstairs.

Now they sat there in silence. All Caroline could hear was the crackle of the fire and the sound of the old Regulator clock on the wall. Big Eddie took a sip of the whiskey and winced. Then he set his glass down on the coffee table and turned to her.

"So when are you going to tell me the truth?"

Caroline looked startled. "What?"

"The truth?"

"What do you mean?" She touched her throat again. "About what?"

"Grosvenor. How you knew him."

She didn't say anything for a while.

The fire crackled. The Regulator clock kept on ticking, and Big Eddie could almost hear her thinking. Is it time now? Do I tell this old man? Finally, she got up and moved to the fire.

She picked up a brass-tipped poker and stabbed away at the logs. Then she stared at the flames, knowing inside that this all had to do with her dream, but not sure if she was ready to let him in. She thought about the mural and the four painters: Esther Schine with the Liz Taylor eyes and the short, thin painter named Julian Krane. The rugged young artist in the tortoiseshell glasses was Grosvenor. She knew that now.

The young woman bringing in the champagne. She knew who she was, too. All those years she'd kept it pent up inside her, sharing it only with Helen as their sessions continued. Even now as she visited the old doctor at the chronic care hospital, Caroline barely mentioned it. But people had died for that mural now and she knew it was time to tell someone. The old policeman in the terrycloth robe was big and warm and safe. And so, finally, she turned to him and decided to let go.

"Grosvenor? How did I know him?"

Another long pause and then, "The other artist who worked with him, the one named D. Hampton. Her name was Dorothea."

"How do you know *that?*"

"Because she was . . . my mother."

Caroline flashed back now to the tall young woman with the bucket of Veuve Clicquot.

Big Eddie looked stunned.

"You mean to say that your mother . . ."

"I told you. That's why I studied the WPA."

Caroline walked to a window and stared out at the lake.

"She met Grosvenor on one of the mural projects and fell in love. They were going to be married."

She flashed on the pretty young painter. The one from the dream with black hair and blue eyes. Liz Taylor, blowing her kiss up to Grosvenor.

"Her friends tried to warn her he'd never be faithful. They said he was a womanizer, but she wouldn't listen. She was struck by his talent. Even then she could see it. The man was a world-class painter."

Caroline walked back and sat down near Big Eddie.

"So why didn't she marry him?"

"I don't know. Something happened . . . just before the wedding."

"Like what?"

"She never told me. Something terrible. But whatever it was, she broke off the engagement. She never saw Grosvenor again."

"Are you sure?"

Caroline nodded.

Big Eddie waited and poured himself another drink. From years of interrogating witnesses, he knew that timing was everything. You had to let them breathe. If you tried to pull it all out at once, they'd freeze up. So he motioned to her wineglass and she shook her head. "Whiskey, please."

He picked up the bourbon and poured until she said, "Fine."

Then he took his time with the ice tongs, dropping one, two, and then three cubes into her glass. "Water?"

She shook her head.

The fire crackled, the clock ticked, and then he picked his glass up and touched hers.

"A hundred years."

"Cheers."

She seemed to shiver as she swallowed it down. Then, finally, when he saw she was ready, Eddie started again.

"So, your mother and Grosvenor fell out. I guess this was around the time that Black Jack came in?"

"Yes," said Caroline. She took another pull on the whiskey. "He was a lawyer back then. In his mid-twenties. A cock of the walk. He represented some of the artists. Quite ambitious, but broke just like they were. They were all so poor, you know. All except Mother. Even after the Crash, she was worth millions."

Big Eddie had it now.

"So your mother saved face on the rebound from Grosvenor, and Drexel got the money to build his empire."

"A marriage of . . . convenience." She dropped her head and turned away from him. This time she couldn't hold back. She was about to break down when Big Eddie touched her.

"Hey. Come on. Whatever their marriage was, it wasn't in vain." He lifted her chin. "After all . . . they had you."

Caroline looked at his face reflected in the light of the fire. He was a big man. A big Irish bear. She hesitated, and then she touched his hand.

Big Eddie pulled her toward him and they embraced.

After a few seconds, when they pulled apart, Big Eddie wasn't sure. Was this a father embracing his daughter or a virile old man holding on to a beautiful woman?

Whatever it was, they hardly said two words to each other on the ninety-minute trip back to New York.

26

IT WAS AFTER MIDNIGHT WHEN EDDIE BURKE PUSHED INTO the lobby of Caroline Drexel's co-op on Sutton Place. The doorman jumped up.

"Hey. Stop. I gotta call up."

But Eddie brushed past him and stepped into the elevator.

He'd been trying to reach her all night. There was no answer. So he tried his father at the bar and at home in Bay Ridge. Nothing. Finally, around eleven, Caroline had left a message at the squad room to say that she was coming home. The message said *she* was coming home. No word of his father. But Eddie knew better. He'd seen the way the old cop had looked at her. How fast he'd volunteered to go up to Columbia. The way that he'd wanted to stay in the case.

All men have demons. Harpies that live inside and feed on the soul. Some men control them, use their energy to reach higher. But most are crippled by them, allowing the demons to sap their strength. All races are afflicted, but few are possessed like the Irish. And there was one, big, world-class leviathan inside Eddie Burke. A demon that had kept him from trusting for many a year now. One that had flushed his career with NYPD and ruined his marriage. And at night, in his dreams, when he looked into the face of that demon, he saw his father.

Eddie jumped out of the elevator now and pounded on the door of Caroline's apartment.

"Open up."

A few seconds went by and then he heard the sound of her heels on the marble.

She swung the door back, dressed in black silk pajamas, and Eddie stormed into the foyer.

"Where the hell've you been? I've been calling for hours. You tell me some guy's following you, then you disappear."

"We just got back. We were about to call you."

"*We*. Right. I knew it."

He moved past her into the living room and then . . .

"Oh, Christ."

He saw his father, entering from an adjoining room.

"This is perfect."

His father shook his head. "Kid, I was just in the john."

"No. This is great. You two alone here."

"What are you *talking* about?" said Caroline.

"We were working the case, for Chrissake," said Big Eddie. "I had a little mishap and she helped me. We just now got back."

"A little *mishap?*"

Caroline looked at Eddie. "What are you trying to say?"

"That I've seen this before."

"Seen what before?"

"What do you think?"

"Oh God." Caroline couldn't believe what he was suggesting.

"Eddie, this is your *father*."

"Yeah. I know. Big Eddie Burke."

He was halfway to the door when Big Eddie grabbed him.

"Kid, come on, will you stop?"

Eddie spun around to confront him.

"I'll stop when you stop, old man."

"Eddie . . ."

"Look. Just do me a favor. Go back to the bar and stay the fuck out of my life."

Big Eddie's face was bright red now. Caroline looked mortified. Nobody said anything. Finally, Eddie threw open the door and stormed out.

The next day, Eddie was sifting through the ashes of a warehouse fire on Pier 92. He looked bad. Like somebody he knew had just died. His eyes were red and he was dressed in the same clothes he'd been wearing the night before. He'd spent the two hours after he left Sutton Place in some bar on First Avenue. The kind of place that served Irish coffee in cute little cups with green leprechauns and whipped cream with chocolate sprinkles. But Eddie was throwing down Jameson's. He was surprised they even carried the stuff in this place. T. J. Laffs it was called. A bar full of guys who sold TV airtime, mid level admen and stewies in heat. A fucking fern bar. You asked for an Irish whiskey in a place like that and they usually poured Bushmill's. Goddamn Orangeman's liquor.

After that, Eddie had staggered over to the Ideal Café, a German lunch counter on Eighty-sixth in Yorkville. He sat at the bar and had knockwurst with red cabbage, washing it down with a Berlinerweise.

He cooped in the Chevy until five, keeping the windows cracked and the heater on, and then drove to Fifty-second and Lex to that all-night drugstore, where he picked up a Brut stick, a bag of Bic Disposables, and a can of Edge gel. He put the FDNY Fire Marshal card on his dash and parked in an NYP space next to the Doral Hotel. Then he slipped into the men's room off the lobby and washed up.

Now it was just after seven. He was back on the job, servicing Kivlihan, pushing his way through the char on that pier. There was a tugboat going by on the Hudson, using its horn, so Eddie didn't notice the man walking up behind him, cracking the charcoal as he walked. But then, when he heard the man speak, Eddie froze.

"Kivie said you'd be here. I need to talk to you, son."

Eddie didn't bother to turn. "I got nothin' to say."

"I tried to beep you all night."

"I had it off."

Big Eddie got in front of him now.

"Look, when you took off like that, I didn't have a chance to tell you—"

Eddie pushed past him.

"I think we ID'd the killer."

Eddie stopped and took a deep breath. He was trying to keep from exploding. He turned around. "No. You don't understand. *You're* the killer."

"What? What are you talking about?"

"You. You killed my mother and right now you're killing me." He started to move toward the Chevy.

But Big Eddie followed him.

"Eddie, what you saw last night. It's not what you think."

"That's just what you said the night Ma had . . ." Eddie hesitated.

"The stroke? Go on. Say it. You're still hanging that over me, aren't you?"

Eddie spun around now.

"Why the hell not? She sat home and said rosaries for twenty-two years. All those nights you were off 'working cases.' Twenty-two birthdays you missed. Twenty-two Christmas Eves you never showed, and that woman forgave you because Big Eddie Burke was out fighting crime. Then the one night she went to the hospital . . . The one night she needed you, I call to find out you're shacked up with some waitress.''

Eddie hauled off and smashed him hard on the jaw. Big Eddie staggered back and instinctively started to lunge at his son. Then he stopped and wiped the blood off his lip.

''Was that for her or for you?''

''It was for both of us . . . Man, I needed a *father,* not just some headline in the *Daily* fucking *News.*''

''If you felt that way, then why'd you join the academy?''

'' 'Cause I thought I'd do better. I promised myself I'd still break the cases and be home for my kids. But you weren't just breaking cases, you were out breaking hearts. When that finally hit me, I quit.''

Suddenly Big Eddie's eyes got wide.

''Wait a minute. You're saying you washed out of police work because of me and some *broad?*''

There was acid in Eddie's voice. ''You're the detective. You figure it out.''

Big Eddie went livid. ''God*damn* you . . . We had cops in our family for three generations.''

''And then came the Bad Seed. Well, you're the one who planted it, Chief. Or maybe you didn't. With you, it must have been hard to keep track. . . .''

Big Eddie tried to swing at his son, but Eddie side stepped and hit him hard with a left to the stomach. The older cop froze, doubled over, and went down.

Eddie taunted him. ''Come on, get up. I've been waiting a long time for this.''

Big Eddie tried to stand up, but he stumbled. Then he spit blood. It was clear now that Eddie had hurt him.

''Pop?''

When he realized what he'd done, Eddie rushed to his father. "Pop. What's the matter?"

Big Eddie was down on his knees now, so Eddie put his arm around him.

"What is it, Pop?"

But Big Eddie was starting to shake; white-faced, sweating, going into shock. So Eddie propped him up against a piling and ran to the Chevy. He pulled out the mike on the Motorola.

"Squad four-eight to base. Come on. Come on. This is Burke."

"Got you Eddie," said Vasquez.

"I got a ten-forty-four code three at Pier 92. Call dispatch."

"What's wrong?"

"My father. He's bleeding internally."

"Ten-four" said Vasquez. "I'm on it."

Eddie rushed to Big Eddie's side now, keeping his head up as the old man coughed blood.

"Stay with me, Pop. Please. Just hold on."

27

THE BLINDS WERE DRAWN AND IT WAS DARK IN THE SEMI-private room at Roosevelt Hospital. Big Eddie was sleeping now, with an IV in his arm, and Eddie was at his side, holding his hand when a doctor came in—a mid-forties Black man with a name tag that said Nathaniel Griffith, M.D., Deputy Chief of Surgery.

Eddie got up when he saw him.

"Do you know what it is, Doctor?"

The man nodded. "Somehow he ruptured an ulcer." He put two fingers on Big Eddie's neck and checked his pulse.

"An ulcer? My father?"

Dr. Griffith motioned for Eddie to wait until he was finished counting.

"Okay. His pressure's good, considering. He's had the ulcer for quite some time now. We had to go in and tie it off. There's been blood loss, but the old guy's a tough one. With sufficient rest and a new diet, he'll come back."

He gestured toward the bed table where well wishers had sent Big Eddie a bottle of Jameson's tied with a bow.

"By new diet, I mean, lose the bottle."

"Of course, Doctor." Eddie handed it to him. "I'll see to it. Thanks."

Dr. Griffith exited and Eddie moved over to the bed. He touched his father's forehead. Big Eddie was just coming out of the anesthesia now.

He coughed up some phlegm and Eddie lifted up a plastic dish for him to spit into. It was the first time in his life that he'd seen his father so vulnerable.

His head ached, and he wished that he hadn't gone on that bender last night. He wished that he hadn't lost his temper. He wished a lot of things as he touched the side of his father's neck. He wanted to feel Big Eddie's heart beating.

It was almost midnight. By now, the room had filled up with flowers and cards. Eddie had put the word out through the floor nurse that booze was forbidden. She'd also been asked to keep visitors away, and she'd been keeping a phone log. There were a half dozen calls from the crowd at the Tam. Two or three from the detective's bureau. Even Kivie had called with get-well wishes. But there was nothing from Caroline. Nothing on his home machine and no calls from her at the squad.

Around midnight, the old man squeezed Eddie's hand and opened his eyes.

"Pop? Can you talk?"

Big Eddie tried to pull himself up on the pillows, then he felt the incision.

"Ahhh. What was it? What'd they do?"

"You ruptured an ulcer. It's okay now. They tied it off." Eddie stopped and then bore a look into him. "Pop, you never told me you had—"

"Huh." Big Eddie cut him off. "There's a lot about me you don't know."

His voice was weak now, like the voice of a man in his sixties, not like Big Eddie Burke. He looked small in the bed. Small and frail. The old cop tried to pull himself up again, but the pain was too much.

"Christ."

"No, Pop. You're supposed to rest."

Big Eddie exhaled long and hard. Finally, he looked up. "There's something I've got to tell you."

"Forget it," said Eddie, looking away.

"No. I need to say this. . . ."

The old cop turned to stare out the window. They were on the twelfth floor facing west, and Big Eddie could see the lights of New Jersey off in the distance. Finally, he turned back to face his son.

"Ever since your mother's stroke I haven't been able to . . ." He looked at Eddie and squeezed his hand. "I've been . . . impotent . . ."

"Pop. You don't have to—"

But Big Eddie waved him off. He wanted to finish.

"I started to tell you the other day. This retirement . . . it's been brutal. The day before I left, I caught a serial killer. The day *after* I left, I helped some indicted bond trader look for his bearer bonds."

He took a breath.

"I was working, but it wasn't the same. So I opened the bar, and you know what?"

Eddie shook his head.

"Every day behind that counter I got older and weaker."

He started coughing.

"Pop."

Some phlegm came up, and Eddie picked up the plastic dish. Big Eddie spat it out, and Eddie gave him some water to drink. When the old man felt better, he continued.

"When you came along with this case, it was like, I was back on the street. Maybe I got a little too pushy. But you've got to believe me, son. There was *nothing* between me and that girl."

Big Eddie began to weep now. "I'd never hurt you like that again."

"Please, Pop. Don't try to talk." He took a tissue and wiped off his father's face. Then he reached down to hug him. Eddie was crying now, too.

Six hours later, the sun was coming through the blinds, just beginning to bounce off the mirrored-glass high-rises near Lincoln Center, when Eddie heard the beep. He'd been asleep in the chair next to Big Eddie's bed when he heard it—the sound of the IV machine: *BEEP, BEEP, BEEP*. He looked up and saw that his father had ripped the IV from his arm. He'd pulled his pants on under the hospital johnny, and he was struggling to put on his shoes when Eddie jumped up.

"Where the hell do you think you're going?"

"After the killer."

Big Eddie started to walk out, but he suddenly got weak and dropped down on one knee. He was half-sedated, half-exhausted, and the incision scar was beginning to tear.

"God *damn* it . . ."

Eddie rushed over and helped him back into the bed. He stabbed at the red emergency call button and screamed for a nurse.

Big Eddie pulled at his sleeve. "I know who did it, kid."

Eddie's eyes widened. "What?" He'd all but forgotten the case now.

He put his arm behind his father's head to prop him up. "Who was it, Pop?"

Big Eddie was having trouble. It was hard to talk. So Eddie leaned in and the old cop whispered it into his ear.

Then, when the nurse came and he was sure that his father had stabilized, Eddie Burke left the room.

He moved quickly down to the Chevy on Ninth. As soon as it started, he slammed on the bubble and hit the siren.

Cutting in and out of the rush-hour traffic, he roared west across Fifty-seventh toward the West Side Highway. From there, he headed north and uptown toward Columbia.

With every hour that follows a homicide, the crime becomes harder and harder to clear. As the minutes tick by, the odds on the killer's side go up exponentially. Witnesses disappear. Alibis harden. Memories begin to fade and forensic evidence gets lost or destroyed. It had been almost five days now since Alex Sloane was found dead in her loft on Prince Street. If his father was right, the killer was now on the run, and Eddie knew if he didn't grab him soon, the fucker would split the jurisdiction. More time would pass. Evidence would be lost or corrupted. Then, even if they caught him, the ADAs would end up pleading manslaughter down to aggravated assault, maybe reckless endangerment, and the killer of Alex Sloane would get away with murder.

28

IT WAS AN EARLY CLASS. EIGHT O'CLOCK IN AVERY HALL. Caroline Drexel barely had time to prepare for it after that night and the whiskey. She'd taken two Tylenol caplets with a few sips of Evian, but her frontal lobe was still throbbing. Usually with the early classes, she'd get to her office by seven-thirty. She'd make a cup of café filtre and light a Gitane as she scanned the *Times* and went through the slides.

But not this time. It was Mai-Ling's day off, and she'd forgotten to set the alarm, so she didn't get down to the garage until seven-fifteen. When she tried to start the Mercedes, the little red light came on, indicating she needed gas. It was four miles uptown to the university and she didn't want to risk getting stalled in the park. So she left it in the garage and hailed a cab.

Now, as the slides flashed and her head ached, she lit another Gitane and tried to forget what she'd seen in her dream. After that business with Grosvenor up at the lake, it was clearer now. Esther Schine, the Liz Taylor look-alike, was the one they'd found dead on West Twenty-eighth Street, and Grosvenor, the one she'd blown the kiss to, was now missing.

Caroline had tried to call him last night after Big Eddie Burke had left. She'd dialed the Connecticut number and gotten the butler, who said that the master wasn't home. That was all. Then she'd tried Grosvenor's private line over on Beekman Place. Nothing.

She was afraid to think what it meant. She'd first met the old painter when they'd served as advisers on the Williamsburg Mural Project. She'd caught Grosvenor staring at her from across a conference table. He'd asked her out, and she'd found some excuse. It wasn't because he was old enough to be her father. She'd dated a number of older men. It was the fact that he'd been arrogant enough to hit on her mother's daughter. Caroline never told him that she knew about Dorothea. She'd merely kept him at arm's length. They'd stayed cordial, exchanged numbers, met once or twice for lunch; professional colleagues on the Williamsburg restoration board. She'd even invited Grosvenor to lecture her class. He'd pressed her again for a date, and she'd asked him to keep it platonic.

Still, with the limited contact they'd had, she was shocked when she found his name on the list of artists who painted the mural. And now her mind was racing as she tried to put it together and still keep her head for the class.

"As you know, many of the American social realists were influenced by the great Mexican muralists," said Caroline. "Orozco, Siqueiros, and Rivera . . ."

She was doing it by rote, unable to bring any energy to it. There were more important things to consider.

She hit the button on the slide remote and the picture changed to a panel from Rivera's Coit Tower murals.

Suddenly, the door to the lecture hall burst open and Eddie pushed in.

"I need to see you."

All eyes turned toward Eddie.

Caroline looked away.

"I'm in class."

There were a few giggles from the female students, but Eddie didn't stop. He was angry. "I need to see you. *Now!*"

A few of the male students looked at each other. Who the hell *was* this guy?

Caroline's face turned from red to white as Eddie lunged forward and took her arm.

"Come on."

"Where are we going?"

"Outside."

Eddie started to pull her toward the door, and one of her students, a burly, six-foot-three linebacker, shot up from his chair.

"You all right, Miss Drexel?"

"Yes, Michael. It's okay. I'll be back in a moment."

She followed Eddie through the door and the lecture hall went into a buzz.

Out in the hallway, Eddie pushed her up against a wall.

"I want to know what the fuck is going on."

"If this is about your father, you can relax—"

Eddie was shouting now. "It's *not* about my father. It's about murder. The Connecticut cops have been all over Grosvenor's house."

"And . . . ?"

"He's gone. I've checked his New York apartment. Nothing."

"So why come to me?"

"Come on. I don't have time for this shit. You *know* the bastard. You took my father to his weekend house. Now, where the hell *else* would he be?"

Caroline hesitated, then pushed away from the wall. She started to walk back toward class, then stopped and turned around.

"Look. You asked me to help with this case and I did. Now it's getting ugly."

"No shit, lady. It started with manslaughter. What the hell'd you expect?"

"I don't know. I don't know what I thought this would be. All I know is that now I'm done with it."

She started to go back into the lecture hall, but Eddie got in front of her.

"The day I walked into that co-op on Sutton Place I knew it."

"What?"

"That you'd quit. You'd go just *so* far, then you'd stop."

"That's absurd. What the hell does the place I live in have to do with anything?"

"It's a five-million-dollar co-op. You're rich."

"So what? Having money's a curse?"

"No. Not all money. Just inherited wealth. People like you . . . they don't go the distance. They don't have the edge."

"People like *me?*"

"Yeah." Eddie was ripshit.

Caroline tilted her head and let that one go by. She wanted to grab him by the throat, let him know how hard she'd worked for what she'd become, how she'd fought her way to the top of an academic discipline dominated by a handful of men, how she'd done it in spite of her wealth and her looks. But she held back. She just clenched her teeth, livid, but she didn't want him to know it.

She took a long breath and opened a spiral notebook. She wrote an address in the corner of one of the pages, then ripped it off and handed it to him.

"He keeps a studio in TriBeCa. The top floor of an old packing house. If he's not there, I don't know where he is. That's it. No more. I'm done."

Then she turned on her heel and marched back into the lecture hall. Eddie just stood there, seething.

"Yeah, and I love you, too, lady."

29

REMSON STREET WAS ACTUALLY A SMALL SQUARE OF WARE-houses on the western edge of the Triangle Below Canal, that fashionable slice of lower Manhattan called TriBeCa. Eddie had responded to a fire there once. A big four-alarm in one of the old butter-and-egg warehouses. Half the loft buildings in that section were built with refrigeration, and Eddie's company had lost two men in the basement of 32 Remson when a cooling unit fell from the ceiling and crushed them to death. The FDNY had put a black wreath outside the building and two black pushpins were added to a map of the five boroughs at headquarters. Eddie Burke had seen death on this block and today he would see it again.

Caroline had written PH on the address, so he pushed the bell down below next to the sign that said Penthouse.

The letters AIR were painted on the outside of the granite doorjamb, indicating that the top floor contained an artist in residence. It was a special designation by the city that gave a rent break to bona fide artists who'd settled in com-mercial spaces. Over the years, the designation had lost its significance as real estate prices shot up and half the loft spaces were gentrified into residential co-ops. Now, negligence lawyers and account executives had moved into the big, high-ceilinged spaces, and many of the legitimate painters were driven to fringe lofts on the Bowery or NoHo.

But this was still a legitimate AIR space and Grosvenor, the multimillionaire, was probably getting the rent-controlled loft for a few grand a month. Nothing compared to what the square footage in lower Manhattan was renting for. It was just another example of a dictum that Eddie had come to know. The rich had their own private playbook, and everyone else paid retail.

He rang the bell again. No answer. So he took out his lock picks and decided to take a chance. If he went into the space and found something without a warrant, it would be inadmissible. After all, Grosvenor wasn't an official suspect yet. Not in the eyes of the NYPD. The worst they could charge him with was reckless endangerment for swamping the boat.

But Eddie didn't have time for a magistrate, and even if he found one, he wasn't sure he could show probable cause.

Besides, officially, he was still off the case. So he decided to do what the cops in New York called a "dirty search." He'd break in, and if he found anything, he'd go back out, get the requisite probable cause for a warrant, and then return to find the evidence that would have been otherwise inadmissible. It was far from kosher, but a lot of big cases got broken that way.

Eddie wondered what his father would think as he jimmied the lock and pushed open the door. Christ. The freight elevator was padlocked. He had six long and very steep flights ahead of him.

By the time he hit the top floor, Eddie promised himself that he'd start going to Gleason's again and get back to the heavy bag. The door outside Grosvenor's loft was painted black. Eddie pounded on it. No response. He called out, "Mr. Grosvenor?"

No answer. He was about to take out the picks when he remembered something his old man had said. "When you're on a search, always think like the perps do. Take the path of least resistance." Grosvenor had been spooked enough to fire a flare at Big Eddie. There was always a chance he'd be standing inside with a weapon.

So Eddie stopped. He looked up and saw that there was half a flight to the roof.

Grosvenor was an artist, and that meant his top floor loft would probably have skylights. Eddie pushed out the bulkhead door to the tar-covered roof—a roof like the one that Carlos Guzman had jumped from a week ago.

Just as he figured, there were two large, six-by-eight skylights facing north. On the off chance that Grosvenor might be down below, Eddie edged toward them cautiously. He stopped and peered into the first one. It took him a few seconds to adjust his eyes to the change in light as he looked down into the loft. At first, all he could see were a half-dozen unfinished canvases, all on easels, all in different stages of completion. So he cupped his hands around his eyes and focused. That's when he spotted it.

"Fuck."

Hanging from the metal crossbeam of the skylight was the body of a man swinging from a piece of bungee cord.

Eddie rushed back downstairs and used his picks on the door. There were two dead bolts, and though he felt his hands trembling, he got them. The first was a Yale. The second a Schlage. He pushed the door open and found it secured by the inevitable brass chain. Eddie reared back and kicked the door in. He didn't need a warrant now. These were exigent circumstances. The door gave way, and Eddie fell into the loft. When he looked up, he saw the corpse swinging.

It was hanging from the shock cord, which had been knotted into a noose. The tortoiseshell glasses were missing, but it was him, all right. The seventy-year-old Yankee with prep school good looks: Andrew Grosvenor, American master.

Eddie picked himself up and looked into Grosvenor's eyes. They were red, full of petechia, the sign of death by asphyxiation. Then he looked down and saw the overturned stool the painter had stepped off from. And below that, he saw a picture. An old five-by-seven black-and-white in a frame made of teak. The glass was smashed now. He must have dropped it in his final breaths. It was the picture of a woman, a black and white photo from the thirties. She had dark hair and piercing eyes. They were blue, Eddie thought. She looked a little bit like Elizabeth Taylor. It was the pregnant painter who had died on an abortion table so many years ago: Esther Schine.

Then Eddie smelled something—something foul. He looked up at the body and saw that Grosvenor's pants were stained. Loss of bladder control was common in deaths by strangling. In the final seconds, he had simply let go. Eddie winced at the urine smell and looked down at the broken glass and the picture of the beautiful artist long dead. Then he started to shiver.

It was cold in the loft—so cold that Eddie could see his breath—but that wasn't it. There was something else: the lost mural. Three people who had touched it were dead. Esther Schine, Alex Sloane, and now Grosvenor. If you counted Carlos Guzman, there were four. Four deaths somehow tied to that painting.

There was a clear explanation now. The case would be wrapped up in a matter of hours. Any other investigator in his place would rejoice, but not Eddie. There was still something gnawing at him. And as he stood there, looking up at the old man in death, Eddie shivered. It wasn't finished. Not yet.

30

THEY WOKE UP THE SUPER TO START THE FREIGHT ELEVA-
tor, and four hours later, there were eleven people inside
Grosvenor's loft. Jelke, the detective so willing to close out
the Alex Sloane death, was holding court near the door.
There were two suits from the Sixth Precinct and a pair of
uniforms along with the ME's team, who were there to
remove the body. But they were early. So the two patrol-
men stood in a corner, smoking and telling obscene stories
while the ghoul squad went to work. The three guys from
the Crime Scene Unit had gotten their name because they
were the rubber gloves who played with "the guest of
honor." That's what the forensic men always called the
deceased, and it was their job to check the crime scene for
prints, fibers, blood splatters, bullet wounds, ligatures, and
other grisly signs of violent death.

In homicides where the body had dropped on the street,
there was pressure to get it into the wagon and down to the
medical examiner's office right away. Public policy dictated
that the shock value of dead people on the street out-
weighed the forensic benefits of leaving the body in place.

In such cases, representatives from the ME's office rarely
had time to get to the scene before the body was shipped

to the morgue at Thirty-first and First Avenue. There, they conducted the autopsy, a ritual known among murder dicks as "the grand opening."

But in cases like Grosvenor's, where the victim had expired far from public view, there was plenty of time to let the blood spatter analysts and joy-boys have their way. Once the old painter's corpse had been photographed in situ, it was removed to the floor and placed facedown in a neoprene body bag. In order to get a precise fix on the time of death, the ME's forensic pathologist made a dime-sized incision in the lower back and shoved a meat thermometer into the liver. This was done after he'd set the thermometer down on the ledge of the skylight above for ten minutes to get the ambient temperature in the loft. The pathologist smoked a True Blue menthol as he compared the temperature of the liver to the temperature in the loft and then consulted a preprinted table. He cross-reference for Grosvenor's approximate age and weight.

The time it took for the body to cool down from 98.6 told him that the decedent had died between 5:00 and 5:30 A.M.

So far, the probe into Grosvenor's death had resembled a homicide investigation. But this was an apparent suicide, and from here on, the drill was modified. Instead of searching for suspects, Jelke's men would now look for witnesses to confirm the deceased's state of mind in the hours before he stepped off. They would fan out from the death scene in concentric circles and conduct a canvass. Since the only people in TriBeCa likely to be awake at 5:00 A.M. were junkies and garbage men, it was unlikely they'd get very far. But that was the book approach to death investigation.

Not that it worked very well anymore. In the halcyon days of Big Eddie Burke, the Detective Bureau was second to none. The silk-suited gold shields prided themselves on clearing 100 percent of their homicides. Murder for them wasn't just a capital crime, it was the line in the sand between order and jungle law. Cops like Big Eddie commanded enormous respect, not only from the public but among the uniforms as well. When men like him ducked under the yellow tape, the crime scene went hush. They had a sixth sense for tracking killers. If there were four roads to go down and three were dead ends, they always picked smart. They had to. It was their job to let "the maggots" know that you just didn't take human life.

But times had changed since then. The Detective Bureau, which once boasted three thousand men, had been decimated to fourteen hundred. Part of that stemmed from the new trend of putting uniforms on the street. "Proactive police work," they called it. More cops in uniform meant fewer detectives. And half the old-timers wanted out. But there was another, more ominous factor. After crack cocaine hit the streets in the early eighties, the homicide rate in New York had tripled.

A precinct detective's squad that might catch a killing a week was now faced with three in a weekend. And it wasn't just the numbers. There were entire new categories of motiveless murders, deaths where the perps never knew their victims—drug deaths, serials, and a whole new wave of thrill killings—that were almost impossible to solve.

You went into a crime scene in the old days, and you ID'd the victim. By the time you checked his family, his lover, and his job, you had a pretty good sense of the perp. But this was a city today where an OG (Original Gangsta) would cap a guy just because he dissed the gangbanger's girlfriend. Or maybe the guy gave him the look, or he just didn't like the guy's cornrows. It was crazy. A war zone.

So who needed the grief? A veteran homicide investigator could command three times his police salary in private security. If not that, then the DA's office paid double plus benefits for plainclothes detectives.

Also, after twenty years on the job, the pension was 50 percent of your salary. You could quit and open a bar like Big Eddie or beat it down to West Palm and cash your checks overlooking the beach. And why the hell not? Nobody gave a shit anymore. A new phrase had crept into the ranks of these once-dedicated detectives. They'd say, "If you're not out after twenty, then you're working for half pay."

And so, as the eighties turned into the nineties, little by little, the veteran gold shields had put in their papers. The Detective Bureau sat on the brink of a manpower crisis so severe that Governor Cuomo had to step in. In 1991, he signed a bill that effectively lowered the eligibility rules. Now you could turn a white shield into gold in eighteen months. In Big Eddie's time, it took five or six years in plain clothes to make detective. Now it was a year and a half.

And that wasn't the worst part. Most of these new men and women had done their time doing no-brainer, buy-bust narcotics work. It was a dangerous job but quite simple. You ID'd the dealer, went under to make the buy, and as you left the buy site, you signaled to the boys in the van to move in for the pinch. A slam dunk. No deduction involved. Basically, if you were young, with a death wish, and you had enough smarts to load a semiautomatic, you could work buy-bust undercover narcotics. It had nothing to do with investigation, and it didn't prepare you for hunting down killers.

So it was no surprise that by the fall of '95, the clearance rate on homicide cases was a paltry 59 percent. Fifteen percent of those arrested were never indicted and another 15 percent would have their cases dismissed or they'd walk on acquittal. You didn't have to be Jimmy the Greek to figure the odds. Half of the people who killed in New York were getting away with murder.

There was a momentary blip in mid-'96 when the actual homicide rate went down. Former Police Commissioner Bratton took credit back then, and so did Rudy, as Mayor Giuliani was known. But the experts believed that the drop in murders had as much to do with an increase in jail cells as it did with the quality of police work.

Jelke had six years in plain clothes, but he was one of the first to make gold from this new pool of homicide cops. That's why he blew the Alex Sloane death, and that's why he would have blown Grosvenor if Eddie Burke hadn't been on the scene.

31

EDDIE HAD HALF AN HOUR ALL ALONE IN THE LOFT WITH
Grosvenor's body to think about it from the time he'd first
called it in.

He had walked down to his car and radioed Vasquez to
call the precinct detectives. That way he wouldn't leave any
prints on the phone. Then he brought his Polaroid back
upstairs and took his own shots before the CSU boys arrived. He'd waited until they had dusted the phone before
calling Caroline.

He figured he owed it to her, but he made sure that Grosvenor's body had been zipped into the bag before they
opened the door to the freight elevator and led her into the
loft. Eddie stood in front of the body and held his hand out
for her to stop.

"You sure you're up to this?"

Caroline just nodded. Her eyes were red from crying.

Jelke offered to bring her over to the body bag, but she
shook her head and motioned toward Eddie. She wanted
him to do it.

The body was up on a gurney by now, so Eddie turned
and led Caroline forward. Then, when she was next to him,
squeezing his arm, Eddie unzipped it quickly, giving her

just enough time to make the ID. When he closed it again, she said "Yes" in a hollow voice, and then she broke down.

"Come on," said Eddie. "I'll take you home."

Caroline nodded limply and clung to his arm as he walked her toward the elevator. But just then, they heard the motor engage from below and the cage started creaking upward. As the weights dropped and the old cables moved higher, Eddie thought about Alex Sloane and the fire that had brought him into this case. He thought about the beautiful dead girl on West Twenty-eighth Street and the frail, birdlike face of Nathan, her brother. He thought about the wide-eyed death mask of Carlos Guzman and the smell of urine coming down off the body of Andrew Grosvenor.

All the signs pointed toward suicide, but Eddie Burke didn't buy it.

Caroline was squeezing his arm now, holding on for dear life, when the elevator arrived on the penthouse floor. The sliding cage door went up, and there, staring at Eddie, balancing himself on a cane, was his father.

Suddenly, the loft went quiet. The uniforms stubbed out their cigarettes. The ME's men straightened their backs. Jelke played with the knot in his tie and the Crime Scene Unit guys stopped taking pictures.

The legend hobbled out of the elevator and onto the floor. He looked at Eddie and Caroline, and stopped in his tracks. Then he smiled. "Eddie."

His son nodded.

Big Eddie turned to Caroline. "How are you doin', sweetheart?"

Caroline nodded weakly.

"Uh-huh." Big Eddie pressed her hand, taking the moment to pay his respects. Then he looked up and began to survey the loft.

"Where was he?"

Eddie motioned up toward the skylight. "Up there. It was a bungee cord. Double-fixed knot. The super said he used it to hold his canvases there in that rack."

Eddie gestured toward a rack along one wall of the loft full of unpainted white canvases on stretchers.

"He leave a note?"

Eddie shook his head. Most suicides didn't.

Big Eddie hobbled around for a minute. He looked down at the body bag as the EMS guys rolled it into the elevator. He sniffed for a second and then shook his head.

"What is it?" said Jelke, suddenly attentive.

"Cigarette smoke," said Big Eddie. "You in charge here?"

Jelke nodded, an acolyte in the presence of the pope.

"Uh-huh. Something wrong, Chief?"

"Yeah," said Big Eddie. "You let these numbnuts smoke. . . . I count one, two, three, four butts on the floor."

"But Chief, I just—"

"You just *what?* This is a fucking crime scene. Next thing you're gonna tell me, you called it in from that phone without gloves."

"N-no sir," said Jelke, nodding to Eddie.

"He called it in from his car. Used the radio."

Big Eddie's face broke into a smile.

"Fucking A. And he's fire department. You people ought to know better."

Just then, from her place near the elevator, Caroline Drexel shook her head. She was staring up at the skylight, almost numb.

"I still can't believe it."

"What?" said Big Eddie, hobbling over to her.

"That he'd do this. I mean, why would he kill himself?"

"Because something hit him from out of the past."

Caroline rubbed the tears from her eyes. "I . . . I don't understand."

Big Eddie started to pace now.

"Think back to it. Grosvenor was going to marry your mother. His life was set. Then he found out the Schine girl was pregnant. She was carrying his child."

Big Eddie reached down on a desk and picked up the shattered picture of Esther Schine in its evidence bag.

"He took her to a back-alley abortionist. They were going to take care of it: no scandal, no mess. Only she bled to death."

"Christ," said Jelke. "Grosvenor was looking at accessory to manslaughter."

"Minimum."

"And this guy went on to become a American Master." Jelke turned to Eddie. "You gotta love it, right?"

But Eddie stayed silent, so Jelke turned back to his father. "Just tell me one thing. How's this tie into the SoHo thing?"

"Simple," said the old cop. "When the lost mural turned up, Grosvenor figured the truth would come out. Be a pisser to have to swap that spread up on Waramaug for a shitbox in Attica. Right?"

Jelke nodded.

"So he broke into the loft and set the mural on fire. The dead girl, the art restorer, just got in the way."

Jelke smiled. "No shit." He walked up and patted him on the back. "Christ, Chief. You were always the best."

Big Eddie accepted the compliment.

But off to the side, Caroline Drexel was shaking her head. She didn't believe it. Not a word. There was fear in her face as she looked down at Esther's broken picture and Grosvenor's unfinished paintings.

And Eddie picked up on it.

"Hey. You okay?"

Caroline didn't say anything. She moved away from him

and stepped into the elevator. She closed the metal cage door, and the elevator went down.

Eddie Burke didn't bother to follow. He just looked up at the skylight and then down at his father, who was chatting lightly now with two of the uniforms. Big Eddie. He was a legend, all right. When *he* called a case, nine times out of ten it was over. But not this time.

This time he was wrong, and Eddie knew it.

32

CAROLINE DREXEL WENT STRAIGHT FROM GROSVENOR'S loft to the Parkview Chronic Care Facility on Fifth at Ninety-first Street. It was just after 9:00 P.M. on a Friday night, and visiting hours had ended. But over the years, since she'd come to see Dr. Liebman, Caroline had grown close to the administrator, Kelsey Richter, so she was taken to Helen's room straightaway.

Kelsey looked through a wired glass window in the door. Helen was inside, staring out at Central Park. The administrator turned to Caroline.

"Are you sure you don't want me to stay? She's been disoriented lately. Since it's nighttime, she won't be expecting you."

"No, that's okay. We'll be fine."

Caroline squeezed Kelsey's arm as she left. Then she knocked on the door. Helen seemed startled, but then, when she turned around and saw Caroline, she smiled.

"So late and you come?"

"I needed to see you." Caroline moved over to her and Helen struggled to get up on her walker.

"No. No. Please. Don't get up."

Caroline knelt down and hugged her. The big woman

squeezed her tight. There were a few yellowed pictures in
silver frames on the sideboard near her bed. Helen's Tante
Ida from Salzburg and the Schinemann twins, two little
sisters from her strasse in Vienna. But nothing of her parents. Only memories. Years before, Helen had recovered
the few pictures she had from the Nuremberg War Crimes
Tribunal. Back when the storm troopers came, Ida had tried
to rescue the twins. She got them out of Vienna, but they
were captured and sent off to Mengele and his monsters.

Now, Helen's sideboard was filled with pictures of Caroline. Smiling atop her first hunter pony, posing at her first
presentation as a debutant, in cap and gown at her graduation from RISD, and in a dark gray suit the day she delivered her first paper at a Whitney colloquium. Helen had
taken them all with her Leica. Black-and-white photographs. This was her family now. From all of her years in
practice, Caroline was the only one who would come.

Helen pulled herself up on the walker.

"Good. Let us go to the terrace."

"But it's dark," said Caroline, "and it's freezing out."

Helen cocked her head to the fox coat that Caroline had
given her on her birthday.

"That is why we have friends, and that is why they give
us presents."

Caroline smiled. At seventy-three, the big woman still
had such bearing. Caroline grabbed the coat and put it over
Helen's shoulders. It was the only thing that the doctor had
ever asked her for. Well, actually, she'd requested something much less. "A nice red fur hat," she said after seeing
a picture in one of the magazines.

But when Caroline went to the furrier to buy it, she'd
seen the matching coat, and though she had her own reservations about wearing fur, Caroline knew that the ensem-
ble would make Helen happy.

Now, on the terrace, as Caroline helped the old woman

ease into a chair, she thought to herself that Helen looked like an Austrian baroness. The white hair, the piercing blue eyes still full of life, even though the fingers on her left hand were still closed and every so often, she'd stutter.

Helen waited as Caroline rubbed her throat, not exactly sure how to begin, so the old doctor broke the ice.

"For three years she comes to see me like a fine clock. Every S-S-Saturday, just so, at ten A.M., and now she comes on a Friday and doesn't even light up."

"Oh . . ." Caroline smiled. She opened her black Fendi purse and took out the blue package of Gitanes. Helen looked at it the way a starvation victim might covet a piece of food. She held on Caroline's every move as she pulled out the lighter and set it on fire, holding the first puff in for what seemed like forever before letting it go.

"Ah," said the old woman, taking in the smoke. "I have often bargained with myself and thought that I might give up a f-f-few days . . . maybe a week at the end . . . in return for one last pack of those things. But then I think that a week for me now is like a year to someone like you, and perhaps I shouldn't be so extravagant."

Caroline smiled and held out the cigarette.

"Why don't you just take this one?"

Helen's eyes grew wide. "What? And betray my handsome young doctor from L-L-Lenox Hill? We are old, my dear, and exceedingly selfish, but we still have integrity."

Caroline looked away and smiled. She took another puff.

"Now, what brings you here on a night when you should be out with a man, having fun, telling lies, getting laid?"

Caroline blushed. She was often shocked at Helen's candor. She smiled again, but soon it faded. She rubbed her neck.

"What is it, child?"

Caroline got up and walked to the edge of the terrace.

"Things have happened so quickly. I almost don't know where to begin. . . ."

But then she did, and she took her time to bring the old woman up to date: the mural fire, Alex Sloane, and now Grosvenor. She made little mention of Eddie Burke. She just wanted to get it all out, and finally, as she stubbed out her second cigarette, she did.

Dr. Liebman took a long time to respond. From the first moment she'd read to Caroline in her office, she knew that someday, some of the truth would come out. She never fully understood the depth of the crimes that were buried, but all bad things find their way to the surface eventually.

Helen burned a look into Caroline as she stood, arms folded and shivering at the chill on the terrace. Then, finally, she asked her, "So the dream . . . you believe that it is somehow t-t-tied to all this?"

Caroline nodded. "I *know* it is. I just can't understand how. I saw that mural *years* before I ever knew it existed. The dream was one of the reasons I studied the field. When I learned it had surfaced, I was thrilled and a little bit scared. Now to know all the death that it's brought . . . well . . . I'm worried."

She sat down next to Helen, and the big woman pushed the hair from her eyes like she'd done so many years ago.

Helen looked out at the tens of thousands of twinkling lights in the buildings across the park. Then she began.

"There was a journal. It belonged to your m-m-mother."

Caroline's jaw dropped. "What?"

"She was . . . she wrote about her life at the time of the WPA. The other artists. The murals they painted. When you were under, I used to read to you from it."

Caroline was half in shock.

"But how did you . . . ?"

"Your mother's attorney. He contacted me after her will was probated. There were things about her life that you were too y-y-young to know. She asked that under the right circumstances you be . . . exposed to it. After you'd begun to see me and we made some progress, the lawyer felt it was time."

"What about my father?"

Helen took a long time to answer that. She chose her words carefully. "Let us just say that it would not have been appropriate for him to see the document."

Caroline became excited now. It was as if she had learned about some long-lost sibling.

"So, what was in it?"

"As I said, your mother's memories from the time that she painted. She put it away when she met your father and then . . ."

Helen hesitated. Caroline pushed forward and squeezed her arm. "What? What else?"

Helen looked away from her. "Later, when you were a child, she began writing again. The entries continued almost up until the time that s-s-she . . ."

"Died?"

The old woman nodded. She was stuttering more now, starting to get tired.

"As part of your therapy I would read to you. I wanted you to understand where you came from, to hear it in your mother's own words. She loved you so much."

"Why didn't you just show me the journal?"

"As I said, you were young."

"But why didn't you mention it to me later?"

"There was no need. We had dealt with the pathology that produced your symptoms, and we'd succeeded in helping you."

Caroline stood up. "Then help me now."

"What do you mean?"

"I need to know what was in it. I want to see it."

"The j-j-journal?" Helen rocked back as if someone had

asked her to betray some sacred covenant. "That's impossible."

"But why?"

Helen looked flustered.

"Well, because it's . . . it doesn't exist anymore."

Caroline began to tremble now. "Why? What happened to it?

Helen looked away. "I destroyed it."

Caroline almost screamed at her. "Why? Why would you *do* that?"

"Because some things are best left uns-s-said."

"I don't understand."

Helen turned away again. "You told me yourself that people had died."

Caroline knelt down in front of her. "Please, Helen. I have to know."

The old doctor covered her face with her hand. As she did, Caroline could see the blue tatooed number from the death camp. Of all the terrible things that Helen had known in life, the horror of the Holocaust, the pain of a thousand patients she'd tried to heal, *this* was a secret that Helen would never reveal. She was sure that if she did, it would shatter Caroline. And Dr. Liebman was simply too old now to help her. And so, for the good of her surrogate daughter, for Caroline's own sense of peace, she just shook her head.

"No, child. I'm sorry. You have trusted me now all your life and you must trust me again. Don't ask me to t-t-talk about this . . . p-p-please."

Caroline stared at her. She could see the pain on the old woman's face. There on that terrace, in the big red fox hat and coat, Helen Liebman was weeping. Finally, Caroline hugged her. They spent a few quiet moments together and then she led Helen back to her room.

Another person might have let it go, let the journal die along with the woman who wrote it, but there was a fire inside Caroline Drexel. It had driven her this far through life, and it was driving her now as she raced across Central Park to the old co-op where Helen had lived.

She had a key to the apartment, because after Helen's stroke, she'd seen to it that her furniture was covered and her files packed away. There was no electricity in the apartment, but Caroline had come in before, to get Helen's clothes size before buying the hat and coat, so she'd left a flashlight by the door.

She let herself in, switched it on, and pushed into the study that Helen had used as an office. Caroline went straight to the closet where she'd packed up Helen's patient files. It took her two hours to sift through the dozens of boxes in search of her own patient history. But by then it was clear that the files were gone. She searched the bookcases and the wall cabinets. Then she began moving through the rest of the apartment, opening anything big enough to hide a journal or her case files. The place was empty. Finally, she came back to the office and started at Helen's big desk. She'd cleaned it out years before when Helen had taken sick, but now she had nothing to lose. So Caroline set the flashlight down on a table nearby and went at it, opening every drawer, turning them inside out. Still nothing.

"Damn it," Caroline slammed the last drawer closed in frustration. And when she did, the flashlight fell off the table. It rolled under the desk, so she had to reach down to get it. It stopped against the wall, and Caroline had to lean in all the way with the tips of her fingers to touch it.

That's when she saw it: the envelope taped to the bottom of the desk. It had Helen's handwriting across it. The note said, *In the event of my death.*

Caroline tore it off and grabbed the flashlight. She ripped open the envelope like an archaeologist who's just cracked an ancient tomb. There, inside, on Helen's letterhead was a single blank piece of stationary surrounding a safe-deposit box key.

33

CAROLINE HAD TO WAIT UNTIL SATURDAY MORNING WHEN
the Park Avenue branch of Chase Manhattan opened its
doors. She rushed to the basement and presented the guard
with the executor's letter that she used in dealing with Helen's other business matters. Then she showed him the key.

He took her into the vault, where he checked the number.

"Boy. It's one of the big ones," said the guard.

Caroline smiled nervously as he went to the end of a row
of safe-deposit boxes and opened one that was the size of
a small chest of drawers.

The guard pulled it out and carried it to a cubicle lined
with green felt.

"Just let me know when you're finished."

Caroline smiled. She waited for the guard to disappear
around a corner and then opened the box.

It was filled with stacks of Helen's old black-and-white
photographs, bound with rubber bands. There was her beloved Leica and some jewelry. Underneath Caroline found
a manila folder with a fold-over flap and a tie string. She
undid the bow and opened it. Inside was an inch-thick stack
of medical files. Her heart began to race.

She ripped off the elastic and searched through them

quickly, recognizing some of the patient names as Helen's closest friends. When she got to the bottom of the stack, she realized that her files weren't there.

Caroline leaned against the wall of deposit boxes and rubbed her forehead.

"Oh God . . ."

The guard, around the corner, called out, "Are you all right, miss?"

Caroline poked her head around the cubicle. "Yes. Yes. Thank you."

She returned to the safe-deposit box and began assembling the contents, arranging the stacks of pictures the way Dr. Liebman had left them. Caroline thought to herself that she would never find the truth in all this. She could never go back to Helen and tell her what she had done.

She was about to call for the guard when she noticed a pictured of Helen smiling, arm in arm with her. The snapshot, atop one of the stacks of photos, was taken at a MoMA cocktail party following a major WPA retrospective. Caroline remembered how Helen had handed her Leica to a waiter and asked him to bang off a shot.

She pulled the photo from the stack and ran her forefinger across Helen's face. This old, white-haired woman was as much a mother as Caroline had ever known, and now she was trying to protect her. But from what?

Caroline pulled the rubber bands aside to push the picture back into the stack, and they suddenly snapped. The elastic broke and the stack of pictures came undone.

Now, inside the stack, Caroline saw a small yellow Kodak slide box. She picked it up, curious, because Helen had never used color or slides. Only black-and-white film.

She flipped up the top of the box and spilled out its contents onto the green felt counter.

She sucked in hard.

There, in front of her, were eight tiny microcassette tapes

from Helen's dictating machine. On the back of the first cassette, in Dr. Liebman's own hand, were the words:

> C. Drexel. 3/28/77.
> Dorothea's Journal. Tape One.

Caroline clutched the tape to her chest like a nun who had just found a relic of the true cross.

Then she quickly repacked the box and called for the guard. She couldn't wait to get out of the bank.

34

EDDIE BURKE WAS STILL ON THE CASE. ANYONE ELSE WHO'D heard the rap his father had given would have folded the tent and gone home, but not Eddie.

The former chief of detectives had tied the Grosvenor death and the Sloane homicide into a nice little bundle. It was logical. It fit, and it was supported by the lion's share of the evidence. But Eddie Burke couldn't let go like that. He had to keep working the case; partly, because he knew that when it was over, he'd never see Caroline again, and partly because his father had declared it now closed.

Still, all that was from the heart. There were other, more practical reasons that had kept Eddie up all night, other reasons he'd followed the ME's wagon up to the morgue on First Avenue, other reasons he'd stood in the autopsy room and watched as the deputy medical examiner cut Andrew Grosvenor apart for the autopsy.

You see, as good as Big Eddie was, there was something he'd missed as he leaned on his cane and held forth on the suicide. He'd seen the split in the doorjamb where Eddie had broken the chain coming in. He'd seen the way the neck had snapped on the body, and most of all, he'd seen motive. With all of those signs pointing toward suicide, a door chained from the inside pretty much tied up the case. But up on the roof, Eddie had noticed one of the skylight windows. It was slightly ajar, and if somebody had taken the trouble to string up a body, it would have been a simple thing to make his way up and out onto the roof. Taken alone, that wouldn't have pointed to murder. But there was another thing that Big Eddie had missed: the look on Caroline's face.

Eddie had watched her as his father went on about the abortion gone wrong and the fire in SoHo. Caroline was shaking her head, but it wasn't disbelief on her face, it was fear.

Someone had been stalking her for days now. Presumably the killer of Alex Sloane. And now Big Eddie was saying he was dead. It was Grosvenor. The man in the body bag. So what was she still afraid of? And why did she take off? Just split without so much as a thank you? If not to Eddie, then his father. No. She knew something. She knew that Big Eddie was wrong.

But that, on its own, was still not enough. There was something that Eddie had seen in that loft, and he wanted it checked through forensic pathology.

When he first started at The Bureau of Fire Investigation, Eddie never would have noticed it, but six months into the job, he'd had the luck of meeting Dinny Walsh. Dinny— Dennis to strangers—was an old-line arson investigator, long since retired and working as a PI for the Firemen's Fund.

Eddie had been poking around in the ash from some duck-shop blaze down on Mott Street when he ran into this salty old Mick who was speaking Chinese.

The guy had the pink skin and white hair of all great Irish ward heelers. In his fine camel-hair coat and Florsheim brogues, he looked like a Court Street ambulance chaser or maybe a State Rep. But here he was, whipping off with some skinny Chinese guy when Eddie walked up with his flashlight and boots and asked if he was the landlord.

Dinny just turned to him and smiled. "Don't tell me. You just hit The Bureau?"

Eddie nodded tentatively, and the old Irishman whipped out a business card. Under the Firemen Fund's logo it said:

Dennis X. Walsh
Investigator
Supv. Fire Marshal FDNY
Retired

As soon as Eddie gave him his name, the old guy stopped short.

"Not The Chief's Kid?"

Eddie nodded and looked away.

But Walsh threw his arms around him. "God love ya, Kid."

Eddie pushed away.

"Wait a minute. Didn't he ever *tell* you?"

"Tell me what?"

"Me and your father. We went to St. Pat's together."

Eddie shook his head. No. Somehow Big Eddie had left that out.

"Fuckin' altar boys," said Dinny. Back when it was still in Latin. Your old man used to cut the wine and we'd drink it up in the alley behind the church. God love ya Kid. You went FDNY. . . . Big Eddie must have been fuckin' ripshit, huh?"

Eddie nodded.

"Let's get out of here, go for some Chink."

Eddie looked at the little Chinese man, and Dinny said, "Don't worry. He only speaks Mandarin."

He took Eddie over to BoBo's for a feast.

It was the first time that Eddie had eaten sizzling rice

soup. And Dinny held him in the palm of his hand for two hours as he unrolled his story.

He was Army Airborne. Dinny had gotten into the war late because of his feet, but he bribed a guy down on White Street to change his physical, and he'd gone off to fly.

When the Japanese had surrendered, he started flying DC-3s full of Brownings to the Koumintang. He flew thirty-six missions over the mainland before getting wasted. "The fuckin' Chicoms" had him in a forced labor camp for a year. That's where he learned how to "speakee Chinee."

Dinny came back after walking three hundred miles to the China Sea and spent the next twenty years at Twenty-six Engine in Bay Ridge. It was his birthright. Twenty-six had been the company where Dinny's father had served and his grandfather before him, and now, his own son was there. The Walshes had *always* been red, and if the money as a PI wasn't so good, he'd be there still.

After that day, Dinny had taken Eddie under his wing. He taught him how to trace a line of volatiles from the point of origin. He showed him how to look for plants, the melted bottoms of plastic milk jugs filled with accelerants. He taught Eddie about the link between demolition companies and arson. That was the best one and it always happened to city-owned buildings, which meant that Mr. and Mrs. taxpayer paid.

Dinny explained it like this: "See, the city's got some tax repo rat shack, right? It's bombed out. Condemned. Unsafe for human habitation, so they contract with a demo company to knock it down. On day one they sign a contract for ten grand for the removal. On day two there's a fire. The shithole burns to the ground. On day three the demo company pushes away the rubble with a 'dozer. Costs them maybe a buck and a half. Now they're up eight and a half Gs. Fuckin' windfall.''

With Dinny it was always "follow the money."

And Walsh had taught Eddie something else—something that had caused him to question his father's conclusion on Grosvenor. In police work, homicides made to look like suicides were rare. The stuff of bad mystery novels. But for fire cops, as many as 10 percent of their blazes were fires set to cover up something else: a break-in, a burglary, or a murder. It was especially true in crimes of passion.

As Dinny put it, "Some KY cowboy finds his boyfriend choking some other guy's chicken, and he drills 'em with holes. For some crazy reason, he figures that if he covers the stiffs with cleaning fluid and tosses a match, the cops'll put it down as an act of God. But people don't realize that you can still autopsy a body that's fried. The MEs call 'em 'crispy critters.' They're tougher to open up, but you can still find the bullet holes.''

So Dinny taught Eddie to always look further. Go past the obvious. And the way that he taught him this lesson was to bring him down to the morgue and have him watch the pathologists as they cut up the dead.

Eddie would never forget his first trip to Thirty-first Street. Dinny had been promising to take him down to the ME's office, but he wanted to wait until "the right body dropped.''

The old leprechaun was late that particular night, and Eddie was forced to wait in the yellow-tiled corridor amid the meat lockers and the gurneys full of stiffs. They'd parked him on a bench just outside the fresh room, and by the time Dinny arrived, he was almost sick. Death has an unmistakable stench, and Dinny told him there were only two things that would make it go away: Vicks Vaporub— a touch in each of his nasal cavities—or sharp provolone cheese. Eddie retched. He hated cheese. So Dinny tossed him the small blue-capped jar. Eddie touched just below his nose with two fingers, then got up on wobbly legs and followed Dinny through the door marked Autopsy.

It was a busy night, and there, on four stainless steel tables, human beings were laid out like mannequins as the deputy MEs cracked their chests and took out their organs while dictating into overhead mikes.

A goateed Russian emigré named Chernakov stood over the last table against the wall. His scrub suit was splattered with blood and there was a Lucky dangling out of his mouth. He nodded to Dinny and motioned Eddie up to the table.

"Hey, Dinny, you hear about the old guy they find in Plaza Hotel?"

Dinny shook his head.

"Must have been eighty. Japanese. Had little shriveled pecker covered with condom. Poor bastard popped embolism while hooker was giving him head."

"Yeah?" said Dinny.

"They were going to charge her with manslaughter, but DA dropped charges. You know why?"

Dinny could see it coming. He shook his head anyway.

" 'Cause it wouldn't stand up in court!' "

The pathologist slapped his sides with a blood-covered glove. "Wouldn't stand up—get it?"

He poked Eddie, who nodded. Who the fuck was this yahoo?

"Don't worry," said Dinny. "We've tried to have Yuri deported, but the Commies won't take him back."

Eddie nodded. Right.

"Okay," said Dinny. "Where's the stiff?"

Dr. Chernakov pointed to a large, three-hundred-pound Black man on the table in front of him. "Here. Had him in cooler five days. One more, you don't show, we send him to Potter's Field.'' Chernakov motioned for Eddie to come closer.

The decedent, identified on the ME sheet as Unknown Black Male Case File #2237221, had been found in a South Bronx single room occupancy hotel with his throat cut from ear to ear. There'd been a bloody knife in his hand and he had been kind enough to leave a note. Ordinarily, in cases like this, where the cause of death seemed obvious, the deputy ME would sign off without an autopsy. Even a partial evisceration could cost the city five hundred dollars in time and labor. So they'd list the COD as a probable suicide and release the body for burial.

If nobody came in a week, he'd end up in Potter's Field, the public cemetery for unknowns on Hart's Island off the Bronx. He'd get a nice bath and a box made of Carolina pine. Then a busload of inmates from Riker's Island would lay him into a ditch with a half-dozen other John Does and cover him up with a backhoe.

But this guy was different. There had been something about the throat cut that caused the Russian refugee to look further.

"Here, look at edge of serration," Chernakov said to Eddie. Eddie leaned in over the body. The Black man smelled of vomit and Aqua Velva.

"See."

"What?" said Eddie.

"No hesitation marks."

Eddie didn't understand, so Chernakov explained in his hard Russian accent. "In ninety-nine out of hundred suicides like this, you see little nicks near edge of fatal serration. Suicide is not natural. It is against human nature. So people will take knife and start to cut. But then they stop and think. No. This hurts. A few seconds later maybe they do it again. And then, finally, they get up the nerve and *hrrrrrrgghh.*''

Chernakov made an obscene cutting sound as he demonstrated with a scalpel.

"So here, no hesitation marks," said Eddie. "Which means—"

"No suicide."

"Sonovabitch," said Eddie. "Then how'd he die?"

The dead man on the table had a huge three-inch Afro. Chernakov smiled and began moving his rubber-gloved fingers through the thick, nappy hair. Finally, at the base of the skull, he found it.

"Here. You see." He pulled the overhead light down and motioned for Eddie to look closer. Sure enough, Eddie could see a quarter-inch circle.

"Entrance wound. It was twenty-two Mercury load. Made to disintegrate on penetration. No exit wound."

The Russian slammed an X-ray up on a light box behind them. As Eddie looked at the dead Black man's skull, he could see fragments of lead in the brain. Somebody had put a gun to his head, shot him execution style, and then slashed his throat. They'd even taken the time to leave a note.

After that night, Eddie had never again rushed to judgment. And after that, when he had a forensic problem, he went out of his way to find Yuri Chernakov.

And so, Eddie thought of Dinny as he pushed through the doors of the autopsy room and found Dr. Chernakov, still smoking, still at the corner table, standing over the body of Andrew Grosvenor.

Standard operating procedure in a death by hanging was to cut off the noose but keep the knot intact, tying the loose ends together with a string and preserving the rope in a separate evidence bag. But Eddie had pressed the CSU guys to leave the noose around the neck and they'd complied.

Chernakov looked up at Eddie as he came to the table.

"To what do I owe this honor?"

"I miss the smell of formaldehyde." said Eddie. "Besides, I've been freelancing on this one, and I've got a question."

Eddie put the liter of vodka in the brown paper bag down on the stainless steel table.

"Okay. Fire." Chernakov started to laugh. "Get it? Arson? Fire?" He was coughing again and the ashes from the Lucky had spilled onto Grosvenor's chest.

"You're a regular Yakov Smirnoff, Yuri."

"Soon maybe I'm ready for Improv, huh?"

"Absolutely. An HBO special. Maybe Leno."

The Russian smiled and exhaled a cloud of smoke. "All right. What do you need?"

"Take a look at this noose," said Eddie. "It's supposed to be a suicide."

"Hmmmm."

Chernakov took his time. He felt around the neck, then raised the noose and examined the skin. Finally, he switched on the overhead mike and began dictating.

"Okay. This is body of white male septuagenarian. Period."

He began feeling along the neck again.

"There is apparent fracture of proximal hyoid bone and thyroid cartilage. Period. Crime Scene report suggests subject body was found hanging from length of shock cord. Period. The noose on examination contains double fixed knot. Period."

He pulled up the noose to examine the neck again.

"There is five centimeter horizontal ligature below level of thyroid cartilage. Period."

Then Chernakov began rubbing his goatee. "Hmmm."

"What is it?" said Eddie.

"Normally, in death by hanging, thyroid and hyoid bone are intact, but this guy's at least seventy, right?"

Eddie nodded.

"In person that age, you'd expect neck to snap. Still . . ."

"What?"

"I don't like noose like this for suicide."

"Why not?"

"Fixed knot is on right side of head, no?"

"Yeah," said Eddie.

"Man was left-handed," said Chernakov.

He picked up Grosvenor's left arm.

"See muscle here in forearm? Larger than right. What did he do for living?"

"He was a painter," said Eddie. "What's the left or the right got to do with it?"

"Left-handed people who hang themselves almost always put knot on left."

Chernakov demonstrated. He held the imaginary bungee cord above his head with his left hand and tightened the imaginary knot with his right.

"So what you're saying is, you don't think that he put the noose on?"

"Dah."

"Which means he was murdered?"

"Dah. It is possible."

"What're the odds?"

"Eddie, you know I don't like percentages."

"Come on, Yuri. I brought you a liter this time."

Yuri smiled at the vodka.

"I'd say at least sixty-forty."

"That he was whacked?"

"Dah."

35

EDDIE RUBBED HIS NAILS ALONG THE STUBBLE ON HIS FACE and checked himself in the rearview mirror. Christ. He looked like some mental patient who'd just been released from Pilgrim State. It was Monday morning at 7:30 A.M. He'd spent Friday night and half of Saturday at the ME's office. Then he'd crawled home and found a few hours of sleep. By Saturday night, he was on the phone to American Express checking out Grosvenor's whereabouts on the night of the Sloane murder. First thing Sunday he dealt with TWA. After that, he'd stopped at St. Paul's on Ninth Avenue for The Eleven. He hadn't been to church in six months, but he felt like he needed it. When Mass was over, he lit a candle for his mother and drove to Manhattan Base.

The squad room was deserted, but there was an in-box full of paperwork to get rid of so Kivie would stay off his back. That had taken him all day, and it was almost ten o'clock Sunday night when Eddie crashed on the old Naugahyde couch in the locker room.

By the time he woke up, it was after five A.M. Rather than go home, he put his head under the locker room shower, dried off, and drove over to Munson's Diner, but it was closed for renovations, so he headed over to Sutton Place.

For the past two hours, Eddie had been parked up the block from Caroline's co-op. He was hungry and thirsty and half dead. There were four disposable Bics in the glove compartment, but he'd left the Edge Gel in the john at The Doral and wasn't sure he could take a dry shave. He'd been wearing the same suit for twenty-one hours. It was the second night out of four that he'd slept in his car. He always kept an extra shirt and some skivvies in the trunk. Two, maybe three pairs of socks. In *his* line of work, you just never knew. But the single-breasted wool worsted was hanging on him.

He'd almost dozed off at seven, and he knew she was prone to leave early, so he used the car phone to call the Knossos Coffee Shop on First Avenue for some food. He'd given the address of the Sutton Place apartment building he was parked in front of and the astonished delivery boy had laughed when Eddie whistled for him. He gave the kid a four dollar tip so he'd exit quietly. No sense getting the Sutton Place doormen riled over some maniac in a Chevy ordering take-out food.

Then he washed down the bacon and egg sandwich with coffee—hot, black coffee—as he got his second wind and checked the rearview mirror. Eddie could just see the door to her building. Still quiet.

He was all set to catch the seven-thirty headlines on WINS when he saw the blue-and-white pull up beside him.

"Shit." Eddie eased down in his seat. She'd be out pretty soon. He didn't need this. There were two young uniforms in the radio motor patrol. The one riding shotgun rapped on Eddie's window with his nightstick.

"What are you doin' here?"

Eddie held up his shield. "Stakeout."

The uniform smirked and looked at his partner. "What

the fuck you waitin' for? Somebody to burn down a co-op?'' The two dickheads traded laughs.

"No," said Eddie. "I'm waitin' here to get cited for decking a fuckin' beat cop. Now take off."

The shotgun uniform started to get out, but his partner grabbed him. He pointed to his Timex. They were due to punch out on the twelve-to-eight tour and it just wasn't worth it. The shotgun uniform had to satisfy himself with flashing the finger, and Eddie just grinned as the unit rolled off.

It was almost another hour before the red light went on above the awning in front of Caroline's building.

It meant that the doorman needed a cab. Eddie perked up behind the wheel and tossed the empty coffee cup on the floor. The doorman jumped into the street and blew his whistle.

A few seconds later, a Plymouth taxi pulled up and Caroline Drexel got inside. She was dressed in a cute little suit with brass buttons, carrying a bag with two C's intertwined. Chanel, Eddie thought. He had dated a buyer from Saks once, and she'd taught him about women's clothes. Caroline didn't look like an art professor this morning. She looked like some bond trader's wife in from Rye for lunch at Lutèce and a facial at Bendel's. It didn't fit.

But Eddie pulled into traffic as the cab made a right turn onto Fifty-third Street and shot west across town.

He was two car lengths in back of it now, crossing First, when his beeper went off. Christ. He'd had his radio switched off on the stakeout. He checked the beeper. It was Kivlihan.

Eddie swallowed hard and made a decision. The case was over now. Even his father would say that, and he knew if he pushed, he'd be dead at the FDNY. He thought for a second as he swerved left to avoid another car and roared west on Fifty-third. Then he took a deep breath and switched off the beeper. He didn't know where this would lead him, but he was sure of one thing: Grosvenor hadn't killed Alex Sloane, and Caroline Drexel knew it.

He had to find out how much *more* she knew, even if it meant his job. Besides, this wasn't about work anymore.

Eddie slammed it into third and kept going.

Few things in the world compared to driving in Midtown Manhattan. Maybe the bull run at Pamplona or the double black diamond run at Gstaad. To make it from point A to point B you had to be quick-witted and reckless. If you had an ounce of concern for the paint job on your '93 Cutlass, you were doomed. Motor vehicles moved through Manhattan the way appartchiks moved through the old Kremlin—with laser-guided ambition and total disregard for human life.

Eddie had learned the unwritten code in his freshman year at CCNY. He'd taken a night job driving for Ann Service Corp., a Checker garage on West Twenty-first Street. The dispatcher was a hard-boiled Iraqi named Youssef. He sent his drivers into the streets with two dictums: "Never pick up young Blacks wearing Nikes and never, ever, give right of way."

The logic was simple: everyone in New York was so base, so craven, so out for themselves, that if a space opened up in traffic, the fastest car had to fill the void. It was axiomatic. To allow another motor vehicle a break at an intersection, to be the last off at the light, or to stop for pedestrians would be self-destructive. If you drove with a fragment of Presbyterian kindness, you'd be risking your life and the lives of your passengers.

Eddie had ignored the admonition about young Blacks way back then, and he'd been held up three times. It happened that the assailants were white, Hispanic, and Asian, but in each case, they were wearing high-topped athletic shoes.

So this time he held to the second rule and he floored it, narrowly missing a Sabrett pushcart as he careened west behind the yellow Plymouth. But the cab just made the light on Second, and Eddie had to skid to a stop as the morning pedestrian mob hit the crosswalk. Shit. He jumped out and tried to follow the cab with his eyes, but it blended into a sea of yellow heading west. When the light changed, a big United Van Lines truck jammed the box, so Eddie slammed on his Mars light and hit the siren, shooting wide and around it. He saw a narrow opening now on the north side of Fifty-third as a delivery truck pulled away. He smashed his foot to the floor and did seventy up the block until he caught sight of the sign on the back of the taxi.

It was a picture of Jim Palmer pitching low interest rates at the Money Store.

Eddie kept his eyes on Palmer and stayed with the cab across Third and Park, but then he lost it again in the block east of Madison. Fuck. When the light turned red, Eddie screeched to a halt. He looked straight ahead west and then uptown, not knowing which way to go. Did she turn or go straight? He couldn't tell. So he decided to follow his gut. Four roads. Three dead ends. Right?

He slammed it into first and left rubber as he peeled out, heading straight. And then something caught his eye on the right. There, up on the top of a black skyscraper, he saw the word Drexel in letters twenty feet high. So he hit the brakes and spun it right, almost crushing a Honda Civic as he did a ninety-degree turn and raced up Madison. He was neck and neck with an uptown bus when he roared left in front of it, just in time to see Palmer, grinning at him as the taxi pulled up outside 460 Madison, and Caroline Drexel got out.

Eddie skidded to a stop half a block ahead at the curb.

He jumped out and threw the FDNY marshal card on the dash as he raced back downtown on foot.

He got to the black tower in just enough time to catch that mane of blonde hair as she pushed through the rotating doors. Caroline moved past a model of a new high-rise complex. There was a sign on the model that read:

Drexel Place
The Madison Avenue of Tomorrow

Eddie held back as she went toward a bank of elevators. On the gray marble wall above the bank it said, The Drexel Group: 68–PH.

Caroline got into an elevator, so Eddie stopped at a newsstand. He looked across the street and spotted a Soup Burg. Then he grabbed a pile of magazines. She'd be up there awhile, and he was dead with Kivlihan anyway, so he'd wait.

36

THE CONFERENCE ROOM ON THE PENTHOUSE FLOOR OF THE Drexel building was lined in burl, an expensive wood, but one that Black Jack Drexel had come to appreciate on his stays in Rome. He always put in at the Excelsior and always demanded tower suite 602. All of the paneling in those rooms had been done in burl. It was Il Duce's favorite finishing, and it was said that Mussolini himself had kept a mistress there during the war.

Caroline was led into the enormous room and shown to a seat at a conference table the size of a carrier flight deck. The surface was done in black Zimbabwe granite and polished to a mirrorlike finish. The dark stone reflected coldly against the soft brown wood.

No less than twenty captains of industry were seated around that table: all in their mid-fifties to sixties, all white, and all male. Caroline was the only woman. They nodded to her politely, and she thought to herself that Chanel had been just the right choice. God. She hated these meetings. But this had been a command performance. Besides, she needed to speak with him now, and it had to be done in person. Alone.

There was a preconference buzz in the air. Talk that Clinton was bringing back the investment tax credit. He was about to do a Nixon-to-China move that would shock the Democrats. But the men at this table weren't surprised. They always knew that Bill was their boy. Men like this were paid to live in the upper reaches, beyond the headlines and the polls. To take the broad view. Buy long when everyone else was selling short. One of the younger men, a boorish cutthroat with slicked-back hair and a red foulard tie, leaned in close to Caroline. He asked if she was still seeing that German. Italian, said Caroline. Some kind of count, wasn't he? Untitled, she said. God, the man's breath reeked of garlic and he was wearing Polo Safari. No, said Caroline. That had ended months ago. She was too busy with her work at the university to see anyone on a regular basis. The man smiled, flicking his tongue like a gecko. He pushed a business card toward her. He was in from Darien a few nights a week. He kept an apartment at the Carlysle. Bobby Short was a personal friend. If she ever—

But thankfully, he was cut short when two of the big burl-covered doors swung open. Drexel's secretary, Le-Stadt, pushed in to announce His Eminence.

"John Charles Drexel," he said, and the old lion walked in. He was dressed in a chalk-gray Savile Row tailor-made—a man with the face of a boxer and the regal bearing of the Ambassador to the court of St. James. He didn't bother acknowledging Caroline as he stood at the head of the table. He took a moment to adjust his tie and shoot his cuffs, then he brought the meeting to order.

"All right, gentlemen. Let's get to it. At the top of the agenda we have the pending merger between Drexel Leisure Group and Mitsumo Corp. Now, we've all learned a lesson from the Japanese, and I think you'll agree; the only way to live with them is to know their history."

He shot a look down to the end of the table where Caroline was sitting rock still, her eyes closed.

"Are you listening, Caroline?"

She sprang to life.

"Yes. Yes, of course, Father."

"Very well."

Drexel began to circle the table.

"Now then. The Japs have a term: *Kuromaku.* It translates literally as *black curtain.* The word comes from Bunraku theater, where an unseen wire-puller controls the stage by manipulating puppets from behind a black cloth.

"That's the way old man Mitsumo operates. In the dark with minimum exposure. And that's the way this merger has to take place."

He was getting closer to Caroline now and she touched her neck nervously.

"We all know the record on Japanese takeovers. They own a third of downtown Honolulu, twenty percent of downtown L.A. Christ, they now own the land that this building sits on, and Mitsumo is coming in for a big piece of Drexel Place. A while back, when all this got out in the press, the Japs began to retrench; take a much lower profile. That little fuck Perot didn't help. When the NEEKAY went soft in ninety-four, they started to drop their exposure. Well, thankfully, now they're back."

Drexel stopped behind his daughter and put his hands on her chair. Caroline's heart began to pound.

"There are no two ways about it. We're goddamn undercapitalized in this country. I don't like to admit it, but we need them. We just have to be discreet. From here on, everything happens behind the black curtain."

Caroline could almost feel the heat of his glare on her neck now.

"I've instructed PR to keep the shades down. Mitsumo will come in through their Houston shell. As far as the Street knows, this project is red, white, and blue. We'll

have our people at Salomon work on the SEC. Understood?''

All of the men nodded their heads. But there was nothing
from Caroline. So Drexel squeezed her shoulder. His hands
at the edge of her neck felt cold.

''Yes, Father.''

''Good.''

He bent down now, and came inches away from her face.
She could see the cigar stains on his teeth.

''You wanted to see me. What is it?''

37

MADISON AVENUE WAS PACKED WITH LUNCHTIME TRAFFIC
as Eddie sat in the booth in the window of Soup Burg and
watched the front door of the Drexel building. The street
was in virtual gridlock now as a demolition crew moved
an enormous crane into place. The crane would be fixed
with a wrecking ball. The old building next to the tower
was set to be demolished to make way for Drexel Place.

Eddie wondered how much of New York had been lost
like this. Beautiful buildings with granite facades replaced
by boxes of curtain-wall glass. Landlords, like the one
down on Avenue C, were to blame. But so were the big
developers who put up those eighty story slabs. It was progress, right? Eddie wondered how many people would
sweat in the summer in a building with windows that didn't
open, people sitting at computer terminals breathing recy-
cled air when the AC went down.

And he wondered how many people would die the next
time a fire broke out on the fiftieth floor and water pressure
dropped and the ladder trucks couldn't reach.

He'd been sitting there almost four hours now. He'd read
every paper cover to cover: the *Times*, the *Post*, and the
Daily News. He'd even grabbed *Newsday* off the counter.

Then he'd been through *New York, Esquire,* and *G.Q.*

He didn't usually read the men's fashion magazines, but as he stared down at his rumpled suit, he figured it couldn't hurt. The beeper was burning a hole in his pocket. He still had it switched off. *Christ,* when the fuck was she gonna to come *out?* He'd had so much coffee he'd been to the john four times, and in a hash house like this, there was only so much food you could order before the arteries started to harden.

The owner of the place, a thin reedlike man named Spiros, had been eyeing him like a predatory bird. He kept a toothpick in his mouth as he stood at the register near the door, and every once in a while he would take it out, point it toward Eddie like he was going to say something, and then stick it back in his mouth.

Finally, when the line of lunch traffic started to back up at the door, he came up to Eddie's booth.

"Hey, mister."

"Yeah?" Eddie kept his eyes on the Drexel building.

"You see the booth you're in?"

"Yeah."

"Normal day, I turn that booth over every ten minutes."

"Yeah?"

"You've been nursing your coffee since breakfast."

"Right, and the place has been empty."

"Why do you think?"

"Your cheese danish is bad?"

"No. We make the best in Midtown."

"So?"

"Because of you. That's why this place is so empty."

"What?" Eddie looked up at him now.

"You don't shave. Your suit smells. What the hell kinda person wants to come in here and sit next to you?"

Eddie's first impulse was to clock the guy, but then he looked down at himself and laughed. The poor bastard was right. Eddie looked like he'd just been paroled. No. That's not right. The Department of Corrections wouldn't let a guy leave Riker's like that.

"All right, so how can I make it up to you?

Spiros smiled now like a ferret. "Well, let me see. This booth is a two. Average check, six-fifty, seven dollars. Seven times five an hour . . . Gimme a hundred, we'll call it even."

"What?" Eddie got up. He was about to go toe to toe with the Greek when he spotted Caroline coming out of the tower across the street.

"Look, I don't have time to argue. Here's my business card. Next time some fire inspector comes in here shaking you down for a bribe, call that number. I'll save you a hundred bucks."

He threw down a twenty for the coffee and split, racing across Madison, dodging the traffic as Spiros stared at him, openmouthed.

Caroline started to walk uptown, but she was forced to stop and move into the street. The sidewalk was blocked by the crane being towed into place. So she waited for the traffic as some men in yellow hard hats backed an enormous wrecking ball up to the crane. One of them burned a look into her and rubbed himself.

Finally, Eddie came up behind her.

"How the hell is he, Caroline?"

She froze at the sound of his voice. Then she picked up the pace. But Eddie caught up to her.

"Your father. I thought you said you didn't speak?"

She started to slow down. "We don't. Not normally."

"But you did today."

Caroline stopped and turned around. "Okay, I'll make it simple. I'm on the board of directors. I never go to the meetings. This time, I decided to go."

She started to walk away, but Eddie grabbed her wrist.

"Why? Why now?"

"It's a family matter. None of your concern."

She pushed away, and Eddie stood there.

"Right, and maybe I shouldn't be concerned about Grosvenor, either. The fact that somebody came in and choked him to death with some bungee cord."

That stopped her. "What?" You're saying he was murdered?"

Eddie moved up and nodded. "That's right, but then, you *knew* that didn't you?"

Caroline touched her neck and turned away. "I don't know what you're talking about. I mean, your own father said it was suicide and—"

Eddie grabbed her. "Stop it. You *knew* my old man had it wrong. I saw the look on your face. So I started checking, and guess what? Grosvenor was in L.A. the night of the fire. A half-dozen witnesses saw him. There's no way he burned that mural. Somebody else killed the girl."

They were right in the middle of Midtown Manhattan at noon now, but Caroline didn't hear anything else. Not the traffic noise or the sound of the crane generator or the jack-hammers at the demolition site. She just stared at him. "So, the killer's still out there."

Eddie smiled. "You're getting good at this."

He started to walk away, but she called over his shoulder, "Eddie . . . wait."

He didn't bother to turn around. "If you need help this time, you can call your old man."

He got to the Chevy. He reached into his pocket, pulled out the keys, and started to open the door, when suddenly, she reached out and grabbed his hand. Eddie looked at her. Their faces were inches apart now.

"I haven't been honest with you."

"No shit."

He started to get in, but she stopped him. "Do you want to hear it or don't you?"

Eddie stood there, suspended for a moment, half in the car and half out, leaning on the door as he thought about it. This woman was world-class fucking trouble. He'd probably lost his job, and now what else would he lose? A shanty Mick like him and a woman like that? For all he knew, she was some kind of coconspirator. But he'd never been this close to a face like hers, and he knew that he had to go with it.

"How long is it gonna take?"

"Long enough."

Eddie looked away. Then finally, "All right. Get in."

She walked around to the passenger side and slid across the seat. The skirt of her suit hiked up, and Eddie caught that piece of lace from her garter. Mother of God. It wasn't fair. He'd been awake for too long. His defenses were down. Eddie touched the stubble on his face. He felt like a week's worth of bad news. Then he climbed in beside her, making sure he didn't get too close. He grabbed the bag of take-out from Knossos and the package of Pez on the dash and tossed them into the backseat. The car was a metaphor for Eddie's own life. A swill pile like him. But he glanced to the side and saw her smile, so he popped it in first and took off.

The man standing in the shadows on Madison waited until the Chevy was moving before he lunged forward and hailed a cab. When he got in, he told the driver to stay with the Caprice. Then the man found a Marlboro. He tapped it down on the back of a gold cigarette case and set it on fire with a gold Dunhill lighter.

38

IT WAS AFTER FOUR-THIRTY AND THE STREETLIGHTS HAD
just flashed on along West Fifty-first Street. Caroline was
sitting in a canvas-backed folding chair, staring out the
sixth-floor window of Eddie's apartment while he show-
ered. It might have been a testament to the dimly lit,
one-bedroom crib. It might have been that she needed to
feel the cold air on her face, or maybe it was because she
couldn't bring herself to look him in the eyes, but Caroline
preferred the view of the dingy block between Eighth and
Ninth to the sight of the place where Eddie lived. It was,
like so many apartments in Manhattan, more of a cell than
a home. The reinforced-steel front door was locked in place
by a Fox lock and a pair of dead bolts. A fire escape ran
up the front of the tenement building, and the three windows that faced the street opened out onto the old, rusted
balcony.

The place was an invitation to home invaders who'd
come down from the roof, and Eddie's apartment had been
robbed twice. On the first hit, all they'd taken were a pair
of nine millimeter magazines without bullets. Eddie had
barely moved in then. But in the second break-in he'd lost
a small Toshiba TV and his one possession worth fencing:

a Marantz CD changer he'd purchased from 47th Street Photo with half a month's pay. It wasn't so much the violation of space that hurt Eddie or the loss of a piece of expensive equipment. But inside the Marantz at the time of the boost, Eddie had all six of his King Pleasure CDs and he knew that it would take months, maybe years, to replace them.

So after the second hit, Eddie had broken down and gone in with the landlord to put up the sliding steel gates. They were bolted to hasps with a pair of Yale padlocks. Big ones, too thick for the standard bolt cutter. Being an arson investigator, Eddie had the presence of mind to keep the padlock keys on an eye hook screwed under the windowsill. He'd axed his way into more than a few blazes in his time, only to find the occupants dead, asphyxiated, hanging from the searing hot window gates, unable to locate the keys, trapped like gerbils in their sweltering cages.

Eddie came out of the shower and pulled on the slacks to his blue worsted suit, one of the two suits that he owned. There was a single clean oxford button-down left from the laundry, so he threw that on and grabbed a tie.

It was blue with red and white stripes. Much too thin for the fashion of the moment, but the last thing Eddie Burke cared about was the width of his tie. He threw on some skin bracer and walked into the living room.

Caroline was smoking, and she had one of her exquisite fingers wrapped around a steel window gate. He watched her for a minute and wondered why fires never seemed to break out on Sutton Place. Christ. She was so out of place in Hell's Kitchen. He'd noticed, as they'd entered the neon-lit hallway of the tenement building, how she'd caught the smell of urine against the wall and pretended to ignore it, how she'd taken the six floors of the walk-up without beefing, though he knew that by three she was cursing the cigarettes. Once inside, he'd offered her a Miller Lite. It was the only liquid he had in the place besides tap water. But Caroline had said no. She was okay. He let her get her bearings, watching as she surveyed the empty pizza boxes and Chinese food containers, and then found the folding chair by the window. It was a relic from his time with Mary Rose. Something from her Crate & Barrel phase. One of two matching forest-green director chairs.

All he'd gotten away with from that marriage was the green fold-out sofa, his collection of *National Geo's,* a broken Mr. Coffee machine, and that chair. Not much of a legacy for six years.

Mary Rose had given the other chair to Goodwill, but this one was left in a closet amid Eddie's debris, so she'd missed it.

Now Caroline Drexel was sitting in it with her legs crossed, the skirt discreetly pulled to above her knees. She stubbed out the Gitane and leaned forward, toward the window. Eddie watched as she pushed her hand through the steel gate and under the sill. She let the cold rain touch her fingers, and then she pulled them back. When the rain was coming down hard enough to reflect against the wall, Eddie decided to start.

"You *knew* Grosvenor didn't kill himself, didn't you?"

She hesitated and then nodded. "Yes."

"How come?"

She turned to face him now. "Because of the work he was doing. There were a half-dozen canvases in his loft near completion. He was prepping a show in L.A. That's why he went out of town."

Eddie walked across the room to her.

"All right. So why'd he run from my father up at the lake?"

"Maybe something scared him."

"Or some*one*. Like the killer."

Caroline looked confused. "I don't understand."

Eddie raised his voice now. "Don't you get it? Whoever killed that girl in SoHo set Grosvenor up. Even Big Eddie fell for it. Esther Schine . . . that abortion . . . Grosvenor was the designated hitter for the SoHo death. But there was something *else* in that mural. Something worth killing for."

"Nothing's worth killing for."

"Maybe not, but this isn't over."

He slammed his Smith into the paddle holster at the small of his back and took off toward the door.

"Where are you going?"

"Grosvenor's loft. It's the best shot I've got."

Caroline got up from the chair and then stopped. "Are you sure? Maybe it's better to let it go."

"Do *you* want to take the chance?"

"What do you mean?"

"You said it yourself; the killer's still out there."

Caroline hesitated. "I don't know . . ."

"Yeah, well I do. You can let yourself out. Just slam it."

Caroline stopped and then moved toward the door. She slammed it like he said, and then followed Eddie into the hallway.

"You'll do better if you go there with me."

"How come?"

"I know the man's work."

She pushed past him down the stairs, but Eddie caught up with her on the fifth-floor landing. He took her hand and spun her around.

"You doing this to prove I was wrong?"

Caroline hesitated again and then said, "I'm doing it . . . for my mother."

She turned and headed down toward the street, and Eddie Burke thought to himself how he'd never seen a woman who looked so fucking good under neon light.

39

IT WAS DARK BY THE TIME THEY MADE IT TO THE TOP FLOOR of Grosvenor's loft building. The single bulb in the hallway had gone out, so Eddie had to feel around for the key. Caroline stood shivering on the top-floor stairwell, but finally, Eddie located it atop the transom. He fit it into the lock and turned the dead bolt. The two of them ducked under the police tape designating the crime scene and went inside.

Eddie felt against the brick wall near the door and found the rheostat. A soft orange glow from a series of overhead spots filled up the thirty-by-eighty-foot space, and Caroline squeezed Eddie's arm. He looked at her and saw that she was staring up at the skylight where Grosvenor's body had swung.

Neither of them went toward the wired-glass windows, so neither of them noticed the man below in the street. He stood in the shadows of a meat-packing warehouse and watched through the rain as the top floor lights came on. He saw Caroline's shadow moving against the light upstairs. Then he stepped back under the packing house awning. He tried to engage the gold lighter, but it needed a new flint.

Upstairs on the penthouse floor, Caroline told Eddie that they were lucky. Few artists would have saved any work from sixty years ago, but Grosvenor was anal-retentive. He'd always had a sense of his place in history, and he'd kept every sketch. She gestured to a series of lateral file cabinets.

"His rough work was filed over here."

She led Eddie toward the file drawers and started going through the line drawings and charcoal sketches. They were neatly categorized by date and cross-indexed by subject matter, beginning at the present and moving back over time.

"A guy who has his shoes organized by color, leather type, and season," said Eddie. "I'll bet he keeps his flies in a tackle box with forty-two drawers. He's got every issue of *Art in America* that ever came out, and I'll give you five to ten they're set up in special folios by month and year. This is gonna be a fucking nightmare."

"What do you mean?" said Caroline. "I should think that a person this organized would be a detective's dream."

"Just the opposite," said Eddie.

"I don't understand."

Eddie set down a canvas marked 2/3/91 and started pacing.

"Look. You take somebody like me. I'm the kind who never puts his car keys in the same place twice. I've got ten years of *National Geographics* shoved into U-Haul boxes. There's a pile of mail on my desk I've been meaning to get to since Bush was in office."

"But what's that got to do with—?"

"Predictability. The most important thing in my life is always at the top of the pile. Unless the pile's been turned upside down. Then it's on the bottom. With guys like Grosvenor, you have to figure his systems. And people like that are prone to subsystems and sub-subs. Life isn't complicated enough for them. They have to fill it with pigeonholes. No. We may find what we're after here, but you'd better not have any dinner plans. This could take all goddamn night.''

And he was right. As they went through the sketches, they saw that they were cross-indexed. But not just by year; by subject and period. It wasn't enough to look chronologically. They had to read Grosvenor's mind.

How would a master like him have filed a 1938 mural? Under the WPA? Murals? Labor rallies? No. It wasn't that easy.

Still, as the hours went by and the rain pounded down on the skylights above, Caroline and Eddie stood witness to an extraordinary body of work. Grosvenor wasn't just a stunt painter like Warhol or Lichtenstein, who figured out a bankable style and stayed with it. He had an amazing range—from neorealism to abstract impressionism to deconstructivism—and as they moved through his life, they could see how he'd always kept growing.

It was after midnight when Caroline found it in a file marked Group Projects. The sketch for the two-panel diptych.

"Oh God. Here it is," she said. "*Workers of the World Unite.*"

It was just a pencil rendering, but Caroline could feel its power. The left panel of the sketch showed the pilot, the nurse, and the stevedore. The right panel showed the Farmer, the teacher and the miner. In front of the nurse was a small child. Because they were simple sketches, the faces hadn't yet been defined. But behind the six in the foreground, there was a crowd of workers carrying flags.

Caroline ran her hand along the back of the mural near the factories.

"Here. You can see the influence of Diego Rivera, the Mexican muralist. The flags are Orozco and the farm in the upper right is in the style of Thomas Hart Benton. Both of the symbols say growth, productivity.''

Eddie just shook his head. ''To me it looks like one of those posters from Russia.''

''Yes. It seems strident and propagandistic today, but back then, in the thirties, the labor movement was young. Almost . . . holy to some.''

Eddie rolled his eyes. Comparing Lenin to Pope John Paul II. These goddamn intellectuals. He took out one of the crime scene Polaroids of the burned mural and matched it to the sketch. He compared them both, trying to find a motive for murder. After a while, Caroline shook her head. There was nothing. But then Eddie turned the sketch over.

On the back, it had the names of the four artists who painted the final mural: D. Hampton, A. Grosvenor, E. Schine, and J. *Krasnoff*.

''Krasnoff,'' said Eddie. ''I thought you told me the fourth artist's name was Krane.'' He checked his notebook. ''Julian Krane?''

''That's what it said in the artists' roll book. Maybe Krasnoff was his real name and he Anglicized it.''

As Caroline stared at the sketch, she flashed on her dream. The short, painter with curly brown hair who'd pinched Esther Schine on the ass. The one who pushed away Esther's advances as if to say, ''Not with me, baby-cakes.'' It was clear to her now. This was Julian Krasnoff/Krane.

Eddie grabbed the sketch and started rolling it up.

''What are you doing?'' asked Caroline.

''When I mentioned the name Krane to Esther's brother, I could see that he knew him. Then he stopped. He wouldn't say any more.''

Eddie shoved the sketch into a long paper carrying tube and moved toward the door.

As soon as the lights flashed out up above, the man in

the shadows hurried east down Remson Street. When he got to Hudson, he jumped into the street and hailed a cab. He eased himself down in the backseat of the Checker as the headlights from Eddie's Chevy turned the corner and headed uptown. The man told the driver that there was a fifty in it if he stayed back in traffic but kept with the Chevy.

When the driver, a Sikh named Jamil, looked into the rearview mirror to see who the fare was, the man turned his head and lit a cigarette. The cabbie pointed to a No Smoking sign on his dash, but the man in the back just said, "Hey. You want the Grant? Then shut the fuck up and stay with that car."

Jamil always drove with a curved Gurkha knife. A piece of tempered New Delhi steel with a blade that cut metal like balsa wood. He felt like stopping the car and gutting this fucker, but it had been a slow night downtown with the rain, so he swallowed hard and pushed the red button on the digital meter. When the Chevy was a half a block ahead of them, they roared off.

Eddie hadn't noticed the Checker behind them when he turned left onto Canal Street heading east. He hadn't noticed it in the tangle of rush-hour traffic as he pulled up to the light on Mulberry in Chinatown. But a half-dozen cars on Mott had blocked the intersection as the light went to green on Canal, and when Eddie did a fast end run around them, he saw the Checker screech forward. By the time he got to The Bowery, he was sure.

For years in the forties and fifties, when huge yellow fleets ruled New York, Checker had been the dominant maker of taxis. But they'd lost out of late to Chevys, Chryslers, and Fords. There were even a dozen yellow Peugeots and Saabs now, most owned by small independents with two-and three-vehicle minifleets. With only a handful of Checker garages left, it was something of an event when you saw one of the big, upright, yellow boxes behind you.

They stuck out in traffic. In this case, all the more because of the driver. A man with a dark face and a beard under an orange turban. The European immigrants who had dominated the taxi industry for decades—The Jews and Italians and fast-talking Micks—were gone now. Men with an opinion on anything from Sandy Koufax's earned run average to the security importance of Quemoy and Matsu. Men who had coined the phrase "fuckin' Lindsay" as an epithet to express one's displeasure with life in New York. A phrase they peppered their speech with every time they hit another pothole.

These were men who knew what was wrong with life and freely offered a thousand solutions to fix it. For one thing, you had to put "the animals" behind bars, bring back the death penalty, and get rid of those judges who were letting the killers walk on technicalities. The fact that these technicalities involved the Fourth, Fifth, and Sixth Amendments didn't matter. The city was becoming a "jungle," a "war zone," and a "fuckin' sewer," and the only way to stop it was to keep out "the coloreds."

What an irony it was, thought Eddie as he drove east with Caroline next to him. Those cabbies had financed their flight to the suburbs by selling out to the same Third World immigrants they'd blamed for the chaos. Irish, Italian, and Jewish cab drivers who'd financed their mortgages and put their kids through Boston College and City Baruch by selling their medallions to the very people they'd cursed.

Now the New York taxi industry was a Third World enterprise, dominated by West Indians, Taiwanese, Liberians, Vietnamese, Eastern Bloc emigrés, Koreans, Pakistanis, and Sikhs. Immigrants from countries with a black market gold standard who had gotten out with the tiny ingots taped to their backs. People who could buy a medallion for cash, with no financing and no questions asked. So it was the orange turban on the driver in the Checker behind him that caught Eddie's eye as he spun the Chevy into a radical arc, shooting left up Bowery and then left again along Grand.

The blocks of the old Italian neighborhood, now a virtual Chinese enclave, were a rabbit warren of alleys and narrow streets. And it didn't take Eddie long to lose the Checker as he sped up Lafayette and east across Bowery again before picking up Delancey.

When he was sure that the Checker was no longer behind them, he turned south into Alphabet City and down toward the Jacob Riis Housing Project.

The credits for *Hard Copy* rolled on the old Zenith in the living room when Eddie and Caroline were finally seated across the kitchen table from Nathan Schine. His head was tilted to one side like some old Hebrew judge as he listened to Eddie state his case.

"When I asked you about Julian Krane, you knew who I was talking about, didn't you?"

The old man didn't answer. He opened his eyes and looked over at a commercial for Preparation H on TV.

"Mr. Schine, I need to know this."

But Schine waved him off and cupped his hand over his ear. For some reason, the ad for the hemorrhoid suppressant was the most important thing in his life.

Eddie motioned for Caroline to shut it off, so she got up and went into the living room.

"What the hell'd she do that for?" said Schine.

Eddie grabbed his arm.

"We don't have time for this, Mr. Schine."

The old man jumped up from the table.

"You think you can come into my house and shout at me?"

Caroline came in from the living room and tapped Eddie on the shoulder as if to say, "Let me try."

She went over to Nathan Schine and touched his arm. Schine blinked behind coke-bottle glasses as he took her all in. He might be seventy-eight and his eyes weren't so good, but this was a beautiful woman.

Finally, she touched his hands. The skin was mottled, but his fingers were long and thin. She turned them over. The old man was a mess; hair growing out of his nostrils and ears, a smell coming off an old plaid flannel shirt, but his nails were perfect, like he'd just had a manicure. Caroline smiled and looked around.

"Where's the piano?"

"What?" The old man drew back, surprised that she had something on him.

"You have beautiful hands. A two-octave reach."

"I . . . I don't. I never play here. At the community center, sometimes, but not here."

Caroline smiled again. "I studied for six years. It took me that long to realize that my hands were too small for the concert stage."

"They look pretty nice to me," said the old man. He allowed himself a half smile, then looked away. It was hard to stare a looker like this in the face.

He moved back toward the table and took a sip of Mogen David. Then he poured some into a glass for her. Eddie got up and shook his head. No *way* was she going to drink that shit. But she did, without a wince. Then she smiled.

"I'll have another."

Nathan Schine pulled his lips back, revealing a set of yellowed false teeth. He poured again. Then, when he set the bottle down, he gestured toward Eddie.

"So what are you doing with him? This cop who raises his voice in my house?"

"I'm an art professor," said Caroline. "I've studied your

sister's work, and I'm worried. People are dying because of that mural.''

Nathan let all that sink in and then nodded. ''I always knew there was something about that picture.''

Eddie moved into the kitchen now, leaning against the counter. Caroline looked up at him and continued. ''We think maybe an artist named Krane was connected. He called himself Krasnoff as well. Did you know him?''

The old man hesitated.

''Yeah. Krasnoff. Krane. Julie had a thing about passing. Couldn't live with his Russian name, so he changed it.''

Eddie risked a question now. ''How well did you know him?''

''He and my Esther were like this.'' The old man crossed his fingers.

''They were lovers?'' said Caroline.

Schine raised his eyebrows. ''You kidding? Julie was *feygele*.''

Caroline shook her head. She didn't understand.

''You know . . . gay now they call it. He was like another brother to Esther.''

Eddie sat down at the table. ''Do you have any idea where we can find him?''

Schine was about to get up when he stopped. ''What? You didn't know?''

Eddie and Caroline shook their heads.

Nathan Schine got up and moved toward the window. He opened it up and looked down the fifteen stories. The curtains blew in from the freezing wind off the East River, and he cocked his head toward it.

''He went out a window like this one.''

''What?'' said Eddie. ''What are you talking about?''

''I'm talking about your Irish friend, Mr. Burke: McCarthy. He put Julie's name on a list. *Pink,* they called him. A fellow traveler.''

Schine stared out at an oil barge going up the river.

"One day he's a big art director on Madison Avenue, next day, *pffft*, he can't get any work. So he goes to some office building, opens a window, and jumps out."

"He killed himself?"

Nathan Schine nodded, and Eddie shot a look at Caroline. "Another suicide. Let's go."

40

THE BELL IN ST. ANDREW'S CHURCH WAS STRIKING TEN when Big Eddie Burke leaned on his cane outside the entrance to One Police Plaza. He'd gotten there five minutes early, and he was kibbitzing with Tommy Haggerty, a uniformed sergeant who'd stood guard like Cerebus in the headquarters lobby for the last fifteen years. They'd been talking about the old days and how the young recruits weren't worth a shit.

Tommy said that it hadn't been right since the sixties. "You know . . . Vietnam and the drugs."

"When I started," he said, "the first thing I wanted to know was how to reload my goddamn .38 under fire. Today, the first thing a rookie asks you is whether bridgework is covered by the dental plan. We got a house fulla fuckin' weenies upstairs, Chief. It's tragic."

Big Eddie nodded, not agreeing, but allowing the sergeant to make his point. Then he got philosophical. He asked Tommy (who had almost thirty in) what he thought the most important quality was in a cop—a good cop.

Tommy flashed the Irish smile and shot back, "There's no question. Not even close. Iron balls. You can't show them fear. You've got to be able to stare them down, even if you've pissed in your drawers. The perception of command is the thing. You lose that, you surrender the line.''

Big Eddie nodded again. He'd always been generous with the opinions of other men. Always a tolerant leader except when it came to his son. He took a few seconds and leaned on the cane, allowing Tommy to give back the question.

''So what do *you* think, Chief?''

Big Eddie smiled and then cocked his head.

''To me, a good cop is somebody who admits that he's wrong. It took me a lot of years and a shitload of cases to come to that, but it's true.''

Haggerty nodded deferentially. He was about to ask Eddie how he got injured, when the night bell rang outside.

Big Eddie turned on the cane and saw Eddie outside the glass door with Caroline.

''Kid's got your taste in women, Chief.'' Haggerty winked as he buzzed them in.

Eddie came into the hallway and hugged his father.

''Sorry to get you up, Pop. But—''

''You don't have to say it. I blew the call.''

He turned to Caroline. ''I don't know which to feel worse about: calling a murder a suicide or having a son that's smarter than me.''

She smiled at Eddie as they walked inside toward the elevators.

They were about to go upstairs when Big Eddie caught something out of the corner of his eye. He turned and looked through the curtain-wall glass of the hallway, out toward the plaza by Borough Hall. There, in the shadows, he saw a flicker of light. It was a man. He was lighting a cigarette.

When the man saw Big Eddie looking at him, he ducked into the shadows.

A few minutes later, Big Eddie and his son were back

in a special section of the records room. Here they stored the dead files, tens of thousands of cases from all five boroughs that had remained unsolved and thus open over the past ninety-five years. It was 1903 when they'd started keeping track, and like many police departments, the NYPD had recently assigned a team of detectives from the Major Case Squad whose sole job it was to shake the old cases. To reexamine the evidence, and contact the witnesses again. The theory was that on open felonies, especially homicides, the assailants might let their guard down. Or maybe witnesses, chilled from talking at the time of the murder, might now come forth. But now, most leads came from science.

There was AFIS, a new Automated Fingerprint Identification System for matching old prints and DNA, the genetic identification process that had figured so prominently in the O. J. Simpson case.

Major Cases had broken a number of derelict felonies this way, and more than a few men, wrongfully convicted, had been freed when the new DNA evidence conflicted with the trial package. Unfortunately, the squad had not yet gotten back to 1938 and the strange, bloody murder of Esther Schine. Nor had they looked into a death from 1952 that was still open but listed as a probable suicide.

Big Eddie told them that the cases were cross-filed under Suicides, but the name Krasnoff would be faster. And after fifteen minutes in the files, he found it.

"Here it is."

The file, on microfiche, said J. Krasnoff, WM 698/52—E, meaning that the victim was a white male. The six hundred and ninety-eighth medical examiner's death in 1952. Big Eddie handed the film to Eddie, who threaded it up on a machine.

"Stop when you get to October," said Big Eddie.

Eddie moved through dozens of cases projected on the

screen of the machine. Caroline started to light a Gitane and then saw the No Smoking sign, so she stopped. She was leaning in over Eddie as he sat at the machine, and he could smell her perfume. Tonight she was wearing Panther.

Finally, Eddie stopped. He moved through October until he came to a black-and-white crime scene photo. It showed a man's body sprawled on the roof of a building.

"Right. Here we go. Krasnoff. 10/12/52. He died on Columbus Day."

"Is that important?" said Caroline.

"Not unless he was Italian," said Big Eddie.

She thought to herself, What is it about the Irish? The way they always put comedy next to death.

Eddie read from the caption on the picture.

"Says here, P.O. twenty-first floor."

"What's that mean?" said Caroline.

"Point of origin," said Big Eddie. "It was taken from the window he jumped from."

"Where was that?"

"A building in Midtown."

Just then, Caroline started touching her throat.

Eddie studied the picture.

"It looks like he fell onto the roof of the building next door."

He moved the cursor on the machine and asked for a printout of the file.

Big Eddie picked up the copy from the printer and handed it to him.

"Yeah," said Eddie. He was reading now. "Subject body found on eleventh floor roof at 480 Madison."

Caroline stopped rubbing her neck. All the color had left her face. She looked like she was about to be sick.

But Eddie didn't notice. He kept reading. "The deceased, reportedly despondent over the recent loss of his job, went to the twenty-first floor and leaped to his death."

"You can get a pretty big headache from a ten-story drop," said Big Eddie. "Where'd he go out from?"

"Four hundred eighty-two Madison," said Eddie.

Suddenly, Caroline got up to leave, but she stumbled.

"Hey," said Big Eddie. "You all right? You look like you're ready to pass out."

Caroline started to slip, but Eddie caught her.

"What is it? What's wrong?"

"I'm . . . I feel sick . . ." She was reeling now, so Big Eddie intervened.

"Look, Kid. All this has been brutal for her. Get her out of here."

Eddie looked at his father's cane.

"What about you?"

"You kidding? I used to work here. I'll catch a ride with the boys."

"You sure, Pop?"

"Come on. There's nothing we can do till tomorrow. I'll meet you at the base. Nine o'clock."

"But what about Kivie?"

"Don't worry. I'll deal with Kivlihan." Big Eddie smiled. "Hey. Maybe I can redeem myself." He looked at Caroline. "Go on. Get her home."

Eddie nodded and hugged his father. He looked at Caroline and wondered why she'd suddenly gotten so ill. Sure, she'd been through a lot. But she'd already seen two DOAs: Alex Sloane, the art restorer, and then Grosvenor. She'd held it together through that. So why now? Why buckle at the sight of a guy who'd jumped to his death forty-five years ago?

Eddie wanted to ask her, but it wasn't the time. She was squeezing hard on his arm as he led her out.

Neither of them knew that there was a man downstairs waiting for them. A man with a gold Dunhill lighter, standing in the shadows of Borough Hall.

But Big Eddie had seen him, and he was wondering if he'd still be there when he got down to the street.

41

BIG EDDIE WAVED GOOD-BYE TO CAROLINE AND HIS SON AS he limped on the cane toward a line of squad cars just going out on the late tour.

He recognized one of the uniforms, a mid-fifties sergeant who used to work the Four-three named Tony Costello.

"Hey, Tone. You got time to give an old cop a ride?"

"What? I'm gonna turn *you* down?" said the cop. "Get in."

Big Eddie hobbled over to the shotgun door of the blue and white. When he pulled it open, Costello noticed the cane.

"What the hell happened to your leg?"

"I cut myself shaving."

Costello laughed.

Big Eddie was just about to duck into the unit when he stopped and shot a look over toward Borough Hall. It was that guy again. Standing there in the shadows.

The man hesitated and then, as if he'd seen the old cop watching him, he darted back behind a column.

Big Eddie turned to Costello.

"Hey Tone, I just remembered something I left upstairs. Gimme a rain check, will you?"

"You sure?"

"Yeah, I'll catch a ride with one of the other guys."

"No problem, Chief. Good to see you." He jerked his head toward the cane. "Listen, do me a favor. Next time you do your legs, use a Lady Remington. They don't cut."

Big Eddie laughed and tapped the roof of the unit as Costello pulled away.

He waited a second and took in a lungful of air. He touched his hand to the side of his neck. Christ. His pulse was racing. He looked over across St. Andrew's Square. Eddie was talking to Caroline near the steps of Federal Court.

By the book, he should call his son, do this with backup, but Big Eddie Burke had thrown the book away decades ago. He opened his coat and pulled out his old Police Special. Most of the young turks packed nines now. Nine-millimeter S&Ws, Glocks, and Sig-Sauers. Semiauto. Ten or thirteen to a mag instead of six. Rapid-loading, rapid-fire. They were nothing against Ingrams and Mac-10's, but they sure beat the six-shot double-action .38s. They had to. The rules of engagement had changed. The feds had even taken to using Colt nines, fully automatic machine pistols. They could unload a clip of thirty-two in four seconds. That was the gun of choice now at DEA.

But Big Eddie still had his snub-nose. Retired cops held on to the right to carry concealed. And if he was going to do this, the simple revolver was all he had. So he flipped out the cylinder and checked it. Then he took in another deep breath and moved off toward Borough Hall.

The Municipal Building. It was one of the boldest government enclaves in New York: rococo, ornate, a wedding cake of Venetian arches that rose three stories above an open portico at street level. At the crown of the cake was a gold-leaf statue of Gabriel blowing his trumpet. Like most of New York, it had fallen into disrepair until the late

1980s, when the city began to restore it. The two-year project that was supposed to cost twenty-two million had risen
to more than sixty and they were still arguing about the
masonry bids eight years later. It was fitting for a building
that looked down on the old Tweed Courthouse, New
York's true monument to malfeasance and greed.

Borough Hall was half dark and in shadow now. Big
Eddie watched as the lights of the cars on the Brooklyn
Bridge played across the granite portico.

He heard a noise and looked up to see pigeons roosting
under one of the capitals. Then he moved into the dark
below the portico and heard it again.

He thought about subway traffic. There was an entrance
for the R train at the center of the building, but the red light
was on, so the token booth downstairs must be closed.

Big Eddie looked through the arches over at the courthouse. Eddie was still there, talking to Caroline. He thought
again about calling him, but decided to move ahead. There
was still a part of this case that belonged to him, and he
wouldn't let go. He leaned on the cane with his left hand
and squeezed the grip on the .38.

Just then, he heard a noise in the corner of the portico,
like a coin had just dropped. He started to move toward it
when suddenly the man lunged out from behind him. He
kicked the cane out from Big Eddie's hand and grabbed
the gun.

The two of them struggled now, Big Eddie trying to grab
him around the neck. The assailant was a much younger
man. Mid-thirties maybe. The old cop got close to his face
for a second and he could smell the nicotine. Then the gun
fell away and Big Eddie had him around the throat, squeezing, choking the guy with his enormous hands. The man
went down on his knees. He was gagging now. Big Eddie
was sure that the guy was done, and then the bastard
reached down and found the cane. He brought it up in one

fast, lethal jab and bore the butt into Big Eddie's stomach.

The wound from the surgery ruptured immediately, and the old cop spat blood. He dropped to his knees and let go of the guy's neck. Then the sonovabitch came at him again, using the cane like a bat, slamming it into his stomach as Big Eddie knelt on the cold brick floor and tried to call out.

But it was too late. The blood was bubbling up through his esophagus.

The man tossed the cane away, and with one swift kick from his boot, he landed a final blow to Big Eddie's stomach. The legendary chief of detectives collapsed on the portico floor and started to go into shock.

The man laughed and bent down, rifling Big Eddie's pockets. The old cop spat blood and started to shake. Finally, the killer found it . . . the wallet. He flipped it open and saw the gold shield. Then he looked at the words embossed in gold and spat bile.

"Chief of detectives . . . fuck."

He tore the badge off and tossed down the wallet in disgust, shoving the trophy in his pocket as he turned to go, not running, just walking away from the crime scene, because he knew that he owned it now.

But there was something he didn't count on. The bulldog strength of will inside the old Irish cop. And Big Eddie was crawling now, ripped with pain and aspirating on his own blood, but he had to get to it, had to put his hands on that .38.

The assailant would be out of his line of fire in five seconds, but he kept on crawling and then he was on it, curling his fingers around the grip and lifting it, trying to focus on the fugitive as he walked away in the dark.

The arrogance of the fuck, thinking that the old cop was finished. And then, Big Eddie sucked in hard and found the trigger.

Another breath and he squeezed off a shot. The sound cracked out like a bomb detonating under the portico.

Suddenly, fifty yards across St. Andrew's Square, Eddie Burke snapped to attention. He heard the echo from the report and saw the smoke from the muzzle flash under the arches. He was running now, and he turned to scream back at Caroline.

"Call for help!"

She ran toward the squad cars at One Police Plaza as Eddie tore off toward the sound of the shot.

When he got to his father, Big Eddie was hemorrhaging.

"Oh Christ, Pop!"

He picked up the old man's head and cradled it in his arms.

"What happened? Who did this?"

Big Eddie looked up at his son and coughed.

"You were right, kid. The fucker's still out there."

"Don't talk."

Just then, Eddie heard sirens.

"There's help coming."

He hugged his father as Big Eddie looked up at him.

"I think I hit him."

Big Eddie coughed up blood.

"Christ, Pop, don't talk."

But the old man was in extremis now and he knew it.

"No. I've gotta . . . I've gotta say this . . ."

"Come on. Please . . ."

"You may think that you're *Fire*, kid, but you're not."

"Okay."

"You're a *cop*. . . . You hear me, Eddie . . . ?"

"Yeah."

"It's in your blood. Only . . . you're *better* than me."

He was shaking now.

"You always were . . ."

"Pop?"

There was another cough, but Eddie knew this was different. He had heard it a dozen times as he carried bodies out of blazing tenements and burning bodegas. The final purge. The death rattle. And Big Eddie Burke, the chief, the legend, let it go.

"Pop. No . . . God *damn* it."

Eddie threw himself over his father's body now as an EMS unit roared up through St. Andrew's Square and screamed into the portico, followed by a half-dozen uniforms.

Eddie laid him down on the granite as the EMS guys tried to give CPR, but it was too late. The paramedic looked up at Eddie and shook his head.

Caroline Drexel stood at the edge of Borough Hall, falling back in the shadows as the EMS team pulled out the body bag. She was shivering, almost paralyzed, because now, for the first time, she understood what this meant.

It had been pulling at her for days now, ever since she'd looked down on Grosvenor's body, the parts of it starting to come into focus. Just like her dream. She'd suspected it when she first saw the mural. After listening to Helen's tapes, she was almost positive. And then, when she saw the picture of Krasnoff's body lying sprawled on that rooftop, she was sure.

Caroline caught sight of Eddie and started to walk toward him. Then she stopped. What good would it do? Whatever this was, she would have to finish it now on her own. Besides, she'd always been weak, unable to cope with death. Always at her worst when people needed her most. Caroline knew exactly what she should do. She should walk up to Eddie and hold him. She should stay at his side through the grief. That's what her mother would have done.

But she wasn't made of that. Caroline knew now that she had come from the other side of the tree. So she pulled up the collar on her trench coat, walked out into Chambers Street, and hailed a cab.

42

CAROLINE STUBBED OUT THE GITANE IN THE ASHTRAY AND reached for the pack, but it was empty. There were ten other butts in the tray, all marked with red on the tips from her lipstick. She'd been chain-smoking now since just after 2:00 A.M. when the guard from security at the Amsterdam gate opened her office. Shit. She searched the drawers of her desk for another pack but couldn't find one. Her office was dark, lit by the green glass of the old banker's lamp on her desk. The black onyx Deco clock now said 4:52 A.M., and she still didn't have it. The thought had come to her on the way uptown in the taxi, so she'd told the driver not to stop at Sutton Place, to continue up to One hundred and sixteenth. The driver had flashed a look at this blonde in the rearview mirror and wondered what kind of white woman in a brown leather trenchcoat rides to Harlem at two o'clock in the morning.

But then, when she said it was Amsterdam, he'd understood. Columbia. Fine. One of them.

She'd been searching for it, almost frantic ever since. It *had* to be here. But she'd gone through two dozen files on the mural projects and she still couldn't find it. She was beginning to think that maybe it was in one of the files in her library at home when she heard the noise outside. It was somewhere on a lower floor, like a door closing on one of the stairwells. She switched off the light and sucked in hard. A few seconds went by as her heart raced. The guard from security said that he'd lock up the building when he left, but that wouldn't stop the killer of Big Eddie Burke.

She waited in the dark. Maybe it was the cleaning man. She'd seen his cart in the hallway when the guard let her in. Sure, he was probably finishing up. He'd come for the cart. So she switched the light on again and went back to looking.

Then the noise came again, on a higher floor, and she was sure there was somebody out there. Wait . . . on the nights she'd worked late, hadn't the janitor always finished by midnight? He'd left his cart behind once before and picked it up the next night.

There were footsteps in the corridor now. Jesus. Caroline switched off the light and dropped down below her desk. Her heart pounded.

Should she risk the call to security? No. Then she looked up toward her office door and her heart sank. Mother of God. It was unlocked.

The footsteps came closer, so she got up, rushed to the door, and threw the dead bolt. It made a noise so loud, she could hear the echo out in the hallway, and the footsteps stopped. Damn it. How could she be so stupid? She looked around her office now, frantic, searching for some kind of weapon. Then she saw it, the metal nail file on the desk near her purse. It wouldn't kill, but maybe if she could get up the courage to push it into his face . . .

She walked to the desk and grabbed the file. Then she tiptoed back toward the frosted glass door and stood behind it as the footsteps resumed in the hall. Footsteps from rubber soles. Heavy, deliberate steps, like a man. She held her breath as he came up outside and tried the doorknob. It turned, but the door held firm. Caroline was trembling now, but the man seemed to turn away. The footsteps started to move back down the hall, and she sighed. Then they stopped. She heard the wheels squeak on the janitor's cart and then he came back to the door and SMASH . . . the frosted glass broke as his hand came through, covered with a cleaning rag he had picked off the cart.

The hand shot to the dead bolt and turned it, forcing open the door as Caroline screamed. The man pushed in, grabbing her from the back and covering her mouth.

He switched on a flashlight and it burned in her eyes as she stabbed out with the nail file, but the man slapped it to the floor with the light.

She struggled with all she had, knowing that this man would hurt her. She'd seen what he'd done to Grosvenor and Alex Sloane.

Caroline reached her hand back, trying to rake him across the face with her nails, and then, when he pulled away, his hand suddenly went to the light switch and the overhead neons flashed on. She looked back and there, with his hand to his mouth, signaling for her to be quiet, stood Eddie Burke.

"You!" She almost screamed it out in relief.

"Keep it down. I had to do a B and E to get in here."

"But how did you know I was . . ."

"I didn't. The doorman said you weren't home yet, so I took a chance, drove up here, and saw the light in your office."

Caroline dropped back against the wall and exhaled hard. Then she thought about it.

"Your father . . . he's . . . ?"

But Eddie ignored her, pushing into the office.

"You know who the killer is. Don't you?"

Caroline shot a look to him. "No. I . . . Why would I . . . ? No . . ."

She walked toward her desk and took one of the butts out of the ashtray. She flicked some dead ash from the tip and lit it, nervously exhaling smoke.

She watched now as Eddie looked the office over. He saw the pile of art books and the files; dozens of them opened, dog-eared, and marked with yellow Post-its as if she'd been looking for something. Then he spotted the ashtray full of butts. All she could think of to say was, "I ran out of cigarettes."

Suddenly, Eddie spun around and grabbed her silk blouse.

"Stop running this shit. You *know*. It has something to do with this Krasnoff, doesn't it?"

She shook her head, but Eddie twisted the blouse at her neck.

"*Doesn't* it?"

She started to say something, then hesitated.

Eddie squeezed even harder.

"Tell me!"

She didn't move.

"*Tell me!*"

She couldn't speak. And so Eddie let go and turned away.

"My father's *dead*."

Caroline was in a trance. "I know . . ." She reached out to touch him and then stopped.

There was a moment and then Eddie turned to her. "Please. Just tell me the fucking *truth*."

Another moment as she stared into space and then: "All right. Yes . . ."

"Yes what?"

She dropped back into her chair.

"*Yes, it has something to do with Krasnoff.*"

Slowly now, almost imperceptibly, she began to weep.

Eddie pulled away from the desk and went to the window.

"All this time . . . Why the fuck did you hold back on me?"

"I didn't know for sure till tonight."

"Yeah. Well, you know *now*. Start talking."

There was a long pause. Finally, she looked up at him, shaking her head.

"Four hundred eighty-two Madison Avenue . . ."

"Yeah?"

"The building where Krasnoff died . . ."

"What about it?"

"My fa . . . my *father* . . ."

"Your father *what?*"

"He owns it."

Eddie reeled as the shock of it registered. His jaw dropped. Then he shot a look to his watch. Almost five A.M. He jerked his head for her to follow him, but she wouldn't move. He grabbed her arm, killed the lights, and pulled her out of the office.

43

THE SUN WAS JUST BEGINNING TO STAB THROUGH THE TOWers of Midtown Manhattan when Eddie and Caroline pulled up in his Chevy outside 482 Madison Avenue. It was an old twenty-one story building next to The Drexel Tower. Granite. Prewar. The kind of thick, impregnable office structure that had lined both sides of Madison until the glass boxes began to go up. An edifice that reflected America in the late 1930s: confident, imposing, and built to endure.

Only on this morning, it was different. When Eddie and Caroline exited the Caprice, they found a plywood wall across the mouth of the building. A fifteen-story crane stood at the edge of the sidewalk while a team of men fixed a round, ten-ton slab of concrete to its cable. Today, 482 Madison, the once-invincible landmark on Advertising Row, was about to go down.

Eddie looked up at the wrecking ball.

"How long has he owned it?"

"Since the forties. He had an office here. It was one of the first buildings he bought."

"Yeah, well, they're about to wreck it."

He led Caroline up to the plywood wall where a two-story sign sat atop an artist's rendering of the enormous new complex. It said:

Drexel Place
The Madison Avenue
of Tomorrow

Eddie and Caroline started to move toward the building when the foreman, a big Black man, stopped them.

"Where you think you're goin'?"

"Inside," said Eddie.

"No way. This fucker's coming down."

Eddie flashed his FDNY badge.

"I'm here to inspect it."

He started to pull Caroline into the hallway, but the foreman blocked their way.

"Uh-uh. We got all our permits."

He looked at the crane.

"That rig's costin' me five bills an hour. I got no time for delays."

Just then, one of the demo crewmen leaned out of a nearby trailer. He called down to the foreman.

"Call on two, boss. That carting guy."

The foreman nodded for Eddie and Caroline to follow him.

"Over here."

He led them over to the trailer.

"You wait."

He went into the trailer and picked up the phone.

"Yeah. Yeah . . ."

The big man was screaming at somebody about transformers. The guy he was talking to was called Carmine. The foreman had two Dumpsters full of electrical capacitors and transformers he needed hauled away. Apparently, this Carmine was asking an arm and a leg because they were full of PCBs, a toxic substance that caused cancer. By law, waste like that had to be buried in special clay-lined land-fills, and the closest one to Manhattan was in Buffalo, New York.

But it didn't matter what this Carmine asked for, thought Eddie, he'd get his price. There was no competition because Carmine was Mob.

For years now the Mafia, which controlled the garbage industry in New York, had taken over carting as well. You had to deal with them. If you were wrecking a building or renovating a loft and you needed a Dumpster to take it away, there was no other choice. The city didn't handle that much industrial waste, so you were locked into paying an exorbitant fee to a carting company controlled by one of New York's five families.

It was price-fixed, noncompetitive extortion. But that's how it worked. Oh sure, you could try to beat it. You'd go to the Yellow Pages and start calling. Comparing prices. Shopping around. There was AAA Carting and Lew-Jac Disposal or St. Albans Refuse. In fact, there were sixty-eight licensed carters in the city of New York. Only they didn't quote prices. They didn't compete. At every number you called, some guy would answer the phone—some ga-vone from Bensonhurst—and instead of quoting a rate sheet for so much a yard, he'd ask your address. First the zip code, then the street and the block number. And as soon as you told him, he'd say something like, "That's Capri's block."

You'd say, "Who?"

And the guy would say "Capri Carting, fuckhead."

Then he'd slam the phone down. And this would happen over and over. It happened to Eddie once when he was calling to get bids on a cleanup after a fire in a city-owned building. The place was down on Hester Street on the Lower East Side. A two-story corner lot taxpayer building with stores below and offices above. It had burned once then turned into a shooting gallery. One of the junkies got careless while freebasing, and the place had gone up. So Eddie started calling the carting companies. Pretty soon, he found out that if the city was going to hire a carter, they'd have to deal with S&V Environmental Services of Ozone Park Queens. Hester Street was their block.

Eddie checked it out with Dinny Walsh and learned that S&V carting was really Salvatore and Vinnie Falcone, two underbosses of the Luchese crime family. A year ago they'd been indicted for hauling waste oil laced with toxic chemicals to Wilkes Barre, Pennsylvania, where they pumped it down the bore hole to a mine shaft.

They'd made hundreds of runs in the dead of night, dumping tens of thousands of gallons of toluene, benzene, arsenic, and dibenzofuranes, even a little dioxin, paying off some shlub in a gas station where the bore hole was located and filling the mine shaft with liquid cancer. Night after night they came, until one night the ground couldn't hold any more. The mine shaft ruptured and the shit poured into the Susquehanna River.

Sal and Vinnie pleaded nolo (no contest), and got six months suspended even though they'd probably ruined the shellfish breeding grounds of the Upper Chesapeake Bay for the next hundred years.

Eddie couldn't believe it.

"Sure," said Dinny. "They were assertin' their property rights."

"What the fuck are property rights?" asked Eddie.

So Dinny told him the story. How the Mob, which ran garbage, got into a fucking war in the early sixties over which family would get the contract to haul away trash from this new complex in lower Manhattan they were building. Place called the World Trade Center.

With two of the biggest office towers on earth and a daily

population of 35,000 workers, you were talking a mountain of swill here, and the company that hauled it would own a contract worth millions.

So Lucheses started whacking Gambinos, and *they* started whacking the Genoveses, and pretty soon the bodies of young Ginzaloons were dropping like pieces of manicotti all over the city. It was a bloodbath that lasted twenty-six months, with a death toll of almost fifty before the five dons held a sit-down.

They met, said Dinny, at a diner in Paterson, New Jersey. And in between plates of stuffed shells, they used the Yellow Pages zip code map to divide Manhattan into zones of property rights, assigning each block to a different capo in a different family. All five families got a piece of World Trade, and soon there was peace again.

The property rights in the Garment District were so valuable that capos would leave them in their wills to their sons. So, too, the rights outside the stock exchanges, where Dumpsters full of ticker tape hit the alleys each day. And don't forget Madison Avenue, where they turned out tons of ad copy and other white-collar waste.

So Eddie had to laugh at this foreman if he thought he was going to muscle some made guy named Carmine into a price. Besides, after he took the demo company's ten grand, he'd probably drive the Dumpsters to the parking lot behind Toys "R" Us in Cherry Hill and flush the shit down the sewer.

I mean, why waste time and money on a haul to some fucking clay-lined landfill in Buffalo, right? Nobody would be the wiser until clusters of leukemia started showing up among school kids in southern New Jersey. But who the hell would ever put it onto the Mob?

And it hurt Eddie to know all this because his own grandfather, his mother's father, had come from Palermo. Guiseppe DeAngelo. A small, kind man with white hair, a

droopy mustache, and coal-black eyes. He used to call
Eddie *Vinzengrile* which meant *scamp*, and he would bring
him round little chocolates in gold foil wrappers. Eddie
called him Nanno, and he loved the old man, loved how
he smelled of Old Spice, and he kept all that gold foil in a
ball until the day Nanno died. His grandfather was an honest, hardworking Sicilian. But every single person who
came from that island had to live with this fucking curse.
La Mafia was the stain on their heritage. A black mark on
the legacy of all Italo-Americans. The one thing that separated them from the glory that was Rome; from Marcus
Aurelius, da Vinci, Michelangelo, and Marconi.

Eddie Burke was the progeny of two separate cultures,
the Micks and the Eye-Tyes, two disparate immigrant
groups who crawled onto Ellis Island with nothing in common except the figure of a dying man nailed to a cross.

Though he actually liked Pavarotti, and though he had a
secret passion for veal scaloppini and cold meatball subs,
Eddie suppressed that part of his blood until times like this,
when it came back to haunt him. His dominant gene might
be Irish, but he was always his mother's son. Mary De-
Angelo's boy. Little Eddie. And it seemed that now Eddie
spent half his life cleaning up behind the murder and may-
hem caused by these twisted Sicilian men.

But that's how it was. Life in the big city. And as he
waited by the trailer out on Madison Avenue, Eddie had to
laugh. This big African-American didn't know what the
fuck he was dealing with here. The foreman screamed at
Carmine one last time and slammed the phone down. When
he got out to Madison Avenue, Eddie Burke and Caroline
Drexel were gone.

44

THE LOBBY OF THE OLD BUILDING WAS LIT WITH A SINGLE sixty-watt bulb in a wire cage. The walls had been stripped of all marble. Only one elevator was working when Eddie and Caroline walked in. They hit the up button and the door opened. The walls of the elevator, once covered in burnished hardwood, were also naked, taken down to the three-quarter ply. Outside in the street, they heard the voice of the foreman screaming to one of his men, so Caroline stabbed at the button for twenty-one, and they started to go up.

They stepped off on the twenty-first floor, and Eddie looked left, then right. The place was dimly lit with another sixty-watt bulb. There was just enough light for the demolition crew to do its salvage work inside. But Eddie had walked into many an abandoned building in his time, and he was ready.

He switched on a quartz-halogen spot and pointed to the right.

"Krasnoff fell from the downtown side of the building." He motioned to Caroline. "Over here. Come on."

The two of them moved down the half-darkened hallway while outside, in the street down below, the crane operator engaged the diesel engine and threw the up lever forward on the winch. Wheels turned, rusted five-inch round cable creaked, and the huge concrete wrecking ball started to rise.

Back on twenty-one, Eddie stopped and listened.

"The crane. We don't have much time."

At the end of the hallway, they came to an old-fashioned 1950s frosted glass door. It read:

Drexel Industries

Eddie tried the door. It was locked. He started to go for his lock picks when he heard the diesel engine again. There wasn't much time.

"Breaking and entering. Twice in one day."

He used the quartz-halogen spot to smash the glass.

"But it wouldn't be criminal trespass, would it? I mean, after all, you *own* the place."

"My *father* owns it," said Caroline as she stepped through the door frame and into the office.

Eddie looked around and found the light switch. He flicked on a bank.

"Good, there's still some AC in the place."

As they walked through the old office complex, they heard a siren.

"What's that?" said Caroline, squeezing Eddie's arm.

"The all-clear warning."

They moved down a central corridor past office after empty office. All that was left were the paint marks on the floor where the old desks had been. A few phone jacks were still visible, but otherwise, the place had been stripped to the carpet padding.

Finally, at the end of the corridor, they came to what must have been the head office. The door was open, so they moved inside. Right away, Eddie went to the windows and opened the Krasnoff file.

Down below in the building lobby, a demo crewman paced back and forth. He checked his watch and waited for the elevator to come down from twenty-one. Damn it. He could have *sworn* that the car was in the lobby a few minutes ago. Anyway, when it came, he stepped in and hit two. When the door opened on the second floor, he jumped out and yelled.

"All clear." He listened, to make sure that the floor was deserted. Then he moved up to the next one.

Upstairs, Eddie took the death picture of Krasnoff out of the file. He opened the center window in the big thirty-by-forty-foot office suite and looked down.

There, ten floors below, he could see it . . . the roof of the adjacent building. He looked back at the "suicide" photo of Krasnoff. The scenes were identical.

"This is where he fell from."

"Are you certain?"

Eddie nodded.

Caroline looked stunned.

Outside the office, the elevator door opened and the demo crewman leaned out. He looked down the hallway and spotted the broken glass in the door to the right. He should have gone to check it, but the foreman would have his ass if this place wasn't empty in five. So he yelled out, "All clear."

Eddie heard him and pulled in from the window. "They're starting. We better get out of here."

Caroline was staring out the window, almost paralyzed. "What is it?"

There was no response, so Eddie shook her.

"What the hell's wrong?"

She could hardly get the words out.

"This was . . . this was my father's office."

"The whole complex says Drexel."

"No. This was the place where he *worked*. Where his desk was. I remember."

"So Krasnoff knew your father?"

She nodded.

"Okay, so he knew him. He probably met him through your mother. So what?"

"He didn't just know him. He . . ."

"What? What are you trying to say?"

Caroline was frozen now.

"That he *killed* him?"

Before she could answer, the lights went out.

"What was that?"

"They just cut the power," said Eddie.

The siren blared again down below.

"Look," said Eddie. "There's no time for this. We have to get out of here."

He grabbed Caroline's hand and started to pull her out, but she jerked back.

"No."

"Come on. They're about to start wasting this place."

"No. I have to *face* this."

The siren was roaring now down below.

"Face what? You father's a billionaire. Christ, even in the fifties he was stinking rich. Why in hell would a guy like that take a low-rent painter like Krasnoff and shove him out a window?"

Caroline just stared into space.

"Maybe because of the Witch Hunt."

"What? McCarthy?"

Caroline nodded her head.

"Esther's brother . . . Nathan Schine. Don't you remember what he said? Krasnoff was pink. He'd been black-listed."

"So where does your father come in?"

She turned away from Eddie. Too ashamed to face him.

"During the fifties, my father became . . . an informant. He gave names to the House Committee . . . Roy Cohn . . ."

"What names?"

"I never knew till just now."

"Oh Christ." Eddie figured it out. "Your mother's friends. All those left-wing kids from the thirties."

Caroline was in a trance now.

"It was good for business, he said. It helped with the banks."

Eddie moved close to her. "How do you know that?"

Caroline looked away with tears in her eyes. "My mother. She kept a journal."

"All right. So maybe your old man gave up a few names. That's *still* not a motive for murder."

Just then, the building shook. The first shock from the wrecking ball.

Eddie lunged forward and grabbed her. He pulled her out of the office and ran down the darkened hallway. When they got to the elevator, he stabbed at the button, but the lights were out.

"Shit. The power."

The building shook again.

So Eddie looked right, then left, searching for an exit. He saw an unlit red globe over a door that said Exit and pulled Caroline toward it.

Seconds later, they were on the twentieth floor, rushing to get to the bottom, when the building shook again. Plaster fell from the stairwell ceiling and Caroline lost her grip on the rail. Eddie ran to the window and looked up.

The ten-ton wrecking ball was just above them now, slamming into the top floors first. Debris was beginning to fall past the stairwell windows. So Eddie took off, pulling Caroline down with him. Down to eighteen and then around to the seventeenth landing. They were just clear of seventeen when the heel broke on Caroline's shoe.

"Oh, God. I think I twisted by ankle."

"Can you walk?"

"I'll try . . ."

But as soon as she went two steps, she pulled back in agony.

"I can't"

Down below on Madison, the foreman, who was spotting, radioed up to the crane operator.

"Drop it to sixteen."

The crane operator said "roger" and lowered the wrecking ball another few stories.

He was about to slam it into the side of the building where the stairwell was on sixteen. The ball rose.

He turned the crane to give it momentum, and the ball started to swing. In a matter of seconds, Eddie Burke and Caroline Drexel would be buried under tons of concrete and twisted rebar.

The ball was moving now, no more than twenty yards from the building, when Eddie smashed the sixteenth-floor stairwell window with his gun butt. He leaned out and fired a shot in the air.

Suddenly, the crane operator turned toward the noise. He touched a lever and the wrecking ball dropped, hitting the building just below the sixteenth floor. The building shook again. Part of the stairwell collapsed. Plaster and debris rained down on Eddie and Caroline, and for a few seconds, there was silence.

Then Caroline felt her heart beating. She pushed up from under the rubble and saw Eddie's finger. The index finger of his left hand, above the pile where he lay, covered in plaster, lathe, wrought iron, and steel. But that's all there was. He was buried, and Caroline screamed, out his name. "Eddie!"

But there was nothing. So she started digging frantically.

She remembered a piece she'd seen once on the Oklahoma City bombing. How the first few seconds in a burial were the key. A short time without oxygen, and there was brain death. So she scraped at the pile that was on him, terrified, but trying to stay calm.

Caroline found a twisted piece of rebar and used it as a pick until she had his arm out, and then she was able to clear an air hole. She reached in to touch his neck, begging for a pulse, and then she felt it. She squeezed his hand.

"Oh God, please."

45

CAROLINE HEARD VOICES NOW. MEN WERE COMING UP THE stairwell with shovels and picks and an emergency kit. And pretty soon they had him uncovered. They told her to back away, but she wouldn't let go of his hand. Please God. Please. She didn't pray very often, but now she was promising God the world if only He'd let this man breathe.

She squeezed Eddie's hand again, harder this time.

And then Eddie squeezed back.

All the way across town in the ambulance, Caroline stayed with him. Eddie was still unconscious, hyperventilating, when they roared into the emergency entrance at New York Hospital. There had just been a head-on collision on the FDR Drive and a gang shooting on Ninetieth and First, and the ER was in a state of bedlam. EMS paramedics, triage nurses, and trauma doctors were running around like the place was a battlefield.

They shoved Eddie onto a gurney and wheeled him into a cubicle. Caroline had to let go as they lifted him onto an examination table. Suddenly, a nurse who was built like a linebacker stepped in front of her, pulling a curtain around the table where Eddie lay. There was an ID badge on her chest that said Mildred Anson, RN. She turned to Caroline and demanded, "Who are you?"

Caroline said, "I'm a . . . friend."

"I'm sorry, but you can't stay here."

"When are the doctors going to . . . ?"

"You have to go to accounting."

"What?" Caroline was still trying to keep from shaking.

"You've got his insurance card, right?"

"No. Why should I?"

"Then who's gonna sign for him?"

"Sign for him? He needs *help.*"

But Nurse Anson ignored her. She had her clipboard out.

"Do you know if he has Blue Cross, Blue Shield? Major Medical? Any third-party payers?"

"What are you *talking* about? The man is un*con*scious."

"EMS said he didn't have a wallet on him."

"Fine. It must have been lost when they pulled him out."

"Then you're gonna have to declare coverage before we look at him."

"This is outrageous. He could die."

"Not in this hospital. Not without coverage."

"But how can you refuse him? I thought you were supposed to . . ."

"Treat them as long as we have the beds. If you look around, you'll see that we're full."

Caroline got angry now.

"What's your name?"

"It's on my badge, lady. Now, you'll have to move out . . ."

Just then, Eddie moaned from behind the curtain.

"Look, he's a fire marshal. I'm sure they have insurance."

"Can you prove it?"

"No." Caroline shook her head.

"Then I'm sorry."

The nurse started to walk away, but Caroline stopped her.

"Wait. *I'll* pay for it."

"Fine. Where's your card?"

"I don't have a card."

"You don't have a card?"

"No."

"Then how the hell do we know *you'll* pay?"

It was the kind of question people get every day from those mind-numbing bureaucrats. But not someone like Caroline Drexel. This was a woman who spent her life commuting between an ivory tower and a co-op on Sutton Place.

Her clothes were handmade. She had a season box at the Met, and she spent every August in Provence. At the places she dined, they served Chardonnay in crystal and the king crab was always fresh. Caroline went to hospitals for *benefits* not for treatment.

But Nurse Anson kept pushing.

"Miss. Are you listening to me? If you don't have an *insurance* card, then how the hell do we know you'll pay?"

And then, Caroline Drexel just lost it.

She grabbed the big woman by the hair and pulled her out through the ER door.

"What the Christ? Get your hands off me lady. . . . Guards!"

Nurse Anson was screaming now. Everybody in the ER looked up. A Pakistani security guard started running from back inside the emergency room, but Caroline wouldn't stop.

She had the big woman through the doors now, kicking and screaming as she tried to break loose, but Caroline had become someone else.

"You want to know if I can pay? You want to fucking know if I can pay?"

Just then, they turned a corner off the ER and came into an enormous hallway, a huge waiting room with white marble walls. There was a portrait of a woman hanging from the wall. A pretty woman in her mid-fifties, with blonde hair, in a velvet dress. A woman with a strange resemblance to Caroline.

And above her picture, cut into the marble in recessed gold relief, there was an inscription that read:

The Hampton Pavilion

The security guard was almost on them now, with his gun drawn, but Caroline took Nurse Anson and forced her to face the wall. The big woman stared up at the portrait, shaking, thinking that maybe Caroline had come down from the fifth floor where they kept the criminally insane. And then, as the security guard drew down on her with his gun, Caroline said, "That's my *mother* up there you *bitch,* and she gave this goddamn wing. Now I want you to get the best neurosurgeon in this hospital to look at that man in there. And if you don't, I will *personally* make sure that they *fire* your miserable ass."

A hundred people sitting in the pavilion froze in their tracks, not knowing what to make of this. Not knowing if this was some kind of hostage situation and maybe they'd all be on *Eyewitness News.* Nobody said anything, and then the security guard cocked his gun.

"You wanna step away from that nurse, lady?"

Trembling now with rage, half in shock herself, Caroline looked at him with the face of a mother lioness after a hyena has fucked with her cubs. Then the crowd of onlookers parted, and a small gray-haired man in a blue pinstriped suit came up to her. A little Brahmin in horn-rims with a nameplate on his lapel that said Foster Hutchinson, Hospital Administrator.

He looked around at the startled crowd and the nurse, who was shaking so hard now she'd wet her pants.

He looked at the Pakistani security guard with the Ruger trembling in his hands, and then he turned to Caroline and smiled.

"Why, Miss Drexel! So nice to see you. How can we be of help?"

46

AS IT TURNED OUT, EDDIE WAS LUCKY. WHEN DR. VANDER-jak, the chief of neurosurgery, was called back from lunch at the Yale Club, he was able to rouse him after a simple pupil dilation test. A diagnostic CAT scan revealed a hairline concussion in the anterior lobe. But after 20 cc's of epinephrine, Eddie was lucid and walking and his speech was clear. Vanderjak usually left such things to ER residents, but he volunteered to close a two-inch gash above Eddie's right eye. He joked with the fire cop that he was using a knot and stitch that he normally reserved for tying flies.

Eddie quipped, "Christ, Doc, if you *tie* the flies, how the hell do you get the zippers down?"

It took the old Dutchman a few seconds to get it.

"Yes, yes. Flies. Zipper. That's rich."

After that, Eddie got up and took Caroline's arm.

As they walked out, Hutchinson called over Caroline's shoulder.

"You needn't worry about a bill, Ms. Drexel."

"That's kind of you, Hutch. I'm sure there won't be any repercussions from this . . . as long as Nurse Anson takes some sensitivity training."

The big nurse smiled bitterly as they disappeared through the pavilion doors, and Hutchinson, the administrator, choked out a nervous laugh.

Half an hour later, Eddie Burke was asleep on the Bill Blass sofa in Caroline Drexel's study. She covered him in a Vittadini duvet and touched his forehead. Good. She drew the curtains and left him a note on rose-colored stationery.

> If you're hungry, there's a cornish game hen in the little Sub-Zero near the bar. Enough wine to put you to sleep again. It's been a long night.
>
> Caroline

Then she went into the bedroom and undressed. She found a pair of Donna Karan silk pajamas, pulled back the Laura Ashley comforter, and crawled in. She was exhausted all right, but there were other reasons why she couldn't wait to get into bed. She wasn't under for five minutes when she started to dream.

It began like it always did, with the music and the image of Julian and Esther Schine.

It had to be you. It had to be you . . .

Now that she knew him as Krasnoff, she could hear his voice clearly.

Yes, there it was, just the singsong hint of the closet queen. After all, this was the thirties, and even among artists, homosexuality was still something of a covert status.

I wandered around and finally found, somebody who . . .

Caroline slipped into REM now, and the dream turned from black and white into color. But the dream was taking too long. It wasn't necessary to have every moment: the kiss blow by Esther, her mother coming in, the champagne toast. Caroline knew these by heart, although this time, she could swear that Esther looked just a little bit pregnant.

'Cause nobody else, gave me such a thrill, with all your faults, I love you still. It had to be you, crazy old you. It had to be you . . .

And there they were now: the four of them, standing back to admire the mural. And for the first time, she could almost make out the faces on the five figures in front: the pilot, the nurse, the stevedore, the farmer, the teacher and the miner.

She was tossing and turning in bed, waiting for the music to end, her pulse racing, because she knew for certain now what she'd see.

Then the doors flew open and the cold rain poured in and the angry young man was upon them. Only now, for the first time, Caroline could hear his voice.

"What are you people *doing?* Didn't you hear about it?"

And Dorothea, her mother, said, "What?"

The young man threw the newspaper down and came face-to-face with her, almost hissing it out. "All this . . ." he looked around at the studio. "It's over."

And now, for the first time, Caroline Drexel was inside her mother, looking out. She felt her pain at the sting of his brutal remark. And now, for the first time, she saw his face: the face of John Charles Drexel, Her father.

And then, he grew older, in his forties, and she was in her little room up in Newport. It was summer. Caroline looked in a mirror above her night table and saw that she was just a child, six or seven years old.

Her father was leaning over her, over the bed. He touched her face, then ran his big hands down along her nightie. She pushed him back, but he lunged at her. So she kicked him and he ripped off his belt, slapping her across the behind until it was red. He put his hand over her mouth so she wouldn't scream, and she tried to pull away, but she couldn't. The little blonde girl was shaking now, almost in shock as the big man pulled down his trousers and forced himself into her. The pain was mind-numbing, and it hurt so much, but she couldn't scream.

Then it all went to black, and Caroline shot up in bed, hyperventilating, shivering. Only now, when she looked up, she saw Eddie Burke.

"Caroline. You all right?"

He sat down on the bed and put his arm on her shoulder.

"What?" She was disoriented and there was a throbbing pain between her legs.

Eddie ran to the bathroom and got her a glass of water. He came back and gently held it up to her lips. She drank some.

"Thanks." She looked up and smiled at him.

"I heard you scream."

"Yes. Well, I'm fine now."

"You sure?"

Caroline nodded, hoping he wouldn't let go, but he did.

"Okay. Listen, what you did for me back at that building . . . the hospital . . . I appreciate it. But I've got to go now."

She reached up and touched his arm.

"Why?"

"I've got to see to my father."

He got up from the bed.

"Wait. Please don't go."

Eddie stopped. "Look. I have to."

He started to walk out, then he touched his head.

Caroline said, "What is it?"

Eddie went to a mirror. There was blood coming down from the bandage above his eye.

"So much for neurosurgeons."

Caroline jumped out of bed.

"Oh God. Let me get something for that."

She went into the marble bathroom and came back with cotton, some Band-Aids, and some iodine.

"Here. Sit down. Please."

Then, ever so carefully, she undid the bandage above his eye. She said "Oh God" again when she saw the wound.

"I can't believe that you're walking."

"Hey. It's on my eye, not my leg."

She took a cotton ball and brought it to the mouth of the iodine bottle.

"Close your eyes now. This could burn."

Eddie closed his eyes.

"That's the story of my life."

"What?"

"Things that burn."

"Hold on."

She touched the cotton to his face and winced at the pain she was causing him. Eddie gritted his teeth.

He wanted to squeeze her arm, but he didn't. A moment passed, then she put a Band-Aid over the wound.

"You can open up now."

"Okay."

He checked himself in the mirror again.

"Christ. An inch lower and I'd look like Peter Falk."

Caroline smiled. "What is it with you people?"

"What people?"

"The Irish. You've got a line for everything."

"Hey," said Eddie. "What are we supposed to do? The glass is either half-full or half-empty. You either laugh or you cry."

He started to walk out when she stopped him. "Wait."

"What?"

"The last few days ... ever since you found me here with your father ... you've been different."

"Oh really?"

"Yes. I know that you and your father had some kind of problem, but—"

"Look. We talked about it. Okay? Before he died. We worked it out. Now I have to go."

He started to exit again, but this time she grabbed his arm.

"No. God damn it. This time *we* need to talk."

Eddie stopped. "There's nothing to talk about."

"Yes there is. That night with your father—"

He pulled away. "I don't have time for that now." Eddie kept walking out.

"Well, *I* do. You've been pushing me in and out of buildings now for three days. You said you needed my help, and I helped you. Now I want to say a few things."

Again, Eddie stopped.

"You may think you know what's going on here," said Caroline, "but you don't."

"Is that right?"

"Yeah. There was something in that mural. It was hidden for fifty years, and now four people have died for it: your father, Grosvenor, that poor girl in SoHo, and her boyfriend. If you count Krasnoff and Esther Schine, six . . . Six people, Eddie."

"What are you trying to say?"

"I'm trying to say I was scared that night with your father. I needed somebody strong. I'm scared now."

Eddie just stared at her. Christ. What a face. She looked beautiful and vulnerable all at once. He could see that she wanted him, and now, finally, he admitted to himself that he wanted her, too. Eddie started to retrace his steps, slowly, keeping his eyes on her. Then, when he got a few inches away, she reached out and ran her index finger along his lower lip.

Eddie burned a look into her, deciding whether or not to do this. Then, with his right hand, he opened the front of her silk pajamas.

Caroline took his left hand and ran it along her cheek.

Slowly at first, he undid each button. Then, before he could get to the last one, she dropped down in front of him and undid his belt. She reached inside and took out his cock. She wet her fingers and rubbed them along the tip of it, and then, when it started to stiffen, she took him into her mouth.

Eddie arched his back. Christ. She ran her tongue along the outside of the shaft. Then he pulled her up by the shoulders and kissed her hard on the lips. Caroline pulled away, and he pushed her down on the bed. They fucked like it was their last day on earth.

47

CAROLINE WOKE UP AND SMILED TO HERSELF. GOD. SHE hadn't been taken like that since her days at St. George's. He was rough, but so goddamn generous.

She opened her eyes and smiled at the ceiling, and then she reached over for him—but he was gone.

"Eddie?"

She jumped up and threw a robe on, rushing out of the room and into the foyer above the marble stairway, then down the steps, two at a time.

"Eddie . . ."

And then she heard him call out from the study.

"Down here."

Her heart leapt.

He was on the sofa, leaning over a low butler's table, the file on the lost mural spread out in front of him.

Caroline walked up behind him.

"When did you get up?"

"About an hour ago."

"Would you like some coffee?"

"In a minute, maybe."

"Really, Eddie, I think you should eat something."

But Eddie was busy, rubbing his chin as he studied the file.

"It still doesn't fit. We've got a ton of circumstantial pointing to your father for Krasnoff. But we don't know why. Even if it *did* have to do with McCarthy. Why would he kill him? What the hell did Krasnoff threaten him with?"

Caroline sat down next to him and rubbed her hand along the inside of his thigh. He was staring at Krasnoff's picture from the autopsy file. And she kissed him behind the ear.

Eddie smiled. "Hey, come on. I'm trying to focus on this."

"Okay." Caroline started going through the pictures.

Eddie thumbed through his notebook, then stopped. "You know, you never said why you went to your office last night."

"Was it really last night?"

"Yeah."

"It seems like ages ago."

"Right. So what were you looking for?"

Caroline got up from the sofa.

"Oh, nothing. This old article I remembered."

She was searching for a cigarette.

"On what?"

"The murals. It was in *Life* magazine, from the fifties."

Caroline lifted up a silver cover from a cigarette box and tapped a Gitane against it.

"It was about the art. How so much of it had been ruined."

"What do you mean, ruined?"

She lit the cigarette now with a silver lighter.

"Don't you remember? I talked about it the first day we met. Most of the artists from the thirties were leftists. During the Witch Hunt, thousands of canvases were destroyed."

She walked to a wall of books across the study.

"Wait a minute. I may have it here."

She started with a shelf of foot-high art books on the bottom and worked her way up. When she stood on a small hardwood ladder, Eddie could see the line of her ass against the silk robe.

Finally, after a few minutes, she went to a series of file drawers at the bottom of the bookshelf. As Eddie looked through the pictures in front of him, Caroline checked the files in the drawers. After a few minutes, she found it.

"Here it is. *Life* magazine, July 1951."

The headline on the piece read: "End of WPA art: Canvases which Cost Government $35,000,000 Are Sold for Junk."

Caroline started reading. " 'Recently, after the government had liquidated its WPA art project, these pictures were sold for four cents a pound to a Long Island junk dealer. Among the users, some plumbers who bought the cheap canvas to wrap pipes with for insulation. . . .' Damn."

"What is it?"

"They don't give the junk dealer's name."

She handed Eddie the article, and he studied the cover picture. Just then, he saw it.

"Christ. There it is."

"What?"

"The mural. A piece of it. See? In the upper right-hand corner."

Sure enough, in the corner of the article with dozens of WPA pictures displayed for the junk men, Eddie pointed to a fragment of the mural. The section with the pilot.

"But what's it mean?"

"I don't know," said Caroline. "I thought maybe if the name of the junk dealer was in the piece, we could see who might have bought it for scrap."

"What would that get us?"

"Maybe the second panel."

"What second panel?"

"Oh, come on, you knew that."

"What?"

"That it was a diptych. Painted in two sections, forty feet wide."

Eddie rubbed his neck and checked the file.

"Jesus, the mural that burned was only ten by twenty."

"Right. The left panel."

Caroline picked up the *Life* article.

"So what were you thinking?"

"I thought maybe if we found the right panel, it might tell us something."

"Like what?"

"I don't know. Something."

Caroline dropped back onto the sofa. She got quiet again.

A few moments passed as they stared at each other. Then Eddie looked from the death shot of Krasnoff to the picture in *Life*. He did it again.

"Wait a second. Let me see that."

He put the picture of Krasnoff next to the magazine.

"What is it?"

Again, Eddie looked from the mural to Krasnoff.

They were the same person.

That's when he understood.

"Oh Christ . . ."

"What?"

"You're fucking brilliant, you know that?"

Caroline smiled. "Thank you, but I don't understand."

"They used each other as models."

"What?"

"When they painted the murals with all those figures, the artists posed for each other. Right?"

"Sometimes. But what does that matter?"

Eddie picked up the two pictures.

"Look. Here."

And sure enough, there it was, staring out from the picture in *Life*: the face of Julian Krasnoff. He was the pilot. The gay little painter, enshrined in oil as a fighter jock.

"I see it," said Caroline, "but I still don't . . ."

Eddie jumped up and ran into the living room. He came back with the picture of John Charles Drexel in the silver frame.

"My father?"

Caroline felt it coming. She'd been this close to putting it together, and now Eddie did it for her.

"They used each other as models. Six figures: Krasnoff, Esther Schine, Grosvenor, your mother and Black Jack Drexel, the captain of industry, the Witch Hunt informant, preserved forever on canvas with all of those pinkos. *Workers of the World Unite.*"

Caroline rocked back on her feet. She felt dizzy, faint. For a second, she flashed on the angry young man from the dream. He was twenty-four then. He threw down the paper and screamed at her mother, and then her mother looked up toward the mural and there he was. Standing amid the red flags.

Caroline had suspected some of this from the moment she'd heard Helen's tapes. She knew he was involved with the mural, but she hadn't known all the rest. How he'd come to her bed when she was a child; how he'd violated her. That was the trauma that had sent her to Helen in the first place. The terrible event that Dr. Liebman sought to uncover by taking her back with hypnosis.

She'd used her mother's journal as a catalyst. And now, all the pieces fit.

John Charles Drexel wasn't just a child molester, he was a cold-blooded killer. He'd taken care of Krasnoff, and then, when the mural surfaced, he'd sent his man to make sure that it burned.

Caroline was on the sofa with her hands across her face.

"Are you all right?" Eddie touch her shoulder. He could see that she was crying. Finally, she looked up.

"But why? I mean, why did he do it?"

Eddie got up and started pacing.

"Why do most people kill? Anger. Revenge. For him it was self-preservation. How would it look to the Committee? The banks? John Charles Drexel, the staunch anti-Communist, up there on canvas with all those . . . fellow travelers?"

Caroline was numb now as Eddie kept pacing.

"After Krasnoff got fired, he went to see your father. Asked him for help. Your father refused him. They argued. Krasnoff threatened to blow his cover. There was a struggle, and Krasnoff went out the window."

Caroline turned away as Eddie went on.

"No one would have known. The secret went out the window with Krasnoff until forty years later when a pipe started leaking in an old subway station."

Eddie stopped.

"If it all came out *now*, do you realize what it would do to him? Forget Drexel Place. Forget the Japs. This guy would finish his life up in Sing-Sing."

"But it was so long ago."

"Unh-uh. There's no statute of limitation on homicide."

"But the art restorer. That Sloane girl. Why would he?"

"It's like I said before. She just got in the way." Eddie sat down, defeated. "Only now it's over."

"Why?" said Caroline. "I don't understand."

"Come on. The mural's gone. There's no way to prove it. The picture in *Life* only has Krasnoff's face. All we found at Grosvenor's was a sketch. If he'd had anything more specific, with faces, the killer took it. No, this is finished."

Eddie stared up at the ceiling, shaking his head. He looked at Caroline, and then finally, it hit him.

"Unless . . ."

"What?"

"What if the wrong half got burned?"

Eddie picked up one of the black-and-white shots of the mural after its discovery in the subway station. He pointed at Krasnoff, the pilot.

"This was the left half of the diptych, right? The three figures are covered in plaster. Whoever burned the mural figured your father's face was one of these three."

"Yes, but—"

"What if it *wasn't*? What if your father was in the other half?"

Eddie jumped up and raced from the study.

"Eddie," said Caroline. "Eddie, wait."

But he was already halfway into the foyer, stabbing at the elevator button.

Caroline threw on a trench coat, jumped into some mules, and ran down the service stairs. In the lobby she caught him.

"Where are you going?"

"The subway station."

"But why?"

"You said it yourself; they sold the canvas as scrap for four cents a pound. If I can find the second half of that mural, I might have a shot."

"But if it didn't come out before, what makes you think you can find it now?"

"Hey, there's a lot of pipe in that station. We know half the mural got used as scrap. What if the other half's there?"

Caroline didn't answer.

"Look. Do you understand?

He grabbed her by the shoulders.

"Your father's behind all this death."

Eddie turned to exit. Caroline hesitated as he rushed into Sutton Place, then she ran out after him.

The doorman watched as she got into Eddie's Chevy. He watched as Eddie threw the Mars light on the roof, hit the siren, and screeched off.

Then he picked up the phone, punched in some numbers, and waited until somebody picked up on the other end. It was the male secretary, LeStadt. It sounded like he'd just woken up.

LeStadt asked why the doorman was calling this late, and the doorman said, "I'm not sure if this is important, but you said you wanted to know everything."

"What is it?" demanded LeStadt.

There was a pause and the doorman said, "It's that cop again. Burke."

"What? The old man? He's dead," said LeStadt, almost spitting it out with contempt.

"I'm not talking about the father," said the doorman. "I'm talking about his prick son."

48

JEAN-CLAUDE POUSSAINT WAS PISSED. THE SPURS WERE IN Seattle tonight, down by ten against the Sonics, and he'd laid his whole fucking check on the game. If he lost, he'd need something extra to cover himself with the shy.

For two weeks now the Haitian had been pulling tit duty for Bell Security, a firm supplying rent-a-cops to various construction sites around Midtown. JC had been doing clock work on a high-rise in the West twenties near Park, and all he had to do was walk the site every hour and key in on lockboxes around the perimeter.

It gave him plenty of time to check the NBA point spread on his Watchman and catch some zzzzs. But tonight some cocksucking West Indian named Kenny had called in sick, so they pulled him up to this city job in a rat-hole tunnel on Ninety-first where there was no fucking way he'd get any reception.

"Shit." He had three bills on San Antonio and he was freezing his balls. At the other job there was always a trailer with a quartz heater, but not here. It was two stories down, and the fucking wind howled through the tunnel like a hurricane off Port-au-Prince. And forget any sleep. Every motherfucking ten minutes another Broadway Local would

come screaming through, and the place would go so bright
with arc light that he felt like he was back in Haiti being
tortured by the TonTon Macoute.

So here he was, a thirty-seven-year-old degenerate gam-
bler with four kids in the Morningside Projects and ten
grand in vig to the shys, down in this tunnel, staring up at
some broken pipe, guarding ten rolls of canvas, a power
scaffold, and a box full of Black & Decker. It had been a
cocksucking life ever since he left his first wife in Bai de
St.-Jean. That's when he quit going to Mass, started doing
poppers, and lost his soul to the fucking sports book.

Jean-Claude sat there on the crate, tapping the earphone,
trying to point the antenna on the FM radio the right way
so maybe he could at least catch a little bit of the Knicks
at Boston. He was up at the north end of the platform, so
he walked south toward the emergency stairs, and that's
when he heard it, somebody dropping the metal grate from
above. JC checked his watch, thinking maybe this was
Jaime Velez, his midnight relief, coming down ten minutes
early. That would be perfect. He fucking deserved it.

This way he'd go upstairs, pop some amies, spank the
monkey, and catch a cup of French roast while he listened
to the final score. He was due. He was fucking due.

Just then, the IRT Downtown Express roared through the
tunnel doing eighty, heading south for the station at Sev-
enty-second. The noise was deafening, so JC had to raise
his voice.

"That you, Jaime?"

There was a quartz halogen light shooting down on the
metal stairs now, but no answer, so Jean-Claude tried again.

"Velez?"

The train was at mid-station now, moving with such
force that the loose canvas blew on the overhead pipes.

"Jaime?" JC was screaming, but there was still no answer, so he drew his gun and moved back in the shadows.

He was about to cock it when just then, coming down the stairs, he saw an incredible pair of legs in spike heels.

He lowered the hammer.

"Who's there?"

Caroline Drexel came down to the top of the platform, followed by Eddie Burke. He showed the Haitian his ID.

"Fire Department. Arson. You private?"

JC nodded and looked at a clipboard.

"They didn't say anything about any Fire—"

"It's not on the sheet," said Eddie. "Unannounced inspection."

JC nodded, then looked Caroline up and down.

"Who's she?"

This was one bitch he'd like to take up in back, do a popper with.

"Consultant on a job we're investigating."

"You people are out a little late."

"Yeah, well we just got a lead on something."

Eddie ran the quartz halogen up along the pipes overhanging the platform.

"That where the break was?"

JC looked up at it. "Guess so."

"They have security here since the break?"

"That's right. First shift comes on at six when the plumbers leave."

"Notice anybody unusual down here the last week or so?"

"Hey. I just started tonight."

Suddenly, he put his hand to the earplug.

"Fuck."

"What is it?" said Eddie.

"Celtics game. Ewing just scored from outside the key. Knicks are in overtime. Fuck."

Eddie traded looks with Caroline.

"Okay. Are we straight on this?"

Jean-Claude smiled and checked out Caroline again. "Yeah. Go ahead. Do what you got to do."

Eddie handed the light to Caroline and pushed the scaffold toward the old break.

"Do me a favor. When I get up there, run it along the pipe."

She nodded, and Eddie climbed onto the scaffold.

"Along here, okay?"

He motioned along the pipe. For ten feet on either side of the break, you could see where they cut in the new canvas.

"Good."

Eddie moved under the insulation and bent down to a case full of tools on the scaffold. He was looking for something to score it with. A box cutter. He found one buried under the tools in a corner of the case.

JC touched his ear again and screamed out, "Fucking A. One twelve to one ten, New York. I knew I shoulda been down on that game."

Eddie reached up toward the pipe. He had to climb onto the scaffold siding to reach it.

"Be careful," said Caroline.

He raised the box cutter up toward the canvas, and for a second, the light from the halogen flashed off the blade.

JC said, "Hey. What the fuck you doin'?"

Eddie made an incision in the insulation.

"My job."

"You fucking crazy? They just put that canvas up."

"Don't worry. You're covered. Besides, I'm only working over here in the old shit."

With Caroline holding the light on the pipe, Eddie scored around it.

Just then, they all heard a noise from above.

"What was that?" said Eddie.

Caroline switched off the light.

Eddie turned to JC. "You expecting somebody?"

JC nodded. "My relief."

Another noise on the metal stairs.

"Jaime? That you?"

But there was silence, so Caroline switched on the light again.

Eddie made another cut in the insulation and then pulled. All he got was a handful of mildewed canvas, so he moved along the scaffold down the pipe another ten feet. Another cut. Another pull. Nothing. Then one more time.

Suddenly, Eddie froze. He pointed at Caroline, who switched off the light. This time he was sure that he'd heard something.

JC raised his hand. "Wait a second."

"What is it?"

"Final score on the Spurs game . . ." He listened and then ripped the plug out of the radio.

"Fuck me. I shoulda gone short on Seattle."

Eddie just shook his head at Caroline and waited another few seconds. They both looked toward the stairs, but there was no other sound, so she switched the light back on, and Eddie moved down another ten feet. He made a fourth cut in the old canvas. Caroline panned the light over it as he pulled.

"Mother of Christ."

"What?"

"We've got it."

Eddie pulled some more, and there it was: the right half of the mural; *Workers of the World Unite*.

The Haitian looked up at it, openmouthed.

"What the fuck's that?"

Eddie moved a few feet on either side to make sure that he didn't cut into the mural itself, then he started to pull.

Caroline sucked in hard.

"I don't believe it. All those years . . ."

As the mural came out, she could see the faces of the three remaining workers. First, the figure of the farmer came out. Grosvenor had used his face for that as well as the likeness of the stevedore in the left panel. Next came the teacher. When she saw the face, Caroline bit her lower lip.

"God."

She was about to cry.

"What is it?" said Eddie.

"It's my . . . mother," said Caroline.

JC was shaking his head now as Eddie pulled out more of the mural, revealing the face of the miner.

It had been almost sixty years, and his hair was jet-black then, but sure enough, there he was, John Charles Drexel.

Eddie said, "We've got him."

Caroline rushed to the scaffold now to receive it, as Eddie pulled the rest of the mural free from the pipe.

"Be careful. It's priceless."

"Yeah. But not the way *you* mean. It's evidence."

He started to hand it down to her when just then, they all heard that noise again on the stairs.

JC was sure now. He pulled out the earplug and ran toward it.

"Hey, Jaime, you not gonna believe this. I got no fucking luck."

Suddenly, there was a gun blast. An ear-piercing crack filled the tunnel as a bullet ripped out of a Beretta and tore open Jean-Claude's throat. The security guard was blown back against the white tile wall of the station and a fragment of brain matter touched the toe of Caroline's shoe.

"Jesus."

Eddie jumped down from the platform and reached for his Smith, but suddenly, there was a light in his eyes, and when he put his hand up to block it, he saw a man on the emergency stairs.

The figure stepped into the light, and Caroline recognized him as her father's secretary, LeStadt.

He was pointing the gun at Eddie's head. And then, behind LeStadt, in the shadows, she saw him. The titan, the Witch Hunt informant, and the face on the canvas from so long ago, Black Jack Drexel.

49

"MY COMPLIMENTS, MR. BURKE."

Drexel walked down the stairs behind LeStadt, who kept the Beretta trained on Eddie. The male secretary was dressed in double-breasted Armani under a trench coat.

Eddie looked at his pockmarked face and nodded toward Drexel.

"I know who *he* is," said Eddie. "Who the fuck are you?"

LeStadt pushed the gun against Eddie's neck and then reached into his pocket. He spat on the ground and tossed something down. Something metal. It hit the hard concrete of the platform and spun like a coin. Then it stopped and Caroline touched her heart.

"Oh no."

It was Big Eddie's shield.

Eddie started to lunge toward LeStadt, but he cocked the Beretta.

Caroline screamed, "No, Eddie!"

LeStadt smiled.

"The old fuck was way past his prime."

Eddie bent down to pick up the badge. He ran his thumb across the words "Chief of Detectives." And then, in a

flash, he came up with the box cutter and slammed the
blade of the razor against LeStadt's neck.

Caroline screamed, "Eddie!"

"What the fuck are you doing?" said Drexel.

"Finishing what my old man started," said Eddie.

It was a standoff. LeStadt could fire and he'd cut a hole
through Eddie three inches wide, but the muscle reflex
would slit his own larynx.

Eddie said, "Go for it."

LeStadt hesitated.

"Come on. It's more of a chance than you gave my old
man, you coldcocking sonovabitch. Thirty years. Thirty
goddamn years on the force and he had to die in a gutter.
You fuck."

LeStadt's index finger touched the trigger. Then he
looked down at the razor and stopped.

"Come on," said Eddie. "You like blood. Let's see
what yours looks like."

He made a pinprick incision with the box cutter and a
trickle of red ran down onto the collar of LeStadt's perfect
white shirt.

Eddie's eyes were wide now. It was a look that said he
had nothing to live for, and LeStadt could see it. A 9 mm
against the heart of a madman meant nothing.

"Let's go, fuckface. *Do it!*"

But just then, Drexel jammed a .44 up against Caroline.
It was a Charter Arms Special. The David Berkowitz gun.

"The Irish were always crude fighters," said Drexel.

He tossed a silk handkerchief to LeStadt.

"Clean yourself up."

Drexel cocked the .44, then turned to Eddie.

"Back away."

Eddie hesitated, then started to pull back, but Caroline
shouted. "No. He won't do it."

"And why not?" said Drexel. "I've done everything else. Now back *away!*"

But Eddie held on to the box cutter.

"It bothers you, doesn't it, Drexel? All that blood . . . It spills out in ways that you can't control."

"Shut up."

But Eddie wouldn't. "Your boyfriend here do the girl? The one down in SoHo? How about Grosvenor? I mean, he was the only other living person who really knew what was in that mural. You *had* to kill him. A bullshit suicide, just like you used with Krasnoff."

Drexel shot a look at Caroline now. Tears were running down her face. She was almost paralyzed by the truth of all this.

"I told you to—"

But Eddie kept going. "When the mural was found, you were afraid there'd be questions. Maybe someone would tie you to Krasnoff's death. The Japs would love that. Their new partner, charged with manslaughter."

"Look," said Drexel. "I didn't come here to debate with a goddamn fireman." He turned now to LeStadt. "I came for the mural. Now get it."

LeStadt pulled away from Eddie and went for the mural.

Drexel screamed at Eddie, with the gun still on Caroline, "Drop the box cutter. *Now!*"

Eddie smiled and let it go.

"Now, up with your fucking hands."

Eddie complied. He started to back away toward the edge of the platform near the subway track.

"So what are you going to do?"

Drexel pulled the gun off Caroline and aimed it at Eddie.

"Why, I'm going to kill you, Mr. Burke."

Eddie looked at Caroline, who was almost in shock now.

"Okay. So you cap me. Then what? She's a witness. You really gonna kill your own daughter?"

Drexel hesitated and then picked up the quartz halogen light. He shined it in Caroline's eyes.

"Kill her? I wouldn't think of it."

He turned toward Caroline.

"He's got a gun in a holster at the small of his back, darling. Take it."

Caroline just stood there.

Drexel was more brutal this time.

"Caroline. I *said* take the gun."

Eddie looked at her and smiled. No way. Not this time, boss. And then, suddenly, she started to move toward him.

Oh no. Christ, no.

She moved up behind him in silence now, the tears streaming down her face.

Eddie couldn't believe it. She opened his jacket, reached inside, and found the Smith. He was awestruck.

"I . . . I don't . . ."

"Understand?" said Drexel. "Of course not, Mr. Burke. What would you know of a child's love for a parent?"

Eddie looked at Caroline, trying to find some denial in her eyes, but there was nothing.

"Is it true? Are you with him on this?"

Still nothing from Caroline. She just stood there, frozen.

Drexel laughed. "With me? Hell, I sent her to *school* for it. She wrote her dissertation on the WPA."

Eddie was almost in shock.

"You see, Mr. Burke, that piece of canvas was always out there. A filthy reminder of a rather embarrassing youth. I *raised* her to find it, and now she has."

Eddie looked at Caroline. The betrayal was overwhelming. He walked up as if to slap her. Drexel aimed the gun at his head. So Eddie spat in her face.

"Caroline!" Drexel bellowed at her.

She just stood there, motionless, unable to wipe the spittle away.

"Caroline!" He yelled louder.

She flinched at the sound of her father's voice.

"Let's go, darling."

LeStadt handed Drexel the mural. The old lion turned and started climbing the stairs with the mural under his arm. Then he stopped and looked down at Caroline.

"I said *come!*"

Another flinch, and Eddie understood their relationship now.

Finally, Caroline turned like a broken child and followed her father up the stairs. When they got to the top, Drexel called down to LeStadt.

"Do it with your hands, and leave him down on the rails. The subway will do the rest."

Then, just before Drexel was about to push up the metal grate, the southbound IRT Local lit up the station down below.

At the sound, LeStadt shot a look toward the train. As he turned, Eddie jumped down off the platform.

"Shit," said LeStadt, running forward with the light, shining it down along the track.

But Eddie had slipped into a crawl space under the platform overhang and the male secretary couldn't see him.

"What is it?" shouted Drexel from upstairs near the street. "What's wrong?"

He started running back down the stairs now, pulling Caroline along. She was moving behind him in a daze.

"He jumped," said LeStadt, panning the light.

"Do you see him?" Drexel was on the platform now. He tossed down the mural and pulled out the .44.

"He's down there, somewhere by the overhang."

Drexel nodded and looked left, following the train south down the tunnel. Then he looked north, assessing the situation. Finally, a tiny smile cracked his lips. The sense of panic fell away, and he tightened his jaw muscles. He knew that he had Eddie now, and the prospect of letting him twist before death gave him pleasure.

"He can't move uptown or he'll run into the next goddamn train. Go down and follow him. We'll wait at Eighty-sixth. Shoot the fuck if you have to. We'll deal with the body later."

LeStadt nodded.

Caroline was staring down into the tunnel, paralyzed. The body of Jean-Claude Poussaint was inches away from her feet. Finally, Drexel pulled her toward the exit stairs.

"Let's go."

Eddie could hear LeStadt's steps as he moved down the platform to a small set of stairs at the end. The male secretary stopped for a second and listened. There was a low wind whistling down through the tunnel from Ninety-sixth, but nothing else.

LeStadt popped the magazine out of the Beretta and reached into his jacket for another one. The bullets in this mag were different. Teflon-jacketed .9 mm rounds with shiny tips. They were hollow-point loads, designed to shatter inside the body on impact. Outlawed in most NATO countries. Devastating on impact with meat. If he did this right, he could blow off the head and the hands. Without prints or a jawline, they'd never be able to ID the body.

LeStadt was a man who believed in efficiency. Two jobs for the price of one. This way, he wouldn't have to go back down the tunnel. He smiled at himself for his cleverness and slammed the mag in the gun. Then he took a long breath and moved down into the dark.

50

THE DIGITAL CLOCK ON THE BANK AT BROADWAY AND
Ninety-first said 11:54 P.M. when Drexel pulled his daughter up through the metal grate at the top of the emergency
stairs. He cocked his head toward the Mercedes 600 parked
at the curb and motioned for Caroline to get in. Then he
opened the trunk and slid the rolled-up mural inside. He
started to move toward the driver's-side door, then he
stopped. He looked over at the open padlock hanging from
the hasp on the metal grate and retraced his steps. Drexel
moved onto the curb, standing over the crosshatched metal
of the grate. He snapped the lock shut, securing the grate.
Now the fucking fire cop would be trapped inside, and anybody else wanting to get into the tunnel would have to go
look for a hacksaw.

Below, in the tunnel, Eddie listened as LeStadt hit the
tracks. He was wearing leather-soled shoes, walking with
just the hint of a limp, as he made his way in the dark with
the halogen light. The limp . . . Maybe his father had hit the
prick after all. Eddie waited until LeStadt was a good fifty
yards north of him, and then suddenly he rolled out and
moved in the dark across the tracks. The only light in that
part of the tunnel came from a string of bulbs run along

the platform wall by the plumbing crew, and Eddie had to step carefully to avoid the third electrified rail. The ribbon of steel ran down the track, pulsing with 600,000 volts.

There was one on the other side, too, and when he got to it, Eddie heard a low rumbling hum. He looked across the tracks to where LeStadt was panning the light. The killer stopped to listen, and Eddie used the moment to jump across the uptown electrified rail. Now he was moving south through the tunnel along the uptown track.

Just then, he heard that unmistakable metal click as LeStadt pulled back on the breech of the Beretta and put one into the chamber. Eddie held his breath and crouched down, listening to LeStadt's leather soles as he moved down along the old wooden ties on the southbound side. Six years in the BFI had taught Eddie one thing. When you were hunting for bad guys, it was best to wear Vibram soles. So he headed south now in silence, watching the killer over his shoulder as LeStadt moved downtown along the opposite track.

Eddie wondered where Drexel had found LeStadt. The guy had the smell of a spook. Maybe Defense Intelligence. One of those expediters that had traveled the world for Uncle starting brushfires and then letting the Company come in to put them out. LeStadt had forensic training; Eddie was sure of that. The crime scene at Grosvenor's was too clean for an amateur. There'd been no signs of forced entry, even though Grosvenor would have been terrified to let him in. No. This was a guy who knew how to use lock picks with latex gloves. How to snap the hyoid bone and make a noose out of bungee to fake a suicide. But only a few in the covert branches could kill with their hands, and if he'd been Bureau, he'd be using a Glock. The Beretta was the side arm of choice for half the world's military. So Eddie figured he was dealing with an ex–Navy SEAL or a Langley spook or maybe even a foreigner. Sûreté, the Mossad. Multinational princes like Drexel always used men like that as expediters. And though the job description was probably secretary/chauffeur, Eddie knew that he was up against a world-class hood.

LeStadt shined the light along the downtown tracks as he inched forward with the gun.

"This doesn't have to take so long, you know. You can show yourself, and we'll finish this."

Eddie caught just the hint of an accent. Belgian. Maybe German.

LeStadt got to the platform overhang that had been Eddie's first hiding place, and he stopped. He shined the light underneath and realized that Eddie'd come out.

"So, you're going to make it hard on me," he said. "I'll have to take a little more time with you at the end."

German. Yeah. The way he pronounced the w. Eddie was sure now. He'd spent a year with the corps in Stuttgart, and he knew a hundred guys named Dieter who spoke like that. The guy might have a Frog name, but he was a fucking Kraut.

LeStadt smiled faintly and spun the light south down the length of the track. With the reflection and the curve of the track, it looked to the German killer like the skeleton of a snake. And that was just how he felt. Like a bushmaster sliding through the grass outside Dresden, hungry for some small bit of game: a rabbit, a field mouse, perhaps. That's all this fire cop was: an incompetent grocery clerk. A tiny burr on the side of a lion. An irritation that had to be excised so that Drexel could get on with his work.

With no place to hide on the southbound side, LeStadt knew that Eddie was across the track, but the line of steel pillars supporting the tunnel blocked his view. So he panned the light left and jumped the downtown third rail, single-handing the Beretta, presenting as small a target as

he could, even though he knew that the rabbit was defenseless.

Then, when he jumped the electrified rail on the uptown
side, he caught just a flicker of shadow falling back against
the tunnel wall down the track. LeStadt smiled.

"You're a Catholic, right? The Irish love wakes, so I'll
make you a deal. Are you listening?"

Nothing from Eddie.

"If you come out right now, I won't use a head shot.
Do you hear me? They'll be able to keep the coffin open
and all your fireman friends can spill whiskey on you as
they look down and tell lies about your miserable life."

Eddie was hardly breathing now. He had pushed himself
into an indentation in the wall. A curvature ten inches deep
and six feet tall. There was one of them every twenty feet
or so along the tunnel wall so that track workers could have
some place to hide if they found themselves staring at an
oncoming train.

Eddie flattened his body, trying not to breathe as the tip
of LeStadt's light beam played along the ties. LeStadt was
quiet now, stalking him, swinging the light with the gun as
he moved down the track, checking each indentation.

Eddie knew that in a matter of seconds the ex-spook
would be on him. He was done. Defenseless. No gun. And
he thought to himself what a goddamn cosmic joke. Big
Eddie Burke and his son both going down because of some
leaky pipe in an old subway tunnel. To die for bad plumbing.

And just then, the halogen light went out. He heard
LeStadt stop, and he heard him kick off his shoes. Loafers,
thought Eddie. This guy was good.

Now all he could hear was that wind whistling down
from Ninety-sixth Street. And then he knew that LeStadt
was moving again in the dark. A few seconds later, he
heard the man breathing. He was no more than ten feet

away now, and Eddie could smell the fucker's aftershave. What was it? Polo? English Leather? No. Paco Raban. This guy was continental, all right. A decade running volatiles had given Eddie an acute sense of smell, and he thought to himself that the last goddamn thing in his life that he was going to remember was the smell of his killer's cologne.

51

UPSTAIRS ON BROADWAY, DREXEL AND CAROLINE WERE heading south in the Mercedes. There was fire in his eyes, a cold, dull stare in hers. All she could think of was the memory of the man as he touched her. The way that he ran his hand down across her tiny neck and found her private parts. She had buried it now for twenty years, but it had all come out again with an old painting in a subway station. At least now she had the tapes of the journal. Another piece of her mother. But as she felt his eyes on her, Caroline knew that she was his property. He had owned her back then, and he owned her now.

As they came to the stoplight at Eighty-ninth, Drexel saw an NYPD squad car riding north up Broadway across the concrete median. He slipped the .44 from his waistband and slammed it into the glove compartment along with Eddie's Smith.

Then he buckled his seatbelt and motioned for Caroline to do the same. The squad car was on routine patrol, but why risk it. When they passed Eighty-eighth, neither of them noticed the man in the uniform of Bell Security running north.

Jaime Velez checked the clock on the VCR in a store

window at Eighty-ninth. Shit. It said 12:03. He knew that the Haitian had money down on the Sonics, and he'd want to be on the street for the final score.

He'd be ripshit that Jaime was late like this, but fuck, he'd missed the D train on Arthur Avenue and had to ride local to Fifty-ninth before he could change for the uptown to Eighty-sixth. Now he was humping fast to get up to Ninety-first. See, Poussaint had a mean motherfucking temper, and Jaime didn't need that kind of shit tonight.

Two stories below, in the subway tunnel, LeStadt was taking his time, moving like a spider through the dark. He was sure that Burke was almost beside him now. Scared shitless, feeling his sphincter contract, quaking at his imminent death. He'd asked around about the fire cop, and the word had come back that he was a loser, a washout, nothing like his old man. And look how easy the father had been.

It was almost pitch-black on the uptown side of the tunnel, and LeStadt couldn't see him yet. Still, he'd made a plan about the way he would do it, and he had to laugh to himself. It was brilliant.

He would move in the dark until he had him, waiting until he could hear the fuck hyperventilating, and then he'd flash the light in his eyes, surprising him, so he could use the gun on his hands. He'd take off the left one first, because he'd seen that Burke was left-handed. Then he'd blow off the right one. Two explosions of cartilage and blood. And only then, after the fucker had seen himself disfigured, would LeStadt go for the head shot.

Then he'd rifle the body, take his shield, his wallet, his jewelry, anything that would make an ID. He'd strip him clean, then he'd leave him there. It might be days before a maintenance crew came through that part of the tunnel. The body would be far enough across the tracks to be out of the plumbers' sight, and with the gaping wounds, the rats would do the rest.

They'd find him missing at work and there would be some kind of manhunt, but Burke had been missing a lot lately, and with his father gone, *maybe* they'd think he'd just taken off. After a month or two, when the search had cooled, LeStadt would drive down to Atlantic City, use the ID, rent a room at Trump's Palace in the name of Eddie Burke, and then run up some markers. By the time Missing Persons made the case, it would look like one more cop had gone wrong. A fire marshal with an attitude problem and a failed marriage who was into the shys.

They'd take the open case jacket marked Eddie Burke and file it away under *disgrace,* and as long as Caroline Drexel held with her father, it would work.

But Eddie Burke was thinking, too, his mind racing to put a profile on this guy coming at him with the gun in the dark. What kind of man was he? Arrogant, Eddie thought. Cocky. Sure enough of himself to keep things from his boss. Otherwise, why hadn't Drexel been down in the tunnel before this? They had security here, but a rent-a-cop wouldn't stop Black Jack Drexel. If he'd known that only half of the mural had burned, why didn't he look for the other half?

Because LeStadt hadn't *told* him, thought Eddie. He'd gone into the loft and set the thing on fire. There was plaster covering the faces, so he couldn't be sure, but his boss had sent him down for a job, and he'd done it, not figuring that the Sloane girl would get in the way.

So when she came off the elevator and surprised him, LeStadt barely had time to kill her and split. He had to know what this thing meant to Drexel. How it had haunted him since the thirties. With only half of the mural gone, there was a 50 percent chance that Drexel's face was still out there. So why not tell the man that he'd only burned half?

Eddie's mind raced as he heard LeStadt on the tracks a few feet away.

And then he figured it out. LeStadt hadn't told his boss because of Caroline. *She* was up there in the loft with the cops. *She'd* seen the mural. If she hadn't told her father, then LeStadt must have figured he'd done it. Burned the side of the mural with Drexel's face. If that was true, there was no need to keep looking.

But *why*, thought Eddie. Why *hadn't* she told her father? Caroline couldn't be sure from that charred piece of canvas she'd seen in the loft. If she'd been in on all this from the start, why didn't she let him know that only half of the mural had burned and they had to keep looking?

Eddie was turning it over and over in his mind when suddenly, the light flashed in his eyes and he heard the hammer cock back on the Beretta. He held his hands out to block the light and then he heard LeStadt say, "Get ready to die, fucker . . ."

Just then, as his eyes adjusted to the light, he heard a man shouting upstairs, across the tracks.

It was Jaime Velez.

"Hey, JC, what the fuck you doin' with this lock, man? How I'm supposed to come down, relieve you?"

And in that second, when LeStadt turned his head toward the noise, Eddie Burke sprang out of the indentation, lunging at him for the gun. He got his hands around it and snapped LeStadt's arm back as that voice from above kept on yelling.

"Poussaint, where the fuck are you, man?"

LeStadt tried to push Eddie back. All he needed was enough distance to straight-arm a shot, but Eddie held on and slammed LeStadt's gun hand against the cold, slimy tile. He bloodied the knuckles, but the killer wouldn't let go. Eddie reached into his pocket with his right hand and came up with his father's badge.

He flicked open the pin on the back and jammed it into LeStadt's cheek. Blood spurted out and LeStadt screamed.

''Aaaaaggghhh.''

He reached up to flick the badge away, and as he did, the gun fell to the tracks.

Both men lunged for it and Eddie was faster, but LeStadt snap-kicked Eddie's fist and the Beretta went flying out toward the middle rails. Eddie could see now that LeStadt was some kind of kick boxer.

LeStadt smiled. With Eddie defenseless, he started stalking him. He would have to kill him a different way. Use his feet. But he was confident that Eddie would die.

And then both men heard that scream from above. ''Hey listen, Homes, I'm freezing my gonads up here. Let me down!''

But LeStadt didn't bother to turn this time. He had his eyes fixed on Eddie as the fire marshal moved back toward the tunnel wall. Eddie searched in the dark for the Beretta.

''JC! It's locked! Let me down!''

But Jean-Claude Poussaint was lying dead across the tracks, and Eddie knew that soon he'd be next. He'd always been good in a bar fight. The left hook had coldcocked Kivlihan, but fists were no match against feet.

Eddie's head rocked back as LeStadt jumped up and threw the first kick.

''Christ.'' Burke tasted blood.

He tried to duck, but LeStadt spun around and slammed his right heel into Eddie's jaw. Eddie reeled and staggered back. Another kick and Eddie went down. He'd lost the hearing in his right ear now, and it wouldn't be long before LeStadt did some brain damage.

''What's wrong, Mick? Nobody ever teach you to box?''

The guy was taunting him now. Eddie got up and raised

his fists to cover his face, but LeStadt just spun around and kicked him behind the ear. He went down again, and the killer delivered another blow, opening up the gash above his eye. Eddie knew that if there was one more kick, he'd go blind.

And then he saw it. A pinprick of light way down the tunnel at Eighty-sixth, starting small and then getting bigger as it ran along the tunnel wall. He heard the low rumble turning into a roar, and he knew that the light was coming from the headlamp of an Uptown Local train careening through the tunnel at sixty miles an hour. A train that was heading right for them. So Eddie Burke used every bit of his strength to stand up. The blood was pouring down from his eye, and he stumbled.

The train operator was squinting forward in the motor cabin. There was something on the track about three hundred yards ahead, so he hit the brakes and pulled a cord and a deafening whistle whined through the tunnel.

As the light got brighter, Eddie struggled to his feet. He looked at LeStadt now, poised and ready to deliver the final blow. And then there it was—the reflection of the Beretta on the uptown express track. The glint of light against the burnished chrome of the 9 mm Italian gun. But LeStadt saw it, too, and he ran for it, just as the train screamed ahead. The headlamp lit up the tunnel now, and Eddie saw that LeStadt was almost on the Beretta, so he slammed himself back into an indentation while the train roared by. Eighty tons of steel, screaming six inches away from his face.

And then, he saw the hot white flash of arc light go up on the other side.

Finally, when the train was gone, Eddie closed his eyes and waited for the shot. He knew he was finished now. One way or another, he was dead. But there was nothing. No footsteps. No breathing. Not even the smell of cologne. He looked out toward the express track and saw only darkness. He dropped down and felt around for the light. The man had stopped screaming upstairs, and the tunnel was quiet. A few seconds went by before Eddie could find the quartz halogen spot that he'd first brought down from the Chevy.

He picked it up cautiously, expecting any second to hear the hammer slam down on the Beretta.

Then he got up, using his handkerchief to wipe the blood from his eyes, and he panned the light left then right. Nothing. He started to move toward the gun now, walking toward the express track, searching in the dark, but it was quiet. Just the sound of the wind whistling down from Ninety-sixth. Then he smelled it. The unmistakable stench of burned flesh. Then the dull hum a few feet in front of him. He panned the light and he saw the figure, something that had once been a man, blackened now from the force of the electric charge. The body was covered in char, with eyes like slits and the fat almost bursting the skin like a hot dog left too long on a grill.

Eddie bent down now. LeStadt was gripping the Beretta. It was frozen in his hand, welded to the third electrified uptown rail as 600 volts of DC passed up and down through his body. There was smoke coming up from the follicles of hair on his pockmarked face. It was gruesome.

Eddie Burke had seen a few disfigured corpses in his time, bodies ravaged by fire or crushed under burning debris, but he'd never gotten used to it—how something as perfect as the human form could be corrupted like this. And even though this was the man who'd been sent to kill him, Eddie stopped and made the sign of the cross. It was the Irish in him. No matter what, you had to do this for the dead.

Then he got up, folded the bloodstained handkerchief, and put it into his pocket. He knew that Drexel would be waiting down at Eighty-sixth, but he didn't care anymore. This thing had to finish.

52

DREXEL PULLED THE MERCEDES INTO A SPACE NEAR THE newsstand on the northwest corner of Eighty-sixth and Broadway. He looked at Caroline. She hadn't said a word since they'd left the old station at Ninety-first. She kept staring down at the floor, fixed on something.

"What is it?"

She didn't answer. There was just the hint of a flinch at the sound of his voice.

"What are you staring at?"

Caroline wouldn't talk. She was frozen.

Drexel shook his head and found a small penlight flash in the console. He flicked it on and shined the beam on the floor at her feet. He saw the tiny piece of brain matter on her shoe. The fragment of tissue from Jean-Claude Poussaint.

Drexel didn't bother to say anything. There was nothing to say. All of this would be over soon. He would deal with his daughter later.

He checked the Rolex on his wrist. It was 12:09 A.M., Wednesday morning. Almost ten days since the girl had first died in that loft. He looked around, scanning the sidewalk on Broadway, then he pushed a button on the driver's-side door. The window dropped on Caroline's side. The air was bitter cold. It rushed in and she shivered. Then Drexel got out. Broadway was almost deserted by now, but he wasn't taking any chances.

He looked up and down the street. There were a few stragglers around the newsstand and a pair of taxis waiting for the light. Two Italians were throwing bundles off a *Daily News* delivery truck, but otherwise, the place was quiet. Drexel walked around to the passenger door and reached in. He opened the glove compartment and shoved the .44 in his waistband. He left the Smith. Then he squeezed her arm.

"Stay here."

She flinched again.

A sanitation truck made its way up Broadway. A few more taxis went by, and Drexel moved down into the subway.

The enormous Black man in the token booth was stuffing his face and pawing through a tabloid when Drexel walked up. The man was disgusting.

Drexel prided himself on sizing up his opponents, taking their measure in seconds. He lived on the thirtieth floor, but he knew the petty details of human existence as well as anyone. The rag that the fat man was reading was called the *Globe*. It specialized in stories about aliens and transsexual nuns. The short, dark chocolate roll he was eating was called a Ring-Ding, a processed food favored by small children and chunky housewives. The man wore a powder-blue Transit Authority shirt with an ID that said Delroy Suggs. He had on a set of headphones plugged into a yellow Sony Walkman. His fingers were tapping like bratwurst on the token booth counter. There were pink blotches on the man's face. His hair was done in an Al Sharpton pompadour and it was dripping with Jeri Curl, that pomade the

Blacks used. It was clear to Drexel that he was staring at a goddamn bottom feeder.

Men like this disgusted him. Not because they were beneath him, but because they had lost control. This one had probably started out as a would-be tight end. The big kid from Lenox Avenue who dreamed of making it in the NFL. And now look at him. He was an obese disgrace. A man who had surrendered his vision.

But not Black Jack. Drexel had *his* dream precisely in focus, and when he dealt with this bothersome arson cop, he'd get on with it. The old lion had to clear his throat to get the fat man's attention. He shoved a crisp new twenty under the arch in the bulletproof window and only then did the man look up.

His enormous head was propped up by an elbow the size of a honey-baked ham, and he was lost in some story about an Elvis sighting in Lancaster, England. A long time ago, Black Jack Drexel had taught himself to read upside down.

But now it was Delroy's turn. He looked Drexel up and down, eyeing him sideways, the way Black men do. Here was this motherfucker, had to be in his seventies, right? The dude had manicured nails, silver, razor-cut hair, and a three-thousand-dollar camel-hair coat. There was a platinum Rolex on his wrist and Delroy was sure the rest of the bills in his money clip were Jacksons or better. It was just after midnight, and here was this motherfucker venturin' down in the killin' zone. Be easier, give the man a razor, tell him to slit his own throat. But hey, this was New York, so go figure.

"How many?" he said.

Drexel said, "Only one."

The big man pushed a token under the arch in the bulletproof window; then eighteen wet singles and fifty cents. He knew this would drive the dude batshit, but he didn't care. He needed his fives and tens.

Drexel wondered if Delroy Suggs had heard any shots. Probably not, with the headphones on. He wondered if he could get the gun through the token arch if things went bad and he had to kill him. The fat fuck must weigh three hundred pounds, thought Drexel.

No. Not enough clearance. He'd have to feign some kind of sickness and get the man out of the booth. Then he'd make it a head shot, to be sure.

Drexel dropped the token into the slot and pushed through the turnstile. He looked left and right down the platform and saw that it was empty.

The uptown side was deserted as well. He pulled the .44 from his waistband and made sure there were six in the cylinder. Fine. He was ready.

53

A HUNDRED YARDS NORTH, EDDIE BURKE CROSSED THE
track and ran through the dark toward the light of the
Eighty-sixth Street station. He'd been turning it over and
over in his mind all the way through the tunnel. Caroline
... How in hell did he miss it? From the minute he met
her, the danger signs had been flashing: the look on her
face at Grosvenor's, the way she trembled at the mention
of her father's name. Eddie had seen that before with the
kids at the fire scenes. Sad-eyed children from rat shack
tenements in the Bronx and East Harlem. Kids with con-
tusions under the eyes and abrasions along the arms and
buttocks when you wiped off the soot.

Eddie would help get them treated for smoke inhalation
and then contact a caseworker from Social Services. They
would interview the kids and more often than not, the children would ask to go home. They'd get released and go
back for more. Eddie understood. That was part of the sickness. As often as their eyes had been blackened, as often
as they'd show up at the ladder trucks with wounds from
the beatings, those kids would go home again. They'd fly
into the arms of their parents. And two or three days later,
Eddie would hear that they were back in the emergency

rooms. It was twisted, dysfunctional, and Eddie had always put it down as a ghetto disease. Poverty, drugs, and alcohol were the real parents of child abuse. At least that's what he'd thought until tonight. But Eddie knew now that income had nothing to do with it. Neither did physical violence. He'd been over every inch of Caroline's body, and she hadn't been touched. Not like that. The pain she felt came from somewhere else. The torment of constant harassment. The belief that she'd never quite measure up. That she was somehow weaker, unable to service the legend. It was an affliction that came to the children of powerful men, and Eddie Burke knew it well.

Still, as bad as it was growing up, Eddie was proud of his father. Proud of the medals he'd won and the collars he'd made. Even on the nights when he didn't come home, Eddie would sit there in front of the tube and get a little rush when he saw him, tall, straight, with cobalt-blue eyes; making the perp walk on the six o'clock news.

After all, his old man was out there keeping the watch, doing God's work, and Eddie was proud—right up until that night when his mother got sick.

But what kind of father could Drexel have been? For a woman who'd studied art that celebrated American labor, what kind of a role model was this? A robber baron? An arbitrage czar? A man who took pride in wrecking companies, not because he'd make money but because they were there to be wrecked? Caroline Drexel had been the victim of child abuse as surely as those little urchins at Engine Company Forty-four. She had scars of a different kind, and Eddie wished he could heal them.

But she'd lied to him. She'd used him throughout the investigation. She'd taken his gun in the end and left him to die in a subway tunnel. She was rich and beautiful and she had a Ph.D., but she was the daughter of Black Jack Drexel, and in the end, that's where her loyalty was.

• • •

By the time he reached the stairs at the uptown end of the station, Eddie was exhausted. The place was deserted, nobody on the platform, and for a second, he asked himself why he'd come. After LeStadt had gone down, he could have walked north up to Ninety-sixth and avoided all this. But he was tired. He carried the smell of LeStadt's burning skin in his nostrils and he wanted this finished. So he straightened up and made his way up the platform stairs.

Eddie stood there a second, then cleared his throat and closed his hand around the tin in his pocket. A safety pin didn't mean much against a Charter Arms Special, and he wondered what his father would do at a moment like this.

Eddie walked toward the center of the station with slow, deliberate steps. He passed the first white-tiled column with the words 86TH STREET in black. There was nothing. He moved past another column. The place was still quiet. He was beginning to think that maybe the station was closed. Maybe Drexel got stopped at the chain-link gate. So Eddie got a little more confident and moved toward the third column. Still nothing.

But then, when he came to the fourth, Drexel jumped out and drew down on him. The old lion smiled.

"Did you really think she'd betray me?"

He pointed the barrel of the .44 at Eddie's heart.

All Eddie could think of were the final words of his father.

"I guess it was in her blood."

Drexel smiled again. "Bet your ass. The girl loves me."

"Right, sure." Eddie looked away.

"No. I mean, she *loves* me. She fucked me." He reached down and rubbed his cock.

Eddie rocked back. "What?"

"Oh, come on. What did you think? A woman who looks like that. Did you think it would matter that I was her fa-

ther?'' The old bastard licked his lips. "She's the best piece
I ever had."

Eddie raged. "Goddamn you . . ."

He lunged toward Drexel, but the robber baron cocked
the .44.

"Stop right there."

Eddie stopped. He was seething. "You fuck . . ."

"Get your hands up."

Eddie bit his tongue, forcing himself to calm down. He
had to kill him now. Rip off his head and piss down his
throat. Someway, he had to get to that gun.

Drexel moved up to him slowly, triumphant. He controlled the scene. So Eddie turned away and thought of his
father. What would Big Eddie do?

He had to buy time, so he took a deep breath.

"There's just one thing I don't understand," said Eddie.

"And what's that?"

"If she was with you on this from the start, why did you
bother to have her followed?"

Drexel smiled like a cobra. It was a question that celebrated his own twisted sense of deception.

"Insurance," said Drexel coldly. "You see, the little
bitch has some of her mother's blood, too."

And that's when Eddie understood. That's when he knew
why she *hadn't* told Drexel the wrong half was burned. She
still had her mother's blood.

He flashed a look toward the bastard. Four feet. He
needed him just a little closer.

But Drexel stopped. He raised the gun and lined up the
forward sights.

"Did you think I was going to let you get me inside?"
Drexel sneered. "I read your file. I know what you did to
your supervisor. It's the left hand, isn't it?"

Christ, this guy had all the moves.

Drexel fingered the hammer on the gun.

And now Eddie knew it was over. The fuck was too far away to lunge at. A scream wouldn't matter. Even if there *was* a token booth clerk on duty, Eddie would be dead before the guy hit the platform.

So Eddie pricked his hand with the pin from his father's shield. He hoped that the pain would distract him. A thousand times he'd rushed into burning buildings and wondered what it would feel like at the end, and now he knew. It would feel cold and dull and not worth continuing. He closed his eyes and whispered under his breath, "O my God, I am heartfully sorry for having offended Thee. . . ."

Then, suddenly, a bullet roared through the station, tearing 150 mph as it ripped into Drexel's neck.

It blew him forward, piercing his carotid artery. His face contorted, his body shook from the shock, and he slammed up against the tile of the column. Blood gushed down past the black words that said 86th Street and Drexel's manicured nails scraped the tile. He was struggling now to hold on.

Then the second shot came, and his right eyeball exploded out from the front of his skull. As the body contorted, the bloody face looked at Eddie in disbelief. A man who'd spent his life plotting every move had been caught in the end by surprise.

Then Drexel dropped to the platform, and Eddie heard the crack as his skull fractured. A second went by, and a small puddle of blood dripped down from his eye. It was just the way Alex Sloane had gone out.

And then, when he looked up again, Eddie saw Caroline down at the middle of the platform. She was double-handing his Smith, shivering, cold, hyperventilating.

There were tears streaming down her face.

54

THEY HAD THREE FLAGS ON THE COFFIN: THE STARS AND Stripes, because Big Eddie had been a veteran; the flag of the City of New York; and the orange, green, and white tricolor of the Irish Republic. An honor guard of two hundred uniforms followed the casket as a lone piper from the Emerald Society stood off to the side at Our Lady of Angels Cemetery in Bay Ridge. The Policemen's Benevolent Association had sprung for a green-and-white tent in case of inclement weather, but it was a glorious day. Eddie sat in the front row next to the mayor, both commissioners (police and fire), the cardinal, a half dozen judges, ADAs, and another fifty dignitaries. Aggie Stein was behind him in the second row. Even Kivlihan had turned out. Aggie put a hand on Eddie's shoulder, and he looked out toward Sheepshead Bay where Big Eddie had once taken him fishing.

And then Monsignor O'Boyle of St. Pat's in Bay Ridge raised the gold censer over the casket and said these words:

> I am the Resurrection and the Life. He who dies
> and believes in Me will live and he who lives and
> believes in Me will never die.

He read the *Dies Ire* in Latin and then blessed the final remains of Edmund Patrick Burke. There was a pause as the honor guard fired a twenty-one gun salute and then they presented Eddie with the three flags, each folded into a tight little triangle. Eddie nodded and looked down the row at Dinny Walsh. The elegant little arson inspector brushed some lint off his navy blue topcoat and got up to speak.

"Your Eminence," said Dinny, turning to the cardinal. "Mr. Mayor. The honorable fire and police commissioners ... distinguished friends and colleagues of Eddie Burke: I've been asked to say a few words about this great man. . . ."

Dinny laughed. "Of course, I've never said a *few* words about anything. But we're all in a hurry to get down to the Tam for the *real* wake, so I'll be brief. . . ."

There were some light chuckles from the crowd. Dinny looked over at Eddie and winked. Eddie smiled.

"How do you measure the life of a man like Big Eddie? Sure, he put down more felonies than anybody else in the history of NYPD. Sure, he made the Detectives Bureau the greatest crime-fighting unit since the Dutch bought the island. But how can you possibly honor a thirty-year career like his in just a few minutes?

"The answer is, of course, that you can't. There's never been anybody like him. No one ever came close. . . ."

Eddie smiled and looked out at the crowd, searching for her as Dinny went on.

"This is *not* to say that the man didn't have his critics. You don't sit in the chief of detective's chair for seventeen years without getting your feet scuffed. Big Eddie Burke knew how to kick ass and take names, and there were a few jealous men in this city who scorned him.

" 'He was lucky,' said some. 'He'd been in the right place at the right time,' said others. And the meanest among them said that he'd been chief of detectives in an age when homicide was still a solvable crime. . . .

"Now, God knows that Edmund was lucky. He was lucky to have the wife he did. Lucky to leave this son who sits here today. Lucky to have kept his faith."

Dinny turned toward the cardinal, who nodded.

Eddie kept searching the crowd.

"Big Eddie Burke never had much time for leisure. He was too much of a workhorse. I don't think he took a vacation in thirty years, and I know that he never set foot on a golf course. The man didn't have the time. But still, years ago, there was another Irishman who said a thing or two about luck, and I think what he said can give us comfort today. His name was Walter Hagen, one of the greatest golfers who ever lived."

"Christ," said Aggie, whispering to Eddie. "Leave it to him to remember your father with a golfing metaphor."

Eddie just turned and cracked a smile. Then he looked out at the crowd again. She still wasn't there.

Dinny went on. "One day . . . I think it was in the heat of the Masters . . . Hagen was facing a sixty-foot putt. It was the eighteenth green. He was one stroke back, and he had to sink it to go into sudden death. But the green had a curve, and he knew that a simple straight shot would go wide. So Hagen had to figure the contour. He had to judge the distance, the speed. There must have been twenty variables and the crowd stood there hushed because everyone knew it was an impossible shot. Hagen was getting old by then, his career had peaked, and there were some who'd suggested he hang it up. You see, all great men have their critics.

"But then, without hesitation, Hagen walked up to the little white ball. He drew back, struck it, and watched as it sailed in a glorious arc all the way to the cup. The crowd went crazy. A couple of fans lifted him onto their shoulders.

It was the most amazing putt anyone had ever seen.

"And then, suddenly, at the edge of the crowd, one of the spectators cried out, 'Hell man, that was luck.' Well, Hagen's loyal fans erupted. Some of them wanted to thrash the bastard, teach him a lesson for criticizing the legend.

"But Walter just smiled and raised his hand and the crowd quieted down. Then he took his club and walked up to the critic. He faced him dead on and said, 'You bet your life it was luck. But let me tell you something, my friend . . . luck is the residue of design.' "

The mayor and the cardinal nodded. The crowd was transfixed.

"And so, that was Big Eddie Burke. A great policeman, a good Catholic, and a man who made his own luck for the people of New York. The city was safer when he was on the bridge and we will not know his likes again."

Then Dinny looked up to heaven.

"Eddie, if you're up there . . . and we know that you are, boy . . . pick out a nice wood for me. I'll be there as soon as they call me, and I'll meet you on the eighteenth tee."

It wasn't the custom to applaud at funerals, but 200 uniforms jumped up. Two hundred and fifty odd voices let out a cheer. The mayor put his arms around Eddie, and the cardinal wiped a tear from his eye. Then the honor guard sprang forward and another twenty-one shots rang out. Finally, when it was quiet, the piper played "Danny Boy" and Eddie Burke felt a lump in his throat as his father's remains were lowered into the ground.

When it was finished, he got up and looked around again. He still didn't see her.

Later, as the cemetery cleared, Eddie stood in a tangle of uniforms, shaking hands, receiving the comfort of friends. The fire commissioner came up and said how proud he was that Eddie had broken the case. He told him to take some time off and then come see him. They ought to discuss his future. Eddie nodded and caught the look of anger from Kivlihan, who turned away. Aggie Stein bent over and whispered in Eddie's ear, "It serves the little fuck right."

Just then, Bobby Vasquez came up and gave him a note. He said a woman in the crowd had handed it to him. It was on rose-colored stationary, and the initials on the outside said C. D. Eddie took a deep breath and opened it. The note read:

> All I knew was, he wanted the mural. I had no idea about the killing. *Please* believe me.
> Always . . .
>
> Caroline

Eddie looked up toward the exiting crowd. Then he saw her, dressed all in black, staring at him from behind a pair of dark glasses. He started to walk toward her, but Caroline ducked into a waiting limo and was gone.

It was almost a year before he saw her again.

55

A STRING QUARTET PLAYED VIVALDI'S *THE FOUR SEASONS* as a thousand of New York's beautiful people crowded into the six-story glass atrium for the opening of Drexel Place. It was a magnificent cathedral of korten steel and curtain-wall glass designed by Kevin Roche, the architect who'd done the Ford Foundation building. A truly public space, now filled with people who rarely mixed with the public. A year ago Eddie Burke would have felt out of place in this crowd, but not now. He walked through the tangle of champagne-sipping glitterati in the enormous foyer and came to a table where three Junior Leaguers in dresses by Valentino were checking names.

One of them said, "Name please?" She didn't bother looking up.

"Eddie Burke."

The woman looked up at him now.

"Oh yes," she said. "Miss Drexel asked us to look out for you."

She got up and took Eddie by the arm, making sure he had a flute of champagne before introducing him to the U.S. ambassador to the United Nations and the violinist Itzhak Perlman.

Eddie didn't worry anymore if people mistook him for his father. More often than not now it was the other way around. *He* was the celebrated fire investigator who had broken that big murder case, and oh yes, didn't he have a father who was once a cop? It had taken him months, but Eddie had gotten used to the recognition. He was another man now: a year older and considerably more polished. It was a transformation that had come over time.

After the funeral he'd gone on leave, found a package deal on a little hotel down in Akumel on the Yucatán coast. Did some diving, baked in the sun, and just rested. When he came back to Manhattan Base, Dinny Walsh called. He caught wind through the grapevine that Eddie was in line for Kivlihan's job, and the old investigator told him that if he was going to be an executive officer, he should look like one.

Dinny knew a tailor at Paul Stuart who fitted Eddie with his first double-breasted suit, a gray one in Italian wool. The tailor's name was Enrico. He came from a town near Catania, where Eddie's Nanno was from.

The Sicilian told him that the pants would ride better with braces and Eddie had gone along. Enrico helped Eddie select a half-dozen pinpoint oxford shirts and the proper accessories. Eddie had always used a Windsor knot, which made the ties look thick at his neck, and Enrico suggested that a single slip knot would be better. A few weeks later, when a lawyer outside 100 Center Street mistakenly called Eddie counselor, he went back and bought another double-breasted, this one blue. The new salary increase would cover it.

Twice a month now Eddie visited a barber who worked on the second floor of the Warwick Hotel. The man combed Eddie's hair back straight and taught him to use a gel. He even got him to sit with a manicurist from time to time. To compensate, Eddie would go over to Gleason's gym and work on the heavy bag. He'd lost almost twenty pounds in six months, and he was down to his college weight. He'd given up meatball subs for pasta and insalata mista with balsamic vinegar. He read the *New York Times* every day and stopped buying the *Post*. A month earlier, he'd found an apartment in a brownstone on West Seventy-sixth off the park, and he'd started listening to books on tape as he drove to the three-alarm blazes.

The fire commissioner had kept his promise. Eddie was now a supervising fire marshal, executive officer of Manhattan Base. Eddie told himself that this new charge toward self-improvement was because of the change in jobs, but it wasn't.

Where was she? He looked around as he moved through the crowd thick with money and famous names. He wondered what he was going to say when he saw her.

Just then, somebody tapped him on the back and Eddie turned around. It was Jelke, the homicide dick. He grinned and offered his hand.

"Heard you're running the base now, kid. The old man would be—"

"Yeah."

Eddie looked past him, searching the crowd.

Suddenly, the music stopped. A man in gray pinstripes was tapping a microphone atop a dais. The platform was set in front of an enormous pair of doors, crowded with dignitaries. Eddie recognized a few faces from SoHo. Leo Castelli was up there and Julian Schnabel, that painter who worked with the broken plates. Eddie had started taking a late supper down at the Spring Street Bar, going to an occasional gallery now and then. Nothing serious. Just trying to learn a few of the buzzwords. Christ. Where the hell was she?

Just then, the man at the microphone cleared his throat.

"Ladies and gentleman, welcome to Drexel Place. We

don't want to interrupt the flow of Veuve Clicquot any more than we have to, so without further ado, I'd like to introduce the person most responsible for this splendid new space, Miss Caroline Drexel.''

Eddie lifted his head to get a look at her over the applauding crowd and there she was, radiant in a little black dress. Her hair was cut short like a boy's now, and there was a new kind of peace in her eyes. A far cry from the trembling woman he'd left that night on the subway platform. She was free now. In control. A woman with nothing but choices.

It hadn't looked so good for her a year ago. That night, after Drexel was sealed in the body bag, detectives from the Twenty-fourth Precinct had taken Caroline into custody. The charge was murder-conspiracy and homicide. The DA was ready to put her away. After all, this was a gigantic scandal involving abortion, manslaughter, homicide . . . and there she was at the center, a beautiful blonde heiress. A Columbia professor who'd killed her own father, one of the richest men in New York. The tabloids and the trash TV talk shows were rabid for it. There were a half-dozen ''true crime'' books in the works. The networks were in a bidding war for the movie rights. It was the kind of case that a smart ADA could ride into the AG's office.

But Eddie Burke stopped all that. He testified at the grand jury that Caroline had fired the shot in an effort to save his life. As to the conspiracy charges, he was certain she had no idea of her father's plan. And in one day, the tabloids turned Caroline Drexel from Lady MacBeth into Mother Teresa. The twisted victim of an abusive father. The noble daughter who had sacrificed all for love.

Eddie had passed her for a moment outside the grand jury room, but they didn't speak, and when it was over, he'd heard that she'd gone off to Italy. Hiding out for awhile in a little place her mother had kept in Ravello above the Amalfi Coast. Months had gone by without a word, and then the invitation had come. And now, here she was, reinvented like Eddie, ready to start again.

"Thank you," said Caroline as she stepped to the mike. "It means so much to me that you've come here."

She was searching the crowd now too.

"It is the nature of beauty that it doesn't last. Perhaps that's why we covet it so much. For ten years in this country there was a fragile experiment in the arts. A government program in which thousands of artists were given a chance to create. Sadly, much of their work has been lost. This is the first step in our quest to preserve what is left."

The MC handed her a pair of silver-plated scissors, and Caroline stepped up to an enormous white ribbon.

"I hereby open the Dorothea Hampton Museum of WPA Art."

As she sliced through the ribbon, the huge doors behind her opened onto a museum space built into the atrium. It was filled with WPA murals and sculpture. Hundreds of works by Arshil Gorky, Willem de Kooning, James Brooks, Alice Neal, Chaim Gross, and Elia Bolatowski.

Just then, 10,000 white balloons fell from the ceiling, and the assembled dignitaries erupted in applause. The string quartet started to play.

Caroline walked to the edge of the dais and stopped. She looked out over the well-heeled multitude and shook her head. Damn it. He hadn't come. And then, just below the platform, she felt somebody touch her. She looked down and saw Eddie Burke.

Caroline smiled. "I'm so glad you came."

"Wouldn't have missed it," said Eddie.

She stepped down from the dais to face him. They traded looks, trying to find each other again. Finally, she said, "You look different . . ."

"So do you."

She touched her hair. "Yes, I cut it."

"I don't mean that."

"Then what?"

"You look happy."

Caroline smiled and took Eddie's arm. He hesitated, but she tugged at him gently, pulling him into the new museum space. She was wearing Obsession again, and she'd had her nails done in red. Christ. Eddie just wanted to grab her, pull her into a corner. He wanted to let her know what the last year had been like without her.

But he waited. He knew better now. That was the old Eddie Burke, rushing headlong into burning buildings, leading with his chin.

Not anymore.

And then, as they passed through the doors, Eddie saw it. There, up on the travertine marble wall, the right half of a two-panel diptych, newly restored. There were farms in the background, a throng of workers with flags raised in triumph, red banners waving, and three figures in the foreground. The sign below it said, *Workers of the World Unite*.

Eddie looked up at the faces. The farmer, the teacher and the miner, all deceased. He focused for a second on the eyes of young John Charles Drexel, then he looked at the teacher and pulled Caroline close.

"Come here." He kissed her gently on the cheek.

"What was that for?" she said.

"Your mother. She would have done it herself if she'd been here today."

Caroline smiled. She bore a look into him, then put her perfect white hand behind his neck.

A second went by as she studied him, then she pulled him close and kissed him hard on the mouth.

"Hey," said Eddie, looking around. "What about your guests?"

"I don't care," said Caroline. "I just feel so lucky."

Eddie smiled and ran the back of his hand along her cheek.

"Yeah, me, too. That's something I know about."

"What?" said Caroline.

"Luck," said Eddie. "It's the residue of design."

She laughed and took his arm. Then they walked together into the new museum. As the music of Antonio Vivaldi filled the space, Eddie Burke looked up at the old mural and thought to himself that his father was right.

It is in the blood. It always was.

ABOUT THE AUTHOR

Peter Lance is a five-time Emmy-winning former correspondent for ABC News. With a master's degree from Columbia University Graduate School of Journalism and a J.D. from Fordham University School of Law, Lance earlier worked as a trial preparation assistant in the Office of the Manhattan District Attorney. During the late 1980s, he was chief investigative correspondent for ABC News, covering hundreds of stories worldwide for *20/20*, *Nightline*, and *World News Tonight*. Lance was a member of the first U.S. network news crew admitted to Indochina after the Viet Nam war. He did major investigations for ABC News on the JFK assassination, the Pershing II Missile Crisis, and the Iran-Contra scandal. His *20/20* investigation of organized crime involvement in the toxic waste hauling industry won the National Headliner's Award. In the mid 1980s Lance spent six months undercover to expose an arson-for-profit ring operating on Chicago's North Side. For the past several years, he's worked as a novelist and screenwriter. He is married with three children.